An [illegible]thor of mo[illegible] ad[illegible] with more than sev[illegible] Ja[illegible] **Kay Johnson** writes about love and family, and pens books of gripping romantic suspense. A *USA TODAY* bestselling author and an eight-time finalist for the Romance Writers of America RITA® Award, she won a RITA® Award in 2008. A former librarian, Janice raised two daughters in a small town north of Seattle, Washington.

Lara Lacombe earned a PhD in microbiology and immunology and worked in several labs across the country before moving into the classroom. Her day job as a college science professor gives her time to pursue her other love—writing fast-paced romantic suspense with smart, nerdy heroines and dangerously attractive heroes. She loves to hear from readers! Find her on the web or contact her at laralacombewriter@gmail.com

Also by Janice Kay Johnson

Hide the Child
Trusting the Sheriff
Within Range
Brace for Impact
A Hometown Boy
Anything for Her
Where It May Lead
From This Day On
One Frosty Night
More Than Neighbours

Also by Lara Lacombe

Ranger's Justice
Ranger's Baby Rescue
The Ranger's Reunion Threat
Colton's Covert Baby
Colton K-9 Bodyguard
Enticed by the Operative
Dr. Do-or-Die
Her Lieutenant Protector
Pregnant by the Colton Cowboy
Colton Baby Homecoming

THE HUNTING SEASON

JANICE KAY JOHNSON

COLTON'S UNDERCOVER REUNION

LARA LACOMBE

MILLS & BOON

First Published in Great Britain 2020
by Mills & Boon, an imprint of HarperCollins*Publishers*
1 London Bridge Street, London, SE1 9GF

Special thanks and acknowledgement are given to Lara Lacombe for her contribution to *The Coltons of Mustang Valley* series.

ISBN: 978-0-263-28031-9

0520

MIX
Paper from responsible sources
FSC™ C007454

This book is produced from independently certified FSC™ paper to ensure responsible forest management.

For more information visit: www.harpercollins.co.uk/green

Printed and bound in Spain
by CPI, Barcelona

THE HUNTING SEASON

JANICE KAY JOHNSON

Chapter One

Lindsay Engle set down the phone very carefully. If she'd given into her emotions, she'd have slammed it into the cradle and potentially shattered it.

The balding man who'd been chatting with another caseworker made his way between desks until he reached hers. Glenn Wilson, mentor and friend—and well able to read her, even when she was stone-faced. "What's wrong?" he asked her.

Quiet had stolen over the room, she realized. Glancing around, she saw that her coworkers' heads had all turned, too. She'd have sworn she hadn't raised her voice.

"I removed a boy from his home two weeks ago."

Nods all around; too often, as employees of Oregon State Child Protective Services, they had no choice.

"I placed him with his uncle, who sounded disgusted with his brother. Shane *liked* his uncle." Her jaw clenched so hard she wasn't sure she'd be able to relax it enough to say another word.

Glenn laid a hand on her shoulder. "Is the boy badly injured?" he asked, voice gruff but also gentle.

Lindsay shook her head, swallowed and said, "No, thank heavens. He collapsed trying to get on the school bus. The driver called 9-1-1, and Shane was transported to the hospital. That was the ER doc calling. Shane managed to tell them that his uncle Martin hurt him." More like beat him to within an inch of his life, from the sound of it.

She opened a desk drawer and took out her handbag. "I need to get to the hospital."

Ashley Sheldon, who sat behind the next desk, murmured, "That poor kid."

"Apparently, brutality runs in the family," Lindsay said bitterly.

"The cops arrest the creep?" Glenn asked.

"He's conveniently not home. I don't know whether he realized he'd gone too far, or whether he thought Shane would make an excuse and he'd skate."

"He fell down the stairs," suggested Matt Grudin, tone acid.

"Had a dirt bike accident," Ray Hammond, another coworker, added.

Dark humor was common in their profession, but all Lindsay could summon was a pathetic smile before she said, "I'm off."

As she walked away, behind her Glenn growled, "There's a reason I took early retirement."

She fully understood. Social workers, especially those on the front lines, burned out all too fast. Maybe she was getting to the point where she should do something else for a living. Something one step removed from children with purple bruises, black eyes and teeth knocked out by a fist, or girls who carried terrible secrets. How Glenn had stood it all those years, she couldn't imagine. She admired him and was grateful that since his retirement he still stopped by the office regularly to say hi and lend his support to anyone who was especially frustrated or down.

At the small community hospital, she went straight to the emergency room, where she was allowed in Shane's cubicle. As many times as she'd seen battered children and teenagers, she never got over the shock. His face was so swollen and discolored, she wouldn't have been able to recognize him as the boy who, despite his wariness, was still capable of offering an irresistibly merry smile.

Maybe she should say, *had* been capable.

The one eye he could open fastened on her. "Ms. Engle?"

At least, that's what she thought he'd said.

"Shane." At his bedside, she reached for his hand, but pulled hers back when she saw that his was heavily wrapped. "I'm so sorry. I never dreamed—"

"My fault," he mumbled through misshapen lips. "I thought—" He, too, broke off, but she had no trouble finishing the sentence. Shane had believed his uncle was a good guy.

"Can you tell me what happened? In ten words or less?"

The fourteen-year-old, tall for his age but skinny, tried to smile, then groaned.

Seized by guilt, Lindsay exclaimed, "I'm sorry! Forget it! We can wait until you don't hurt so much."

He gave his head the tiniest of shakes. "S'posed to clean the kitchen last night, and I didn't. He dragged me out of bed and..." He made an abortive gesture. "You know."

"I gather you talked to a police officer."

"Kinda."

"Okay. Did you have the MRI?"

She thought that was a nod.

"Has the doctor talked to you yet?"

"Waiting for you."

"Oh. Okay." She smoothed sandy blond, shaggy hair back from Shane's battered face. "You know this isn't your fault."

His face twisted slightly and one shoulder jerked in a shrug she had no trouble interpreting. Did Shane even believe the cruelty he'd lived through from his father was anything but normal? As with most abused children, he wouldn't have talked about it to his friends. For all he knew, the same crap might be going on behind closed doors in their homes. Now, having the uncle Shane had liked and trusted react so violently to his minor offense had to make him think men were always this violent…or else there was something about *him* that caused both his father and uncle to lose it.

Neither interpretation was healthy.

The original call regarding Shane had been referred to another caseworker, Emmett Harper. Emmett had thought Shane would respond better to a woman and transferred his case to Lindsay. Whether Emmett was right or not, Lindsay had never had any trouble with the boy, and thought he trusted her as much as he could trust anyone.

She hated that his ability to trust had taken another blow.

Lindsay hid a wince. Bad pun.

"*I* say it's not your fault," she told him, but saw his disbelief.

AN HOUR LATER, she'd talked to the doctor, a gray-haired, reassuring man who said Shane had suffered a concussion, two broken ribs, a broken cheekbone, three broken fingers, probably from blocking a punch, and a great deal of soft tissue damage. Nothing permanent, but he'd be in significant pain for weeks to months as the broken bones healed.

Shane was admitted for the night because of the head injuries, which gave Lindsay almost twenty-four hours to find him a new placement.

She also talked to the Sadler police officer who had responded to the call from the bus driver and who had driven to Martin Ramsey's house on the outskirts of town. They used a small room off the ER to talk.

"Shane says, after his uncle beat the crap out of him, he told him to take a shower and get ready for school. Sent the kid out the door to catch the bus."

"Did he really think nobody would notice Shane's face?" Lindsay said incredulously.

Middle-aged and seemingly steady, Officer Joe Capek shook his head. "If he did, he's delusional."

"Do you think he took off?"

Sounding doubtful, he said, "If he'd been afraid of trouble with authorities, he could have kept the kid home from school for a few days. Threatened Shane with what would happen if he told anyone."

Lindsay thought the same. "When do you plan to go back to the house?"

"I gather he works as a handyman?"

"More like he does remodels, but yes, he said he takes small jobs, too."

Capek shrugged. "Figured I'd try five thirty, before my shift ends."

"I'll meet you there," she said, rising to her feet.

"Is that smart?" he asked.

"I want to look him in the eye when you cuff him," she said grimly.

His mouth twitched into an almost smile. "Let's meet there, then."

By the time Lindsay drove to the old farmhouse on the outskirts of Sadler, a headache had begun climbing the back of her neck. She could feel the pitons being pounded in.

Unfortunately, Martin Ramsey did not appear to be home. As Officer Capek circled the house to knock on the back door, Lindsay peered into a dusty, small-paned window on the side of the outbuilding that appeared to serve as a garage. She spotted a lawn mower and a flatbed trailer, but no car or pickup truck.

They met back at their own vehicles.

"I can send a unit around later," he told her, and she nodded. Truthfully, there was no huge urgency to get their hands on Martin. He had no other children in the home who might be potential victims.

The next morning, she drove Shane to a receiving home, intended to be temporary. Late afternoon, she called Capek to learn he'd had a family emergency. Sadler was one of the larger towns in eastern Oregon, which meant only that it had a handful of traffic lights downtown and an array of essential businesses as well as a bunch of churches and taverns. The police department consisted of seventeen officers as well as a chief and captain. The resources weren't unlimited, and the county sheriff's department was stretched even thinner patrolling lonely miles of rural roads and highways. Lindsay had always found both agencies to be cooperative to the extent of their capabilities. This time, though, it appeared that in the absence of Officer Capek, nobody else had made any effort to catch up to Shane's uncle.

Too mad to wait, she decided to follow up herself. She wouldn't make contact, just check to see if there were indications the man was home. The situation was beginning to strike her as really strange. Had he gotten home yesterday evening and not wondered at Shane's absence? Or had he gotten nervous and gone to stay with a friend?

Or could he be at his brother's empty home? Austin Ramsey was serving a disgracefully short jail sentence for what he'd done to his son. Knowing that, Martin might have thought he could stay there for a week or two with no one the wiser.

Martin's own home first.

The aging house and barn and additional small outbuilding looked as deserted as they had yesterday. Even forlorn, Lindsay thought, although that was surely all in her head.

Disturbed, she turned her car around and went back out to the road.

Shane had grown up in a somewhat more modern rambler that was also set on two or three acres. As Lindsay turned into the long dirt driveway, she became uneasily aware that, without binoculars, the nearest neighbors wouldn't see what was happening here.

Her foot went to the brake. Maybe coming out here alone wasn't the smartest thing she'd ever done. But after a brief hesitation, she made sure the car doors were locked and went ahead. Why would he be a danger to her? He probably thought he was fully justified in punishing his nephew.

She rolled to a stop in front of the house, which at first sight showed no sign of life. Here, a double garage could be hiding his pickup truck.

Lindsay turned her Subaru Outback around, so that all she had to do was stomp down on the accelerator to escape. Then she leaned on the horn and watched the front door and windows through her rearview mirror.

Wait. Was that a light on inside?

Her internal debate was brief. This was hardly the first time she'd gone alone to speak to an abusive parent. Assaulting her wouldn't advance Martin's cause. To the contrary, in fact. He still technically had visitation with his own children, albeit they lived with their mother and a stepfather in Pennsylvania. Given his poor impulse control, it probably hadn't occurred to him that he had put that visitation in jeopardy by beating up his nephew.

Lindsay left the key in the ignition, her engine running and the driver side door open to facilitate a hasty escape. She wasn't even sure why she felt so tentative as she climbed the two porch steps and approached the front door.

Ringing the doorbell produced a sound inside she'd call a gong. When nothing happened, she eased toward the large front window. The blinds were down, but slanted to allow her to peer in. The interior was dim, but a light was definitely on deeper in the house. The kitchen?

She dialed 9-1-1 and clutched her phone in her hand with her finger poised over the screen as she left the porch and went around the house to the back. On the way, she reasoned with herself. Austin might well have left a light or two on in the house to make it appear someone was home. He could even have lights on timers. Lindsay didn't understand this instinct insisting that, all evidence to the contrary, someone was here.

The quiet seemed unnatural when the road wasn't that far away. She stopped in the middle of the overgrown lawn and looked around. Movement in the trees caught her eye, chilling her despite the heat of the day. She stared. She'd been imagining things; no one was there. A few leaves quivered, probably because a bird had taken off from that branch.

Taking a deep breath, she turned to the back stoop, which was just that: a concrete pad with a small extension of the roof sheltering it. She was only a few feet away, about to take a last look over her shoulder, when she saw that the door stood open by an inch or two.

She froze, eyes fixed on the thin band of light. Her finger twitched, but…what if she called the police, and it turned out Austin just hadn't latched the door when he left the house?

Somehow, Lindsay knew better and knew, too, that she was going to look inside. Her mouth was suddenly dry. She used her elbow to nudge the door. It swung silently inward, revealing a utility room with a bench for the owner to sit and remove boots. Two pairs had been neatly placed beneath the bench. Several coats hung on hooks on the wall. An empty plastic laundry basket sat atop the dryer. An open doorway led into the kitchen.

Lindsay tiptoed forward, straining to hear any faint sound. As she scanned the room, her nostrils flared at the sharp scent of something burning.

For a moment, she didn't understand why two feet clad in white athletic socks were in such an odd position. She took one more step as she grappled with the question…and saw a man sprawled on the kitchen floor. At the sight of his head and the blood pooling on the floor, her stomach lurched.

Dear God, he was dead. Murdered. And…he was at least the same general size and shape as Martin Ramsey.

DETECTIVE DANIEL DEPERRO groaned as the canned voice on his cell phone assured him he could go the company website and discover a wealth of information, freeing him from any necessity of bothering an actual person.

He'd listened to the lengthy spiel and the ensuing elevator music six times now.

Since waiting on hold was a chronic time-waster for all detectives, he was mostly inured, but his mood hadn't been good today for no particular reason. His leg ached, although there was nothing new in that. When a high-caliber bullet shattered your femur, putting the pieces together was a little bit like trying to patch up poor Humpty Dumpty. And yeah, he hadn't enjoyed informing the parents of a high school senior that he had arrested their son for selling cocaine, and oh, by the way, the kid would stand trial as an adult since he'd turned eighteen three weeks before.

His desk phone rang and he picked it up, leaving his mobile phone on speaker so he wouldn't miss a single note of the music.

"Deperro."

"Detective, this is Officer Bowman. I just responded to a call from a CPS worker who found the man she was looking for dead. Head smashed like a jack-o'-lantern someone dropped. I don't see a weapon, but someone killed him."

"Address?"

Daniel committed the street address to memory and asked if the CPS worker was certain of the victim's identity. A murmur of conversation in the background was replaced by Bowman's voice.

"She thinks she knows who this is, but can't be positive."

"Okay. The name?"

Martin Ramsey rang some bells for him. Coming in to work yesterday, Daniel had taken note of the report of a severe beating given a fourteen-year-old boy and that the teen had tagged his uncle as the perpetrator.

Checking his computer, Daniel saw that an Austin Ramsey owned the home where the dead body had been found. Austin, however, was currently in the county jail. Interesting.

He grabbed his cell phone, cut off the beginning of the spiel, version seven, and walked out of the station to his car.

The drive didn't take ten minutes.

Somebody had filled potholes in the dirt driveway. Ahead, he saw a brick rambler with a double-car garage at one end. Two vehicles sat in front, one an SPD car with a rack of lights on top, the second a common crossover that would handle well in snow and ice, which they would certainly see plenty of this winter. In the crossover, he could see the back of a woman's head.

Officer Aaron Bowman came around the side of the house. He was young, twenty-eight or twenty-nine, and had impressed Daniel before with his steadiness and common sense.

When the two men met up, Daniel said, "That the caseworker?"

"Her name is Lindsay Engle. She took a boy named Shane Ramsey from his father, who owns this place, and placed him with the uncle. According to her, a couple weeks later the uncle beat the boy bloody. Nobody has picked up the uncle yet, who apparently hasn't gone home. She thought he might be hiding out here."

"And that's who she thinks is dead in there."

"Yeah."

Daniel asked a few questions as the two men went to the back door, which according to the woman had been open. Bowman hadn't gone past the entrance between the utility room and the kitchen.

"Didn't need to check for a pulse," he said, his jaw tightening.

Daniel immediately saw why. Half the victim's head had been obliterated. He also understood Ms. Engle's doubts. If the dead man had any face left, it couldn't be seen from this angle.

The odd note was a small metal wastebasket sitting in the middle of the kitchen floor, only feet from the body. He took another step until he was able to see the burned, broken flakes inside, like blackened sheets of paper-thin, delicate phyllo bread.

Crumpled paper, he realized. A fire that had been deliberately set, and gone out when all fuel had been consumed.

Daniel called for CSI. He wanted to walk through the house, but found the front door locked and didn't want to contaminate the kitchen by tromping through it. He asked Officer Bowman to stay and to start a log of who came and went. Then he went to the caseworker's car and knocked on the passenger side window. She unlocked once he asked if he could get in to talk to her.

He turned in the seat to survey her, and felt an odd stirring he identified as surprise. In some inexplicable way, she didn't look like a Child Protective Services caseworker, yet he knew that was ridiculous. He'd worked with enough of her colleagues to be fully aware they could be young, middle-aged, near retirement, outwardly cheerful or glum, blue-eyed or brown. The stereotypes didn't work. About all he knew for sure was that in the local office, a majority of the caseworkers were women.

This one had medium brown hair worn in a roll on

the back of her head, blue eyes and a voluptuous body he thought could be a problem when she worked with unstable men and hormone-ridden teenage boys. But that was none of his business.

What did make him curious was her guarded air. He wondered if she was ever completely open. The fact that he sensed she had secrets might in fact be his business.

"Ms. Engle?" He held out a hand.

Hers was icy cold. "That's right."

"Tell me what brought you here." He smiled, hoping to relax her. "Start at the beginning."

She spoke succinctly, her voice pleasingly husky. Mostly, what she told him was a recap. He listened intently when she explained her reasoning for checking out this house, and for deciding to get out of her car and ring the doorbell.

"You didn't consider calling for police backup?" he asked.

"I should have." Her cheeks warmed. "I don't like to do that unless I know something's wrong, though. I mean, that's a waste of your time. This was just..."

He waited through her hesitation.

Her eyes met his. "I really don't know. Just a feeling, I guess. I almost chickened out when I first came around the back of the house. I could have sworn someone was standing in that wooded area. But I don't know, when I kept looking I didn't see anyone."

Was she tossing out the possibility that someone else had been watching her to keep him from focusing on *her*? Or had a killer really been there, and she'd been an idiot to disregard what her instincts had surely been telling her?

She continued. "When I saw that the back door was

open a crack, I justified going inside." She made a face. "I actually tiptoed, believe it or not."

Yeah, he could see her doing that. He wanted to say, *You know walking in that way was stupid, don't you?* Instead, he settled for an "uh-huh."

"What I don't understand is who could have killed him. It doesn't make sense."

She *sounded* sincere. Was she that good an actor? He must have hidden what he was thinking, because her expression didn't change until he asked, "Is Shane still in the hospital?"

Her mouth dropped open. "You're suggesting *Shane* would do this?"

"I'm asking where he is."

She didn't look very friendly now, but said, "I picked him up at the hospital late this morning and took him to a receiving home. I assure you, he's in no shape to borrow a bike, pedal across town and beat a man to death."

"But he has excellent motivation," Daniel said softly.

Her anger, or dislike, flared from a simmer to a rolling boil. "That's ridiculous! He never even fought back when his father abused him. He's a good kid. You might as well accuse me."

He didn't say a word, because yes, the thought had crossed his mind that she might have cracked and killed a man who epitomized everything she hated.

She retreated without moving a muscle. The rest of her answers were single syllables. He couldn't even blame her, but the reality was that he had to consider her a suspect at this point.

Ten minutes later, already on his phone, he watched her drive away. If she intended to call the receiving home, he'd beaten her to the punch—and what he learned in a brief conversation set a red flag to flapping.

Chapter Two

Shane was missing.

Lindsay learned as much when she reached the receiving home. Althea and Randy Price had never been among her favorite foster parents, but they'd seemed capable for short-term placements. Live and learn. Apparently Althea had shown Shane to his bedroom and then failed to notice his absence until four or five hours later.

The woman's round-cheeked face flushed. "I assumed he was sleeping."

Scared for Shane, Lindsay said, "You didn't check even once on a boy you knew had suffered a head injury and had spent the night at the hospital."

Randy Price glared at her.

Althea's chin rose defiantly. "You'll have to forgive me if I thought he needed sleep more than lunch!"

"He needed care, Mrs. Price. And I'll admit I'm disturbed to learn that he walked out without either of you seeing or hearing a thing."

She sniffed. "Well, I'm sure that detective who called will find him."

Oh, crap. That detective had probably called before Lindsay had made it down the driveway. He wanted to pin the murder on her or on poor Shane. Why work when you can go for the easy answer?

She knew what she had to do: find Shane before Detective Deperro did.

But first she had to figure out why Shane had taken off. Only one possibility leaped to mind. He could have gone out to the highway to hitch a ride to some bigger city where he imagined he could live on his own until he turned eighteen. When she thought about it, Randy was a big man who might have reminded Shane unpleasantly of his father and uncle. Lindsay had thought Shane understood that he'd be with the Prices for only two or three days until a suitable foster home was located, but even if he sort of trusted her, believing that the next placement would be any better might be beyond a boy like Shane.

It bothered her that he hadn't had any stuff of his own to take with him. Thanks to police planning to search his uncle's house, they couldn't get into it at least until tomorrow to collect the duffel with his belongings. He wouldn't have any money, either—unless he'd taken some out of Althea's purse. Lindsay wasn't about to ask and put any ideas in the woman's head.

"If you'll excuse me, I need to look for him," she said. "Obviously, I won't be bringing him back here."

Randy's jaws bulged. "We wouldn't have a boy who'd sneak out like that."

Walking down the sidewalk to her car, Lindsay rolled her eyes. Really? Every kid they'd taken in was a saint? She was angry enough; she intended to contact a colleague and suggest they reconsider the Prices' receiving home license.

She hadn't reached her car when an unmarked police SUV rolled up behind her bumper. Deperro got out and watched her approach. She felt a tiny bump in her chest, because there was no denying he was a magnificent male specimen—six foot two or three and broad-shouldered, with dark hair and eyes and bronze skin—but he'd done or said nothing to make her think she'd *like* him. So she nodded vaguely in his direction and went around to her driver door. She couldn't think of a thing she wanted to say to him.

His deep voice carried well. "Ms. Engle."

That tone would scare Shane, too. She really had to find the boy first. "Detective."

"Can we talk?"

Gee, he'd asked.

Only after she opened her car door did she face him. "We've already done that. You may research my background and job performance to your heart's content, but I think I'll get an attorney before I sit down with you again. Now, if you'll excuse me." Not looking at him again, she climbed in behind the wheel and gave a yank to the door handle, only to meet resistance.

Somehow, he'd moved fast enough to grab hold of the top of the door.

Lindsay turned a blistering glare on him. "What do you want?"

"You to tell me where I might find Shane."

"How can I? My best guess is that he decided he can't trust any adults. It would appear he's right."

Those espresso-dark eyes narrowed. "His uncle was murdered. You don't think it would be irresponsible of me *not* to sit him down for a talk? To think, oh, his caseworker says he's a *nice* boy. He couldn't have anything to do with this, and think how much I'd upset him by asking where the hell he was while someone was beating Uncle Martin's head in."

Lindsay tried very hard to hold on to her dislike, but that was hardly fair. Of course, his job demanded he find out where Shane had been while Martin was being killed. Ask Shane if he knew who might hate Martin—or benefit from his death.

Her keys were biting into her palm. Not looking at him, she said quietly, "I really don't know where he is. I'm…scared for him."

There was a moment of silence. He moved again, squatting inside the open door so he was closer to her eye level. Lindsay was painfully aware of the way the fabric of his black cargo pants stretched across powerful thigh muscles. She hated being torn between so many conflicting emotions and impulses.

"I understand," Deperro said, in an entirely different voice. "Believe it or not, I'm concerned about him, too."

She made herself meet his eyes. "Why?"

It was obvious the detective wasn't sure he wanted to tell her, but after a moment he rolled his shoulders as if to release tension. "What if the uncle saw him on the street and grabbed him? Shane might have had reason to fight back. Or what if he was there in the house when someone else killed his uncle? Did he run before that person had a chance to get a hand on him, too? Or did he see something he's afraid to tell anyone?"

Lindsay was afraid her mouth had dropped open. He was right. Those were real possibilities she hadn't considered. Shane might be in danger because he was only a kid standing with his thumb out beside a highway. But he might be dead, too, or running from a killer.

All the air in her lungs left her in a rush. "None of that occurred to me," she admitted.

"You could help me do my job."

If Shane were here, wouldn't she encourage him to answer Deperro's questions?

Of course she would. "For the third time, I really,

truly, cross my heart, *don't* know where he is. I don't have the impression he has any good friends. How could he, when he didn't want anyone to know how bad it was at home?"

"Yeah," the detective said gruffly. "I get that."

"My best guess is that he's running away because he didn't like the Prices and is afraid of what will happen to him once he's placed again. He might think he can get by as a street kid in Portland or Seattle until he ages out."

Deperro swore. "I'll put the word out to watch for him. Damn. We want to stop him before he gets too far."

Again, he was right. And he was able to marshal help from sheriff's deputies and even the state patrol in a way she couldn't. Had she really thought she'd find Shane by driving aimlessly up and down local roads?

Deperro frowned. "Could he have gone by his uncle's house to pick up his stuff?"

"Would he dare?"

"It's worth looking." He rose easily to his feet and stood gazing down at her.

"I can go out there while you—"

"Head out there, too." His eyebrows rose, giving him a devilish look. "You're welcome to join me."

Lindsay closed her eyes. As much as she hated to surrender, she just about had to.

"One question," he said.

She braced herself.

"Has Shane ever been caught setting fires? Even small ones?"

Remembering the smell of something burning at the Ramsey house, Lindsay was profoundly relieved to be able to shake her head. "No. Never."

The detective's eyes stayed narrow and intent, but finally he nodded.

That didn't mean he believed her.

DURING THE DRIVE, Daniel coaxed Lindsay—she'd stiffly given him permission to use her first name—into telling him what she knew about both Martin and Austin Ramsey.

Shane's mother had died when he was nine. When Shane came onto Lindsay's radar, he'd admitted that his dad hurt his mother, too. He thought Dad had killed her, but didn't know for sure.

Daniel gave her a startled glance. "Did you report his suspicion?"

"No. I made a note in his file, but he wasn't home when his mother died, and he said his father denied having anything to do with it."

"How did she die?"

"She was helping paint the exterior of the house. Supposedly, Austin heard her scream and raced around to find her on the ground. She'd been atop a tall ladder, painting the trim on the eaves."

"A fall." Daniel heard how expressionless that came out.

"Hard to prove anything."

"Unfortunately." The odds of a woman whose husband had been battering her dying in an accident struck him as about a hundred to one, but there really wasn't much he could do all these years later.

"I should have done more of a background check on the uncle," Lindsay admitted after a minute, not looking at him. "Martin's ex-wife didn't return my phone call then, and I depended too much on Shane's confidence in his uncle. While I was at the hospital this morning,

I finally reached Martin's ex-wife, who has remarried and lives back east. He hadn't abused the kids, who were really young when the divorce happened, but he'd hit her a few times, she said. He hasn't demanded visitation, but she said there was no way she'd let their kids go for an unsupervised stay with him."

"Have you let her know he's dead yet?" Daniel asked. Fingerprints had already confirmed the victim's identity.

"No, I thought you might prefer to do that."

"I would." He was surprised at her restraint, although it was possible she just hadn't wanted to do a death notification. Who did? "You're sure she wasn't here in Oregon when you talked to her?"

"Pretty sure. I reached a cleaning lady at the house, who gave me Mrs. Schulze's work number."

"Took the new husband's name, huh?"

"Apparently."

He kept eyeing Lindsay sidelong, wondering if she'd just tamped down the hostility or whether she had let some of it go. Not all, or she'd be willing to look at him. And why would she, once she guessed he had to consider her as a possible suspect in the murder of the man who'd brutally beaten the boy under her charge?

Truthfully, Daniel couldn't see it. He'd walked out to the woods where she thought she'd seen someone watching her, but found nothing. Given the extremely dry ground, the guy would have had to do something as stupid as drop a cigarette butt to leave any evidence of his existence, and he hadn't. That's if he existed at all. But Daniel wouldn't hold it against her if she'd been scared enough to imagine someone.

Earlier Daniel had gotten the quickie summation of her job history. Apparently, she had received nothing but sterling reviews by supervisors in Child Protective Services. A few quotes from her annual reviews said things like, "Really cares for the kids," as well as "Lindsay is practical, kind and refuses to let down a child who counts on her." If the supervisor was to be believed, she was adept at dealing with the abusive adults as well as the children. She had a talent for matching adults and children with the right therapists, too.

She'd done social work for nine years, the last three with CPS. If she hadn't yet cracked and knocked off a vicious abuser, why would she now?

Of course, cops were known to break eventually, too, and do something they wouldn't have ten years before or even a month before. While Daniel couldn't entirely rule her out as a suspect, he was more interested in Shane, and then in gathering information from neighbors, friends and people who'd hired Martin along the way. If the man had been capable of losing it with his nephew the way he had, he could have lashed out at other people as well.

At Martin's house, Daniel parked, turned off the engine and looked at Lindsay. "I'm taking you in with me because you'll have a better idea what Shane had with him and whether anything is missing. I'll ask you not to touch anything and to stay with me."

She retorted, "Why are you treating this like a crime scene?"

"Because trouble could have started here and followed him to his brother's house."

Her clipped nod managed to convey surface agreement underlaid by skepticism.

Daniel had the keys that had been in Martin's pocket. It took him a few tries to find the right one to open the front door. It led directly into the living room, which lacked any suggestion of a woman's influence. Scratched, worn hardwood floors were matched by dingy off-white walls, unadorned by art. Instead, a big recliner faced a flat-screen TV. The sofa seemed an afterthought.

His nose twitched at the trace of an unpleasant odor. Lindsay's eyes widened and her head turned. She locked her fingers together at her waist. "Is that…?"

"Something dead? I don't think so." That would be an all-too familiar odor for him. This wasn't the singed smell that had permeated the kitchen at the crime scene, either.

She didn't look all that reassured but followed him to the kitchen. He almost gagged when he pulled the trash from under the sink.

"Can we relax the 'don't touch' rule long enough to throw this out?" she asked, making an awful face.

"Once I poke through it." He'd found useful evidence in garbage cans or dumpsters before, but felt certain that wouldn't be the case here.

When he donned latex gloves, Lindsay retreated a few steps. "You're braver than I am."

He smiled. "I doubt that. Cowards don't do your job."

Those blue eyes flashed at him. "You're right about that."

Beneath dirty food containers and a bunch of beer cans, he found a pound of hamburger that was now gray and all too clearly the source of the stench. Daniel took the plastic bag out to a garbage can he'd noted during the earlier visit. Lindsay stayed on the back porch, sucking in fresh air.

"None of that looked recent," she said when he returned.

"No." He'd noticed the same.

"But...does that mean neither of them had dinner the night before last?"

"Let's look in the fridge."

"Do we have to?" she mumbled.

Daniel outright grinned as he swung open the refrigerator door. Another package of hamburger wasn't looking good. Otherwise, racks held mustard, mayonnaise and ketchup, a half gallon of milk—nearly empty, he discovered, when he lifted it—onion and celery in the vegetable drawer, and a pizza box on the top shelf. He took it out and decided it was still edible. He tipped the open box toward Lindsay.

"I suppose that was dinner."

"His, maybe. More would have been gone if Shane had had some. He's a teenage boy."

Her eyes glittered with anger he understood. "You're saying the creep beat him because, what, he didn't throw away some wadded paper towels and a few beer or pop cans?"

"Something like that," he agreed.

"I assumed Uncle Martin had cooked, with the understanding that Shane would do the clean-up." That anger still carrying her, she said, "Can we check out Shane's room?"

"You know which one it is?"

"I was with Shane when Martin helped carry his stuff up. Saying how glad he was to have Shane, and how he wished he'd known how his brother had treated his own son." She shook her head in disgust. "Apparently, the abuse was okay for him because Shane wasn't his."

They started up the stairs. To distract himself from the sway of her hips in front of him, Daniel commented, "In my experience, it's not usually the good guys who get murdered. It's drug dealers, gang members, people trying to screw other people over. The exception is victims of domestic abuse."

She waited for him on the landing, a crinkle forming on her forehead. "This is a turnaround for you, then."

"When this happens, it's usually because a woman or an older kid fights back. Grabs a knife or gun." He shrugged.

He almost regretted saying it, because wariness showed on her face again. "That's why Shane is at the top of your list."

"I'm afraid so," Daniel admitted. "I won't railroad him, Lindsay. I promise."

She searched his eyes with an intensity that shook him. He wasn't used to suspecting someone might have actually seen parts of his psyche he'd rather keep hidden. As a cop and a former soldier, he had plenty he never talked about. He didn't look away, though; he wasn't sure he could.

Finally, she dipped her head, indicating—what? Acceptance? Belief in him?

He could only hope.

One step into Shane's room and Daniel knew the boy had been here today and was gone. Dresser drawers remained open. Lindsay peered under the bed, urged him to open the closet door. Empty.

Finally, staring into the closet, she said, "At least he has his stuff."

If that was the good news, he didn't want to hear the bad.

His phone rang while he was locking the front door, Lindsay having already started down the porch steps. Unfamiliar number, but local area code. He answered.

"Detective Deperro, this is State Patrol Officer William Lasher. I have the boy I was told you're looking for."

"That's good news." He was aware of Lindsay stopping, turning to look at him. "Where did you find him?"

"The kid had gotten a surprising distance from Sadler. He'd had his thumb out on Highway 97 near Redmond."

"I'll come pick him up," Daniel said.

"Oh, we're on our way to you. Can't say the boy is happy—" there was a smile in Lasher's voice "—but he's gobbling a double cheeseburger and fries, so I'd say he's okay."

Daniel laughed. "Hey, he's a teenage boy. Bottomless pit."

"That's for sure. I have two of 'em at home."

Daniel thanked him and they agreed to meet at the Sadler police station. He could see from Lindsay's expression that she thought he'd isolate the kid in an interrogation room and take out his rubber hose.

"I want to sit in on your talk with him," she said firmly.

"You're entitled," he agreed. "Unless you or we come up with another family member willing to take responsibility for Shane, you'll need to stand in as his guardian."

She eyed him suspiciously, then climbed into his SUV. Lindsay Engle was one feisty woman, who wouldn't appreciate his smile.

THE BOY STARED anxiously at Daniel. Small for his age, he looked downright pathetic with the bruising in full color, the swelling that distorted his face, and the way he held one arm across his torso as if protecting it. Daniel had broken ribs before and knew how painful they were. Shane's right hand was wrapped to immobilize several fingers, which would rule out writing or texting. The still grossly swollen lips turned his speech into a mumble.

Lindsay had very gently hugged him and murmured something in his ear. Now she sat on the boy's side of the table, where she could fix a distrustful gaze on Daniel.

"Are you making me go back to that foster home?" Shane asked her.

Lindsay shook her head. "No, we've found a permanent placement for you. You'll like this family."

Not hard to see Shane's doubt.

"Why did you leave the Prices' home?" Daniel asked. "Ms. Engle has been worried about you."

Shane shot a quick look her way. "I'm sorry. I just thought…" He didn't finish.

"Did either of the Prices do or say anything that frightened you?" she asked him.

His shoulders hunched. "Not really. He—Mr. Price—looked mean."

Enough chitchat. "When did you last see your uncle Martin?" Daniel asked.

The kid's puzzlement appeared genuine. "Yesterday morning. When he said I had to go to school and to get out of the house."

"Has he contacted you?"

"How could he?" He sounded confused. "I don't have a phone or anything like that."

"He could have had his call put through to your hospital room."

"The only person who called was Ms. Engle." His expression changed. He drew into himself, appearing to shrink. “Is he trying to get me back? Like, claiming it wasn’t *him* who hurt me?”

“No—” Lindsay broke off at Daniel’s signal.

He said bluntly, “Your uncle is dead, Shane.”

Shane gaped. “*What?* How?”

“He was murdered. Ms. Engle found his body.”

His wild stare swung between Daniel and Lindsay. “But… I don’t get it.” And then he drew in a sharp breath. “You think *I* killed him?”

Daniel modulated his tone. “I have to ask, Shane. The fact that you were missing at the same time he was murdered doesn’t look good.”

“I wouldn’t! I never saw him!” He focused on Lindsay. “I didn’t!”

She reached for his uninjured hand. “It’s okay. Just answer Detective Deperro’s questions so he can eliminate you as a suspect.”

Well, at least she hadn’t said, *I believe you,* although Daniel felt sure she did.

Trouble was, despite a usually cynical nature, he believed Shane, too.

Chapter Three

Shane eyed the molasses cookies Rhonda Manning had set out. She and her husband, Lyman, both beamed at him. Lyman designed games for a small software company in Bend. He worked remotely three days a week, only going into the office the other two days. Maybe five foot nine or ten, he was as scrawny as Shane, and certainly not physically prepossessing, which made him a good choice for Shane.

Lindsay thought this was the perfect home for Shane.

She smiled at Rhonda. "If you don't mind me snitching a cookie or two, I'd better get back to the office."

"Of course not. I'll grab a napkin."

Lindsay turned to Shane. "Remember your promise to the detective."

Shane ducked his head. "I won't run away again. If I freak, I'll call you."

She laughed, hugged him and murmured in his ear, "You do that." Lindsay thought he was smiling when she let him go, although given the swelling on his face it was a little hard to tell.

Shane was shyly reaching for a cookie when she thanked the Mannings and left.

Unfortunately, she'd lied; she wasn't going to the office. Her destination was once again the hospital. As medical personnel were legally required to do, an ER doctor had contacted Child Protective Services to report his belief that a twelve-year-old girl was being sexually abused by her stepfather. Lindsay's supervisor, Sadie Culver, had asked her to take this investigation. The only other caseworker free to pursue it was male, and Sadie assumed the girl would feel more comfortable with a woman. Given that Deperro had allowed Lindsay to take Shane, exacting only the promise that he stick around, she thought she had the boy settled. She couldn't forget that she had dozens of other open cases, but the most urgent leapfrogged to first place on her agenda.

Nobody in Kaila Kelley's family had appeared on the Oregon Department of Human Services' radar before. That wasn't unusual in cases of sexual molestation; those children rarely told anyone what was happening. Shame and threats were such an effective one-two punch that a father could work his way through three or four daughters before even a hint of the ugly situation surfaced. Lindsay hated knowing that Kaila had an older sister, Kira.

She learned at the hospital that the observant ER doc had admitted Kaila over the objections of her mother. Going to her room, Lindsay found Mrs. Norris sitting solicitously at her daughter's bedside. The slight figure in the bed lay curled on her side, looking toward the window instead of her mother.

When Lindsay introduced herself, Kaila rolled over, her small face with delicate bones drawn with anxiety. The mother jumped to her feet.

"I just don't understand why that doctor insisted on calling CPS!" Anxiety underlaid Mrs. Norris's anger. "My husband thinks of Kaila as his daughter. He'd never do anything so awful! She had to have been raped, maybe by a boy at school. It's the police who should be investigating."

They would be, but Lindsay didn't tell her that. Rather, she said calmly, "I'm here to find out what Kaila says happened."

Mrs. Norris turned her head to look at her daughter. "Tell her." Her voice rose to near-hysteria. "Tell her your daddy wouldn't hurt you."

Before the girl could open her mouth, assuming she intended to, Lindsay took two steps to place herself between the mother and child. "I know this is difficult for you, Mrs. Norris, but I need to speak to Kaila alone. You can wait in the hall or go down to the cafeteria and get a cup of coffee or lunch. If you give me your phone number, I can—"

"I have a right to be here! I'm her parent," the woman cried.

"Under usual circumstances, that's the case. However, we need to offer the children we protect the chance to speak freely to us. I feel sure you understand that."

Paige Norris understood no such thing, but eventually, reluctantly, withdrew.

"Hi, Kaila." She sat in the chair pulled close to the bed and smiled sympathetically. "I'll bet you have awful cramps."

Wary brown eyes focused and unblinking, Kaila nodded.

"Are your parents divorced? Do you have contact with your biological dad?" Lindsay already knew, but this seemed like a good way to edge into the difficult part.

"Daddy died," Kaila said in a small, husky voice. "In a car accident."

Lindsay touched the girl's nervous hand. "I'm sorry. It's hard to lose a parent."

Tears shimmered in Kaila's eyes but didn't fall.

"When did your mother remarry?" Lindsay asked.

"Four years ago. I was eight."

"That's been a long time. Do you think of your stepfather as your dad now?"

The girl shook her head vehemently. "He's mostly nice. You know? But he always liked to hug us and we had to sit on his lap and stuff like that. Mom said he's just touchy-feely. Like that. I didn't like it, but I just—" She broke off.

I just endured it. That's what she wasn't saying. And her mother had sent the message that she should ignore her own instincts and allow a man to handle her any way he wanted. Lindsay had to struggle for a moment with her temper.

Once she had it mastered, she asked, "What about your sister? Kira? Does she like him?"

"Uh-uh. She hates him. She never said anything, but I think he did *this* to her before. I'd find her crying, and she'd tell me to go away."

"And what is 'this'?"

Getting a child her age to spell out the details took patience. But Lindsay sat quietly and allowed Kaila to take her time. Finally she admitted to the molestation, but her eyes glistened with tears when she said, "He told me I couldn't tell *anyone*, or bad things would happen."

Starting to weep, she exclaimed, "But I can't go home! I can't!"

Lindsay took her hand and said firmly, "No, you won't be going home unless and until we're certain you'll be safe there. I'll call the police, and they and I both will talk to your mom, your sister and your stepfather. In the meantime, I'm placing both you and Kira in a foster home. She can't stay at home, either."

"Really?" Those wet eyes held a glimmer of hope. "Mom says I'm lying. That's what she'll tell you, too."

"You know what?" Lindsay smiled. "I've heard that before. What *you* tell me is what counts the most."

Kaila cried afresh, but less with despair than relief, Lindsay thought.

"Now, you'll be staying here at least overnight," she said. "I'm going to talk to your mother now. I'm also asking the nursing staff not to allow either your mother or stepfather in to see you. Okay?"

She gave a big nod and started swiping at her face with her sheet.

Lindsay squeezed Kaila's hand and turned her mind to foster placement options.

DANIEL TIPPED BACK his desk chair and brooded. Not surprisingly, he'd had little luck finding any of Martin or Austin Ramsey's neighbors at home midday. He'd have to canvass the neighborhood in the early evening. So far, he hadn't come up with names of friends, either. He supposed he'd have to start with clients who had hired Ramsey to work on their homes or businesses; the guy had kept records of his jobs and payments. Daniel wasn't optimistic about learning much from them. The brutality of the beating shouted rage. This crime was personal. It had to be.

Most murders weren't mysteries. Wife shot husband after he hit her one time too many. Brawls got out of hand at bars. A creep holding up a convenience store panicked and shot the clerk.

On the face of it, Shane was the likeliest—and best motivated—suspect, and Daniel couldn't yet 100 percent rule him out. The fire in the trash can was typical for the budding arsonist. Nonetheless, Daniel thought the kid was sad more than angry, and the timing wasn't right. After all, Daniel couldn't be sure the fire was connected to the death, although setting a can in the middle of the kitchen floor to, say, burn papers didn't strike him as logical.

Anyway, now that the medical examiner had established time of death, Daniel didn't see how the boy could have managed to knock off his uncle while also picking up his stuff from his former home and getting so far from Sadler. Suspicious by nature, however, Daniel reminded himself that Shane might have an older friend who helped by driving him around…and possibly even with murder.

He couldn't rule out Lindsay Engle, either, if only because he had to look twice at the person who'd found the body. He considered her unlikely, in part because, while CPS workers had a tough job and did burn out, what happened to Shane wasn't extreme or anything new to her. He hadn't read any undertones in what she'd said. In fact, he liked her determination to protect a boy who'd taken some hard knocks—literally and figuratively. He liked a lot more than that about her, but kept that kind of interest tamped down.

"Hey." Another Sadler detective, Melinda McIntosh, tapped her knuckles on his desk.

He straightened with a jerk. Damn, he should have noticed her approach. Way to go.

"What's up?"

"I just caught an investigation that involves a woman I hear you know. Lindsay Engle?"

Unexpectedly jolted, he said, "Tell me about it." Had he read the social worker wrong?

Melinda grimaced. “The lieutenant likes to give me anything that involves female victims.”

“That’s…sort of logical,” Daniel pointed out.

“Yeah, but it’s also sexist.” She shook her head. “Forget I said that. This involves a girl who was apparently raped. She’s named her stepfather.”

Daniel shook his head in disgust. He also relaxed, although he hoped not visibly. “And Ms. Engle was assigned to the case.” He was proud of himself for not calling her Lindsay, for keeping his distance.

“You got it.”

Midthirties, Melinda was divorced and attractive, with hazel eyes and dark hair kept in a severe bun. There was a time Daniel had considered asking her out, but her appeal hadn’t overruled the likely complications. Instead, they’d become friends who worked together well when partnered on investigations. That was happening more since Daniel’s previous partner had turned out to be corrupt, taking money to protect drug traffickers. Daniel never would have called John Risvold a friend, but he had trusted him. Being shot, twice, by his partner had been convincing evidence that the guy had betrayed not only Daniel, but everything else they were supposed to stand for.

“Ms. Engle is good at her job,” he commented now. “Really good. Don’t get between her and the kid she’s protecting.”

Melinda laughed. “You mean, if I don’t want to lose a hand?”

He grinned. “Something like that.”

Her smile faded. “With these kind of accusations, it isn’t easy hanging on to any objectivity.”

“No, it isn’t.” He hesitated. “Yell if you need backup.”

She waved off his offer. “No reason I should.”

Didn't that sound like famous last words? Unsettled, he watched her walk out of the cramped detective bull pen.

AT FIRST MEETING, Doug Norris seemed a likeable man. Lindsay saw what Kaila had meant. He was medium height, his body soft without being fat, his smile friendly. His handshake was soft, too, and possibly a little damp. Nerves?

Lindsay hadn't expected him to admit to having a sexual relationship with one or both daughters, and she'd been right. Instead of outrage, he went with deep disappointment. He loved the girls, had done his best to fill in as their father, couldn't understand what had set Kaila off.

"You are aware of the reason she was hospitalized."

"Don't some girls have heavy, er, cycles?"

Cycles? He couldn't possibly be that prudish, given that he was married and outnumbered in his home three to one by females.

Lindsay repeated the doctor's observations, with his conclusion: Kaila's bleeding had denoted an injury from an act of nonconsensual sex described as brutal.

"Brutal?" he repeated. *Now* he sounded outraged. "I can't believe that. Her mother said Kaila looks fine. She couldn't understand why that doctor wanted to keep her."

His reaction cemented Lindsay's certainty. He didn't think what he'd done was brutal; he'd probably convinced himself that his stepdaughter was happy to have greater intimacy with him. He wouldn't consider himself a violent man.

She asked further questions. Well, yes, he'd been home with Kaila when the alleged assault occurred, but all they'd done was watch TV. If it was true that she'd been hurt, she must have slipped out of the house later, met up with some friends. She was protecting one of them.

Kira insisted her stepfather had never done anything like that to *her*—until she found out that she was being removed from her home along with her sister no matter what she said. Then she cried and admitted he'd been molesting her for several years. She hated him, but Mom wouldn't listen and she didn't know what to do.

The phenomenon was all too familiar to Lindsay. Life was tough for a woman raising two children on her own, especially if she didn't have the skills to make an adequate living. Once she'd found a nice guy who treated her well, she didn't want to admit to his dark side. If she pretended even to herself that her daughter's accusations weren't true, that said daughter was acting out as she entered her teenage years, then everything was fine. Kira would be ashamed someday at the awful things she'd claimed. So would Kaila, who must have gotten the idea from her older sister.

Lindsay had also encountered plenty of women who leaped immediately to their children's defense and called the cops themselves. Unfortunately, Paige Norris wasn't of that breed.

By the end of the school day, the foster care coordinator she liked best to work with had found a foster home that could take both girls. Keeping them together was important.

She spoke several times to a Detective McIntosh. Honestly, Lindsay had been surprised that Sadler PD had any women on the force, never mind one promoted to detective. This was a traditional, conservative town, to put it mildly. Melinda McIntosh must be both tough and determined to have earned her place.

They'd agreed to interview family members separately, since their goals and authority differed. Detective McIntosh strongly supported Lindsay's decision to remove both girls from the home while the investigation progressed.

Late in the day, Lindsay checked on Shane, learning that he was in the middle of a computer game designed by his new foster dad, and was in awe at how impossible it was to beat.

She also spoke to Kira and Kaila's foster mother, who said they were settling in well. Kira came on the phone to say, "Mrs. Simpson is really nice, except she says I have to go to school tomorrow even if Kaila doesn't."

Laughing, Lindsay said, "Since Kaila spent last night in the hospital and you didn't, that sounds fair to me."

The silence that followed sharpened her attention. Finally, voice small, the fourteen-year-old said, "I wish I'd told, 'cuz then this wouldn't have happened to her."

"Kira, when the person you most rely on doesn't believe you, you have to ask yourself why anyone else would. You also have to know that, if someone in authority actually *does* believe you, it'll mean your family getting torn apart. That's scary."

"How do you know? Did…did this happen to you, too?"

"I had an abusive parent—" not something she often admitted "—but it wasn't sexual."

"Oh." Kira was quiet for a moment. "I guess it hurts either way."

"It does."

The conversation stayed with her when she returned to the office to do some online research and write reports. For a girl at such a tumultuous age, Kira Kelley was astonishingly insightful and mature.

Lindsay felt confident that the two girls were telling the truth about their stepfather. His "poor me, I'm just trying to be a great dad" crap confirmed their stories. Mom's emotions and responses were off, too. Still, there wasn't any more Lindsay could do until results came back on the rape kit and Detective McIntosh tied up her investigation.

A thought slithered into her head. Too bad Doug Norris hadn't been murdered instead of Martin Ramsey. After this last beating, Shane would never have been sent back to stay with his uncle, but a judge might decide to return Kira and Kaila to their mother and stepfather if no proof was found to support their accusations.

Guilt rushed through Lindsay. How could she even *think* something like that? Yes, she despised men like Doug Norris with every fiber of her being, but violent impulses were foreign to her. She had vowed long ago never to be anything like her mother.

Besides, it was unlikely Martin's abuse of his nephew had anything to do with his murder. He had to be involved in something shady, or he'd hurt someone who wanted revenge, or maybe he had been sleeping with a married woman. The timing would turn out to be coincidental. She refused to believe otherwise.

Chances were good Detective Deperro was pursuing other avenues of inquiry—wasn't that the right term?—and she wouldn't hear from him again.

And no, that wasn't a twinge of regret she felt. It was probably her stomach reminding her she hadn't stopped for lunch.

THE ONLY UNEXPECTED finding once the medical examiner opened up Martin Ramsey was several tumors in his lungs.

"Squamous cell carcinoma," the M.E. remarked. "Those tumors can extend into the wall of the chest."

The blackened lung gave away the dead man's lifetime of smoking. Daniel had seen the ashtrays in his house, smelled the tobacco smoke that had seeped into the walls.

"Didn't get a chance to kill him," he said.

The small fire set in the wastebasket hadn't had anything to do with Martin's smoking. No cigarettes had been found in his pockets, and Daniel hadn't smelled even a hint of tobacco smoke in Austin's house.

Dr. Stamey had already expressed his belief that the weapon used to bash in Ramsey's skull was an old pipe, perhaps two inches in diameter. He had plucked flakes of rust from the mess that was the victim's head.

In his first pass through Austin's house, Daniel hadn't seen anything like that, nor had the CSI crew.

Now that he knew what to look for, he intended to return to the house. He had yet to search the several outbuildings, although he didn't really expect to find the weapon. The killer had probably brought it with him, and taken it home when he or she was done. He or she would have worn gloves, too. His gut said this murder had been planned; it wasn't an impulsive act. The rage was there, but it might have been boiling for a long time.

What made Daniel uneasy was the fact that Martin had been beaten to death, as he had beaten Shane only the day before. Hard not to connect the dots. Coincidences didn't sit well with him.

He didn't make a habit of jumping to conclusions, though, or accepting easy answers like a fish snapping up the fly. He had work to do, and plenty of it.

An hour later, he was sitting in a conference room at the county jail questioning Austin Ramsey, who sat across the table from him. Austin was close to Daniel's height and breadth, as his brother had been. His hair was barely stubble and he had a cauliflower nose. Either he'd been in a lot of fights or he'd boxed in his younger years.

"Martin's dead?"

This was the third time Austin had said that, as if he kept hoping for a different answer. He was even shedding some tears, swiping angrily at them with the back of his hand. He could beat his own kid but cry over the death of his brother. Sentiment came in many guises.

"He is." Daniel hesitated, then told him about the cancer. "If you're a smoker, too, you might want to see a doctor."

"Nah, I never started up." He scowled. "You gonna find who killed my brother?"

"Yes, I am. I'm hoping you can help."

"Any way I can," Austin agreed.

As the big brother started spilling everything he knew about Martin, Daniel reflected that sometimes you had to dance with the devil, like it or not.

And then he wondered how Melinda's investigation was going...which brought him to thinking about Lindsay Engle. He gave his head a hard shake to get her out of it, causing Martin to pause midsentence and gaze at him in surprise.

"Sorry," Daniel said. "Just...had a passing thought. You were saying that he hadn't been seeing any woman steadily recently. Anything stand out about the women he did see?"

"He didn't say nothing about anyone. Maybe he was taking a rest."

A rest. That was one way to put it. Daniel had been taking a rest, too, no one catching his eye.

Until Lindsay Engle had, at a highly inconvenient time.

Chapter Four

"I know it's frustrating that the job was left unfinished," Daniel said drily.

Perched on the wingback chair facing him, Cathy Haugen showed her embarrassment with a flush. "I'm so sorry. Someone murdered him, and I'm complaining because he didn't show up here the next morning and finish spackling the wall around my new window."

He was interviewing the homeowner because Martin Ramsey had been working for her the week before he was killed. So far, Daniel hadn't learned much from her. As a detective, he wasted too much time talking to people who didn't turn out to know a thing. Sooner or later, he had to remind himself, something useful would pop.

Ms. Haugen agreed that she and Martin had chatted. He'd mentioned a nephew living with him, but she didn't recall the boy's name. No, Martin hadn't seemed any different the last few days he'd worked here. Well, the last day, maybe. He'd been quieter than usual.

After thinking, she said, "Brooding." And then he just hadn't showed up the next day.

Because he was dead. Daniel chose not to remind her of that cold, hard truth.

Time to wind this down, he decided. He'd opened his mouth to thank her when his phone rang.

"Excuse me," he said, rising to his feet and walking toward the patio doors before answering the call from Detective McIntosh. "Deperro."

"Daniel, I told you I'm investigating the sexual molestation of a girl, Kaila Kelley."

His interest sharpened. Kaila Kelley, whose caseworker happened to be Lindsay Engle.

"I had an interview scheduled with the stepfather," she said tersely. "I found him dead. Murdered. I thought you'd be interested."

"I am. Are you still at the scene?"

"CSI hasn't even arrived. I called you right away. There might be a connection with that murder you're already investigating."

Because of Lindsay's involvement, or did this guy's injuries resemble Ramsey's? Daniel didn't ask. He'd see soon enough.

"Address?"

After committing it to memory, he made his excuses to Ms. Haugen, gave her his card in case anything should occur to her and left.

Ten minutes later, he pulled to the curb behind the crime scene unit's van and a marked SPD car. The unmarked maroon sedan at the head of the line was Melinda's. Curtains were probably twitching up and down the block.

At this house, blinds were drawn on the front window. The minute a uniformed officer opened the door and handed him a clipboard to sign in, Daniel smelled smoke. Through an archway, he saw the body and two crime scene investigators he knew in the living room.

One was taking photos. Although Melinda wasn't in here, he detoured to take a look at the victim.

He winced at what he saw. Doug Norris had been stripped naked and posed. The handle of a knife stuck out from his chest. From the quantity of blood, Daniel guessed the blade had torn right through Norris's heart.

He had no trouble interpreting the message. Norris had been raped and his heart broken. Exactly what he'd done to his stepdaughter.

This fire had been set in a copper kettle on the hearth that probably held newspapers or kindling during the winter. Today, it had been stuffed with paper of some kind that had burned down to ashes. The fire had leaped up high enough to char the white-painted brick fireplace surround. Not intended to burn down the house, but then this killer had staged the body with care. He—or, damn it, she—wouldn't want that effort to go to waste.

One of the techs glanced up and greeted Daniel, who nodded in return. This was an ugly crime, but they would all do their jobs. Compartmentalize, which meant tucking away what they'd seen before they went home to their families.

He found Melinda in the kitchen on her phone. He waited until she ended the conversation and set down the phone.

"You saw?"

"I saw," he said. "This wasn't subtle."

"No. I gathered that Martin Ramsey was beaten, just like he'd beaten the kid. That could have been chance, but when I saw what was done to Norris..."

"We have two kids who were badly injured. Now the assailants are dead in a way that resembles what they did to the kids. I couldn't be sure about Ramsey, but after this—" Daniel shook his head. "I hope you don't mind working together. The small fires at each scene are as good as a signature. We have one killer."

She nodded. "I agree. But what is he trying to tell us with these fires?"

"I wish I knew," he said in frustration. "How old is the girl?" If she'd said, he didn't remember.

"Two girls," she corrected him. "Kaila and Kira. Twelve and fourteen. Turns out he's been raping Kira for a couple of years. Now, Kaila. I don't like to say a victim deserved what he had coming, but I'll make an exception for this creep." After a discernible pause, she added, "That's assuming, of course, that he really was guilty."

Daniel knew what she believed. "This killer didn't wait for you to gather enough evidence to be ready to file a charge. We have a sort of vigilante who has killed twice now, and only four days apart. That's fast for someone who has never before committed murder."

"Are we sure he hasn't?"

Turning so he could see a slice of the living room, Daniel grimaced. "I looked for anything similar in Oregon. Choice of victim, use of a fire as part of his MO, attack meant to mimic what was done to the victim. Unless our killer's a recent transplant—"

"And then how did he learn about the assaults on these particular children?" Deeper than usual lines etched her face. "No, you're probably right. We just have to figure out what triggered this guy to start now. The assault on Shane Ramsey sounds as if it was savage, but not that unusual."

He knew what she meant. There was a reason Child Protective Services had a unit here in Sadler the size they did. Child abuse was all too prevalent, pretty much everywhere.

He didn't like saying this, but had to. "Is it coincidence that Lindsay Engle is the caseworker involved in both instances?"

Melinda frowned. "She's been with the unit for several years. Besides, she's been good to work with. I don't want to believe she's capable of anything like this."

"I don't want to think she is, either," Daniel said roughly. "But I can't help noticing that, except for the wastebasket fires, she's all that ties these two murders together." He frowned. "She know about this yet?" He nodded toward the living room.

Melinda shook her head. "I haven't even notified the wife. I suppose we'd better confirm the whereabouts of the two girls, although I can't imagine…"

He couldn't, either. Doug Norris had been average size rather than big and brawny, but he'd still have been a lot stronger than any young girl—even two of them trying to take him on at once. Just thrusting the knife in so deep required more strength than most people realized, as well as some knowledge of how to direct the blade under the rib cage and upward to reach the heart. As a method to kill, it wasn't for the squeamish. And then there was the suggestive staging. By two kids with no history of trouble or gang affiliation? No.

A woman who had spent years building rage toward this kind of offender? Who'd had plenty of time to do her research, who although slim had appeared fit, whom Norris would have let in the front door?

Like it or not, Daniel and Melinda had to seriously consider Lindsay as a suspect.

LINDSAY WAS LESS than thrilled to pick up the phone to hear the receptionist say in a hushed voice, "There are two detectives here to see you."

Wonderful. Was Detective Deperro still fixated on her, or did he have more questions about Shane?

"Send them back," she said, then wished she'd asked for their names. This could be different detectives, here to see her about another case—except the SPD didn't have a very big investigative unit.

She rose to her feet and braced herself. Maybe she wouldn't feel any impact from Daniel Deperro's presence this time.

Wrong. Even though he allowed Detective McIntosh to precede him into the room, she saw only him. Daunting shoulders, dark eyes, unreadable expression. She had the sense that he saw only her, too. She couldn't be imagining that.

The other caseworkers present lifted their heads from whatever they were doing to watch the pair of detectives weave their way through desks to Lindsay's. Silence fell over the room.

Detective McIntosh nodded civilly, although she, too, had an air of reserve Lindsay hadn't felt when they talked yesterday.

Deperro said coolly, "Ms. Engle."

So much for being on a first-name basis.

"I can grab another chair." Lindsay looked around.

"Do you have a conference room available?" the woman detective asked. "It would be better if we had some privacy."

A chill spreading inside her, Lindsay said, "Of course." They followed her to a room designed for small groups. She took a seat and waited, from long practice keeping a pleasant expression on her face. Once they, too, had taken seats around the table, she asked, "What can I do for you?"

Detective McIntosh jumped in. "Well, first I wondered if you'd had a chance to talk to Doug Norris again."

Surprised, Lindsay focused on her. "No, I haven't even tried. As I told you, until you've completed at least an initial investigation, I won't make any further contact with either the girls' mother or stepfather."

"That's what I understood," she said.

Deperro didn't bother with the niceties. Without any trace of the warmth she'd glimpsed in him when he persuaded her to work with him to find Shane, he said, "Can you tell us what you have done and who you've seen this morning?"

The chill deepened to the point where Lindsay wondered if her core temperature had dropped.

"I had to put a bunch of investigations on the back burner for Shane and then Kaila and Kira. I've managed today to talk to half a dozen people regarding allegations made by neighbors, teachers, in one case a school nurse."

"Did you speak to them here?" Deperro asked brusquely.

"No. I made appointments to meet them at a coffee house or at their homes. In one case, at a school." She looked from one face to another. "I've worked with officers from SPD often and been cooperative, but I'm getting a bad feeling here. This meeting is over unless you tell me what happened to bring you here this morning with your current attitude."

They didn't even exchange a glance, and yet she could feel communication humming between them.

It was Detective McIntosh who inclined her head. Big surprise there; she made a far more natural "good cop" than would her partner.

"I had an appointment this morning to speak to Mr.

Norris. When I arrived at the Norris home, I found him dead." She paused. "Murdered."

Lindsay quit breathing, only stared. Dizzy, she sucked in air at the same time as she pushed her chair back from the table. "And you think *I*—"

In his deep voice that now sounded like a growl, Deperro said, "I'm sure you'll agree that we should be concerned by the fact that you're the caseworker for both children whose guardians were murdered within forty-eight hours of you removing the kids from their custody."

She couldn't look away from his hard, accusatory face. It was absurd to feel hurt, even if they'd worked together and she'd caught him watching her in a way that surely meant he was attracted to her. Maybe all he'd been doing was softening her up. Face it, he'd made no bones about his suspicion after Shane's uncle was killed.

Doing her best to shake off the hurt, Lindsay rose to her feet. "I won't meet with either of you again until I have an attorney present. You know your way out. Please excuse me."

"Ms. Engle."

Her back to him, she stopped in the doorway.

"If you'll just give us your schedule for the morning, let us verify that you didn't have a gap of time—"

She kept walking.

"SHE *HAS* BEEN COOPERATIVE," Melinda said mildly. "Did you have to come on so strong?"

He'd been a jackass, Daniel knew that, without quite being sure why. He'd been…relieved earlier on to be able mostly to dismiss her as a suspect in Martin Ramsey's murder. He liked her. He could more than like her, which had to be the problem. Now, after the second murder, he was infuriated to suspect she'd played him, manipulated him from the get-go. Maybe he was mad most of all because she exerted a pull on him that was damn near irresistible. Now he felt betrayed—and that was dumb as hell. In his heart, he couldn't believe she was a killer. To eliminate her, he had to ask questions—but if he'd come at those questions differently, he wouldn't have alienated the woman who was, at the least, a central witness in their investigation.

A woman who was unlikely to lower her guard around him again.

Melinda had every right to come down a lot harder on him than she had so far.

He scraped a hand over his jaw. "I'm usually smoother than that."

Perturbed lines showed on her forehead. "Yes, you are."

"Maybe if I leave, she'd talk to you."

Her eyebrows lifted. She didn't have to say, *Fat chance.*

Lindsay was nowhere to be seen as he and Melinda passed back through what resembled a squad room, the half dozen occupants unashamedly staring. Had he thought she would return to her desk and continue calmly doing her job? She was probably closeted with her supervisor…or out shopping for a criminal defense attorney.

He called himself a few names, but he kept his mouth tight and his face blank. Out front, they passed the reception desk, Melinda nodding politely to the woman who was on the phone but also keeping a sharp eye on them.

He pushed open one of the double glass doors to let Melinda go first.

Behind him, the receptionist called, "Wait!"

He turned to see she had hung up the phone. "Yes?"

"Ms. Engle left something for you."

A mousetrap, to break a few of his fingers? He doubted she could come up with a cherry bomb that fast.

The receptionist handed over a manila folder, so thin it couldn't hold more than two or three sheets of paper. He didn't open it until he was in the car. Behind the wheel, Melinda leaned toward him so she could see, too.

Two pages. The first was a copy of today's page from a day planner showing that, indeed, Lindsay had jam-packed her morning with appointments. Page two, scrawled names and phone numbers.

Though angry, she'd still given them what they had asked for.

"If she actually met with all these people, I don't see how she could have worked in a detour to kill Doug Norris." Tone still mild, Melinda was going out of her way not to sound critical.

Squeezing a murder into this schedule looked pretty damn unlikely, Daniel had to concede. His mood lightened a little—but they still had to verify that neither Lindsay nor another party had canceled one of these meetings.

"Do we know TOD?" he asked.

"Jim Stamey texted me. Said his best guess for time of death was three to four hours ago, but may change his opinion after the autopsy."

Daniel nodded. Stamey would have checked the body's temperature and half a dozen other indicators before venturing his opinion. In Daniel's experience, the guy had never been far off.

"That puts Norris's death at somewhere between nine and eleven this morning," he calculated.

"Yes. I suggest we notify the wife and find out when she left for work. That might narrow the window."

"I'll make some calls from this list while we're on our way." That would also serve the purpose of distracting him. He hated being a passenger.

Without further comment, Melinda backed the department-issue car out, swung around and made the turn onto the street that led to the light at the highway. He didn't know where Paige Norris worked, but obviously Melinda did.

By the time they pulled up at an insurance office downtown, Daniel had spoken to three of the people Lindsay had met with that morning. So far, so good... but he had yet to reach three more people, one of whom hadn't answered or responded to the message he'd left.

Inside the insurance office, he had his first look at Paige Norris, who didn't yet know she was a widow. From behind a desk she lifted her head to beam at them before she really saw them.

If not for Ramsey's murder, he'd be looking hard at this woman. With the abuser now out of the picture, she might get her daughters back. What if she really *hadn't* believed the girls' claims, but her husband had given himself away and now she knew they'd told the truth? Women were known to do the unthinkable to protect their children.

This woman, though...she was petite and appeared ultra-feminine, wearing a fuzzy pink cardigan over a matching pink top. His gaze fell to her long fingernails, also painted pink. It would be hard to kill a man without breaking a nail or chipping the polish.

Unless she'd managed a quick visit to a manicurist on her way to work. Could those be fake nails?

Sometimes he wished he didn't so readily suspect people of the worst behavior.

In this case…he couldn't imagine she'd beaten a large man to death as a cover for when she murdered her own husband.

Alarmed, Paige Norris shot to her feet. "Why are you here?" She was all but whispering. "My bosses don't know anything about the girls and…and all the ridiculous stuff they said. I could lose my job if—"

"We need to speak to you." Melinda could sound tough when she needed to. "Is there a conference room available?"

"I—" Mrs. Norris drew several deep breaths as if to steady herself. "Yes. I suppose." She hustled them halfway down a short hall and into a plush room with a table surrounded by six upholstered chairs. "I'll be right back."

Daniel heard her talking to someone a short distance away, explaining that she needed to speak to someone about an issue at school and could this someone else please answer the phone for a few minutes.

Apparently the coworker agreed, because she reappeared, whisking into the conference room and yanking down a shade over the inset window before taking a seat and gazing at them anxiously. "Now what?"

Daniel deliberately chose a chair off to one side. Melinda was familiar to the woman; she'd respond better to her questions. Observing felt like the smarter tactic.

Too bad he hadn't kept his damn mouth shut earlier with Lindsay.

"First, let me ask what time you left home this morning," Melinda said.

Her anxiety increased. "I don't understand." It took some low-key urging, but finally Mrs. Norris said,

"Eight forty-five. I usually leave at eight-thirty, but Doug was unsettled about having to talk to you, and—" She stopped. "Wasn't he home? I know he intended to be."

"Mrs. Norris—Paige—I'm afraid I have some bad news for you."

She pressed a hand to her throat. "What could possibly—"

"When I arrived at your house, the front door was unlatched and open a few inches. I called for your husband, and when I didn't receive a reply, I stepped inside. I found him dead, Mrs. Norris. He was murdered."

The woman let out a piercing cry, the kind that haunted cops who made too many death notifications.

MAD AS HELL but also a little scared, Lindsay explained to her supervisor what was going on.

Her boss for a year now, Sadie Culver had been brought in from the Bend office when Glenn Wilson retired. She'd been thrilled with the promotion and especially the transfer, because she and her husband, a third-generation cattle rancher, already lived near Sadler. Lindsay guessed her to be in her early forties, and both liked her and had found her to be a supportive manager.

Sadie was aghast to learn that the police might suspect one of her caseworkers of a crime as horrific as murder.

"You're the last person I could imagine going off the deep end like that," she exclaimed. "I mean, with this job, burnout is always an issue, but you haven't exhibited any sign at all."

Lindsay sat facing Sadie's desk, feeling like a school child called in by the principal. "Thank you for saying that," she said, relaxing a little. "I understood why after the first murder the detective had to look at me, because I found the body. Now it's come down to me being the caseworker involved with both families."

"We don't have that big an office. If someone is knocking off abusive parents, it could be chance that you were investigating both."

Lindsay shuddered. "What if someone really *is*? These two murders weren't even a week apart."

Sadie studied her with obvious concern. "Good Lord. I'll look to be sure our records haven't been hacked. Otherwise, how do you want to handle this?"

"I did give them my schedule for this morning. Unfortunately—" she hesitated "—that won't let me off the hook, unless Doug Norris was killed way earlier this morning. The problem is, I ended up with a break at about ten-thirty, when a mother I was to meet with wasn't home."

Her supervisor got an odd expression on her face. "You don't think there's any chance that woman, too, is…?"

It took Lindsay longer than it should have to understand. Sadie wondered whether the woman she'd had the appointment to meet with had been murdered. "Oh, dear God." She closed her eyes. "No, I can't imagine. Her son has had some bruises, but nothing that awful. I'm thinking the family might need counseling…but maybe I should ask the detectives to do a, um, welfare check on the woman."

"Have you tried calling her?"

"I did at the time and got voice mail, but I'll call her again right now." Her hands were actually trembling when she took out her phone.

A woman answered immediately. "Oh, is this Ms.

Engle? I'm so, so sorry I didn't call to let you know I had to rush into work."

Jennifer James was a hairdresser.

"Mrs. James, I don't think you understand the gravity of the concerns that led to Child Protective Services being called in. You do realize we're authorized to remove children from their home if we believe them to be in danger."

Across the desk from her, Sadie let out a whoosh of air. Lindsay shared her relief, although her annoyance almost drowned it out.

Mrs. James expressed anger at the tattletale school nurse but also agreed to meet with Lindsay the next day.

Lindsay ended the call. "Well, she's alive."

Sadie leaned forward. "What can I do to help?"

"I can't think of anything at the moment, except to express faith in my mental health if either of the detectives shows up to talk to you." She made a face. "I think I need to take an hour of personal time right now, though, to find myself an attorney."

"Of course." Sadie stood and came around the desk, reaching out a hand to squeeze Lindsay's. "I can just imagine what Glenn would have to say about this."

Lindsay knew exactly what Glenn would say. Loudly. Probably to the police chief. "Let's not tell him yet, okay?" she suggested.

Sadie mimed zipping her mouth.

Lindsay produced something like a smile and headed back to her desk. She'd wait until she was in her car to do a search for attorneys and make her calls. Her fellow caseworkers did *not* need to know she was a suspect in a murder investigation.

Once she reached her car, she had to start it and turn on the air-conditioning to combat the August heat.

Maybe, she thought, as she flipped pages until she found “Attorneys—Criminal Law,” whatever lawyer took her on would advise her not to speak to either detective at all. The burning in her chest told her how glad she’d be never to set eyes on Daniel Deperro again.

Chapter Five

When Lieutenant Matson walked out of his office the following morning, his gaze locked on Daniel. It didn't waver as he stalked across the bull pen, ignoring support staff and the only other detective present.

Uh-oh.

Daniel leaned back in his chair and waited.

The lieutenant came to a stop in front of Daniel's desk and crossed his arms. "Seriously? You've named a CPS worker as a suspect in two murders?"

Did he sound plaintive or annoyed? Daniel couldn't quite decide.

"We—" He cleared his throat. He had to leave Melinda out of this one. "I didn't go that far. All I did was ask Ms. Engle for her whereabouts around the time of the murder."

Middle-aged, Matson was softening around the waist but still formidable. "And do you have any real connection between her and these murders?"

"She's the caseworker involved with both families. Plus, these murders are to all appearances expressing rage at the abusers. In neither instance do the children have any family defending them, far less expressing anger. I questioned Ms. Engle after Martin Ramsey's murder but didn't take her seriously as a suspect. After the second murder…how can I not? Who else has reason to feel that kind of hate for two men who likely didn't even know each other?"

"Her supervisor is not happy. She feels we're endangering any future of interagency cooperation."

That was a load of crap, and Lieutenant Matson had to know it. Nonetheless, Daniel said, "You can assure her we're doing our best to eliminate Ms. Engle as a suspect as quickly as possible."

"Are we succeeding?"

"Unfortunately, she had a break in her schedule that would fit into the current estimate of time of death. I just reached the woman Ms. Engle was to have met with. This Mrs.—" he glanced down at his notes "—James says she had to rush into work and didn't think to let Ms. Engle know she wouldn't be home."

"Ms. Engle couldn't have counted on having any time."

"That does argue against her being the perp. Still, if she planned to go after Norris later, she could have decided to seize the chance."

Matson scowled, said, "Keep me informed," and walked away.

Everyone around them managed to look really busy.

THE ATTORNEY LINDSAY had decided on, Jeff Eimen, did indeed instruct her to refuse to meet with either detective without him sitting in. She had thanked him and paid a retainer.

Because she was a murder suspect.

You never knew what kind of new life experience might come along.

She decided to work from home for the rest of the day,

making follow-up calls and reviewing files. Why not? That's what she did several evenings a week anyway.

Sometimes she felt as if she was drowning, but if she slowed down, a child somewhere would suffer. It was reality that abused or neglected children occasionally fell through the cracks. A caseworker left the job, another one replaced her but was somehow never given that particular file. Or a caseworker got involved in something messy and time-consuming, as with the Kelley girls, and assumed lower priorities could wait. She could be fooled by a seemingly sincere parent, misread a situation. The possibilities for disaster were endless, and ever-present. What if Shane hadn't survived the beating his uncle gave him, for example? How would she have lived with that?

Lindsay made herself push back from the desk in her home office and go to the kitchen to pour a cup of coffee and think about what she could make for dinner. That part didn't take long; a microwaveable meal it was.

She used to enjoy cooking. That was just one of many small pleasures and hobbies that had gone by the wayside over the past few years. She couldn't help wishing sometimes that she hadn't jumped onto the hamster wheel that was CPS, except she was always aware how urgently the job needed to be done.

Sighing, she took the fresh cup of coffee back to her desk. Her phone rang as she was sitting down. Since she recognized the number, she didn't answer. To hell with Detective Daniel Deperro.

The second time he called, she was on the phone with the grandfather of a child living with a drug addict mother. Deperro hadn't left a message the first time. She waited to see if he would this time.

Nope.

Five minutes later, her phone rang again and his number came up. Gritting her teeth, Lindsay answered coolly, "Detective."

"You've been ignoring me."

"Astonishingly enough, I haven't been sitting here playing computer games and waiting for you to call. I'm busy, Detective."

"I need to talk to you again," he said brusquely.

Annoyed to have his deep voice awaken a small thrill inside her, Lindsay said as distantly as possible, "I'll have to look at my schedule and coordinate with my attorney to find a possible time."

The ensuing pool of silence gratified her.

"Who'd you hire?"

"Jeff Eimen of Eimen and Sloan."

"Huh."

"You thought I was bluffing?"

"I hoped," he admitted. "You're making this more complicated than it has to be. For obvious reasons, I need to clear you. I'm not hounding you for the fun of it."

"Really? You could have fooled me." She let out a huff of air. This was pointless. "What I think, Detective, is that you tend to jump to quick conclusions. I'm right in front of you, so it's got to be me." She paused. "Now, if you want to suggest some times that would work for you, I'll call Mr. Eimen and run them by him."

"You were…good enough to cooperate today and provide us with your schedule. I need some clarification, that's all."

Even as she weakened, she knew she'd be a fool to believe that.

"I suppose you want to know what I did with the hour I should have spent with Jennifer James."

"That's one question," he agreed.

She closed her eyes and kneaded the painfully tight muscles in her neck. "I bought a chilled latte and a scone—orange-cranberry, if that matters—at the drive-through coffee place two blocks from the library. I then went to the city park by the Boys & Girls Club. I found a bench in the shade and ate my scone. To my current regret, I didn't see a soul."

"Did you receive or make any phone calls during that hour?"

"That's two questions, Detective Deperro. This is your last. I ignored several calls that weren't urgent, and I didn't call anyone. I enjoyed a slight breeze and meditated." The pain pinging up her neck hadn't relented. "Good bye, Detective."

"Wait!"

She ended the connection with her right thumb, then sat tensely waiting for him to call again.

He didn't. Not that he was done with her, of course.

"DAMN WOMAN," DANIEL GROWLED.

"I can guess who you're talking about."

Startled, he looked up. Once again he hadn't noticed Melinda's approach. Lindsay Engle was distracting, and more.

Jump to quick conclusions. That really had him stewing.

He told his partner how Lindsay claimed to have filled the hour she'd unexpectedly been given.

"We can check with the coffee kiosk," Melinda said thoughtfully. "Maybe find out who was patrolling that part of town this morning. He might have noticed her car, especially if it was the only one in the parking lot."

"Yeah. We can do that."

She perched on the edge of his desk, one foot braced on the floor, the other dangling. "What's wrong?"

"Has it occurred to you that she might be a target of the killer? Either he's trying to get her in trouble…or he thinks he's doing her a favor and she'll be thrilled."

Melinda frowned at him. "That's a leap considering she's a link between only two murders."

The chair squeaked as he leaned back, raising his eyebrows. "Only?"

She frowned. "You know what I mean."

"I do, and you're right. Her name coming up in both investigations really could be coincidental. I looked over the past few months to see what child abuse cases CPS has needed to involve us or the sheriff's department in."

"And?"

"Five, and three of them weren't anywhere near as horrific as the beating Shane Ramsey took or the sexual molestation of the Kelley girls."

He'd felt some relief at learning that. The odds were eight to one that the next really nasty case would be handled by a different caseworker. Nine to one if the supervisor directly handled investigations as well as managed the caseworkers.

He twitched at having to acknowledge how much he didn't want Lindsay to be a part of this.

"You expect more murders," Melinda said.

"I don't think this killer will stop. Do you?"

She pressed her lips together but finally said, "No."

"Unless we catch him."

"Does the lieutenant know what you think?"

"He hasn't asked, but he's not stupid."

They looked at each other for a minute. Finally, she said, "I've only been involved in a couple of murder investigations. One was a stabbing during a tavern brawl and the other a domestic. Not exactly mysteries. I'm not sure what to do next," she admitted, with a frankness that surprised him. Melinda hadn't made it to detective in the face of bias by displaying any uncertainty.

Daniel knew she'd just given him her version of a compliment.

"We need to continue investigating the people around each victim. One of the two killings could have been committed as a way to muddy the waters."

If he wasn't mistaken, Melinda tried to hide a shudder.

"That's kind of drastic."

"It is, but it's happened."

"You're saying the fires were just a trick," she said.

"A not-so subtle way to convince us we have a single killer who has an agenda that's related to the abuse allegations."

"When really one of the two victims was murdered for an entirely different reason."

"It's conceivable."

Melinda hesitated. "Do you really believe that?"

He told her the truth. "No. Especially given the question of how this killer knew about both abuse allegations and so quickly. My gut says we need to quietly look at the other CPS caseworkers, indignant supervisor included."

"Burnout," she said slowly.

"And maybe someone who doesn't like Lindsay Engle."

"Or likes her a lot."

He wasn't happy with either scenario.

LINDSAY DIDN'T HEAR a peep from the detectives over the following several days. Rather than reassuring her, the quiet made her more nervous. It felt like the eye of a hurricane.

She decided, for once, to take the weekend off. Truthfully, she'd rather not be assigned any more investigations for the time being. If something awful came in, Sadie could give it to someone else. Just in case the abuser was murdered, that would ensure the cops knew she didn't have anything to do with the killings.

Still…it was strange that she was the caseworker in both instances.

The first question to ask was why Sadie had chosen her to talk to Kaila Kelley, when she was still tied up with Shane's case.

Because I'm a woman, she reminded herself, but she knew that wasn't all. Since Glenn's retirement, their office had only three male caseworkers, five female, six counting Sadie.

Two of the female caseworkers were newbies. The others… In her heart of hearts, Lindsay knew she was the best. The most perceptive, the most patient, most skilled at dealing with all parties, from the endangered child to the abuser and any other family members. She was also one of the most experienced.

Hey, growing up in a succession of foster homes had taught her plenty.

If Sadie did prefer her, well, it wasn't like getting gold stickers on her paperwork or being trusted to run errands to the principal's office. No, it meant her getting assigned to the most shocking cases.

She knew what she had to do now: refuse any new assignments. Sadie would understand her reasoning. Lindsay had plenty to keep her occupied for a few weeks, at least. And think how wonderful it would be to catch up. That wouldn't last, of course, but just once, she'd like to come home at the end of a workday and be able to take the evening off without guilt. Or even put in for vacation! The last one had been three whole days so she could attend her college roommate's wedding two years ago.

So she'd enjoy this weekend, even if it was already Saturday morning. Go somewhere overnight. Drive to the coast, maybe? After enduring two months of central Oregon's usual summer heat, it would be bliss to walk on a rocky beach in the fog and mist. More blissful if she had someone to walk *with*, but she couldn't get greedy. After all, her last date had been with…

She couldn't even remember his name. A firefighter, who'd had to cut their evening short for a callout. A forest fire, not a home fire, she remembered. A lightning strike had ignited it, and people had been evacuated from rural north county. Every local fire department had fought that one. He'd promised to call her when life was back to normal, but never had. She'd only vaguely noticed, because it turned out they had nothing in common except some sexual sizzle that burned out, on her part, after listening to him brag about his hunting prowess for forty-five minutes.

Come to think of it, the long drive to the coast didn't sound all that appealing. So maybe she'd go up to Mt. Hood. There were a lot of bed-and-breakfasts in the area, she knew. Surely she could find a vacancy.

Decided, she started throwing a couple of changes of clothes into a small suitcase. She'd added toiletries and pulled the suitcase to the small entry when her doorbell rang. She hesitated, between one blink of the eye and the next seeing Martin's body lying on the kitchen floor.

For heaven's sake, it was midday and there must be

neighbors out gardening, kids riding bikes. The spurt of fear was an overreaction.

A fist rapped hard on the door.

Really?

She swung it open to find Daniel Deperro on her doorstep.

DANIEL ANTICIPATED LINDSAY'S REACTION. If she'd let him speak, he'd explain. But she didn't.

Eyes narrowing, she snapped, "Since my attorney didn't happen to drop by for breakfast this morning, you need to leave." She tried to shut the front door in Daniel's face.

He was too quick, inserting a booted foot. "Damn it, will you give me a minute?"

"I'll report you to your captain. This is harassment." She glared at him. "Or are you prepared to arrest me?"

The heightened color in her cheeks made her even more beautiful. Appealing. Unfortunately, anger was responsible for the warmth tinting her cheekbones, not arousal or shyness.

He kept his foot between the jamb and the door. "I'm not. I…actually have good news for you."

No relenting was visible.

"Uh…can I come in?"

Her expression was about as friendly as a jagged chunk of lava.

Suddenly appalled, Daniel wondered why he was really here. He could have called. *Should* have called, not shown up on the doorstep.

"Okay," he said, pulling back his foot. As he'd hoped, she didn't slam the door. "We verified your purchase at the Java Stop." They'd been able to do that right away. "An hour ago, I was finally able to talk to Officer Capek. Do you know him?"

Terse nod.

"He saw your car at the city park. Passed it three times during the forty-five minutes you told us you were there."

Her eyebrows challenged him. "Maybe I sneaked out the back side of the park and called a cab."

"An old lady lives right across the street from the Norrises. She'd have seen the cab." Unless Lindsay had had it drop her a street away. But Daniel didn't believe that for a minute. What killer would dare take a cab to a murder scene? Ask the cabbie to wait for him? What if he returned covered with blood?

Daniel knew Lindsay was smarter than that.

Her grip on the door eased. "*Somebody* was in the house, so why didn't she see them?"

Good question. If Mrs. Knudson had caught even a glimpse of the killer, he and Melinda would have had other leads to follow and not gone straight to the state Department of Health Services offices.

"Back slider was unlocked."

"But he still took a chance that someone would see him—what? Jumping the fence?"

"He did, but if he was watching and, say, saw two adults leaving for work from the same house, he could be pretty safe in thinking he wouldn't be seen."

"If only people paid more attention..."

Catching the dark tone, mixed bitterness and sadness, Daniel nodded. "Both of our jobs would be easier."

"How can people not see long-term abuse?" Lindsay's expression softened to bewilderment that he understood.

"Hard to figure," he said quietly.

She'd let the door fall open far enough for him to notice the suitcase behind her.

His eyebrows climbed. "Going somewhere?"

"Going...?" Her head turned to follow his gaze. "Oh, yes. I'm fleeing from the law, obviously."

His grin clearly startled her. "Took your time about it."

Lindsay scrunched up her nose. "I haven't gotten away even overnight in months." One shoulder lifted. "Seemed like a good weekend."

Keeping his voice soft, Daniel said, "May I come in?"

"I was just leaving... Oh, fine." She stood back.

The front door of the small rambler opened into the living room. Gleaming hardwood floors weren't usual for the era of the house. He bet somebody, maybe Lindsay, had added them at a later date. A huge braided rug in muted shades of rust and peach centered the sofa, an easy chair and two antique rocking chairs. The brick fireplace would be great in winter. He guessed the TV was in the antique armoire, the door of which was firmly shut. Two built-in floor-to-ceiling bookcases to each side of the fireplace took pride of place.

"Nice house," he said.

"Thank you." Now she did look shy. "Will you be here long enough for a cup of coffee?"

"I'd love one."

Instead of sitting, he followed her to the kitchen. Bright red tiles formed the backsplash beneath old-fashioned white cabinets. A red enamel teakettle and red-and-white-checked curtains accented the tiles and made this room, too, homey.

She had her back to him while she started the coffee, giving him a chance to admire her curvy body in tight-fitting jeans and a thin red T-shirt that hugged her generous breasts.

She definitely pushed his buttons, and not only physically. Daniel just wished she wasn't mixed up in this mess somehow. While she couldn't see him, he let his mouth twist. Okay, by being such an ass to her he might have squelched any possibility of taking this attraction somewhere even when this was over.

Assuming she shared it.

After standing on tiptoe to take two mugs from a cupboard and setting them on the counter, Lindsay faced him, her expression turned wary. "It occurs to me I surrendered too quickly. You still have questions, don't you?"

He could tell she knew the answer before he opened his mouth.

Chapter Six

"I do," he admitted, but held up a hand before she could shove him out the door and slam it in his face. "But they're the kind of questions I'm asking because you know the people concerned."

"You mean, the families?"

Her wariness would have deep roots, in part because keeping information about cases confidential was her default. And then there was his hot-and-cold behavior. Why would she trust him?

"If necessary, but I'm thinking more of people working in your field." He hesitated. "Your coworkers."

"What?"

She hadn't put quite enough force into that. Lindsay had to have some of the same ideas he and Melinda had.

Daniel rolled his shoulders. "Can we go for a walk? Or—" No, she'd never agree. But, damn, he felt restless.

She glanced toward her suitcase. "I really wanted to get away." She sounded wistful. "Do something fun."

"Do you ride?" he asked.

"You mean, horses?"

He smiled. "Of course, horses. I'm not a big fan of motorcycles, not after scraping so many bodies off the pavement as a patrol officer. I live on some acreage outside of town, where I can keep my horses."

"More than one?"

"Five," he said. "Quarter horses. I breed my three mares. Only one of them has a foal by her side right now, though. A two-year-old is about ready to start under a saddle. I'm letting him put on some size to be sure he's up to my weight."

He'd swear that was wonder he saw on her face. He hadn't screwed up after all. She might not like him, but she was obviously horse-crazy.

"If you mean that, I'd love to go for a ride. Heck, by the time I got up to Mt. Hood, I probably wouldn't be able to find a place to stay anyway."

"In August? Maybe a cheap motel."

Lindsay made a face at him. "Give me a minute to change clothes."

While she raced upstairs, he studied the books on her shelves and speculated as to why she didn't have any family photos on her fireplace mantel or walls. They might be on display elsewhere in the house or tucked in a photo album she often perused, but somehow he doubted it. Her own history might explain why she'd committed to her line of work.

That got him to thinking about social workers in general. Or, more specifically, Child Protective Services caseworkers. How many were motivated to do such a difficult job by backgrounds as abused children? That would surely make them more likely to burn out in a big way—and to feel the kind of rage this killer so obviously did.

Something to ask Lindsay, except he didn't want her to think he was digging into *her* background.

"Sorry to be so slow." She took the steps at a clip that had him instinctively moving to the foot of the staircase to catch her if she took a header. "My boots weren't where they're supposed to be."

Not cowboy boots, but brown leather ones clearly made for riding. Right now, he wore the flexible tactical boots that were most practical on the job. Once home, he'd change into worn cowboy boots.

She grabbed her purse and car keys. "Should I follow you?"

"No, I can bring you home later. Maybe we can stop for lunch." If he hadn't gotten her back up again by then.

Once on their way, she surprised him by expressing curiosity about his background.

"I grew up in this part of the state," he told her. "Near Prineville. My father was a second-generation citizen. My mother came to the US from Guatemala as a teenager with her parents, who were migrant workers. Dad has a cattle ranch, which wasn't for me. I have an older brother who will likely take over when Dad retires, if he's ever willing to." He smiled. "Mama will no doubt put her foot down at some point. Cooking for half a dozen ranch hands for years and years must get old."

Lindsay chuckled. "I would have said I like to cook, but not that much."

"What about you?"

"Oh, I grew up in Portland. Ended up here only because I was offered a job in Sadler right out of grad school."

"Family still there?"

Out of the corner of his eye, he saw her hands flex, as if she wanted to tighten them into fists but had stopped herself.

"No," she said finally. "Never knew my father. My mother drifted in and out of my life until the court finally terminated her parental rights when I was ten. I learned later that she died just a few years after that."

"Drugs?"

"Alcohol."

Daniel took a hand off the wheel and laid it over hers on her thigh. He gave her hand a gentle squeeze and then made himself let her go. He wasn't much for touching and rarely did on impulse, but her tone had bothered him. She'd sounded so damned composed, as if she were talking about a casual acquaintance's troubled childhood, not her own.

"I suppose I'm a cliché," she said after a minute. "Trying to fix other families because I couldn't fix my own."

He thought about that. "Given that you work for CPS, isn't it more that you're trying to rescue abused children because nobody rescued you?"

The glance she flicked at him was both startled and shy. "People did occasionally try to rescue me. Thus the foster homes. Actually, I learned to ride at one."

He really wanted to reach for her hand again. Just touch her. Again. But this was too soon, even assuming he ever decided to act on his attraction to her.

Uh-huh. When was the last time he'd taken a woman out to his place for a ride?

He had to struggle to remember, which meant he'd kept any women he'd been involved with at a distance.

Lindsay and he were both quiet for the last five minutes of the drive.

LINDSAY LEANED FORWARD after he turned onto the packed earth of a long driveway. "Is that your home?"

"Yes. I converted an old barn." His satisfaction showed on his face as he looked at the structure.

Lindsay felt a sudden pang of jealousy. She liked what she'd done to her house, but this… The exterior appeared to have been stained and a protective coat undoubtedly applied, but the lines of the old barn remained, up to the peaked roof that would shed snow. The hayloft appeared to be a balcony now. Huge windows and skylights no doubt opened up the interior, both the main floor and what looked like a loft.

"It's spectacular," she said, unsure if it would be appropriate to ask for a tour.

Smiling faintly, he parked by the converted barn rather than the long, low one that was presumably a stable and said, "Come on in and take a look if you're interested. I need to change my boots."

The interior was rustic enough that she guessed he'd used reclaimed wood for the few walls and the floor, which was glossy but not planed to the completely smooth surface she was accustomed to. Kitchen, dining and living areas flowed in a way that felt natural. Cabinets had been crafted of a knotty pine and the counters were brown granite streaked with gold. Daniel disappeared up an open staircase to the loft, and she ventured to explore the back of the main floor, where a few rooms were walled off by rough, aged lumber that might have come from the original stalls. She found a full bathroom, a home office and what was probably a guest room.

Lindsay sighed with pleasure. This wasn't anything she'd have expected from him. Especially when he was being a jerk.

When he came back downstairs, she asked if he'd done the work himself.

"A lot of it," he said, his head turning as if he assessed the quality of that work. "My brother helped, as did a couple of friends. I did a hell of a lot of research before I started. The idea isn't original, you know."

"I do, but it isn't common, either. This really is gorgeous, Detective."

His smile became crooked. "Can we go back to first names?"

Stung by a sharp memory of how she'd felt when he went on the attack, she said, "Maybe that's not smart," and with her head held high, went out the front door.

Daniel—Detective Deperro, she reminded herself—grabbed a black Stetson from a hook by the door, set it on his head and followed her. He didn't comment as he led the way to the stable.

He saddled two horses, both easily identifiable as quarter horses from their powerful hindquarters, one a blood bay, the other near black. The bay was for her. Giving Lindsay a boost up, he said, "Nessa is good-natured. Not a slug, but she'll read your mind whatever your skill level."

His gelding was Max, although both horses had lengthy names under which they were registered. The two-year-old, which he pointed out grazing in a nearby pasture, was Nessa's son.

They set out at a walk, broke into a trot and then a lope. Lindsay gradually let her body relax and flow with the horse's rhythmic gait. The sun shone, not yet as hot as it would be by midday, and the sharp scent of ponderosa pine and juniper was one of the world's finest perfumes as far as Lindsay was concerned. She felt happy, in a carefree way she rarely did. Beside her, Daniel rode as if he'd spent half his life on horseback—which he probably had, growing up on a ranch.

The land was gradually rising, the pines growing taller and closer together. Daniel drew his gelding back to a walk, and Nessa did the same without waiting for permission from her rider.

Lindsay stiffened, knowing that Daniel slowed to a pace that would allow for conversation. Still, she turned to look at him. "Thank you. I don't get to ride often enough. If I had a horse—"

His mouth quirked. "You'd ride every day?"

"Do you?"

"When I get home before dark."

The weight of her job settled back on her shoulders. "I…don't have much time for recreation."

"I'm sorry this can't be just for fun." He sounded as if he meant it, but his dark eyes were, as always, hard to read.

Lindsay only nodded. "What is it you think I can tell you?"

"It's probably occurred to you that one of your co-workers might have gone off the deep end."

She pressed her lips together and stared straight ahead, not really seeing the landscape before her. It seemed wildly improbable that one of the men or women she worked with could have committed such grotesque crimes, but…*somebody* had. She couldn't help thinking she sounded like the shocked neighbors after a serial killer was arrested.

But he kept his lawn neatly mowed, and there was that time when my garbage can got knocked over and he picked it all up without asking for thanks.

Even so, Lindsay argued, "It's hard to imagine. We're a small enough office that I know everybody pretty well. Two are relative newcomers, but they're both young and idealistic."

"You must have started that way."

She still didn't want to look at him. Talking about

herself always made her feel uncomfortably vulnerable. She tended to avoid it whenever possible.

"Not in the same way. Growing up the way I did doesn't leave you with many illusions."

"No." He sounded thoughtful. "I don't suppose most people last long at CPS."

"There are some who make it a career. My former supervisor, for example. Sadie—the current supervisor—has been with CPS for almost ten years now. If I had to guess, it's the idealists who burn out the quickest. Their expectations are unrealistic. I see a lot of what I do as achieving small victories. Sometimes I change lives, but not often. Some of the calls we get are for suspicions of abuse that are true, but not as severe. If the parent or parents will agree to counseling, there's a chance to change the family dynamics before we have to take more drastic action."

"So your instinct isn't always to want to yank the kids from the home."

"If there's any hope, I prefer not to. The foster care system is less than ideal, you know."

"I've read about the problems."

"At some point, I might like to go back to licensing and supervising foster homes. It's another kind of intervention, and really important." Lindsay gave her head a shake. "I've been rambling. This doesn't have anything to do with what you asked."

"Not true," Daniel denied. "The more I know, the better I can judge whether a particular social worker is covering up serious rage."

She had to ask. "I want to think it's chance that I'm the caseworker for the two families involved in the murders."

He was quiet longer than she liked. Somehow, the

sharply defined angles of his face gave an impression of grimness. Lindsay wondered if he knew that the half roll of his shoulders was something of a tell. Stress didn't go to his stomach; it rode his shoulders and neck.

He glanced at her, his gaze somehow sharp. "I'd like to think so, too."

Speaking of stomachs, hers knotted.

"Somebody could be trying to please you," Daniel said slowly, "or get you in trouble."

She'd prefer option C, if it existed. Hoping he didn't see her shudder, she said, "Those are both horrible possibilities. I've already decided that when the next call comes in where the kid is hospitalized, I'm asking Sadie to assign it to someone else."

He tipped the brim of his hat. "Good idea."

Then, of course, he queried her about her coworkers. She felt as if she was betraying them by talking about them to a police detective behind their backs. She wouldn't have done so at all if she hadn't understood his reasoning so well. She dreaded going back to work Monday, when she'd have to look around and wonder. Was dark humor a healthy outlet, or a hint at hidden anger? Was outward serenity nothing but a cover? She'd evaluate expressions, feel uneasy whenever she caught a coworker's eye.

Would she dare get together with any of them on an evening or weekend?

As it was, she didn't share everything she knew. A couple of people had told her in confidence about their own backgrounds, in each case as bad or worse than hers. Those stories she didn't even consider sharing.

Finally, in frustration, she exclaimed, "I just can't believe any of them would do something like this."

Ignoring her outburst, he asked, "Have any of the

men asked you out? Expressed interest? Watched you in a way that feels sexual?"

She knew he was hinting at his earlier option B. Somebody had given her a couple of very twisted gifts, but—

Please, no.

She blew out a breath. "Ray Hammond flirts with me, but he flirts with some of the other women, too."

"He hasn't asked you out?"

"Just for coffee. That kind of thing. I've…taken to making excuses."

She'd swear his jaw muscles had tightened.

"Anyone else?"

"Matt Grudin was already in the office when I joined CPS." As if that made any difference. "He really wanted me to go out with him. He was pushier than I liked." She turned her head to meet Daniel's narrowed eyes. "And don't you dare tell him I said that. He got the message. I think he's seeing another woman now. Anyway, I have to keep working with him."

She wasn't about to tell Daniel that she still caught Matt checking her out. Some women would have been flattered, but she didn't like it. She never encouraged him and tended to avoid crossing his path if she could help it. Unfortunately, his desk was just across the aisle from hers.

This time, the repeat of "Anyone else?" came out as a growl.

"No." The only other man in their unit, Emmett Harper, was at least five years younger than her, easy mannered and enthusiastic.

"What about the women?"

She explained that she liked some of the women she worked with better than others, but that was normal.

He asked a few more questions, but then let the subject go with an "Okay." His legs tightened, and the black gelding went straight to a lope.

Once again, Nessa followed suit. The mare knew who the boss was here, and it wasn't the stranger on her back. Nonetheless, the faster pace exhilarated Lindsay, especially as they gained speed to a gallop.

Despite everything, she felt herself grinning, maybe even laughing, and when Daniel glanced over his shoulder, she saw the flash of white teeth. For this moment, they felt connected.

When she slid off Nessa by the open doors into the stable, she said, "That's the most fun I've ever had being interrogated."

Daniel's laugh kicked off an arrhythmia in her heartbeat.

HE KNEW WHERE to start now: with Mr. Pushy, Matt Grudin, and Ray Hammond, who might or might not have gotten the "no" message from Lindsay. Once Daniel had taken her home, he would run background checks on the two men.

And, yeah, he was letting this get personal. Some stalkers never openly expressed interest in a woman; she was just supposed to suddenly see him and exclaim her wild attraction to him. Her continued indifference was a crime in that man's eyes.

Daniel wasn't ruling out the women, either. Most if not all in the office were smaller and weaker than the two male victims—especially Martin Ramsey—but they had an advantage. Men tended to discount women. Not hesitate to let them in the door, turn their backs when they wouldn't on a male stranger.

Which got Daniel speculating. How *had* Norris been

overpowered? Had there been a tap on the head that wouldn't be noted until the autopsy?

Right now, Daniel wasn't in any hurry to get back to work. Lindsay had unsaddled Nessa without any prompting, cross-tied her and was now brushing her. He smiled at the sight of the mare, head low, twitching her skin here and there to make sure especially itchy places got appropriate attention, lips drooping.

Now, if Lindsay had put her hand on *him*, he'd probably do the same.

"She's about to fall asleep on you," he said.

Lindsay's unshadowed smile felt like a kick to his chest. "I noticed," she murmured. "She loves this. Max looks annoyed instead."

"He has sensitive skin and is maybe a little lacking in patience." Hoof pick in hand, Daniel bent to lift a foreleg to check for small stones or any kind of debris that could irritate the frog. He was pleased to see Lindsay doing the same, then sliding a hand over Nessa's hindquarters before beginning to comb her luxuriant tale.

"Do you show any of them?" she asked.

"Max and I enter cutting horse competitions. Otherwise, no. I bought one of my other mares from a college student who didn't have time for her anymore. Apparently, they rated well barrel racing."

"That looks fun." Lindsay sounded wistful before she went to the mare's head and gently rubbed her poll and ran her fingers through the black forelock. Nessa responded by butting her head against Lindsay's shoulder, then nibbling at her braid. Lindsay laughed. "Sorry, I'm not edible."

Daniel had a contrary opinion on that, but he could hardly say so.

After they turned the horses loose in a pasture, Max

trotted off and bucked just for the fun of it, while Nessa ambled to a spot of shade beneath an old oak tree and settled down, hip shot, for an apparent nap.

Lindsay was still smiling as she turned away. "Maybe I'll do that when I get home, too."

And maybe strip to no more than panties and a tank top, given the heat of the day. Daniel stayed a couple of feet behind to be sure she didn't notice how interested he was in the idea of her sprawled on her sheets.

The buzz at his hip was the distraction he needed, even if he didn't want it. He opened the driver side door of his truck and glanced at the screen of his phone.

Dispatch. Never good news.

Lindsay had opened her door, too, and pulled herself up onto the seat, but she was watching him.

Even as he answered, he held her gaze. "Deppero."

"Detective, we just had a call from the sheriff's department. They have a body, and they're wondering if it might be connected to the two murders here in town."

He'd actually intended to call the new sheriff, a rancher he knew named Boyd Chaney, to discuss the two murders. Gossip must have done that for him.

Chaney co-owned a ranch with a friend, who a year ago had helped hide a little girl who witnessed her father's murder. Once her whereabouts were discovered, all hell erupted. At the memory, Daniel felt an unhappy twinge from his thigh. That was the day when he'd been shot in a gun battle worthy of the Old West.

Chaney had been so pissed off at the lack of help from the sheriff's department, that fall he'd mounted an election challenge and unseated the slug who'd held the office for twenty-four years.

Shaking off the thought, Daniel asked, "Address?"

When the dispatcher told him, he said, stunned, "There's a murder victim *at the sheriff's ranch*?"

Lindsay's vivid blue eyes widened.

"If I understood him correctly," the dispatcher said primly.

"They have a name for the dead guy?"

He couldn't look away from Lindsay, who he'd swear hadn't blinked in at least a minute.

"Yes," the dispatcher said, "he's apparently an employee. Howie Haycroft. That's all I know." Next thing he knew, she was gone.

"Damn," he said softly, swinging in behind the wheel. He stowed his phone between the seats and slammed his door.

"Did you get a name?" Lindsay asked, her apprehension not well hidden.

In the act of inserting the key, he went still. "Can I count on you not repeating what I tell you to anyone at all?"

"I swear."

He wouldn't have told her at all if he hadn't wanted to find out if she knew the victim. Specifically, whether she'd ever investigated him for child abuse.

And, man, he wanted her to look puzzled and shake her head.

"Howie Haycroft."

Her forehead creased as she thought. "Howie…? No, I don't remember…" Horror crossed her face. "Haycroft. Howard Haycroft. Oh, dear God."

He could echo that. "Your case?"

"Yes, but… Oh, it has to have been three years. It was one of my early ones."

"Crap." Daniel could have said something a lot stronger. "Whoever this is has access to the CPS files."

Her teeth chattered before she squared her shoulders, pulled on her seat belt and lifted her chin. Composure restored—on the outside.

“Will you tell me what you remember?” he asked.

“I can tell you the basics. You’d find it in court records anyway.”

“Let’s have it,” he said grimly, and fired up the engine to take her home.

Chapter Seven

Daniel parked in front of the sprawling log ranch house that was County Sheriff Boyd Chaney's home. The second partner of the ranch, Gabe Decker, had had Daniel out to his own place for barbecues and the like a few times. Daniel would call Decker a friend, but despite several meetings he didn't know Chaney as well.

Chaney must have heard Daniel's truck coming, because he waited on the deep porch that ran the length of the house. A big, fit man, he came close to Daniel in height.

Climbing the porch steps, Daniel said, "Chaney." He let a crooked smile form. "Or should I say Sheriff?"

The man grimaced. "Make it Boyd."

"Where's the body?" Why waste time on small talk?

"Bodies." Boyd's eyes met his. "We found a second one."

What the hell?

"I'll ride with you," Boyd said. "Worker housing is half a mile or so north, beyond the barns."

Daniel didn't say anything until they were on their way. By then, he'd decided where to start. "What makes you think these killings have anything to do with the ones I'm investigating?"

"Now that I have access to law enforcement databases, I found background I didn't uncover when I hired Haycroft and his son Colin 'bout two years ago. Neither of them had ever been convicted of a crime, a red flag I look for. Boy was only eighteen then, but a hard worker. Increasingly lousy attitude, though. He didn't like being told what to do, especially by women. Resented our foreman, too."

"Leon Cabrera?" Like Boyd and Gabe, Leon was an ex-army ranger and had been or should have been a sniper.

Boyd's face set in hard lines. "I was about to let him go."

Was? Strong hint that Howard Haycroft's son was the other victim, not a surprise after Lindsay's description of the mess the Haycroft case had been.

"How about Haycroft?" he asked.

"Smart enough to keep his mouth shut, but kids learn from their parents."

Ahead, what had to be twenty log cabins had been built scattered about among a few acres of tall ponderosa pines. Each would feel private, not institutional like most company housing. Native plants formed an understory beneath the trees. The soil itself was tan and gritty, bright green lawns and flower beds conspicuously absent.

Boyd nodded ahead. "Last cabin on the end."

Turning in, Daniel parked again, but neither man moved to get out.

"Colin was almost seventeen when he spoke out for his father," Daniel remarked. The background Lindsay gave him explained why the son had been condemned to share his father's fate. Despite the evidence to the contrary, Colin had insisted the father wasn't abusive.

"It was three against one." Anger glinted in Boyd's eyes. "Why did investigators believe the one kid?"

"I haven't taken the time to dig into the police investigation yet. I was a detective at the time, but I didn't work that one. I'll pull out records once I'm back at the office. When you called, though, I was with the Child Protective Services caseworker who did her own investigation after the death."

The word *death* being a euphemism in this case. Howard Haycroft's wife had been executed. Hands duct-taped behind her back, ankles duct-taped, too. There'd been a single, fatal shot to the head from behind. Classic.

Expression arrested, Boyd said, "This the same caseworker in both of the recent investigations?"

"Yes. We had to look at her, but we're ninety-five percent sure she's no killer. That said, we've passed the point where we can pretend it might be coincidence that she was the caseworker involved with all three families."

Boyd grunted his agreement. He opened his door, but before getting out, said, "I think you can guess how they were killed."

Yes, that wouldn't be a surprise.

LINDSAY COULDN'T SETTLE down after Daniel dropped her at home. Not Daniel, she reminded herself; she'd be a fool to drop her guard yet. Detective Deperro.

Since it was lunchtime, she heated a can of soup but ended up dumping most of it down the drain before rinsing the bowl and putting it in the dishwasher. She couldn't concentrate on the mystery she'd been reading. Daytime TV held zero interest for her. Every sound from outside had her skin prickling for no reason she could name.

All she could think about was Howard Haycroft and the destruction of his family.

He'd killed his wife. Lindsay would swear he had. The scene had been carefully constructed to look like a home invasion, from what she'd heard. Thank God she hadn't seen that body.

The police determined the back door had been jimmied *after* Marcia Haycroft was killed, not before. She had either let the murderer in or he'd already been in the house. Lived there.

Police suspicions explained Lindsay's involvement. She temporarily removed all four kids from the home, although the oldest boy refused to stay in the receiving home, and she had eventually given up and let him go back to his father.

The three younger children, two girls and a boy, cried abuse. Their bodies showed evidence of enough healed broken bones, scars and burns to back up their claim. The oldest son, though, whose name she couldn't recall, had insisted furiously that the mother had been the abuser, not his dad. The others were making up stories, he'd insisted.

She got the feeling the younger children were afraid of their brother as well as their father.

In the end, the DA declined to file charges of murder against Howard, claiming a lack of forensic evidence. No witness stepped forward. That left the fate of the children in the hands of family court. Howard wanted them home, but in the end the judge ruled that the three youngest children would go into a foster home, having supervised visits with their father until they regained confidence in him.

Her stomach had lurched at the idea of the children pressured into agreeing to go back to him, but the visits didn't go well and finally petered out.

Last she'd heard, Howard and his almost adult son sold the house and moved away. Idaho, she thought. She hadn't heard anything about the Haycrofts in a couple of years. Now she wondered if Howard had resumed contact with his younger children. Tomorrow, she'd contact the foster care supervisor with DHS.

But unless something had changed drastically—if one of the younger Haycroft children had been killed or committed suicide, for example—why punish Howard now? And who would care enough to bother? There'd been no adult relatives willing to take in the children, far less avenge them.

And, dear God, what did *she* have to do with it? Lindsay would rather think that somebody hated her than that these murders were supposed to please her.

It almost had to be one or the other, didn't it?

She paced, going from window to window, not seeing what was in front of her eyes. Instead, she grappled with an ominous sense of losing control. She felt horribly as if she were stuck in a web, waiting for the spider.

MELINDA MADE IT out to the ranch while the crime scenes were still being processed. Daniel had forgotten she, too, had met Boyd Chaney at least once, in her case when she'd come out to the ranch to question three-year-old Chloe Keif about how much she'd seen when her entire family had been wiped out. Despite a necessary, tough veneer, Melinda was good with children. He was puzzled by the tension he read between her and Boyd, but made sure neither would guess he'd noticed it.

Both men accompanied her when she studied the two

scenes. With the CSI crew borrowed from the state still working, neither body had been moved. Howard's was in the cabin, requisite trash can with the ash of burned papers beside him, while Colin's body was in a storage shed. The fire there had been set on the dirt floor, a safe distance from anything else flammable. Seemed the killer hadn't wanted to start a forest fire.

Melinda waited until they reached their vehicles to ask, "Could he have been involved in his mother's murder?"

"Lindsay says he appeared to be shocked and grieving her loss. No indication from the younger kids that he had anything but a good relationship with her."

"So you're suggesting this boy was brutally murdered just because he defended his father?"

Boyd said, "More because he single-handedly saved his father from being charged with murder or child abuse. *And* labeled his brother and sisters as liars."

She seared him with a glare. "You know he was probably scared, too."

"I didn't find him very likeable," Boyd commented with a mildness belied by the razor intensity of the stare that answered hers.

"So it's okay he got killed?"

"I didn't say that."

Time to intervene. Daniel pushed himself away from the fender. "Can we focus?"

Melinda took a deep breath, then another. Looking toward the cabin, she said, "I guess the first thing we have to ask ourselves is who is taking primary on this one."

Boyd's eyebrows climbed. "It's my jurisdiction."

The two of them were going to start another pissing

match? Daniel barely refrained from rolling his eyes. Instead, he shook his head and offered a solution.

"We cooperate. We bring Sheriff Chaney up to date with our investigations so he doesn't have to start from scratch. We don't keep anything from each other."

Boyd smiled slightly.

Melinda's lips thinned, but she kept her mouth shut.

"Do you plan to assign a detective to this?" Daniel asked Boyd. "Or work it yourself?"

"I'll assign my senior detective, but look over his shoulder. He has zero experience with a murder investigation, but he might as well learn."

"Unless you were military police," Melinda put in, "you don't, either."

"I've killed people. Seen friends go down. Does that count?"

Daniel was starting to get a headache. Clearly, he needed to take point where the sheriff's department was concerned.

"We don't have many murders in the county, not counting domestics or bar brawls. We all learn as we go." He was the one exception, having worked major crimes including homicide in Portland for a couple of years before deciding to come home to eastern Oregon, but he didn't say so. Melinda probably knew, and the last thing they needed was this to become a three-way tug-of-war.

"Fair enough," Boyd said. "I'd like to join you to interview the caseworker, even if you've already talked to her. I'll have my detective canvass my other employees to find out if they heard anything or saw anyone around the Haycrofts' cabin. Or, for that matter, anyone unfamiliar out here on the ranch. If you can email me whatever you have so far, I'll let you know what I learn from the CSI team."

"Good. Let me give you my phone number."

Melinda offered hers up, too. Daniel couldn't help noticing that Boyd didn't enter it in his phone. Because he had no intention of talking to her? Or was it already in his contacts because they had some sort of previous relationship?

None of my business.

MONDAY MORNING, LINDSAY parked as close to the front door of the office as she could manage. If only the back door wasn't kept locked.

Two journalists with microphones in hand and cameramen to back them hovered by the double glass doors. Did they know what she looked like, or could she slip in with a head shake and "no comment"?

The latest murders had been the lead story on local news and featured in eastern Oregon newspapers as well as the *Portland Oregonian*. Unfortunately, journalists had been able to access public records and find her name.

She grabbed her briefcase, closed her eyes and took a few deep breaths, then jumped out. Her car beeped behind her as she used her key fob even as she hurried toward the entrance.

"Excuse me!" one of the men called. "Are you Lindsay Engle?"

The second journalist, a woman, stepped between her and the door. "How do you explain your involvement with the families preceding all four murders?"

"I have no comment for you. Please let me by."

"Have the investigating officers interviewed you?"

the man demanded to know. "Do you have the sense you're considered a suspect?"

Shaking inside but outwardly composed, Lindsay met the woman's eyes. "If you don't step out of my way, you'll be speaking to the police yourself."

The reporter moved, her expression huffy. "We're giving you an opportunity to share your perspective."

Hand on the door, Lindsay paused. "You should respect the fact that Child Protective Services keeps names and the results of investigations confidential. Speak to the police detectives."

She slipped inside, the closing door cutting off their voices.

Dear God. How could she keep coming to work? But how could she not? This was what she did. Hiding out would make her look guilty. No, it wasn't an option.

Celeste Klassen, the receptionist, hurried around her desk, her wary gaze darting to the view through the glass. "Lindsay! You're okay?"

"Hasn't been the best week," she admitted. No, nearly two weeks now.

Celeste hugged her. "We've all been worried about you. What's happening is weird. And creepy."

Lindsay smiled wryly. "I totally concur."

"Sadie asked to see you as soon as you came in."

There was a surprise.

"Thanks." Lindsay went to her supervisor's office and found the door standing open.

Sadie glanced up from some paperwork on her desk. "Oh, Lindsay. Come on in. Take a seat." She set aside her reading glasses. "I'm sorry you had to run the gauntlet outside."

"Everyone else must have, too. Can't we ban them from the property?"

"That's easier when it's private property. State property is theoretically owned by all taxpayers."

Lindsay wrinkled her nose. "We still shouldn't have to be harassed coming to work."

"Did they recognize you?"

"They asked questions as though they did."

"Tell me about the Haycrofts. I wasn't assigned here then. I've read about it, but that's not the same."

Lindsay repeated what she'd told Daniel, and added a few details she'd withheld from him.

Her supervisor listened, interjecting only a few questions. At the end, she shook her head. "I'd say why now, but it was obviously one of our agency's more dramatic cases."

"And now it's even more so."

"Yes. What's most disturbing is that this murderer either has to be an insider or has somehow got access to our records. The IT department has looked but found no indication a hacker gained entry," she added. "That said, we both know there are people out there who can sneak past any safeguards."

Lindsay nodded her agreement.

Sadie picked up her glasses and began fiddling with them. "For now, if I have to assign any new investigations to you, I'll keep them routine." She held up a hand, although Lindsay hadn't protested. "This is no criticism of you. I hope you know that. But…let's not tempt fate."

The ban, if that wasn't too harsh a word, might not be meant as criticism, but it didn't feel good, either. Call it a pointed finger, because she might not be at fault but was, in some roundabout way, responsible.

Since Lindsay had already made the same decision-but not yet discussed it with Sadie, she nodded and rose to her feet. "I'm going to try not to step out the door today. I'll have lunch delivered."

Sadie laughed. "I may do the same."

Easy for her to be amused. She wasn't the one being hunted.

IT WAS A WEIRD, unsettling day. Lindsay pretended to work more than actually accomplishing anything. Her ability to concentrate was shattered; like light bouncing off so many irregular fragments of glass, it was impossible to focus on one thing.

To start with, she couldn't slip quietly in from Sadie's office and go to work. Instead, the moment she appeared, the five caseworkers who happened to be at their desks all lifted their heads.

"Wow," Ashley Sheldon said. "I don't look *anything* like you, but I had to practically produce ID to prove I wasn't you." Ashley preened, as if anybody with eyes couldn't tell she was far prettier.

Or maybe Lindsay was just feeling sour.

"Yes, having the press hanging out in our parking lot is a nuisance," she said, without elaborating.

The newest hire, Jenn Armstrong, asked, "Is there anything you want us to say?" She flushed. "I mean, what *should* I say?"

"'No comment,'" Lindsay told her. "Just keep repeating it. I already reminded them that our work is kept confidential."

"Yeah, like that'll work," Matt Grudin sneered.

Unless she was imagining things, his gaze held acute dislike. Had she just never seen it before? He might have moved on from her refusal to go out with him, but did he hold a grudge?

She raised her eyebrows, refusing to look away. "Do you have a better suggestion?"

"Yeah, tell them to shove it up their—"

Before he finished, Gayle Schaefer, a quiet woman in her fifties, interrupted. "Sure. Sadie might have something to say about that."

Lindsay felt a physical relief when Matt turned his sneer toward the other woman.

"Then I'll tell her where she can go, too. I've started looking for another job anyway. I can hardly wait to get out of here."

Gayle shrugged and turned her attention back to her laptop.

Ray Hammond caught Lindsay's eyes and grimaced, his expression friendly.

She smiled back, but not so widely as to encourage him.

And then, having opened her laptop, she stared at her screensaver and asked herself if any of her coworkers could be hiding enough rage to kill so ruthlessly. Could someone so brutal be hiding behind an ordinary mask?

Jenn—no. Lindsay really hadn't gotten to know her, but she was straight out of grad school and had only worked here at CPS for six or seven months. She'd inherited Hank Cousins's caseload, but otherwise hadn't been assigned any of the heartbreaking cases. Of course, she could have grown up in some kind of sick situation and had plotted for years—four years for an undergraduate degree, another two to three for her master's—just so she could be in a position to punish every man like her father or uncle or whoever it was that hurt her. If so, she was the best actor Lindsay had ever seen. No, she wouldn't believe it.

Ashley Sheldon wasn't one of Lindsay's favorite coworkers; she could be a bitch. But Lindsay couldn't see her as a possible suspect, either. She was too self-centered. How would these murders help her?

On the flip side, she didn't seem to like Lindsay, either.

Gayle was quiet enough to hide a fuel tank full of rage, but Lindsay couldn't see it. Gayle was kind, efficient...and used a cane. She'd returned to CPS a year and a half ago after a several-year absence. Lindsay had been told that Gayle had multiple sclerosis and was currently in remission. If that was true, she wouldn't have been strong enough to overpower any of the four men.

Lindsay sneaked a look toward Matt Grudin, still at his desk typing furiously on his laptop. Updating his résumé, maybe. *He* was obviously angry, and some of that was directed her way. More than she'd realized, in fact. At about six feet, he was solidly built. Physically, he was capable, she thought. But if he were the killer, wouldn't he be trying *not* to gain attention?

Ray Hammond was more of an enigma to Lindsay, a handsome guy and a little too cocky for her tastes. That said, he seemed dedicated to his job and she'd seen him handling difficult people with ease and showing compassion to scared children. But who knew? He could be more burned out than was apparent.

That left the three coworkers not here at the moment, probably meeting with witnesses or family members. And she couldn't forget Sadie, who had worked in Child Protective Services longer than any of them, albeit not in this office, and who did still take on some investigations. Oh—and Celeste, of course, although that stretched credulity.

Work, Lindsay told herself, but five minutes later her

mind had circled back to the beginning. Could Matt really hate her that much…?

She looked up from her laptop but again, as with every time she did, she found her coworkers surreptitiously watching her. Her eyes flew back down to her screen.

She thought her day couldn't get any worse. Untill Daniel—Detective Deperro—and Boyd Chaney, Granger County sheriff, showed up to escort her into the conference room again to interview her.

Chapter Eight

Thursday, Daniel parked at the curb two doors down from the Norris house. More accurately, from the house where Paige Norris would soon live alone if she didn't sell it. For the moment, yellow tape still stretched across the front door; Paige was staying in a hotel.

There were a few neighbors he had yet to catch at home. Some had apparently been away for the weekend, and unavailable the other times he'd knocked on their doors.

Today, Melinda was tied up with another investigation. Daniel had figured lunch hour might be a good time to find someone home who hadn't been at other times of the day.

With the sun high in the sky, the heat hit Daniel as soon as he stepped out of his unmarked SUV. This was one of those moments when he wished he didn't have air-conditioning in it, not to mention the police station and his home. The plunge from low to high temperatures was what got to him. He'd be sweat-soaked in no time.

What were the odds he'd learn anything at all helpful from random neighbors who hadn't thought to call 9-1-1 and say, *I saw this man carrying a bloody ax running out the back door?* Sure, and the witness also saw the make, color and model of the car the ax-wielder hopped into.

Daniel was not optimistic.

Here they were, nearly two weeks since the first murder, and they now had four bodies. And no leads. No witnesses. Nobody had heard anything, noticed an unfamiliar car in the vicinity. Nothing in the background of any CPS worker jumped out at him to justify formally interviewing him or her.

Monday, after he and Boyd had talked to Lindsay at the CPS offices, he'd managed to start casual conversations with Matt Grudin and Ray Hammond. A couple of the women had jumped in, too, but he'd focused on the men. Hadn't taken him thirty seconds to discover how intensely he disliked Grudin, but he knew he'd started with a bias. That said, the guy did carry a boatload of anger coupled with arrogance. The fact that most of his coworkers must know Lindsay had turned him down wasn't something he took lightly. He didn't succeed in hiding how pleased he was that Lindsay was in trouble, an attitude that shot him straight to the top of Daniel's list of suspects. Grudin ticked a lot of the markers Daniel was looking for.

Hammond maintained a bland facade that made him unreadable. Unremarkable, too, if Daniel hadn't known that he, too, had unsuccessfully pursued Lindsay.

His next stop had been to talk to the IT unit, who claimed there'd been no hacking of the database, and to Sadie Culver, who wasn't surprised at his interest in the caseworkers she directed but either didn't have so much as a nugget of suspicion toward any of them or chose not to share it.

After the interviews, he'd ruled out a couple of the women he didn't see as physically able to commit the murders. And he hadn't been able to narrow his interest in the others enough to justify going beyond background checks and some general questions about the caseworkers' schedules and whether any of them had been involved, even in a secondary role, with any of the CPS investigations that had ended in murder.

Although Melinda and Boyd were as baffled as he was, frustration didn't seem to ride them the way it did Daniel. Boyd was mostly peeved that a man like Howard Haycroft had slipped by the employment vetting at the ranch. Melinda's dark mood had to do with her determination to be the one to crack the case. Proving she was more competent, smarter, than Boyd Chaney was her reason for getting up in the morning, as far as Daniel could tell. She hadn't done or said anything so far that would compel him to issue a warning, but her simmering competitiveness irritated him.

Monday hadn't been improved by the gauntlet of journalists, some with TV cameras, he and Boyd had had to run to get into the state DHS offices to talk to Lindsay. "We are not at this point prepared to make a statement" didn't even slow the shouted questions. Daniel hated knowing that it had to have been worse for her. He had called her several times during the week, ostensibly to ask additional questions of his own but really to find out how she was doing. Every time, the strain in her voice had been a reminder of her face during the Monday interview: too pale, the bones seemingly more prominent than usual, purple circles beneath her eyes.

He'd wanted to do a lot more than call her, but had reined himself in enough to know he needed to keep his distance. He shouldn't have taken her riding at his place that one time.

The week had passed with excruciating slowness.

Now here he was on Thursday, waiting for the other shoe to drop.

Who was next to die?

Shaking his head, he rang a doorbell, stepping to one side of the door while he waited for a response. No, he didn't suppose the middle-aged man who resided at this address intended to whip out a shotgun and blast him through the door, but better safe than sorry.

To his mild surprise, he heard footsteps and a minute later the door opened.

Daniel held out his badge and elicited the information that this was the homeowner, Ralph Brown.

"Sir, I'd like to ask you a few questions." He nodded toward the Norris house. "I'm sure you heard about the murder."

"You kidding?" The guy stepped out on the porch and followed Daniel's gaze. He looked older than his years, his face weather beaten and heavily lined, his hair steel gray. "That's all anyone talks about. I only knew those folks to wave at, but it shakes you up."

"I understand. Is there any chance you were home between, say, eight-thirty and eleven in the morning that day? Might you have seen Mrs. Norris leave for work?"

"Yeah, I did. Real pretty woman. Always friendly."

Daniel smiled. "Yes, she is." *Allows her husband to sexually abuse her young daughters, but hey—she smiles at the neighbors.* "Did you see anyone arrive at the house, before or after she left?"

"No, I left probably twenty minutes after she did. I remember running a little late. I can't see their house from any of my windows, you know. It's blocked by my next-door neighbor's place. I only noticed Mrs. Norris because I happened to be looking out when she drove by."

"Yes, I understand. But, say, while you were backing out of your garage, or if you drove past their place..."

Ralph shook his head. "Only thing I remember was a car parked on the side street. Never seen it before, haven't seen it again."

Daniel determined that he wasn't a car guy. He said it was an older sedan, he thought a Toyota but couldn't be sure. He might have seen the symbol, but didn't Mazda or some other maker have a similar one? Car was white, but not real shiny. His eye had been caught because houses in the neighborhood all had double garages and driveways. Hardly anybody parked at the curb except guests when someone was holding a party.

After thanking him, Daniel walked back to his own vehicle. Back in the direct sun, he was barely conscious of being hammered by the heat. This wasn't a direct lead to a suspect, but at least he had something to go on. A white maybe-Toyota.

The driver could have easily slipped through the gate into the backyard and entered the house through the slider, if it hadn't been locked. It wasn't locked when Melinda found Norris dead.

Getting behind the wheel, waiting for his air-conditioning to kick in, he felt energized. He thought Ralph Brown had seen the killer's car.

It was a start.

BACK AT THE STATION, the first thing Daniel did was look to see what everyone working for Child Protective Services here in town drove. He wasn't really surprised to find that none of them drove a white sedan of any kind, much less a Toyota. That would have been too easy.

After some thought, he pulled up the list of vehicles stolen in the past month. He blinked when he came upon a Toyota Corolla, 2008, white. Researching it further, he learned it had not been recovered. It had gone missing seventeen days ago. Right timeline, if the killer had also driven it when he murdered Martin Ramsey.

The car's owner lived in an older neighborhood on Grouse Street, a few blocks from the business district. It had evidently belonged to the seventeen-year-old daughter. He called her and she told him she'd been leaving for her summer job at Dairy Queen when she'd discovered her car was no longer parked in its usual spot in the alley.

As a cop, Daniel wasn't a fan of alleys. They were too private. Backyards tended to be fenced. Garages accessed by the alley also blocked any view of it from the houses. Trash left out for pickup created great places to hide. In fact, alleys were perfect sites to commit just about any kind of crime and were cordially hated by CSIs.

He couldn't be certain this was the right car, but he thought the chances were good it was. He'd put out the word for patrol officers to sharpen their watch for it.

His desk phone rang, and he signed off with the teen and switched calls. "Deperro."

He allowed himself a fleeting moment of hope that this was about any other crime. He did have quite a few investigations gathering dust in stacks on his desk. When he recognized the voice of a lieutenant on the patrol side, that hope gained altitude.

"Detective? This is Griggs. We just received a call requesting a welfare check. Something the woman said got me thinking. I did a background check and found the man we're supposed to check on was involved in a nasty child abuse case a couple of years back. Name's Bradley Taubeneck. You want to ride along, just in case?"

Daniel resisted the temptation to thump his head on his desk. "I do." Because he loved finding mutilated bodies, he thought sardonically.

He drove himself, following a patrol unit, taking the opportunity to do some quick research. He didn't learn as much as he'd like. Taubeneck had been charged with child abuse, but those charges were later dismissed. Lot of backstory, Daniel was willing to bet.

The landscape west of town was dryer than out Daniel's way. Here, an occasional herd of cattle grazed on high desert scrub behind barbed wire fences. The patrol car turned onto a dirt track that led toward a distant house and barns. Daniel was soon enveloped in a dust cloud. He couldn't see a whole lot until they both parked behind the ranch house.

He knew the patrol officer Griggs had assigned to the welfare check, a guy about his age named Keith Shead. They greeted each other and walked to the back door. Shead knocked firmly, waited and did it again. No response. After a brief consulation, they separated to circle the house and meet in front.

Daniel saw no movement inside the uncovered windows of what appeared to be a bedroom and an empty room. At a third window, he went still, his hand sliding to the butt of his weapon. This, too, had been a bedroom but was now trashed. It was as if someone in a rage had thrown furniture against the walls. Even more cautiously, he moved forward, ducking to sneak a peek before rounding the corner. Shead waited for him on the front porch.

"See anything?" Shead asked in a low voice.

"Somebody threw a mighty big temper tantrum in one of the bedrooms. Looks like it was a little boy's room. A lot of fury there."

"Blinds were down on a couple of the windows, but the kitchen looked okay, just…empty. No remnants of a recent meal or anything like that."

Daniel nodded and rang the doorbell. A gong sounded from within. He pulled a latex glove from his pocket and put it on before trying the doorknob. Locked.

"We may have to break in, but let's try the outbuildings first."

Shead agreed, following Daniel back around so he could see the evidence of the epic temper tantrum.

Giving a low whistle, he said, "I wonder if that's recent or happened a long time ago."

Had Taubeneck lost his family? Crap. He wished he'd called Lindsay on the way.

In fact…

"Give me a minute," he said, and Shead nodded, walking toward their parked cars. Daniel dialed Lindsay's mobile number and waited through five rings before she answered, sounding tense.

"Detective?"

Forget being on a first-name basis. He was still in the doghouse.

"What can you tell me about Bradley Taubeneck?"

The silence that ensued raised the hairs on the back of his neck.

"Is he dead?"

"We're doing a welfare check. I'm told he was involved in a mess that brought CPS in." He frowned. "Were you the caseworker?"

"Of course I was." Her voice had lost all life, sounded numb. "You think you'll find him dead."

"That's a possibility I hope you'll keep to yourself for now."

"Yes."

"What happened to the child?"

"It was a little boy. He wasn't in his bed come morning. They…found him dead outside in the snow. Doors were locked."

He swore. "Did the father throw him out as punishment or something?"

"That's how it appeared at first. I ended up having some doubts about what really happened."

Daniel let another expletive slip out. With the weather currently so hot, how would a killer have replicated the poor boy's death? "Okay," he said after a minute. "I'll let you know what we find."

He and Shead stuck together to search, given that they didn't know what they were facing. Maybe the guy just wasn't answering his phone and would be hostile to have law enforcement officers prowling around his property.

The barn was a washout. Daniel did notice no animals were inside. He climbed the ladder to the hayloft, even moved a few bales to be sure a body wasn't wedged behind them. Shaking his head, he dropped back to the barn floor.

Another outbuilding held farm equipment: a tractor and more. The last one, closest to the house, had buckets, some tools and a white appliance it took him a second to recognize. A chest freezer. His gaze arrowed in on a hasp that had not been original…and the closed, heavy-duty padlock.

As if there was any doubt, a metal bucket filled with ashes sat right in front of the freezer.

Shead was the one swearing up a storm now. He ran back to the other outbuilding and returned fast and sweating, bolt cutters in hand. Daniel doubted speed was going to accomplish anything now. The ashes in the bucket were cool.

The padlock didn't want to surrender. They took turns, untill finally it snapped in two and Daniel wrenched it off, lifted the hasp and pushed open the top.

With ice crystalized over his eyes, nostrils and mouth, the man inside was very dead.

"I'M SORRY," SADIE SAID, her expression sympathetic. "You know this isn't punishment, and I don't believe for a second that you played any part in these murders. I hope you understand that I just can't let you near a case until this is cleared up."

Lindsay wouldn't touch a new investigation with a ten-foot pole. But to be blocked even from working on ongoing cases came as a shock, despite the fact that she'd tried to prepare herself for this outcome. Once details about the latest murder topped local television news broadcasts, Sadie probably hadn't felt she had any choice. The news of the most recent murder had spread like wildfire on social media even before news sources had picked it up.

While Lindsay understood where Sadie was coming from, she was still furious. Not at Sadie; in her shoes, Lindsay would have made the same decision. No, most of her anger was directed at the killer, who seemed determined to destroy her career if not her life even if he didn't add her to his murder tally. But she had plenty of anger left over, simmering beneath the surface, choking her.

She nodded and rose to her feet. "I'll clean out my desk."

She'd almost escaped her supervisor's office when Sadie said from behind her, in what was presumably meant to be encouragement, "You'll be back at work before you know it."

Sure she would. Lindsay didn't even pause. Feeling the heat of humiliation and anger in her cheeks, she marched into the large space occupied by her fellow caseworkers, trying not to make eye contact with anyone. Of course, silence fell at her appearance.

Sitting down at her desk, she wished she had a box, then thought, *Do I really have anything here I really value?* The answer was no.

She opened her already hefty handbag and shoved a few things in. A framed photo of her last foster mom. Two paperback books. A handful of energy bars that might go stale before she made it back—if she ever did.

She was already carrying her laptop. After opening and closing the final drawers, staring in and seeing nothing but the detritus of work she'd allowed to become her entire life, she stood abruptly enough to send her desk chair rolling back.

For the first time, she let herself notice the gaping stares of every single caseworker here in the office.

And her anger rolled over her until she literally saw red.

"Yes," she said loudly, "there's been another murder. I've been suspended, in case you're wondering." Without fault, but that wasn't the point. She looked from face to face. "It would appear that somebody expects me to be pleased because he's making child abusers suffer the same pain their victims did. He's punishing them the way he must think they should have been punished in the first place. The way I failed to do, with my silly insistence on following the letter of the law." Her voice continued rising as her grip on any self-control slipped. She should shut her mouth and leave...but why? she thought recklessly. *I have an audience. The perfect audience.*

One that might well include a serial killer.

"Well, you know what?" She turned in a slow circle to take in everyone in the room. "I'm *not* pleased. I'm enraged. Who does this person think he is, to sit in judgment on people he's never even met? People who haven't been convicted of a crime?" In fact, most of the murder victims hadn't been. Not yet, anyway. "You know he cold-bloodedly murdered a very young man only because, when he was a kid himself, he defended his father?"

They all gazed at her, rapt, unblinking. Movement caught out of the corner of her eye told her Sadie had appeared. And, oh Lord, was that Glenn behind her?

Well, right this minute, she didn't care.

"The latest victim—" Her voice broke. "From almost the beginning, I've believed he was innocent of the accusations. I was responsible for the charges being dropped, although his wife left him and took his other child with her. But this time, the arrogant monster who has named himself judge and executioner murdered *an innocent man*. Think about that."

She slung her laptop over her shoulder and grabbed her handbag. "Maybe I'm no better person than he is, because I hope he—or she," Lindsay added, again glaring from face to face, "suffers the same agony he's inflicted on other people. The difference between us? Unlike this sick creep, I won't be taking justice in my own hands."

She noted the ducked heads, the eyes that no longer wanted to meet hers. Did everyone in this room guess they were under suspicion, because they were among the very few people who had access to the details of the original abuse cases?

She opened her mouth again but regained enough self-control to do nothing but shake her head and stomp toward the exit. Sadie and Glenn stepped hastily aside before she could knock them out of her way. Seconds later, she was out in the heat of the day and pulling open her car door.

"Lindsay."

Recognizing the voice, she closed her eyes and her shoulders sagged. She hated knowing how disappointed Glenn would be in her for making such a spectacular scene. She couldn't even say she felt better for having vented.

I can't go back to work with those same people.

She tossed the two bags onto the passenger seat and turned to face the man who'd given her so much support and encouragement.

"Bet you didn't know I had it in me," she said wryly.

Astonishingly, his smile was as kind as ever, his presence as steadying. He had the same quality Daniel Deperro did, she was surprised to realize, one that made her want to believe, deep inside, that he wouldn't let her down. It wasn't just physical, although like Daniel he was solidly built. Well, not counting the roll around the middle he'd been acquiring since his retirement.

Although she liked and admired Glenn, she was disturbed to realize she had never let herself absolutely, 100 percent, believe she could trust and depend on him. She wouldn't be able to where Daniel was concerned, either. Some scars ran deep.

"'Course I knew you did," he said, his brown eyes compassionate. "You always had a fire. That's what this job takes."

"Uh-huh."

"I know how much stress you've been under. I'm sorry I haven't called."

"I didn't expect you to. It's just…been strange. You know? Why me?"

"Maybe because you've been given the toughest cases from the beginning," he suggested. "Somebody admires you."

"Or resents me."

He waggled a hand. "Possible, I suppose."

"I'll be okay." She forced a smile and rose on tiptoe to kiss his cheek. "It's about time I took a vacation, anyway."

He laughed, kissed her cheek in turn and said, "This *is* a paid break?"

"Yep." This second smile came more easily. "Maybe I should take an Alaska cruise, escape the heat."

"Go for it." He hesitated. "I'm just sorry you don't have a partner to go with you."

Suddenly curious, she asked, "Have you ever been married?" He'd been single as long as she'd known him.

"Sure. Divorced." He grimaced. "Job can do that to you."

"Job can keep you single, too," Lindsay said in exactly the same tone.

Then she saw someone else emerge from the state offices and start across the parking lot in her direction. Matt Grudin. Maybe he intended to be supportive, too… or maybe he thought she'd be vulnerable right now and he could get her in bed. Eager to avoid him, she said hurriedly, "I need to go, Glenn. Talk to you later."

He glanced over his shoulder and turned back with his bushy gray eyebrows high. "Grudin, huh?"

"Just don't want to talk to anyone. Except you," she added hurriedly.

He contemplated her for a minute, then nodded and stepped back. "Better step on it."

She hopped into her roasting hot car, started the engine and, uselessly, the air-conditioning and pulled out of the parking slot before Matt reached Glenn's side.

As she drove away, she didn't look in the rearview mirror even once.

Chapter Nine

Daniel's hands clenched and unclenched on the steering wheel as he drove from the police station to Lindsay's house. She couldn't call and tell him she'd been suspended from her job?

The call from her supervisor, Sadie Culver, had come out of the blue, catching him just as he was leaving to go home. She seemed like a nice lady and had sounded apologetic.

"I think everybody was gaping at her, like drivers do an accident on the highway, and she blew her top. Told them all she didn't think for a minute that knocking off child abusers was a good thing. Said the killer was monster and a sick creep. Glenn was here and followed her out to be sure she was okay, but I still thought you'd want to know."

Yes, he did. And he sure as hell didn't believe she was "okay." As deeply committed to her job as Lindsay was, she had to be feeling lost. Pissed, too, obviously, which he understood.

If she wasn't home… He didn't know what he'd do. Wait? Come back later? She'd had all day; who knew, maybe she'd thrown some bags in her car and taken off, the way she'd planned the Saturday he'd talked her into horseback riding with him instead.

But he saw her car in the driveway as soon as he turned onto her block. Now he just had to hope she didn't ignore his knock on the door, always a possibility given their occasionally adversarial relationship.

He parked in her driveway, blocking her car in. Not likely she'd feel like going out tonight, anyway, unless she had girlfriends who'd insist on dragging her out to a bar. He didn't believe that, though; he couldn't be mistaken about her quality of aloneness.

Daniel strode up to the porch and leaned on the doorbell. He was just about ready to do it again when he heard movement inside. She opened the door and gazed at him without any visible emotion.

"What can I do for you, Detective?" she asked after a minute.

"I heard you were suspended."

"Who told you?"

"Your boss." He hesitated. "I think she was worried about you."

"Because I ranted and raved."

"Yeah, that was probably it." He nodded toward the door opening. "Can I come in?"

She gave it some thought but finally said, "I suppose," and backed up.

Until then, he'd kept his gaze above her shoulders, but now he couldn't resist a look at her spectacular legs revealed beneath cutoff shorts. He liked the effect of the body-clinging tank top, too. She was fine-boned but had ample curves. They were on display right now, which might be one reason she had been reluctant to open the door to him.

"You alone?" he asked, stepping in.

"Yes. I just poured myself a glass of white wine. Can I interest you in one?"

Daniel wasn't much of a wine drinker, but he said, "Sure, why not. I'm off the clock."

Her solitary glass of wine sat on an antique kitchen table, so he pulled up a chair opposite it.

Her feet were bare, too, he noticed while she was pouring another glass and putting the wine back in the fridge. Narrow feet, long toes. He moved a little uncomfortably as his gaze traveled upward.

She turned just then and caught him looking. Her eyes narrowed, but she set the wine down in front of him and plopped into a chair without comment.

"What? Did you imagine I'm suicidal, and you had to rush to the rescue?"

He smiled. "Not for a minute. You're tougher than that."

"Yes, I am." She stared at him with defiance, just long enough to make her point, but then she lifted one shoulder and her mouth twisted. "Crappy day, though."

"Yeah." He had to clear his throat. Somehow, he saw looking down, he'd reached across the table and covered her hand with his. "Told everyone how you really feel, huh?"

She didn't turn her hand over to clasp his, but she didn't pull away, either. "Did Sadie tell you what I said?"

"More or less. I want to hear about it from you." He wished she hadn't made herself a target if the killer had happened to be there when she let loose. But he also understood that Lindsay wasn't much for pretending. Her directness was one of many qualities that attracted him. As a cop, he sometimes thought he heard nothing but lies all day, every day.

So she told him, possibly verbatim, what she'd said before stalking out of work.

Daniel snagged on the last part. "You're sure this

Bradley Taubeneck didn't lock his kid out of the house that night?"

Vivid blue eyes haunted by memories met his. "Without a doubt? No. But… I'm pretty sure. I had suspicions I couldn't prove, so I left them out of the file. His wife accused him, and it was really unlikely the kid slipped out of the house and got locked out accidentally. Of course that happens, though. If the parents locked up and didn't bother to check on their kids before they went to bed."

"What did they say when you asked?"

"The mother claimed she had a migraine."

"But you didn't believe her," he said slowly.

"At first I bought into her story. She was weepy, grieving, even as she darted accusing looks at her husband." Her eyes appeared unfocused now. "Because of her headache, he was bearing more of the child-care responsibilities than usual, and Max was being really loud and wild. They were starting to wonder if he might be hyperactive. Anyway, the more I spoke with them, the more I saw genuine shock and bewilderment and grief on the dad's part and something a little off on hers. He seemed…stunned that she'd point a finger at him. Once he started to say, 'You know I'm always patient with Max. It's you who—' He didn't finish the sentence, but he didn't have to." She sighed and took a swallow of the wine. "It was the kind of investigation I hate the most. They didn't have any near neighbors, which meant no witnesses."

"Plus, Max couldn't have gone to a neighbor's."

"Right." Lindsay shrugged. "I convinced the DA to drop the charges, but I couldn't prove Bradley was innocent any more than I was able to prove his wife was the one who lost it with her own kid."

"Did people you worked with know about your doubts?"

She frowned. "I'm sure I expressed some concern, but they may have thought I had to let him off because there was no way to be sure what happened."

Daniel swore and rubbed a hand over his face. "So our killer thinks Bradley was guilty as hell and got off scot-free." More slowly, he said, "Or, I guess I should say, he *thought* Bradley was guilty." After an even longer pause, he added, "Or else he doesn't care one way or the other. The victims are just…symbols."

"That's even more sickening."

He looked away for a minute. "Yeah."

Sounding stricken, Lindsay said, "You really think somebody at CPS is doing this."

"You have any better ideas?"

She shook her head, gazing into her wineglass as if she'd find answers there.

"Can you tell me who was there to hear your blowup?"

She explained that it had been early enough in the morning, only three coworkers had been missing: Ashley Sheldon, Gayle Schaefer and Ray Hammond. "Well," she said, "I'm sure Celeste heard every word out at reception, too, and so did Sadie—I guess you already knew that—and Glenn Wilson, my last supervisor."

Daniel frowned. "What was he doing there?"

"He pops in once a week or so, just kind of keeping a read on our emotional stability, I guess you could say. Truthfully, I think he's bored."

"Ms. Culver doesn't mind? She doesn't feel like he's looking over her shoulder?"

"No, she says that when she first started, he was really generous when she had questions. I've seen them go out for coffee together, even."

"Does he still have access to the database?"

Her surprise was obvious. "Of course not! You aren't thinking *he* could be—"

"It's going to turn out to be somebody you know, Lindsay."

"Lovely thought."

They looked at each other in silence for what had to be a minute. Damn, she was beautiful. He wanted to stand up, go around the table and pull her to her feet. Hold her—although he was too likely to kiss her once she was in his arms.

What he ought to do was go home. Daniel already knew he wouldn't be doing that. Not until he had no other choice.

"Listen," he said, "what if I order a pizza? Or that Thai place delivers."

Her chin lifted in an all-too familiar gesture of independence. "I'm okay by myself. Don't feel you have to stay to, I don't know, prop me up."

"I want to stay."

She searched his face again, finally nodding. "Then pizza sounds good. Can I have my half veggie?"

"You don't eat meat?"

"Sometimes. It just sounds good. Less greasy."

"Works for me, too." He had the number in his phone and dialed immediately. While he was talking to some kid at the pizza joint, her phone rang. He turned to see her eyeing the caller's number with puzzlement.

She answered anyway. "Hello?"

Color drained from her face.

"'I THOUGHT YOU, of all people, would understand.'"

Daniel crouched next to her chair at the table. "That's all he said?"

"No. Then he said, 'It's not like *you've* never made a mistake.' It was a whisper." Lindsay's voice shook. So did her hand, she saw distantly, as she reached for her wineglass. "I think it was a man, but I'm not positive."

"Damn."

"Damn?" That suddenly struck her as almost funny. "A serial killer knows my phone number? He thought *I'd* understand? 'Damn' doesn't seem to cover it." She shuddered.

"I know some worse words."

His eyes were steady on her face, but sharp, too, as if seeing more than she wanted to give away. One of his big, warm hands rested on her thigh, the other on her lower back. His touch felt so good, it took all she had to hold her spine straight, refuse to succumb to such temptation.

"Not sure those words would help," he added.

"No."

"Lindsay, you know you have to tell me what he meant about you making mistakes."

She shook her head. "I don't know. Truly. I think we're all afraid a child will die because we didn't act or maybe thought counseling would be enough. Or didn't do an adequate background check, like me with Martin Ramsey. As bad in a different way would be taking a child from a parent who was innocent but you hadn't done a thorough enough investigation. Bradley Taubeneck is an example of someone who suffered even though we *didn't* charge him."

Daniel's knees must hurt, as long as he'd crouched there beside her, but he didn't move. "Maybe that's the kind of thing this guy thinks was a 'mistake.' You didn't nail the guy when you had the chance."

She shivered. "So he took care of it."

"Yeah."

She went for what had to be a pathetic smile. "Did you get the pizza ordered?"

"Yeah." The expression on his angular face hardened, and he rose to his feet, looking down at her. "You're too vulnerable here. I think it really is time for a vacation, preferably far, far away. A cruise. Norwegian fjords. The Caribbean. Even Alaska would do for the short-term."

For a moment she imagined it. She'd lie back on a deck chair and sip some fruity drink to try to mute her worries. Dolphins would frolic beside the ship. She wouldn't turn on her phone at all. She'd go to glitzy shows every night, stuff her face, read all the books she never found time to get to.

Assuming she could concentrate, what with the fruity drinks and the fear gnawing at her belly and constricting her heart.

"I can't," she heard herself blurt before she'd really made a decision. "I'm in the middle of this. You know I am."

"I want to take you out of the middle." He looked and sounded grim.

"I know. I understand. It's just...none of it is my fault, but I still feel responsible, in a way." She held up a hand to stop the comeback rising to his lips. "No, listen. Somehow, I must have given the impression that I wished abusers would die. Of course, it's not something *I* can do, but I must have given off the idea that I wouldn't mind if someone else did it for me."

Daniel swore. "Have you ever felt that way?"

She swallowed. "As mad as I sometimes get, no. No. But maybe I complained too much. All I know is that I can't run away now. It's better if he focuses on *me* instead of...whoever he might already be stalking."

He swung away, paced the length of the kitchen then back, his expression dark. "You infuriated him today. He can't kid himself anymore that you're secretly grateful to him for having the guts to do what no one else will, that you'd throw yourself into his arms in gratitude if he revealed himself to you."

The idea made Lindsay's stomach lurch. "I know," she said softly. Her fingernails bit into her palms.

"You saw one of the bodies. You think you know what he's capable of, but you don't," he said harshly. "*Monster* is the right word for him. Can you imagine finding yourself locked in a freezer? It's dark and hopeless and you get colder and colder until ice forms in your nostrils and eyes and lungs?" He planted his hands on the table and bent forward, eyes dark and boring into hers. "How do you think he'd kill *you*, Lindsay, now that you've violated his worldview?"

Her throat closed. Her teeth wanted to chatter.

"What is it you think you can do by staying in town?"

"I..." He was right, in a way. She had no idea why she felt such certainty. Was she trying to prove something to herself? "Maybe he'll stop now, since he knows it's not what I want."

Daniel's laugh was incredulous. "Get real. *You* were only peripheral. Nobody does what he has been doing unless they enjoy it. He's had more than a taste now. He'll keep killing. If you were one of his victims—" He shook his head and turned his back.

Suddenly angry, she said, "Do I stay away forever? How are you going to catch him? If he does focus on me, that might give you a chance."

A growled obscenity expressed his opinion of that

as he turned back to glare at her. "If I thought I could get away with it, I'd take you into protective custody."

"You wouldn't."

"No, but by God you aren't going to be alone for a minute from now on. Do you hear me?"

"Isn't that protective custody?"

"The kind that doesn't involve a jail cell. Count your blessings."

She did. A sudden realization of how petrified she'd be if he walked out on her cracked the wall that she hid behind. She hadn't needed anyone since she was a child, but now she needed this man, and not only to keep her safe.

"I'll definitely count my blessings," she managed.

His expression changed. Whatever she saw on his face was unfamiliar, made her weak, vulnerable.

"Damn it, Lindsay." He wrapped his hands around her upper arms and lifted her to her feet. "Do you know how much I want to kiss you?"

Panicked, she shook her head. Sex, she could do. But with Daniel, it would be more, and she didn't dare.

He muttered something she couldn't make out and pulled her close, tucked her head against his shoulder and held her against him. His body radiated heat. For an instant, she stood stiffly, fighting against the pure seduction of powerful arms, hard thighs and a muscular chest. Then a hitch of breath escaped her and she couldn't do anything but wrap her arms around his torso and quiver with tension even as she tried to soak in some of his strength.

"You'll be okay," he murmured in her ear. "We'll catch this vile excuse for a human being. I swear we will."

Lindsay actually believed him. She might not later,

when she was alone in bed, but right now, she did. Her head bobbed. At least she wasn't crying.

He rubbed his cheek on her hair, or maybe it was his lips. If she lifted her face to his…

No, no, no! What a horrible time to start anything with him. It was classic; little woman desperate to please the man who gave her the best chance of survival. Later…maybe. Now, she breathed in his scent and gathered herself to pull away.

DANIEL LAY STRETCHED out on Lindsay's sleeper sofa, which was both too short for him and ribbed with what felt like steel girders. He'd given up trying to find a comfortable position; there wasn't one.

Hell, he couldn't sleep anyway. Either he was thinking about how to catch this killer, or he brooded about Lindsay. In between, he remembered how she'd felt in his arms, actually allowing herself a minute or two of human contact, of physical support. Probably just as well she'd retreated when she did, because he'd been getting aroused and she'd have noticed any moment. He loved every lush curve on her body along with the taut muscles and a strength so much a part of her; he worried about why she was so wary of him, not to mention every other man. Maybe women, too. The concept of trust didn't seem to be in her frame of reference. Her kind of strength was born out of necessity.

He clasped his hands behind his head and stared up at the dark ceiling. He could be patient. He thought he'd made some inroads already. Tonight, she'd clutched him with fierce strength. She'd let him hold her hand. The situation gave him some proximity, too. Harder for her to resist him when they were all but living together.

Any satisfaction sank under the weight of the real-life situation. He had a deeply bad feeling about that whispered reprimand from the killer. Lindsay was right to be scared that he had her personal phone number—and the confirmation that part of his motivation had been pleasing her. No surprise, Daniel had confirmed that the killer had called from a burner phone, probably already in a dumpster.

Would he come after her? Daniel considered the possibility realistic enough that he intended to provide protection for her twenty-four-seven. Tomorrow, he'd talk to his lieutenant and the police chief if necessary. In the meantime, he had already lined up Melinda to stay with her tomorrow, although it was the detective's day off. As dedicated as she was to her job, she hadn't seemed to mind. He'd spend nights here. He couldn't opt out of a callout, but he'd worry about it when it came. If he had to, he'd take Lindsay with him. Maybe drop her at one of his other cop friends' houses. They'd manage.

She obviously had some idea of being bait, but that wasn't happening unless he could come up with a foolproof plan. Something else to worry about tomorrow.

He listened hard, but heard only sounds that ought to be there. A car passing several blocks away, the refrigerator humming, the gurgle of the toilet flushing down the hall.

Apparently he wasn't the only one who was having trouble sleeping.

He lay rigid, listening for footsteps, but he heard nothing until a faint creaking told him she'd crawled back into bed.

Daniel groaned, wishing he was in that bed with her.

LINDSAY HADN'T FALLEN asleep until at least four in the morning. There was so much to think about, from the whispering, angry caller to the fact that Daniel was there, and not because he had an urgent need for answers. That thought warmed her. Still, she circled on to her state of unemployment, and then back to Daniel staying the night so she didn't have to be alone. Around and around and around…until she dropped into a deep, dark hole and didn't surface until strong beams of sunlight made their way into the room through the window blinds.

Blinking, she focused on the clock. 10:23. She couldn't remember the last time she'd slept so late.

After showering and dressing, she found a cop in her kitchen, just not the same one who'd slept on the sofa last night. Melinda McIntosh perched on a tall stool at the island, a laptop open in front of her.

Melinda lifted her head. "Good morning. Coffee's ready."

"Thank heavens." Lindsay poured a cup for herself and refilled Melinda's. "Don't you ever have a day off?" This *was* Saturday.

"I'd have been working no matter what. I can't turn my mind off."

Heartfelt, Lindsay said, "I know what you mean." They weren't the only ones, either; she doubted Daniel had gone home to laze around. Had he taken a full day off since the first murder?

Silly question.

"Daniel mentioned this Glenn Wilson," Melinda remarked.

"It can't be him. But I've been thinking. Do you know how many retired caseworkers, or ones who switched to another job, are still in the area?"

Melinda set down her mug with a click. "No. Do you?"

"I don't, but I've run into several. I saw…" She

frowned. "Oh, why can't I remember his name?" She pondered. "Barry. Barry… Hill, that's it. Anyway, we talked for a minute in the produce department at Safeway. That was probably two months ago, but I know he's still here."

"I'll request the names of caseworkers who have left in the last couple of years."

"Why just the last—oh." Duh. "Because they have to have known me."

"Right. Think back, will you? Who did you get along with? Have friction with? Any strange interactions?"

The questions kept coming. Had she ever dated a colleague? Had anyone besides Matt Grudin and Ray Hammond—Melinda had to glance at notes on her laptop for those names—ever seemed interested in her? Did she have a close friend among the current coworkers? In the past? Had anybody in particular ever expressed the wish that abusers suffer like their victims had?

That one had Lindsay making a face. "I imagine almost everyone has in a bad moment. Plus, we indulge in a lot of black humor when nobody else can hear."

Melinda sighed. "We do, too. Cops, I mean. All first responders, and I guess you're close to being one."

"I never thought of it that way, but yes."

Lindsay toasted a bagel for breakfast and then made them both sandwiches when lunchtime rolled around. In fact, while they talked, she started baking. Pumpkin bread first, then oatmeal raisin cookies.

"I have to do something or I'll go crazy," she admitted.

When would she get to run again? Do anything by herself? Maybe Daniel—or one of her babysitters—would take her to the gym where she could use a treadmill.

He called midafternoon, speaking first to Melinda

and then Lindsay. Lucky she hadn't expected tender concern for her welfare.

"I've been thinking it might be possible for us to be proactive," he said when she came to the phone. "Do any cases you've handled stand out in your memory?"

Horrible thought.

"Lots of them." Clutching her phone, she closed her eyes. "But you mean ones where the abuser appears to have gotten off lighter than was justified?"

"Yeah." Daniel's deep voice had become gentle. "That's what I'm thinking."

A couple came to mind, one in particular where she'd *known*, with bone-deep certainty, that the mother had smothered the baby she hadn't wanted. Lindsay had never been able to prove it, though, and the autopsy didn't provide the conclusive results needed to try the woman in court.

"I wonder if he'd kill a woman," she said.

The silence told her what Daniel was thinking. A shiver crawled up her spine. *She* was a woman...and he wouldn't be guarding her around the clock if he weren't very much afraid that this killer intended to punish her, too.

Chapter Ten

The ringing phone jolted Daniel out of a typically maddening, surreal dream that ratcheted up his frustration. He sat up, for a fleeting instant unsure where he was, why the nightstand with his weapon and phone wasn't where it should be.

Then the phone rang again, and it all came back to him. Lindsay's sofa. Four more days of investigative dead ends. Four more nights at her place, struggling to keep his hands off her.

He fumbled for the phone. Damn, it was almost three in the morning. Good news never came in the middle of the night.

"Yeah," he answered huskily. "This is Deperro."

"Detective. Sorry to get you at this hour, but I had to tell you that you were right. As you know, the Mehnert woman blew me off when I talked to her the other day. Her baby died tragically. It was a travesty that Child Protective Services came after her. Even *they* had to admit they were wrong, so why would we think for a minute that some crazy vigilante would come after her, an innocent, heartbroken mother?"

Daniel had recognized the voice right away. It belonged to Detective Lee Nakamoto of the Washington County Sheriff's Department. Daniel had traced the woman Lindsay told her about to an address just outside Portland, Oregon, and contacted Nakamoto. The Mehnert woman had been Danica Lashbrook when Lindsay investigated her after the death of her two-month-old child. Turned out, she and her husband split barely a month later. The guy had probably shared Lindsay's suspicions. She'd remarried less than a year later and had taken up residence in western Oregon.

Nakamoto had agreed to go talk to her, tell her what had been happening in Sadler, suggest this would be a good time for her to make herself unavailable for a while. The woman had pretended shock. The detective had a feeling husband number two hadn't known anything about the CPS investigation. They'd had no child yet in the new marriage.

"She dead?" Daniel asked.

"Oh, yeah. Husband travels for his job. Got a late flight from San Francisco instead of spending another night the way he'd planned. He found Danica dead in bed."

"Let me guess. Smothered."

"Pillow over her face," Nakamoto agreed. "The ME may have more to say, but that's what it was set up to look like."

Daniel swore and scrubbed a hand over his scalp. "Keep me informed, will you? I'll try to determine if anyone on our list was out of town yesterday afternoon. Trouble is..."

"It's not that long a drive. Yeah."

"This is the sixth murder, and that's assuming we know about all of them."

"Clearly, he's willing to travel."

"How'd he get in the house?"

"Broke the pane on the kitchen door. Reached in to turn the dead bolt."

Daniel didn't need to comment on how ludicrous it was to put a dead bolt on a door with an easily shattered pane of glass. Why lock it at all?

He turned his head sharply when he caught movement out of the corner of his eye. Watching him and undoubtedly listening to his side of the conversation, Lindsay stood in the kitchen doorway, wearing what was essentially a long T-shirt with a cartoon cat on front. She hugged herself, and he saw that her toes were curled. From cold or shock? How much had she heard?

He and the other detective wound up the conversation and Daniel set his phone down on the table beside his holster and gun. He hadn't bothered to pull the bed part out last night. The couch definitely wasn't long enough for him, but the cushions were reasonably comfortable. Now, he patted the cushion beside him.

"Hey. Come here."

Her hesitation was brief, although he suspected she was being made shy by the sight of his bare chest. Then she came, sitting down with one leg curled under her so that she faced him, carefully keeping her gaze on his face.

"Someone's dead," she said.

"Danica Lashbrook."

"But you warned her."

"Yes. The local cops did at my request."

Her expression somber, Lindsay seemed to be struck by a memory. "She was really calculating. She'd turn this weepy, big-eyed look on her husband, a 'why are they treating me this way?' look, then turn to me with a dignified expression but with her lower lip trembling. But in between, I'd see flashes of anger or coldness.

She thought she could get away with killing her baby, and she did."

"But not for long."

"No." Her gaze had turned inward. "I really detested her."

"Are you saying you understand our killer's motivation?"

"How can I not?" she responded with devastating honesty. "But I wanted to see her behind bars, not dead."

Daniel reached for her hand, exclaiming when he found it icy. "For God's sake!" The air-conditioning must have been running all night. He captured her other hand, too, determined to share his warmth. If she noticed, she didn't look down.

"How will you ever catch him?" she asked.

"If he doesn't make a mistake—and everyone does sooner or later—one of us will make an intuitive leap, or we'll just get lucky. There are cases that go cold, but in a county like this where we don't get that much murder, they're the minority."

Lindsay searched his face. Daniel didn't have a clue what she was thinking.

"I should go back to bed," she said, but didn't move.

"Lindsay—" He didn't know if it was smart or incredibly stupid, but his self-control had been crumbling by the day. He went with his impulse, gently tugging her forward.

Initially, she stayed stiff, her unfathomable gaze never wavering, but then she scooted closer. Daniel did his best to suppress his urgency as he brushed her lips with his, came back to savor them, finally dampening the seam of her lips with his tongue.

She made a funny little sound as she rose to her knees and wrapped her arms around his neck. With a groan, he lifted her onto his lap so that she straddled his hips.

Against her mouth, he mumbled, "Do you have any idea how hard it's been keeping my hands to myself?"

Lindsay pulled back enough for him to see her tiny smile. "I suspected." She rocked her hips, and he groaned again.

"I want you."

"I need you tonight," she whispered, and they came together in an inflammatory kiss that put an end to all qualms, all pretense.

SHE'D NEVER FELT anything like this. It was like being hit by a tsunami, so powerful she couldn't have broken free. His tongue thrust into her mouth, and she stroked it with her own. His hair was thick silk, her fingers tangled in it. One of his big hands gripped her hip to pace her involuntary rocking. The other moved restlessly, exploring her back, the nape of her neck, sliding around to cup one breast.

He started to roll her beneath him but checked himself.

"No. Bed," he said roughly, and straightened with her in his arms.

Lindsay locked her legs around his waist, grabbing hold of his powerful shoulders for more security. Yet as he strode down the hall, he carried her as if she weighed next to nothing. He knew which room was hers; every night, when she headed for bed, she'd been aware of his heated gaze following her.

After being awakened earlier by the ring of his phone and the deep, low sound of his voice, she'd thrown aside the covers when she got up. Now, he let her slide down his body until her feet touched the floor. Within seconds, he'd pulled the long T-shirt she wore over her head.

Voice thick, he said, "You're beautiful."

If anyone here was beautiful, it was him. She explored the sleek brown skin stretched over amazing muscles with her splayed hands. His hands, in turn, lifted her breasts, gently squeezed them, his palms rubbing her taut nipples.

Next thing she knew, she was on her back and he was suckling one of her breasts. She whimpered and arched, fingertips digging into his shoulders. Lindsay found she had no patience. She urged him on, her hips pushing up, seeking.

When Daniel lifted his head, she was glad for the light from the bedside lamp so that she could see his face, transformed by passion. The skin seemed to stretch tighter than usual over the strong bones, and his eyes had the hot gleam that had so tempted her all those nights when she'd known what he was thinking.

"Please" she heard herself beg.

He groaned again and said, "Hell. Give me a minute."

A minute? He walked out of the bedroom, leaving her incredulous. Only when he returned, something in his hand, did she understand he'd gone to the living room for a condom. Condoms plural, she saw, as he dropped several on the bedside stand.

He was magnificent in stretch boxer briefs, but he shed them in an instant and climbed into bed with her. She felt so desperate, she didn't care that he didn't give her any more chance to explore his body. She parted her legs and welcomed him.

She whimpered at the first pressure, unable to look away from his piercing dark eyes. Her fingernails dug into his back. How could she feel so much so fast? His weight on her, the way he filled her, the rhythm that was somehow just right, meant release came with stunning speed, dragging him with her. He rolled to one side, gathered her close and mumbled, "Damn."

Was that good or bad? It sounded as if he was as stunned as she felt. Lindsay wasn't sure she could move and didn't want to. She hardly knew what was happening to her.

Why him? She'd never been drawn to the kind of domineering man who assumed his orders would be obeyed instantly. Except that wasn't totally fair; Daniel Deperro, she had come to realize, was a complex, intelligent man capable of compassion and kindness. And passion that had overwhelmed her.

Giving a heavy sigh, he let her go and got out of bed. To return to the sofa, now that he'd had what he wanted? she wondered, stung. But he disappeared into the bathroom and returned less than a minute later. Of course he was coming back to bed. Lindsay didn't understand her volatile emotions. This wasn't like her.

But then, she'd never known anyone who had been murdered, never mind six victims now. She'd never known a killer before, or annoyed one. She'd never been fired or suspended from a job for any reason. And she'd never had a cop move in with her because he was afraid for her, either.

Live and learn.

Daniel's expression was harder to read now, as he gazed down at her for a minute before slipping beneath the covers as if this was where he belonged, reaching out a long arm to turn off the lamp and pulling her back to snuggle against him.

"Sleep," he said, his voice a soft rumble against her ear.

To her astonishment, she did.

He made love to her once more during the night and wanted to do it again when he awakened to early light. This time, though, she had curled away from him and slept so deeply, he didn't allow himself to wake her up at—he looked past her to the digital clock. 5:43. Good God. Why was *he* awake?

He'd been going to bed earlier since he'd come to stay at Lindsay's, though, and getting up earlier, too. This morning, he had even more to think about than usual. He lay still for a long time, looking at the back of her head, the silky mass of her hair, the tight curl of her body, and felt an echo of last night's shock.

Would she be annoyed or hurt that he hadn't managed to say the kind of thing a man probably should? "Damn" could be appreciative, or not. She hadn't said a single word, but she might have been waiting for him. Or she could be as shaken as he was.

He'd wanted her from first sight, but hadn't been sure he even liked her. For God's sake, he'd suspected her of murder! Lindsay wouldn't have forgotten that.

What was he doing here anyway? Last night's murder suggested the killer's focus remained on the abusive parents. Maybe he still believed Lindsay would swing around to his way of seeing things. In the days since the ominous phone call, Daniel hadn't seen even a hint that someone was watching her or the house. There'd been no more phone calls, no mail, no fire in a small trash can on her porch.

What if he arranged for regular patrol drive-bys and went home himself? Or at least let Melinda and the two deputies that had been helping out off the hook?

Maybe—but he knew he'd continue staying here at night. For a lot of reasons. And, yeah, he'd just gotten into her bed, and he wanted to get back in it.

What kind of bastard did that make him?

Disturbed, he eased out of bed now, picked up his briefs and slipped out of the room. A few minutes later, dressed and pouring his first cup of coffee, he opened his laptop and found several emails from Detective Nakamoto with attachments.

Sipping the coffee, he became absorbed in studying photos and reading what little trace evidence the CSI had found. What Nakamoto hadn't mentioned last night was the fire, this time in a wicker wastebasket. It had burned through but hadn't spread because the flooring beneath it was a laminate that seemed to be impervious to flames. The caption for that photo was, *Tell me this means something to you.*

Daniel wished it did. All he could do was respond, *There's a similar fire at every murder scene. Don't know what it means yet.*

He forwarded the information to Boyd and Melinda, then texted them to suggest that the three of them get together today. He asked Boyd if he'd mind driving into town. Daniel wasn't surprised to have Boyd respond within minutes; as a rancher, he was likely up with the sun no matter what. Given that he was now holding down two jobs, he especially had to take advantage of every daylight hour.

Eleven work? he had texted.

Daniel responded as quickly. *Let's plan on it.*

Frowning, he tried to remember who he'd lined up to stay with Lindsay today. It was getting tougher to find anyone as the days passed without any overt threat. So far, it had been all volunteer. The department was stretched too thin to make paid protection feasible. He'd requested it anyway and been turned down.

He cocked his head at the sound of the shower running just as Melinda called.

"Has Chaney done a single useful thing on this investigation yet?"

Daniel's temper flickered. "I suggested the meeting so that we can try to figure out what we can do that we haven't already done. He may have a fresh perspective."

"What are the odds?" she muttered, but then said, "Sure. Eleven is good for me."

"You might show up with a better attitude," Daniel suggested.

She was quiet long enough he'd have thought she had cut him off except that he could hear her breathing.

"You're right," she said at last. "Chaney rubs me the wrong way, but I can be professional."

The shower went off. Picturing Lindsay stepping out of the bathroom wearing nothing but a towel, he fought to stay focused. "You want to talk about it?"

"No."

Truthfully, that was a relief. His guess was that Boyd and Melinda had gotten personally involved but it hadn't worked out. He'd felt obliged to offer to be a sounding board, but he didn't actually want to know what happened between them.

"Check your email. There was another murder last night," he said. At her exclamation, he gave her the basics, then said goodbye just as Lindsay appeared in the kitchen, looking shy.

Daniel rose to his feet and greeted her with a kiss that he managed to keep gentle. Much as he'd like to go back to bed with her, he didn't have time. Catching this piece of scum had to be his priority.

Lindsay scrambled eggs while he toasted and buttered blueberry bagels. They sat down with their plates and looked at each other.

"When will he stop?" she asked.

Daniel had to shake his head. "I doubt he will. He's killing with scarcely a pause between victims. That's unusual. That he's acting so hastily makes it more likely he'll screw up, but it also has us stumbling behind without time to thoroughly investigate each individual murder the way we normally would."

Poking at her eggs with her fork, Lindsay frowned. "I know you suspect my coworkers, but given that they were working full time, could any of them really pull off this kind of crime spree?"

"It's barely possible," he said. But not likely. He'd been eliminating one after another while cross-referencing their schedules with the likely times of the murders. Increasingly, he agreed with Melinda that they should be looking at ex-employees, not current ones, who had somehow figured out how to get into the database. He'd verified that no ex-employee still had access. That didn't mean they couldn't have an in: either a current employee who sympathized or just liked to complain about all the scumbags who'd gotten off.

Alternatively, a now-retired employee whose rage had been building might have kept a list, dating back years. Who Deserves to Die. That was a realistic possibility…except that the killer had started with two men who had barely gotten into the system. Those identities could only have come by word of mouth.

He was a little surprised at how high the turnover had been in the office. The list of former employees who'd quit or retired in the last three years was keeping him busy. He needed to locate each, find out what they were doing now, run background checks, get some idea of personality and levels of anger. He hadn't attempted to go any further back, because there was one thing Daniel could be sure about: the murderer knew Lindsay.

He surfaced from his brooding when she rose from her chair and said she'd clean. "You're busy, I'm not," she said.

Daniel hid his wince. In her shoes, he'd have been pacing like a tiger testing the bars of his cage, unable to resign himself to inaction. Lindsay hadn't complained recently, but she had to be bored as well as frustrated. She might need a vacation, but home confinement hardly qualified.

Since he needed to get going, he found the protection schedule he'd worked up on his laptop. Theoretically, Phil Chavez, a forty-year-old sergeant on the patrol side, ought to be here any minute. His wife was out of town, leaving him free to spend his day off with Lindsay. He'd encountered her on the job in the past.

Daniel was already reaching for his phone when it rang. Chavez's name came up.

Instead of apologizing because he was running late, the sergeant growled, "I can't make it. I tripped over my own damn slipper and fell. Threw out my back. I can hardly crawl. I had to call Cecelia and ask her to come home."

Daniel told him not to worry, made sure the wife would be home in time to get him to the doctor, and wished him well. He told Lindsay that Chavez couldn't make it and why before he went back to the schedule to see who he could substitute.

Frowning at the monitor, he said, "Maybe you should just come with me. The police station is a fortress." That wasn't literally true, but close enough; it was built with brick, and getting in past the lobby took electronic gymnastics.

She wrinkled her nose. "I think we've gone overboard. Why can't I stay home? Is he really going to break into my house in broad daylight?"

"Most of your neighbors will be at work," he pointed out. "That leaves you isolated."

Those blue eyes fastened beseechingly on him. "I swear, cross my heart, I'll lock up, keep my phone close, call 9-1-1 if I hear anything out of the ordinary. I'm not totally defenseless, you know."

He had to remind himself that in her job, she walked into ugly situations as often as any first responder. That took guts and an ability to ease tensions.

"Do you have a gun?" he asked.

She blinked. "No! But if I hear the back window break, I'll dash out the front and run."

Resigning himself, he said sternly, "While calling 9-1-1 *and* me."

Lindsay rolled her eyes. "Yes, Detective."

He kissed her, said, "Be smart," and left, taking half a dozen looks in his rearview mirror before he lost sight of her small rambler.

SILENCE SETTLED WITH Daniel gone. Lindsay talked herself out of her ridiculous state of unease. It wasn't as if she hadn't spent much of her life alone. Anyway, she heard a neighbor's garage door rising and then descending, traffic on the street in front. People going about their usual business.

Too bad she couldn't.

What she could do was linger over another cup of coffee and the morning newspaper, do some laundry, then read a good book that wasn't true crime or a mystery. At least she didn't have to make forced conversation with near-strangers who had felt compelled to take a shift protecting her.

During those years in foster care, she'd hated knowing how dependent she was on other people—and the necessity of being grateful to them. She hadn't even realized as her stress level rose the past week that it was in part because she'd been thrown back to those old emotions.

Evenings with Daniel here had been…different. Her feelings for him were complicated. He'd passed the point of being a near-stranger, that was for sure, or last night wouldn't have happened. Even so, she wasn't assuming that having sex with her meant that much to him.

With an effort, she kept her attention on her book until lunchtime. Not all that hungry, she still made a salad and ate most of it. The afternoon opened ahead like a stretch of the Sahara. What did she usually do on her days off? she asked herself desperately.

She did errands. Grocery shopped, stopped by the pharmacy and the library—in fact, she had several books that were now overdue. All activities forbidden to her.

Lindsay glanced at her closed laptop. Really, she'd worked. Work was her life.

Had been.

Something had shifted in her. She wasn't sure she wanted to go back to her former life.

She could make lists. She was good at that. Pros and cons of staying with CPS. Potential alternate jobs. Some goals. What did she want out of life?

Right now, a nap sounded really good. Unfortunately, Daniel had been right; in some ways, she was isolated.

She had a suspicion napping wouldn't fall under his "be smart" directive.

Okay, she'd finish her book, then maybe do some baking. She didn't have any better ideas, short of painting the kitchen, but that would require her to go out and buy paint.

Settled cozily on the sofa, she opened the book again. Twice in the next hour she caught herself starting to nod off. No surprise—she hadn't gotten very much sleep last night, after all.

After pouring herself a glass of iced tea, Lindsay went back to reading and to fighting off the sleepiness.

The next thing she knew, she jerked, and realized she'd lost the battle, but something had tugged her awake. What...? Her nostrils flared. Was that smoke she smelled? And...did her eyes burn a little?

The sudden, earsplitting screech brought her to her feet. Her heart thudded. Fire alarm. Oh, God, it *was* smoke stinging her nostrils. And...gasoline?

She took a tentative step toward the hall and reared back when she saw flames licking up one wall. She had to get out of the house. Now.

Except, would somebody be waiting for her out there?

Chapter Eleven

Lindsay snatched up her purse and her laptop, looked around hopelessly at everything she couldn't take the time to try to save and raced for the front door. Her hand on the doorknob, she hesitated.

With the fire consuming the back of the house, the arsonist would expect her to exit out the front. Heart racing in fear, she edged over to the picture window and cracked the blinds. Nobody was visible in the slice of the porch and lawn she could see…but that didn't mean somebody wasn't there. Waiting for her.

She turned as thick, oily smoke billowed into the living room. It smelled terrible. Taking a deep breath, she willed herself to hold it as she desperately scanned the house for options. Her gaze locked on the dining room window. She could get that one open.

Of course she had to pull up the blinds before she could wrench the sash upward. She didn't see anybody waiting outside here, either, but belatedly realized that the old wood-framed window didn't exactly glide upward. A man hidden just out of sight would hear it.

She was out of time.

The air escaped her lungs in a rush. In exchange, she sucked in smoky air. In seconds she began to cough. Eyes watering, she shoved the screen outward. Hungry for fresh air, she tossed her purse and laptop onto the lawn, then swung a leg over the sill and lowered herself gingerly to one side of the thorny old rose bush. Falling to her knees, she couldn't stop coughing.

Movement out of the corner of her eye brought her head up—but she heard multiple sirens, too.

Lights flashing and siren screaming, Daniel drove like a madman. He wouldn't get there soon enough, but he had to try. Firefighters and a patrol officer would have been dispatched and were sure to beat him to Lindsay's house. He hoped like hell they would. The idea of her terrified as she tried to hide behind a neighbor's garden shed or crouch in shrubbery scared him so much his foot pushed down hard on the gas pedal even though the light ahead of him had just turned yellow.

The column of black smoke rose to the sky like a beacon. Midsummer like this, even the grass and foliage would be bone-dry. This time of year, the fire department would be on high alert, but the color of this smoke was a dead giveaway. Gasoline or another accelerant had been used to start the fire.

Arson, and not just the kind of small blaze a troubled kid might start in a wastebasket.

EXACTLY FOUR MINUTES LATER, Daniel turned onto Lindsay's block, where a red fire truck initially blocked his view of her house. Arcs of water crisscrossed to meet the flames as firefighters dragged hoses around the small rambler. Half of them were turned on the walls and roofs of neighboring houses, an acknowledgement that her place was a goner.

He parked behind a squad car and jogged forward, searching frantically for Lindsay in the small crowd that had gathered. Though he desperately needed to find her, at his first full sight of her house he had to stare for a moment. Despite the water combating the fire, voracious flames still shot upward. It was hard to hear anything but the crackling of those angry flames and the splintering sounds as walls and trusses gave way.

Sickened, he resumed his search for her. She'd just lost everything. What Daniel cared about right now was that help had arrived in time to save her. If so…where was she? He'd made plain that she was the priority over the fire. He couldn't believe—

At that moment, he spotted the ambulance. Relief felt like a blow to the chest. He stopped dead where he was on the sidewalk, unaware of the action around him, focused utterly on her. Lindsay sat in the open back, her stricken gaze fixed on the destruction of her home. She couldn't have had time to rescue much of anything before she got out. For a fleeting moment, Daniel tried to imagine how he'd feel, knowing everything he owned was gone: photos and keepsakes from his parents and past relationships, the dining room table he'd spent hours restoring and the oak floors in his home that he'd sanded and stained himself. His favorite riding boots, his leather jacket, the ceramic bowl from a local artisan he used for mixing pancakes.

Once in a new home, Lindsay might spend years reaching for something that had burned to ashes long ago. In her case, she didn't seem to have any family. Anything she'd had to remind her of her parents or grandparents was gone unless she'd stored it in a safe deposit box at the bank. At last he started walking again. She looked worse the closer he got. It had to be shock that had bleached her so pale. A black smear ran from one cheekbone down over her chin. A thick bandage wrapped an upper arm. She held her hands, closed into fists, pressed against her belly. No tear tracks on her cheeks, though. Would she let herself cry later?

As he watched, she began to cough harshly.

Ten feet away, he said her name. He doubted she could hear him, but her head turned and she saw him. She quit hacking and didn't so much as blink. He didn't think he did, either, as he closed the distance.

Either she launched herself into his arms or he snatched her up, he didn't know, only that he held her tight. He lost awareness of their surroundings, the hose snaking inches from his feet, raised voices, even the heat.

"Damn, Lindsay," he murmured, his mouth by her ear. "You're all right. I've been so afraid—" He broke off, as much because his throat closed as because he didn't want to admit that he'd never been scared for another person the way he had been for her.

"I didn't hear a thing," she mumbled. "Somebody set this, didn't they?"

"Oh, yeah," he said grimly.

"The first thing I knew, there was the smoke and then my alarm. I was reading and…" She sounded ashamed. "I think I'd nodded off. I didn't get very much sleep last night. Um. I guess you know that."

He was to blame for her lack of sleep. He didn't want to think about how he'd have felt if she'd died in this fire.

"How'd you get out?" he asked.

"The dining room window."

"Did you see anybody?"

She went utterly still, as though she'd quit breathing. Then, so quietly he could barely hear her, she said, "I think somebody was right around the corner of the house. I saw movement, but then sirens blasted close enough, it must have scared him away."

His grip tightened. "I'm sorry about this. So damn sorry. If I'd had somebody here today—"

"He might have set the fire anyway."

She was right, but he still doubted it was coincidence that the fire was set the first time she'd been left alone since the phone call.

He felt her draw a deep breath, after which she started hacking again. An EMT he recognized helped her back to her seat in the ambulance and covered her face with an oxygen mask.

Daniel promised to come back as soon as he talked to several people.

The fire chief grimaced when Daniel tracked him down. "I'll be surprised if the accelerant isn't good, old-fashioned gasoline. Smell kind of hits you as soon as you get here."

"I noticed," Daniel said. "Damn, I wish we could get our hands on this guy."

"Detective McIntosh just got here. She seems to think this fire is connected to one of your investigations."

"There's no doubt. Especially..." He hesitated, not wanting to put any ideas in Chief Randolph's head. "You notice anything unusual?"

"One of the firefighters mentioned something odd. It's around back, near the point of origin."

Daniel followed him, the two circling onto the street and around the house on the corner to avoid the activity. Fortunately, neither backyard was fenced in. Both stopped when the roof of her house collapsed with a deep groan, but the water seemed finally to be knocking back the fire, albeit too late. Soaking the neighboring houses looked like it had saved them from dangerous sparks.

This wasn't a wastebasket, Daniel saw immediately. Instead, a full-size metal barrel, blackened by the fire, had been placed in the middle of her lawn. The barrel was full of water now because of the hoses, but charred bits of something unidentifiable bobbed on the surface.

"My firefighter says there was a fire in it when he first came around back." Watching Daniel, Randolph lifted his eyebrows. "You don't look surprised."

"I'm not." Although, damn, he didn't like the escalation implied by a large metal barrel versus wastebaskets. "I'd appreciate it if you and anyone else who saw this keep it to yourselves."

"No problem." The chief's gaze touched on the barrel, then swept the still smoldering ruins of Lindsay's small rambler. "Your guy really likes fires."

"So it seems."

"A BARREL?" LINDSAY REPEATED. "Metal?" It was hours later; she'd finally been turned loose from the ER and was beside Daniel in his truck, on the way to his house. He had been telling her what little he'd learned thus far. "Where did he get one?"

"They're readily available. The recycling place used to sell them, although I don't know if they still do. I have a burn barrel myself," he said tersely. "In rural areas, a lot of people do."

Clutching the seat belt with both hands, she gazed ahead through the windshield as a troubling memory stirred without quite taking form. What was it she remembered about a fire in a barrel? Was this from college? Or one of her foster homes? She suddenly recalled one of her foster fathers burning trash in an ugly, rust-ing barrel back behind their house. It always stank, and the smoke was an awful color, but they'd lived on acreage, so there was no one near enough to be bothered.

But that wasn't the memory that niggled at her. It refused to surface, however, either because of her headache or because it was something she'd heard about secondhand.

Finally defeated, she shook her head.

"You know something," Daniel said.

"No, just..." She lifted one shoulder. "I feel like I heard something, but I can't remember what."

"Hmm." He put on the turn signal, his ranch road ahead on the right. "It'll come to you."

He sounded tense, and she understood why. He probably wanted to turn her upside down and shake her until the memory fluttered loose. This was important. Somebody else might die any time.

She shuddered. Who was she kidding? *She* could have died today. If she'd really fallen asleep, she might have been overcome by smoke and never awakened at all. She'd read somewhere that most fatalities in home fires succumbed to smoke long before the flames reached them.

Her dismal mood retreated somewhat when Daniel's converted barn home came in sight. The work and imagination that had gone into it was part of what captivated her.

Between one blink and the next, she had a vision so real, fear gripped her. Flames roared out of the loft, climbing toward the roof, intent only on devouring the structure. The reclaimed wood floors and walls had to be dry. There was no hope—

She blinked again, and there was no fire. Of course there wasn't.

Even so, that fear metamorphosed into panic. She cried, "Stop! You shouldn't have brought me here. I should go somewhere else."

"What?" Daniel didn't brake.

"He could be following us, or guess this is where I'd have gone." Her voice rose with urgency. "He'll burn down your house, too. You know he will."

"Over my dead body," he said grimly.

"Daniel, please!" She was horribly afraid those were tears stinging her eyes.

Instead of parking in front, he backed into a structure with weathered board siding that she only now realized was a detached garage with a concrete floor and a door that ran on rails overhead. He still held the remote in one hand.

Daniel turned off the engine and, instead of getting out, looked at her. "Nobody followed us. I kept an eye out. And why would this guy assume I'd have brought you home?"

"Because we're—" Wait. Nobody else would have any way of knowing they had slept together. People at CPS probably thought their relationship was still antagonistic. It wasn't as if they'd dined out or gone dancing. "He must have been watching the house," she said more slowly. "He knows you've spent every night there."

Gaze unwavering, he said, "I'd have done the same even if we weren't involved."

He'd guessed what she had almost said. "When you got to the fire tonight, you…you came straight to me. You held me."

He didn't say anything for a minute. She couldn't imagine that he comforted every distraught woman the same way in the course of his job.

"It's unlikely he was close enough to see us. The place was swarming with cops and firefighters."

"What if he *is* a cop?" she asked. "We've been assuming he'd gotten into the CPS database, but the police were involved in the investigations of all the murder victims. If he's in law enforcement, he wouldn't *need* our records."

Suddenly, she couldn't read Daniel's face.

THE SAME WORRY had struck him, but Daniel had so far pushed back at it. Now, he had to ask himself whether he just hadn't wanted to admit a possibility that was so close to home.

The silence stretched. He had to break it.

"The thought has occurred to me," he admitted. "There are a few problems with it, though. Some of those investigations weren't Sadler PD, they were sheriff's department. We talk but don't share full access to records." Lindsay opened her mouth, but he held up his hand. "Second, no one officer has been involved with even two of those cases. Neither we nor the county have an officer who specializes in child abuse investigations."

"Maybe he didn't investigate any of those cases. He just heard about them, and it rankled. If he'd been abused as a child, and authorities had failed him—"

He cut to the chase. "Then why the obsession with *you*? Why did he believe you'd 'understand'? Do you have cops as friends? Anyone you've worked with enough, he might think he knows you?"

Lindsay shook her head. Twice.

Daniel narrowed his eyes. "Do you have any friends who were abused as children? Maybe you exchanged stories?"

"No," she whispered. "I mean, there are a few foster parents locally who have that kind of background, but I only know that secondhand. I don't deal directly with foster parents, except those who take only emergency placements."

He opened his mouth, then shut it. No, he couldn't ask if she had any friends at all. That would be cruel, and he had a suspicion that the answer would be no. She undoubtedly had women she considered friends, the kind she might meet for a movie, say, but that wasn't the same as close friends who knew you through and through, flaws and all, who'd be there for you in any crisis and knew you'd rush to their aid, too. Lindsay, he thought, had learned to be solitary a long time ago and still maintained the emotional distance that had saved her as a child from the crash when hope and trust were betrayed.

Alarmed by the sudden certainty that he wanted to be the person she could trust, he only nodded and got out of the pickup. Clutching two bulging shopping bags, Lindsay followed suit and met him at the back bumper.

"I hope the stuff fits," he said, feeling awkward. Melinda had offered to pick up a few necessities for a woman who now owned absolutely nothing that hadn't been in her handbag or laptop case. He hoped she'd taken into account the fact that Lindsay's figure was curvier than hers.

He kept a sharp eye on their surroundings as they crossed the short distance to a side door that let directly into his kitchen. No movement caught his eye, except for the horses that grazed nearby, unconcerned.

The usual sense of peace enveloped him inside the house once he closed and locked the door behind them. High windows filled the kitchen with light. The well-used wood for cabinets, walls and floors gave him a sense of continuity, the knowledge that the past was all around.

Looking at Lindsay's dirty, strained face, he said gently, "The house has sprinklers. Using all reclaimed wood the way I did, it seemed prudent."

She stared at him as if she didn't quite understand what he was saying.

"I'm going to put you up in the loft. If you'd prefer, I can sleep down here." He put a hand on her back and steered her toward the stairs.

In the end, he found scissors for her to cut tags off the new clothes and left her alone to take a shower while he started dinner.

As he sliced chicken breasts, he brooded about the deadly intent behind today's assault on her. That was what it was. The fire was attempted murder, not meant only as a warning or to scare Lindsay. He grudgingly supposed it was possible the killer assumed that since it was daytime she would be awake and would flee the house sooner. But once the fire gathered strength and she hadn't appeared, he could have called her or made a noise to draw her attention. Instead, whoever the SOB was, he'd stood back and waited with a spider's patience for her to come to him—if she made it out of the house at all.

Filled with angry tension, Daniel realized he'd sliced the chicken into slivers instead of the thicker pieces he'd intended, but maybe this was a task made for his mood. He grabbed a bell pepper and started in on it.

Whack. Whack. Whack.

By the time Lindsay showed up, he had himself under better control. The stir-fry came perilously close to being a puree, but she didn't seem to notice. He had to keep reminding her to eat.

"I should have called my insurance agent today," she said out of the blue.

"Tomorrow is soon enough."

Her gaze finally met his. "I don't suppose I can look for a new place to live, or go shopping, or..."

He shook his head. He didn't want her appearing anywhere the wrong person might see her. Now that she wasn't even surrounded by her own stuff, her own space, she'd feel imprisoned even more, but he couldn't think of another solution.

Except that cruise. Too bad he'd discovered how much he'd hate not knowing where she was every minute of the day, not being able to talk to her when he needed to. Not being able to see her would leave a huge hole that he feared had nothing to do with the threat to her.

Didn't it figure, that was the moment where she burst out, "You were right. I shouldn't have stayed in town. I'm a burden, not a help! I don't even know what I thought I could do. If I'd put the pieces together, I could have called you from Alaska or the Caribbean or wherever I'd gone." She pressed her lips together, then said, more quietly, "It's not too late for me to go. After dinner, I'll—"

"No," he heard himself say. "I need to be able to ask you questions. Bounce ideas off you." Was he being selfish? Daniel didn't know. "Have you where I can see you."

She stared at him in shock, and he thought she'd heard more than he'd said. Seeing beneath the surface—she was good at that.

Chapter Twelve

"Do you have to sleep downstairs?" Lindsay hovered on the second step leading to the loft. She knew she sounded anxious. Well, so what. She didn't think she could sleep in Daniel's big bed with no idea where he was or what he was doing. What if somebody slipped by him? The staircase was so solid, she wouldn't hear even a single step squeak a warning.

"That's up to you." He regarded her from those dark eyes. "I'd rather sleep with you."

"Please," she said shakily. Right this minute, she needed him as she'd never needed anyone.

He turned out lights and followed her. She was already under the covers when he set down his phone on the bedside table followed by something that landed with a clunk. His big, black pistol. Maybe that should disturb her, but instead it reassured her. He disappeared into the bathroom, emerging with his chest bare above a low-slung pair of flannel pajama pants. She couldn't look away, but he gave her a crooked smile as he lifted the covers and joined her in bed.

"Don't tempt me," he said in a low, growly voice.

"I wasn't injured."

"Walking upstairs was enough to set you off coughing." He reached out a long arm and turned off the bedside lamp, then drew her into his arms, carefully arranging her half sprawled on him, her head on his shoulder.

The tenderness in his touch made her eyes sting. Lindsay shifted her hand until she could feel the slow beat of his heart beneath her palm.

She dropped off to sleep with astonishing speed.

WHEN SHE AWAKENED with a jolt, she discovered she was alone in bed. Sitting up, clutching the sheet to her chest, she battled panic. Where was Daniel? He would have told her if he had to leave, wouldn't he?

Then it registered that sunshine flooded the loft through the skylight. Oh. It was morning. In fact, when she spotted the clock, the display said 8:55.

Lindsay hustled to take a brief shower and get dressed in a pair of crisp new jeans that fit surprisingly well and a pale russet, V-necked T-shirt. Melinda had even provided a hairbrush and elastics. Feet in new flip-flops, Lindsay took a last look at herself in the mirror, amazed at how good she felt. Apparently ten uninterrupted hours of sleep worked miracles. Despite everything, she was smiling as she went downstairs.

Daniel stood by the kitchen table, looking down at a newspaper. His jaw was clenched so hard, she expected to hear molars cracking.

"What's wrong?"

He glanced up, clearly angry. "Somebody has a big mouth. A reporter found out about the trash can fires."

"Oh, no." That was the one detail police had determined to withhold. "But…who?"

"God knows."

She frowned, sitting down and turning the front page so she could read the article, too. Last night, there'd been more witnesses than usual, but the smaller fire had not only been in back, it had been set in the barrel. To anyone who didn't know better, it would look as if flying embers from the house had blackened the metal.

Daniel controlled himself well enough to pour her a cup of coffee and ask if scrambled eggs and toast were okay.

She'd done most of the cooking when he'd stayed at her house, so she only nodded.

His back to her as he cracked eggs, he said, "I told the fire chief about the previous fires. I asked him to keep it to himself. I can't believe he'd turn around and spout off to a reporter immediately."

She'd spoken to the man, too, and he'd been really kind. "It had to be somebody else. I mean, how many crime scene investigators and cops have seen them? If one of them told a friend, or a couple of them were overheard talking about it..."

"I'll see their asses fired if I find out who gave out this information," he snapped.

She kept quiet for a minute as he dumped the beaten eggs into a hot pan. Finally, she asked, "Does it really matter?"

He huffed out a breath. "I don't know. Maybe we'll get lucky now and someone will step forward and say, 'I knew this guy who liked to start fires in wastebaskets at school, and even sometimes as a joke when he was at friends' houses. I wonder...'"

"That's possible."

He grabbed thick slabs of toast as they popped up from the toaster and slapped on butter. "You're more optimistic than I am."

Lindsay blinked at that. "I don't think anyone has ever called me an optimist."

The smile that creased Daniel's cheeks was a big improvement on his previous grim expression. "There's always a first time."

She examined how she felt, expecting devastation because of everything she'd lost yesterday. But Daniel gave her a sense of hope. Maybe deep inside she *had* been nurturing a sense of optimism. Who knew she could?

DANIEL SIPPED COFFEE and watched as Lindsay checked messages on her phone. There were obviously a bunch, and he was intrigued by her ever shifting expressions. Wrinkled nose, surprise, annoyance, quirky smile.

When she reached the end, she said, "How bad news does fly. Twenty-six messages, seven of them from eager reporters."

Curious, he asked, "The others from friends?"

"Mostly. Well, and people I work with. Celeste and Sadie both left messages asking if there was anything they could do."

Celeste, if he wasn't mistaken, was the front desk receptionist.

"Melinda, wondering if the clothes fit right. She said to let her know what else I need. Glenn saying how shocked he was when he saw my house burning on the five o'clock news. He and several other coworkers want me to let them know how I am."

Daniel nodded. That was expected.

Her crinkled forehead and hesitation sharpened his attention.

"Ray Hammond left a message, too. He said he has a spare room if I need someplace to stay."

Daniel snorted. "Spare room, hell. That's not what he has in mind."

"He can't possibly imagine I'd leap into bed with him out of gratitude," she said indignantly. "Although it does seem strange. We're polite, and that's about it. So why would he think…?"

"That you'd be desperate enough to take him up on his offer?" He mulled the question over. "You're right. That is strange."

"Sadie offered me a place to stay, too. She and her husband have a big ranch, pretty isolated. It might not be a bad idea."

He shook his head. "Not happening. Sheriff Chaney offered, too, but someone got out there and murdered the Haycrofts without a soul on the ranch seeing a stranger coming or going."

"But you can't stay with me constantly," she argued.

"No." Frustration roughened his voice. "Today, I think I'll take you with me until I can get a new roster of bodyguards arranged. Worse comes to worst, you can sit in the break room at the station, eat vending machine snacks and read a good book."

She looked as thrilled as she had the last time he'd outlined the same proposal. "Am I safe there if the killer is a cop?" she asked dubiously.

"I don't think he'll turn out to be in law enforcement. No matter what, the station is a busy place in the daytime."

He couldn't blame her for her dubious expression. And she didn't know yet how bare-bones the break room was, or that the only available chairs were designed for a quick sit while you ate your lunch, not a six-or eight-hour stint.

He reminded himself there weren't a lot of choices here.

When he grilled her about how she felt, she claimed

to be fine and insisted that she hadn't coughed yet this morning.

He told her she should bring a sweatshirt or sweater since the police station was air-conditioned. Lindsay disappeared upstairs. When she returned, she'd put on socks and bright white athletic shoes and carried an Oregon State University Beavers sweatshirt. Daniel seemed to recall that Melinda had graduated from OSU.

During the short drive into town, he and Lindsay discussed calls she needed to make and what she should and shouldn't tell her friends. Where she was staying topped the "shouldn't" list.

He'd just pulled into the parking lot behind the police station when her phone rang.

"Gayle," Lindsay murmured. She answered, said, "Thank you for calling," then listened with only an occasional interjected word. "Really?"

Gayle was the older caseworker in Lindsay's office. Daniel hadn't gotten a read on her.

He turned off the engine but made no move to get out. He did shift his gaze from mirror to mirror and the windshield, watching for movement. The parking lot might be reasonably safe, but he still felt exposed. He'd have hustled Lindsay into the station, midconversation or not, but he could tell this was no idle chat.

Finally, Lindsay thanked her and said, "I can't believe I've never heard about this before. I really appreciate you telling me."

A moment later, phone still clutched in her hand, she turned in the seat to face Daniel. "Gayle has been with the local office of CPS for, oh, eight or nine years, with an intermission of a couple of years when she couldn't work for health reasons." She took a deep breath. "She says in her early years here, when anyone was especially angry or frustrated, they'd be encouraged to start a fire in a burn barrel out back. Glenn thought it was a healthy outlet. He'd say, 'Every time you're ready to lose it, start a fire.'"

Daniel swore. Way to go for a supervisor: tell his people to start fires to express their rage.

Lindsay bit her lip, then continued, "They had celebrations, too, when a particularly vicious abuser was convicted in court. They'd, um, do things like roast hot dogs or make s'mores. She said it was usually lunch hour, so nobody got drunk or danced naked around the fire, but..."

But overt celebrations couldn't be PC—and Gayle had just tied those small fires firmly to the local CPS.

"Did she say whose idea it was?" he asked.

"Glenn at least condoned it." Lindsay sounded reluctant to say even that much. Now she took a deep breath and met his eyes, her own turbulent. "She also said there'd been a series of fires set in wastebaskets in our offices. Gayle thinks that's why Glenn allowed the burn barrel thing. Eventually, word got out and he was ordered to stop it and get rid of the barrel."

"The surprise is that they got away with something that insane for more than a day," he growled.

Lindsay only nodded.

"Damn." He'd quit paying attention to the people coming and going in the parking lot. "We need to get inside. Wait for me to come around."

Compliance wasn't in her nature, but she didn't argue. The way he hustled her the short distance to the back door probably scared her, but it beat the alternative.

THE DAY WAS incredibly tedious, lanced with occasional anxiety when someone wandering into the break room seemed especially interested in her.

Of course Lindsay knew a number of the officers. Joe Capek sat down to keep her company for a few minutes and commiserate about her house fire before he went out on patrol. Evidently he'd crossed paths with Daniel, who told him that she was condemned to near-solitary confinement here—or, as he put it, hanging out.

Otherwise, the first stranger in uniform she met was a man who had to be near retirement age. He was barely inside the door when he saw her and came to a halt.

"Who are you and what are you doing here?"

Taken aback not by his question, but rather by his near hostility, Lindsay said, "Detective Deperro brought me here for the day as a safety measure."

"Yours the house that burned down yesterday?"

She nodded.

Finally moving on into the room, he said, "So you're the CPS worker."

"I am."

He grunted, grabbed a plastic dish from the refrigerator and heated it in the microwave, his back to her. When the microwave beeped, he took his meal and left the break room without another word.

"Nice," she mumbled.

An interminable hour later, a tall thin officer around forty entered, his gaze going right to her. "You must be Lindsay Engle."

"I am.".

"Heard you got fired."

She stiffened. "I was suspended with pay only until Detective Deperro arrests the killer."

The cop watched her with enough intensity to have her nerves prickling, especially since he didn't pour himself coffee, go to the refrigerator or drop coins in either of the vending machines. She had the uneasy feeling he was here for the sole purpose of getting a good look at her.

"You can't possibly be mourning any of the scumbags who've died," he said.

Her tension ratcheted up. "Who've *died*? You think they just tipped over when their hearts inexplicably stopped? Surely you know how brutal these killings have been."

He shrugged. "Pieces of shit we won't have to arrest again."

Lindsay felt sure his attitude was as, if not more, common in law enforcement circles than social services. Frustration was inevitable. Either way she didn't like it. Many of the abusers she dealt with had been abused as children themselves, or their anger control issues had other understandable roots. Some were alcoholics—but stopping drinking wasn't as easy as a lot of people wanted to think. She'd dealt with several men who were recently returned veterans battling PTSD. She had also seen plenty of abusive or negligent parents who did kick their drug habit or their alcoholism, or who got a handle on their personal problems in counseling because they loved their children.

Lindsay did not like Officer… She strained her eyes to read his badge. Jones? James? Something like that.

The door opened behind him and Daniel appeared, taking in the situation with a glance. "You need something in here, Jonas?"

The other cop's lip curled in a sneer even as his flat gaze remained on Lindsay. "Nah." Without another word, he left. The door swung shut behind him.

"Wow. Great guy."

"When I saw him heading this way, I thought I ought

to intervene." Daniel pulled out a chair beside her. "How are you holding up?"

"Bored but fine. What's his problem?"

"Lousy attitude. He's had a couple of warnings."

"Are you sure that's all?"

He grimaced. "Yeah."

Annoyed, Lindsay said, "You know, all those online videos you see of a cop slamming a teenage girl to the sidewalk seem surreal, until you meet a charmer like Officer Jonas."

He cocked an eyebrow. "And all of your colleagues are compassionate, dedicated, professional and unfailingly patient with the people they have to investigate?"

She wrinkled her nose at him. "Point made."

As always, his grin warmed her. "I ordered lunch from Sandwiches and Such. Hope you're not picky."

"I'm not."

She had to admit she looked forward to lunch after a morning of doing nothing. She hadn't even returned more than a few of the calls that had filled up her voice mail. She didn't feel like talking to anyone she had to suspect. "Have you called Glenn or Sadie about the burn barrel thing?"

"Glenn. He admitted it was his idea. He really thought it was a stress reducer, but he understood why he had to ditch it." Daniel spoke carefully, as if trying not to let his opinion leak into his voice.

"He wouldn't have known about the connection between these killings and the fires until he watched his morning news," she pointed out, ignoring the obvious.

"I'm not jumping to conclusions about him," Daniel said with equal care. "You have to be aware that he does fit the profile in some ways, though."

Lindsay fired back, "Except that he was an amazingly supportive supervisor who taught me everything I know. I can't believe—"

"Whoa!" Laughing, Daniel held up his hand. "I didn't say I was going to arrest him. The truth is, anyone around when everyone in the office vented their frustration with fire could see it now as a symbol. I'd look harder at caseworkers who were here then but have retired, except—"

"For the fact that the killer must know me. Or *thinks* he does." She'd thought about the symbolism in those fires. "What if he's protesting, in a way, that he's being denied the chance to burn away his frustration?"

Daniel shoved back his chair and stood, lines deepening on his forehead. "He's crazy. He could have gone home and lit a damn fire in his fireplace."

Well, yes, that was true, but…

Daniel didn't give her a chance to argue. "Call people back. Get a sense of how they felt about the famous CPS bonfires, why don't you?"

Then he was gone, leaving her alone with her phone.

As Daniel buckled his seat belt, he contemplated the fancy building housing the real estate office. He'd just interviewed Hank Cousins, a guy who'd quit his job with Child Protective Services only ten months ago. That meant he'd worked in the same office with Lindsay for two plus years, yet she hadn't mentioned him. He'd be asking why.

Daniel had run the names of former caseworkers—specifically, the ones who still lived locally—by Sadie Culver and Glenn Wilson. Sadie knew Cousins only by reputation. Sounding tolerant, Glenn had said, "Classic burnout. Last thing he said was that no amount of money could make him keep spending his days talking to people who didn't deserve the space they took on this earth."

Cousins interested Daniel more than other names on his list for two reasons: he'd studied for his real estate license for months without anyone in the office knowing he intended to leave, meaning whatever his level of rage he was capable of restraint—and the very nature of selling real estate meant he was hard to track down during the day.

Daniel's phone rang before he left the parking lot. He recognized the number, not surprised when the fire marshal confirmed that Lindsay's house fire had been started with gasoline.

"From the burn pattern, it's obvious this guy wet down a good part of the back wall of the house with gas, and I wouldn't be surprised if he didn't splash some on the roof. Looks like the homeowner had a woodbox out back, the kind with a plywood lid. That would have given him something to boost himself up on."

"No gas can found, I presume."

The fire marshal thought there had to have been at least two five-gallon cans, which would have been heavy.

"He didn't have far to go if he parked on the side street," Daniel pointed out. "The two houses along with the trees and shrubs would have given him some protection from being seen by a passing car. Besides, I'm guessing this SOB had been watching her place and knew which neighbors were gone daytimes."

The marshal grunted his agreement. "My job is easier when arsonists get fancy. This fire could as well have been set by a teenager. The barrel is the only thing we can call a signature, but it may be relevant only to these murders. I have to wonder if he's set fires before that didn't result in fatalities. Maybe just for fun."

Daniel had thought the same. Quite a few years had separated the burn barrel at the CPS office from this outbreak of murder. As fixated as the killer was on fire, it was hard to imagine he'd gone without all that time.

"You plan to look back for similar fires?"

"Damn straight. If I find any strings to pull, you'll be the first to know," the fire marshal assured him, and signed off.

Fifteen minutes later, Daniel arrived at the home of another ex-CPS employee who had caught his attention. This one lived on acreage outside the city limits. The multiple, deep potholes in the long dirt driveway didn't seem to encourage visitors.

Daniel parked in front of a log house with a carport extending from one side. It had been converted into a workshop. Ross Zeller had left the security of state employment to carve wood with a chainsaw. In fact, in the shade of the carport, a brawny, bearded man was currently working on a six-foot-high log standing upright. Looked like it might become a leaping salmon. He turned when he saw Daniel getting out of his SUV, letting his chainsaw idle.

Daniel didn't rest his hand on the butt of his weapon, but he kept it close. This was the first time he'd found Zeller at home, but neighbors and his former coworkers described him as a strange man. The postal worker had seen him pacing his acreage yelling at someone who wasn't there. His wife had apparently left him about the same time he'd changed careers. Was that one more thing he could blame on the high-stress job and the abusers who were the reason for his burnout?

Any of several outbuildings on the property could be hiding that stolen white Corolla.

The chainsaw coughed and died. Zeller didn't sound friendly when he said, "What's a cop want with me?"

"If you've heard about the string of murders locally, you know fire is part of them."

The big man waited warily.

"I'm trying to talk to everyone who worked at CPS when the burn barrel was being employed as a stress-reducer."

Zeller snorted. "That was the best idea Mr. Follow-the-Rules ever had. Surprised me, to tell you the truth."

"Anybody seem to especially enjoy the fires?"

"You're kidding, right? We all enjoyed them. Fire awakens something primitive in all of us. You must know that."

Daniel couldn't deny it. Who didn't stare with fascination into the leaping, multicolored flames of a campfire? "Tying them to a rage to kill is a little different," he said, keeping his tone conversational.

Zeller's expression went chillingly flat. "Wouldn't know. If you don't mind, I have work to do."

Daniel had no excuse to push the guy, so he thanked him for his time and retreated to his vehicle.

As he jolted back down the driveway, Daniel saw in his rearview mirror that Ross Zeller hadn't returned to his carving. Instead, he stood unmoving, watching the cop drive way. Daniel wished he had a clue what Zeller was thinking.

Funny thing: self-employed, living alone, Zeller too was next to impossible to eliminate as a suspect by alibi. Who was there to provide him with one?

Chapter Thirteen

Hustling Lindsay out to his truck at the end of the day, Daniel had to wonder how safe she really had felt here at the police station today, stuck having to deal with cops like Al Jonas. There was a good reason he'd asked only a select group of trusted fellow officers to guard Lindsay.

Maybe he should consider taking her out to the sheriff's ranch after all. Chaney had several men working for him who were retired army rangers—his partner, Gabe Decker, and foreman, Leon Cabrera. Daniel had fought at their sides in the gun battle when they'd been surrounded by the forces of a major drug trafficking organization. If one or the other could assume bodyguard duties…

But Decker was now married and stepfather to Chloe, the little girl he'd been protecting back when Daniel encountered them, and Cabrera had a family, too. Daniel wouldn't want to bring trouble down on them. Besides…damn it, Lindsay would be nothing but a job to either of them, while for him—

He shut down on that thought.

He had more confidence in himself. Right now, that's what mattered.

"Daniel?"

At her soft query, he turned his head. Seat belt fastened, she was watching him.

"Is something wrong?"

Yeah, something was wrong. He had started the truck but not put it in gear. Shaking his head, he lied, "No. I need you to get down on the floorboards, though, just until I'm sure we're not being followed."

As she unfastened the seat belt and crouched down, he grimaced. Like most cops, he tried to keep his address unlisted. Didn't mean he couldn't be found. He entered cutting horse competitions and judged and refereed them, too, ensuring that he was well-known among local horse owners. In fact, too many people knew him. Still, cops didn't take witnesses home with them. Lindsay had been careful to stay away from windows. Unless the guy was staking out his place twenty-four-seven and saw Daniel ushering her into the house, why would he suspect she was staying with him?

Daniel had made the decision to be sure Lindsay had a guard when he couldn't be there, but even though he'd have liked someone else to be there nights, too, adding a bunch more vehicles coming and going would be the equivalent of him waving his arms and shouting, *I have something to protect.*

All the time he brooded, his gaze flicked from mirror to windshield to mirror...and to his passenger.

"Okay," he said gruffly. "You can get up now."

She untangled herself and settled in the seat. "That was fun."

He liked her attitude, a cross between humorous and snide. Under pressure, she didn't buckle; she got mad.

Taking advantage of this uninterrupted time together, he asked about both Ross Zeller and Hank Cousins.

"Hank was friendly, almost too talkative. It was kind

of annoying when I was trying to concentrate. I guess I wasn't that surprised he quit. He looked for any distraction from his job, you know? Um. Ross Zeller. He was…unsettling. I don't mean violent or anything," she hastened to say, "just weird." Her nose wrinkled. "It seemed like every time I looked up, he was staring at me."

Daniel mentally ticked off one of the boxes on his list.

"The only thing is, other people told me the same thing, so it wasn't just me. And he never came on to me or even suggested coffee. He was married, though I heard he and his wife split right before he quit."

"I was told the same," Daniel said. "Was he good at his job?"

"I…don't really know," Lindsay said hesitantly. "He was…volatile, I guess is the best word. I think Glenn only assigned him low-level abuse accusations."

Serial killers were often categorized as "organized" versus "disorganized." Lindsay was implying he fell on the "disorganized" side—except that from what Daniel had seen and heard, his carvings were fine and sold for substantial amounts. That meant he was disciplined enough to work hard. He'd been cagey when Daniel talked to him, too.

But disciplined in one way didn't mean he could study to commit a series of murders without being seen, without leaving any trace evidence.

Cousins might have that kind of discipline if he was truly dedicated to a goal—but nothing about him had sent up a flare for Daniel.

And then there was Glenn, who still hung around the CPS offices, continued to befriend Lindsay in particular, but offered advice and support to other caseworkers, too. Glenn, Daniel had only recently discovered, had been there the day Lindsay got the call about Shane Ramsey collapsing after his uncle beat him.

Daniel hadn't so much as hinted to Lindsay recently that Glenn was still on his radar. Her affection for the man she called a mentor blinded her where he was concerned. On the other hand, Daniel had gained a lot of respect for her ability to judge people. Glenn might be as great a guy as she thought he was.

Deciding this was a good time to change the subject, he smiled. "Hope you like quesadillas. That's what we're having tonight."

"You mean I don't have to cook?"

He laughed. "Your house, you cooked, my house, I cook."

"Works for me," she said. "Might be a long time before I have to cook again."

The humor didn't quite come off.

He reached for her hand, and she returned his clasp.

"YOU EVER DONE any shooting?"

Daniel's question came out of left field, but she should have expected it.

Spreading pico de gallo atop her black bean quesadilla, she said, "Yes, when I was thirteen… No, maybe fourteen. I wasn't in that home very long. The man was a gun nut, and after the police came out to the house because he'd taken his AK-15 along to issue a threat to a neighbor, we kids got moved."

Daniel offered her sour cream. "Sounds like a winner."

"He freaked us out." She wrinkled her nose. "I swear the guy owned fifty guns or more. He talked about being ready to defend his family when the government came to try to take away his weapons." She paused. "He must not have mentioned them when he was interviewed by social services."

Daniel laughed, although he was watching her more perceptively than she liked. "Another reason behind your career path."

"Maybe. He wasn't abusive, though."

He said something harsh under his breath, and she realized she'd put too much emphasis on the *he*. Yes, she'd been placed in homes where people meant to protect her had hurt her instead. In one home, she'd had to drag her dresser in front of the bedroom door at night to keep the man out. That one had been bad; she'd just reached puberty and been self-conscious as it was about her developing body. Vulnerable, afraid to speak out, she'd gotten lucky when the foster mom complained to the caseworker about the scratches on the bedroom floor. The caseworker had her pack up and removed her from the home within the hour.

Yet another reason for her life choices, of course.

"Weren't you ever in a home where people were good to you?" he asked, a roughness in his voice.

"Yes, I stayed in the same home my last three years. I still call and occasionally visit my foster parents." She hesitated. "I'm sure they'd take me in now, but—"

She could tell he didn't like the idea, but he said, "But?"

"They always have three or four kids living with them. I couldn't put them at risk."

"I wouldn't let you," he said shortly, and resumed eating.

She did the same. He continued with the questions about her childhood, and she told him more than she'd intended. More than she usually told anyone. If she had caught even a whiff of pity, she'd have shut down, but Daniel's reactions were never what she considered the norm.

They had finished eating and she was clearing the table as he started the coffee when her phone rang. Made instantly wary, she went to grab it from her handbag. Glenn was the caller.

Relaxing, she signaled to Daniel, who nodded, and she took the phone into the part of the open space situated to form a sort of living room.

"Glenn," she said, as she sank onto a leather sofa, one foot under her. "You calling for an update on the latest exciting turn my life has taken?"

His familiar chuckle was reassuring. "Tough lady."

"What, you thought I'd sit in a corner and suck my thumb?"

Glenn laughed again. "Not for a minute. I just wanted to find out how you're holding up, but I guess I don't have to ask."

"I'm okay. Really."

"I assume you've had plenty of offers for places to stay."

Aware that Daniel had come from the kitchen to lean against a wall where he could hear her, she said, "Yes, I have. Is that why you called?"

He snorted. "You don't want to move in with a crusty old man like me. I hope you know I'd offer if you were desperate, but I'm sure you have younger, more gallant men eager to take you in."

Uneasiness stirred for the first time. Was he angling for her to say, *Sure, you've met Detective Deperro, haven't you? I'm staying with him.*

Instead of too obviously evading her question, she said, "Like Ray Hammond, you mean?"

"You're serious?"

"Yep. I'd have sworn I'm low on his list of favorite caseworkers."

"I knew there was tension between you," he admitted. "He probably means well…"

Somehow, she wasn't surprised that he trailed off midsentence. White lies weren't Glenn's style.

"Well," she said briskly, "I've had so many invitations, I'll probably hop from household to household so I don't wear out my welcome. I do need to start figuring out whether I'm going to rebuild or…" She was the one to break off this time. That was a big *or*. If she didn't plan to go back to her job, maybe she'd be better off moving, starting afresh.

Painfully aware of Daniel's presence, she knew she wouldn't be going anywhere until she found out whether their relationship might become serious.

Seizing her chance, she said, "Detective Deperro told me the burn barrel out behind the office was your idea. Did you really think you'd get by with that?"

He laughed. "Got by with it longer than I expected." His tone sobered. "I never imagined anything like what happened to you. I was trying to manage creatively. We were having trouble retaining caseworkers. You know what it's like. If they could learn to vent, I thought they'd quit repressing the anger and frustration, not throw in the towel so quick."

"That actually makes sense," she admitted.

"I'm glad you understand. You know how highly I think of you."

All she could think to say was "thank you."

To her relief, Glenn didn't press her for her current or future whereabouts, just ended the conversation by saying, "Call if you need to talk."

Off to the side, Daniel said unexpectedly, "It's not just women who feel scorned when they're rejected, you know."

Lindsay swiveled on the sofa. "What?"

"Ray."

"You think he was, I don't know, trying to apologize or something when he offered me a place to stay?"

"Maybe."

She thought about it. "I was polite when I said no, thanks."

Daniel kept his distance. "Learn anything from your call?"

Lindsay told him about Glenn's rationale and her reaction before hesitating. "There was only one thing."

He lifted his eyebrows.

"When he said 'I'm glad you understand.'"

"'I thought you of all people would understand,'" Daniel quoted.

"Yes." She found herself shaking her head. "I won't believe Glenn would do any of this. Why would he now that he's retired, putting the job behind him?"

Offering no reassurance, Daniel watched her for a minute before pushing away from the wall. "I'm going to have you start carrying my backup handgun. For now, forget Glenn and Hammond both. Let's go upstairs."

To bed, remained unspoken.

"THIS WAS AN ugly one," Daniel said tersely.

Lindsay had pounced on the phone when she saw his number on the screen, but hearing his news about the latest murder, she quailed. "Who is it?"

Of course she wasn't alone at Daniel's house. Officer Alvarez, today's bodyguard, was currently at the back of the house walking from window to window, watching for anything out of the ordinary. For all she knew, Daniel had already called or texted him about the latest murder.

In answer to her question, Daniel said, “Ryan Olson.”

She felt a brief moment of hope that she might not have been the caseworker involved with this victim. “I don’t remember that name.”

Daniel killed her tentative hope. “You’re the caseworker of record. It was… Let me check. Three years ago.”

Ryan Olson. Dredging her memories, she still came up short.

“I must have just started working here—” Her heart sank. “Wait. I do remember. I wasn’t involved in the investigation. I was handed nominal responsibility for the case because my successor left for a new job. Olson took a plea, so that was that.”

“He got a slap on the wrist.”

“Well, even though he hurt those two boys pretty bad, it was a one-time event.” The details were coming back to her.

“His kids?”

“His son and a friend. They were wild, and he blew his top and burned them both.”

Daniel was quiet for a minute. “How?”

“Um…forced their hands down onto the top of the wood stove. He started to push his boy’s face down, too, but came back to himself in horror. He tried to treat the burns he’d given them, but didn’t take them for medical care.”

“Bet that didn’t look good.”

“No. When his wife got home, she took them. I seem to remember that he was a veteran who came home in bad shape. Couldn’t sleep, screamed at his wife and kids. You know. But he hadn't hurt anyone until then, which is why he got away with probation and counseling."

"Did the wife stay with him?"

"I won't swear to it, but I think so." She'd already been wrapped up in other investigations, grateful this one wasn't her problem. "The other family was angry he didn't get time in prison."

"Don't suppose you remember their names?"

"Not a chance." She frowned. "Are you thinking this could be a copycat murder?"

"Crossed my mind." Daniel continued, "He was killed inside the Sadler city limits, which makes me primary. It'll be a while before I can get away. I'll call Alvarez and make sure he can stay."

"I can talk to him—"

Daniel interrupted with a brusque "I'll do it." When he added, "We'll get this piece of crud," he sounded considerably gentler.

If only she could help instead of being a burden.

She heard a ring tone and turned to see Officer Tom Alvarez already putting his phone to his ear. He watched her with eyes as dark as Daniel's during the brief conversation. His end consisted of "uh-huh" and "sure." When he set down his phone on the tiled countertop beside his perch on a stool, he said, "Another murder?"

Lindsay nodded. "I hardly remembered the victim. Ryan Olson."

He shook his head.

She told him what she remembered, and saw the same puzzlement she felt.

"Unless something worse happened later, he seems like an unlikely victim."

"Very. Plus...the killer has targeted abusers from my caseload. I never even *met* this guy."

"Huh."

Alvarez had been really nice, making an effort to be companionable as well as perform his bodyguard duties. Now he suggested they play poker for paperclips. He talked about his children with pride that made something in Lindsay ache. Of course, he showed her pictures on his phone of his four kids, from a ten-year-old to his oldest, a girl wearing her prom dress.

"She's really beautiful." Lindsay handed him back his phone. "Is that her boyfriend?"

"Not for long." Alvarez flashed her a grin. "She's been accepted at Stanford. The little punk is heading for a community college."

Despite everything churning inside her, Lindsay laughed. "He can't be that bad if she likes him."

"He's okay, but not good enough for my little girl."

"I'll bet he's scared of you, too."

"Of course he is. I carry a gun."

Lindsay knew he was trying to distract her, and she let him think he'd succeeded. Once he made the rounds inside the house, going from window to window, her thoughts reverted immediately to Daniel's call and the grimness and revulsion she'd heard in his voice.

This was an ugly one. She didn't think of herself as a coward, but she wasn't sure she wanted to know any more.

"HE'S LOSING IT," Chaney growled.

Daniel would call that a major understatement. He wasn't alone in having trouble tearing his gaze from the gruesome sight of what had been a big, strong man in his late thirties. For all that Chaney must have seen in war zones, he looked sick. Melinda was hiding her feelings better, probably because she'd developed that to an art form. As a rare woman cop in these parts, she had to appear hard even when she was grieving, horrified or scared.

Daniel let out a long breath. "What if our killer knows the parents of the other boy Olson burned?"

Melinda answered. "Maybe it's just the use of fire—burning the kids—that stuck in his memory."

"Could be this murder gave him a chance play with fire," Chaney muttered.

They all watched in silence as the body bag was zipped up and lifted onto a rolling gurney. Daniel wanted to be relieved, but he wouldn't be forgetting anytime in the near future the sight of what this victim had suffered. The number of burns… He pushed the images away.

Overpowering this victim wouldn't have been easy. Zeller was the suspect who leaped to mind. He had massive arms and spent his days hefting logs and controlling a chainsaw.

What it came down to was that the man who had tortured Ryan Olson was still out there, still furious at Lindsay for failing to appreciate his multiple "gifts." This feeling of helplessness wouldn't have sat well with Daniel at any time, but it was intolerable given his fear for her.

"Not a single witness so far, and I'm betting we don't find one," Daniel said flatly. "He plans. He has to be cold-blooded as hell even with the anger driving him."

"He burns," Melinda observed, her tone strange.

Daniel waited for Chaney to jump on her, but all he did was turn his head to look at her. His expression was odd, too, Daniel thought.

Hell. They were all in a mood. How could they help it? The killer hadn't just escalated; he'd become more vicious than a rabid wolf. Why?

Daniel hadn't realized he'd spoken his thoughts aloud until Melinda answered.

"Because Lindsay escaped. He needed to punish her, and he failed. Maybe this—" she gestured toward where the body had lain "—was a roaring temper tantrum."

The ball of fear knotted even tighter in Daniel's gut. Had this been a message to Lindsay? Or had this bastard used another man's suffering to make himself feel better? Powerful. In control.

It was maddening to know that a serial killer *was* in control. To think how much pleasure he must be taking as he watched the cops flail around incompetently.

Distantly aware his hand was shaking when he lifted it to rub his jaw, Daniel wanted to walk away from this crime scene. Just get in his car and drive, to hell with speed limits, until he could see and touch Lindsay. And then he wanted not to leave her side until the killer fixated on her was behind bars or dead.

Preferably dead.

It was the first time in his career as a law enforcement officer he'd thought that.

Gaze intense on his face, Melinda said, "Are you sure he doesn't know you took Lindsay home?"

"How can he?"

She lifted her eyebrows. "If he was watching the night her house burned, he saw the way she walked into your arms, how you held her. I wasn't there, but I've heard people talking."

"But even if he hung around long enough to see me drive away with Lindsay, I could have dropped her anywhere." Damn, he wished he didn't share Melinda's unease. Logic was on his side, but the uncanny way the killer had gotten each victim alone, committed his horrors without anyone hearing a sound or catching a glimpse of him coming and going…

"What's the alternative?" he growled, arguing with himself as much as with Melinda. "Anywhere I take her, we could be seen. As it is, I have her covered day and night."

They threw around ideas, but the truth was, there were only so many alternatives. Sending her off on a world cruise would have more appeal if he really believed they'd catch this monster by the time she returned home.

As it was, the killer was playing them.

"We need to keep canvassing," he said abruptly.

Chaney snorted. "We're not going to find him that way. We all know that. He's had hours to vanish." He raised a hand to prevent Daniel's retort. "We have to do it anyway, but why don't you let us handle it?"

Melinda nodded. "Go home, Daniel."

He was primary. He should work this investigation until he was ready to drop. But moved by their unusual unified stance, Daniel said hoarsely, "Thanks."

The urgent need driving him to get back to Lindsay was a little bit of a shocker. Wanting to believe she was safe at his place wasn't the same as being deep-down convinced. Heading for his department-issued vehicle, it was all he could do to keep his pace to a walk.

No, he wasn't going to stop at the station to switch to his pickup. What he did intend to do was go by Ross Zeller's home, see if his strangeness was any more evident. And maybe ask if *he* had a burn barrel.

Chapter Fourteen

Lindsay rocketed out of sleep, for a moment disoriented. What had she heard? She strained for any sound out of the ordinary, but the night was quiet. A bad dream, she decided, her heart still pounding, but she'd woken Daniel, who also sat up.

"What is it?"

"I—probably nothing. A nightmare."

He slid out of bed and went to the French doors, easing the blind to one side. After a minute, he said, "I don't see anything, but I'm going out to walk the perimeter."

Her fingernails bit into her palms. He kept doing this, scaring her every time. "Please don't. What if—" She couldn't finish. He'd know what she hadn't said. *What if he kills you? What if he sees you leaving the house and comes in?*

Already half-dressed, he paused. "I know how to be a ghost."

Shakily, she said, "So does he."

He went still, his shirt half on. "He could be ex-military. I don't know why that hasn't occurred to me."

As far as she could tell, Daniel was energized by the idea and unswayed by her fears.

After yanking down the shirt, he shoved his feet in

his boots, grabbed his gun and murmured, "Stay here." Then he was gone.

Discovering she felt trapped up here, Lindsay got dressed, too. If something happened—gunshots fired, Daniel's house burst into flames—she could deal better if she wasn't naked. Then, like him, she peeked through the blinds.

The view was severely limited, but the moon cast a silver light tonight that illuminated open ground leading toward the impenetrable darkness of the woods.

Her heart took an extra beat. Something had *moved* in that darkness.

Her eyes burned as she stared. She flashed back to the day she'd found Martin Ramsey's body and first thought someone was watching her from beneath the trees.

In fact, these past few days she'd kept feeling eyes on her. The hair on her nape would prickle, and she'd whirl around but never actually see anyone. Her imagination was working overtime, but so far she'd failed to squelch it.

Right now, she couldn't stand the suspense. She slipped to the head of the staircase, unsure if the darkness inside allowed her to feel safe…or had the opposite effect. *Don't be a coward,* she told herself, and descended, her bare feet silent on the solid steps.

In the kitchen, she saw the lighted numbers on the microwave. 4:39. She wouldn't be going back to sleep.

Which door had Daniel gone out? Would he have left it unlocked?

She stood still, waiting. Tension rose as she pictured him slipping through the night, unafraid.

Only the faintest whisper of sound told her the kitchen door had opened. She eased backward into the hall, so she couldn't be seen if it wasn't Daniel who'd entered so quietly.

The kitchen light came on, she heard a familiar clunk, like a gun being set down, and then water running in the sink.

Swallowing fear she hated feeling, she said, "Daniel?"

"It's me." He stepped into sight, his dark eyes locking onto her. "Why'd you come down? You could still get some more sleep."

Lindsay hoped her laugh sounded less broken to him than it did to her. "Sure. That's going to happen."

He studied her for a moment. "Okay. I'm making coffee." He didn't move, though, instead holding out a hand.

She took it and let him draw her close. She wrapped both arms tightly around him, gripping the T-shirt he wore in both fists. His strong embrace calmed her, as did the steady beat of his heart beneath her ear. He couldn't have seen anything even slightly alarming or he wouldn't be so relaxed, would he?

Finally she drew a deep breath and straightened, letting her arms drop to her sides. He did the same but never looked away from her.

"This is getting to you," he said in a soft growl.

Denial seemed pointless. "I guess it is. What are we going to do, Daniel? We can't go on like this forever."

He shook his head. "I'm not moving you."

Shock zinged her. "I didn't mean that." Accustomed to solitude, she had been surprised how comfortable it was to live with Daniel. No, not just comfortable; the truth was, she loved their quiet talks, his heat and solidity in bed at night, his gentle touches, his openness with her.

Making love with him.

What she had no idea was whether he was as happy or hankered for his lost privacy and quiet.

"We'll get through this. He'll make a mistake or one of us will have an epiphany that leads us to him. I admit, I don't like feeling outsmarted and outmaneuvered."

"You know it's not that. If you could predict his next choice of victim, it would be different, but how can you?"

"We did once. We *warned* the stupid woman, and he still figured out when she'd be alone, killed her and waltzed away without leaving so much as a flake of skin or strand of hair behind."

"That means he's using gloves and… I don't know." A Tyvek suit?

Something changed on Daniel's face. Of course he wasn't telling her everything. Should she push?

He turned and went back to where he'd been filling the coffeepot. After a moment, however, he said, "We're speculating that he's shaved his body, at the very least."

Having followed him, she found herself staring at his back.

"His head, too?" she asked.

"Best guess is a hood. Maybe the kind divers wear."

"Oh." Glenn, for one, didn't have much hair on his head to start with, she couldn't help thinking. He did have a hairy chest, though. She knew because when he left the top button of his shirt undone, curly gray hair showed. He would have shaved that if—

Shame curdled in her stomach. She *knew* him. He wasn't capable—but then she remembered their last conversations. She hadn't known he'd ever been married. In fact, his personal life was pretty much a mystery to her. But wasn't that kind of stuff really superficial?

He'd demonstrated his caring, his leadership, his determination and kindness day after day on the job. *That* was what counted. Nausea swirled through her. Think how hurt he'd be if he knew that, even for the tiniest moment, she'd considered the possibility that *he* might be the monster torturing and murdering people.

"What are you thinking?" Daniel leaned against the counter and regarded her, his arms crossed.

She shook her head. "He can't pull the hood up until he knows no one will see him."

"That's true." He hesitated, watchful again. "I've eliminated Hammond and Grudin once and for all."

She gaped. "How? When?"

"They were both in the office when your house was set on fire. This time, there's no doubt."

Lindsay discovered she didn't know how to feel about that. She hadn't wanted either man to turn out to be so horrible or to find her judgment was that off. She didn't like either of them, but she'd respected them as coworkers. But at least… Well, circle back to the fact that she didn't like either of them. That gave her a few degrees of distance. Given the certainty that the killer would turn out to be someone she knew—

"I should be glad," she blurted out, before she could censor herself.

Daniel's dark eyes narrowed, but he kept his mouth shut. And why not? He had to know what she was thinking.

The next thing he said was almost irrelevant. "If only I had more manpower."

Reluctantly, she asked, "To do what?"

"Put a tail on suspects."

"Do you have suspects?"

"You know I do."

Her lips parted, but he shook his head before she could ask who.

"You've told me what you know about people. You already have enough to stew about," he said.

Normally she would have argued, but she knew he was right. Since she was jittery despite the ridiculously early hour of the morning, she went to the refrigerator. She might not be hungry yet, but she had to do *something*, and they'd have to eat sooner or later.

Daniel relaxed, so subtly most people wouldn't have noticed, but she'd already become an expert on reading his body language. He wanted to steer her away from what he was thinking, and for now she'd let him get away with it.

TIREDNESS WAS BECOMING an issue. There was a limit to how long he could go on this way, Daniel knew, working all day, taking more what he thought of as brief combat naps at night than really sleeping. He'd learned his capacity and limitations during his deployments in battle zones. He could pace himself only so long before he had to have a good eight hours of deep, truly sustaining sleep.

Assuming the killer was, or had been, a Child Protective Services employee—and Daniel had little doubt—two men had risen from a more general field of possible suspects to become his favorites. Both male, one retired, one who had quit. Both had displayed possibly aberrant behavior on the job, and now that they'd left it, neither had a schedule that made it possible to pin down alibis with any certainty.

Ross Zeller and Glenn Wilson.

A few others were still in the running, but trailing well behind.

Zeller might have been in the number one position, except that Lindsay didn't sound as if she'd been very close to him. He'd stared at her—but he'd stared at other people, too. Some people, especially a man described as strange, lacked the intuitive knowledge of social cues and boundaries.

Daniel couldn't forget that Glenn had been there the day Lindsay got the call about Shane Ramsey collapsing after his uncle beat him. He hung around the office enough to know what was going on and remained friendly enough with the caseworkers he'd formerly supervised to hear about the child rape case that followed so soon after Martin Ramsey's murder.

Glenn had also proved to be remarkably hard to pin down. Nobody really knew whether he'd had hobbies back when he was still working. Because he hadn't talked about any, the consensus was that he lived for his job. If that was so, the puzzling part was that he had chosen to retire sooner than he had to.

Unless, of course, he'd decided it was time to start hunting the worst abusers in a more satisfying way than slapping them with too-short prison terms.

The two men were a contrast in that Glenn was helpful whenever Daniel called, while Zeller had yet to answer a call from Daniel or answer the door when he made follow-up visits. Ross Zeller's behavior should be more suspicious…but a serial killer who hadn't yet made a mistake might well be an Oscar-worthy actor.

AFTER CLEARING THE dishes that evening, Lindsay sat down again at the table, not happy to see that Daniel was already on his second cup of coffee, and said, "That'll keep you awake."

He smiled crookedly. "That's the general idea."

"You can't—"

"I can."

Refusing to back down, she suggested, "Why don't I keep watch for a few hours tonight so you can really sleep? I can take a nap tomorrow."

"You can't leave the house."

"Is that necessary, if I make your usual rounds inside?"

"You have no experience with patrolling, sentry duty, being a bodyguard," he said flatly.

She crossed her arms and held his stare. "I have good eyesight, and I'm highly motivated. What else is required?"

"This is my job."

Absorbing that, she hid how much it hurt. As calmly as she could manage, she said, "Well, that puts me in my place. If you'll excuse me, I think I'll go read for a while. That'll give you peace and quiet to mainline your caffeine." She stood and started toward the doorway.

Behind her, a chair scraped across the polished wood floor. "Damn it, Lindsay, I didn't mean it the way you're thinking."

She paused briefly, closing her eyes. Why had she said that? She was hugely in debt to Daniel. Yes, they were sleeping together, but that didn't mean he was thinking of her as part of his future beyond nailing a killer. The last thing she should do was add any awkwardness to the relationship when they couldn't avoid each other.

She flapped a hand. "Forget about it. I'm irritated that you won't let me help, that's all."

"Would you turn around?" His voice came out huskier than usual.

Lindsay swallowed, took a few deep breaths and summoned her inner actress before she faced him.

Even more lines had deepened in his face. "*You're* not a job to me. You have to know that."

"Sure." She smiled. "I didn't mean to start something. Don't worry about it."

"I will worry about it." He held out a hand.

Barely hesitating, she reached out. His much larger hand engulfed hers, and he tugged her toward him.

"I've been trying to focus on keeping you safe," he said in that almost gruff voice. "I figured the rest could wait."

"It can," she whispered.

"I've never brought anyone involved in one of my investigations home with me."

Lindsay nodded. She'd assumed as much.

"You're depending on me right now. Putting pressure on you would be a crappy thing to do. Just know that the idea of something happening to you—" He swallowed. Shuddered, if she wasn't mistaken. "I don't know how I could live with that."

The melting sensation inside her rib cage made her eyes sting, too. "I'm not very good at saying thank you. If not for you—"

He cut her off. "Damn it, you're not listening! Gratitude is the last thing I want from you."

"I've been afraid of assuming anything," she said honestly. "So…maybe it's better if we hold off on this conversation."

"We can do that, but you need to know that you're not an obligation to me. You're…important."

Her head bobbed. "You're important to me, too. I—" *No, don't say it.* Instead, she changed gears. "I want the right to worry about you, too, though."

He bent down until his forehead rested against hers. “You can do that,” he murmured. “I’ve been doing plenty of worrying about you.”

He wouldn’t be able to see her mouth, but she summoned a shaky smile anyway. “I know.”

The next moment, he was kissing her. The passion and raw need ignited a response from her as powerful as his. The kiss went on and on as she did her best to mold her body to his, to tell him without words how she really felt.

Suddenly, though, he lifted his head and looked down at her. “You’re right, and I was wrong,” he said, sounding as if somebody had taken sandpaper to his vocal cords.

Lindsay blinked. How was she right?

“I need you now, but after that I also need some sleep. As long as you promise to wake me up if anything at all catches your attention.”

Despite his dominant personality and strong, protective instincts, he was backing down. He intended to trust her enough to allow himself to sink into a deep sleep.

She gave him a smile. “Those are magic words, you know. I should have them tattooed where I can see them forever.”

Showing a hint of wariness, he cocked his head. “Which words?”

“‘You’re right, and I was wrong.’ What else?”

Seeing her full-fledged grin, he laughed. “Later I may have to deny I ever said that.”

“Just try it.”

His mouth still curved, he kissed her again. This time, he steered her toward the stairs.

In the next few days, boredom took a toll on Lindsay. She’d never been sick or injured enough to be confined to her house for any length of time. Vacations? Who had time for those? And on the rare occasion when she'd managed to take one, she didn't use it to huddle inside.

Here, even when she walked around inside the house, she had to avoid passing in front of a window. She loved to read—but not all day long, every day. She'd taken to baking ridiculous quantities of breads, cookies, cakes and pies. The other cops who took turns guarding her took some of the bounty home. Daniel took some to work, too, but he didn't want other cops and employees to start wondering where he was coming by so many obviously home-baked goodies. Bread and cookies she put in the freezer. Whether she was here down the line or not, Daniel wouldn't lack for desserts.

She browsed job openings on the internet, and the reputations of local contractors, just in case she decided to rebuild her house. She looked up blueprints and designs—if she did build, she might as well improve on the basic rambler she'd bought when she'd first moved to Sadler.

She studied the latest model cars. She ordered a dozen new books from an online bookseller. Clothes, too. Daniel wasn't thrilled to learn how often the UPS or FedEx truck rumbled up the driveway to his house, but the packages all came in his name and he scrawled notes to stick to the door permitting the drivers to leave everything on the porch.

"I've turned into a shopaholic," she told Melinda as she ripped open a shoebox. She was pretty sure these would fit. Even so, when she took out the riding boots, she made a face. "As if I'll ever get to ride again."

Melinda laughed at her. "Gloom and doom. Hey, don't forget the bright side. You're alive and you have a sexy boyfriend."

"Those are definitely silver linings," Lindsay admitted. She wouldn't have said anything to the woman detective about her relationship with Daniel, but he'd taken to kissing her when he got home, right in front of Melinda or Tom Alvarez or the couple of other cops who'd become her best—and only—friends.

Not true. She still had her phone, and Glenn and Sadie, at least, hadn't forgotten her. Most of the rest of her coworkers quit calling, no surprise when she couldn't meet up for coffee, had no idea what was happening at work and dodged any questions about where she was staying and when she'd be back.

Pursuing her earlier thought, though, she said, "Poor Daniel doesn't get to ride, either. Even if he had time, he'd feel bad abandoning me." He did still have to feed his animals and check on them, but probably astonished them with his haste.

"The horses don't look like they're in mourning." Melinda was right in front of the kitchen window, where she could see the pasture.

"I know that's true." Lindsay kicked off her flip-flops and tried on the boots. They were amazingly comfortable, thank goodness. She lifted a foot, admiring the glossy black boot. "I'll look good when I do get paroled."

Melinda laughed at her again and talked her out of making another batch of cookies.

THREE TENSE DAYS LATER, Lindsay was clinging to Melinda's reminders of what she had to be thankful for as if it were a talisman holding magical properties. Face drawn, Daniel had less and less to say. She didn't have anything to say, either. She kept wondering how long his cop friends would be willing to give up their days off for a woman they hadn't even known before all this started. She kept wondering when the next body would be found…and who it would be.

Most often, she and Daniel made love before she got dressed again and began the assigned rounds he'd agreed to making routine. There was an increasing desperation to the way they clutched each other, a silent intensity to every touch.

Tonight, as she went downstairs in the dark, Lindsay was ruefully conscious of how well used her body felt and how relaxed. It and her brain had a real disconnect right now. Although she would never tell Daniel, she was growing to hate these dark hours on her own. At each window, she stood still, eyes burning with the need to see even the tiniest movement or anomaly through the slit of the blinds. That shape behind the fence was too big for a horse… But then she saw a foal bounce toward her, and after that, she recognized the larger bulk of what was probably his dam.

Tonight the moon was only a sliver from full, which helped. When it became a crescent, how would they see anything?

She moved to the next window and the next. Was that a car engine she heard? Quivering, she listened, but it wasn't close by. People were out on the roads at night. It wasn't really even that late.

An hour later, she'd circled the house again several times, sometimes seeing mirages that faded away when she looked hard enough. Once she saw what she first thought was a dog trotting across an open stretch of land before realizing it had to be a coyote. Were coyotes a threat to foals? She watched until it vanished from sight.

With a sigh, she wandered down the hall toward the open living space. The kitchen seemed…bright. Puzzled, her inner alarms flaring, she reminded herself there were lit numbers on the stove and microwave. Only none of those lights were orange.

Lindsay ran the last few steps, where the window framed a hot orange light. Fire.

"Daniel!" she screamed.

Chapter Fifteen

Daniel's feet hit the floor before he was fully awake. He grabbed the pants he'd left draped on a chair and yanked them on, pulled on a Kevlar vest over his bare torso and shoved sockless feet into boots. Gun in his right hand, fumbling to close the Velcro strips on the vest, he ran for the stairs.

She waited for him at the bottom. "The house is on fire! I don't know how it happened so fast. I looked out the kitchen window not that long ago, and now flames are climbing the wall. We can't go out that way."

"Have you called—"

"Yes." Stress thinned her voice, but she held on to outward calm. "What can we do?"

"I'm going to arrest this excuse for a human being," he snapped.

She wrung her hands. "What if he's waiting?"

"I'm counting on it," he said grimly.

"How…how will you get out?"

A shrill scream hurt his ear drums. Fire alarm, which meant that in seconds… With a hiss, sprinklers came on.

He had to shout with his mouth at Lindsay's ear. "A window. Come with me."

He hustled her to his office in the corner on the opposite side of the house from the kitchen. There, he slid the wood-framed window open and shoved out the screen. He was already wet and saw that her hair hung in dripping hanks.

"Do you have the gun?" he asked.

He couldn't hear her answer, but she nodded and reached to retrieve it from the waistband at her lower back.

Holding her close, he put his mouth close to her ear. "Stay here unless it looks like the fire will trap you. Okay?"

"What if he gets in the house?"

"Shoot him." Daniel's hands tightened on her shoulders as he fought the need to stay with her. His best chance of catching this monster at last was to hunt him down outside.

He looked out, seeing nobody, before he planted a hand on the sill and vaulted out the window. A shrill neigh carried from the pasture, then another. What if the fire roared across the dry grass to surround his horses?

Daniel gritted his teeth.

Instinct had him trotting toward the back corner of his converted barn. The fire burned on the opposite side. It didn't seem likely the arsonist would be standing on the front porch. Unless he had already fled?

Daniel rejected that thought. This killer was here for Lindsay. Why would he leave now when he had them on the run?

Yeah, and where was his car?

Daniel flattened himself against the rough board siding, gun held in a two-handed grip and took a quick look around the corner. Damn. He didn't see anything but the horses cantering in panicked circles out in the pasture. The fire hadn't reached there, thank God.

Moving fast, he crossed the distance to the other back corner. He flattened himself there before fear crawled up his spine. Had he just behaved predictably? Leaving Lindsay alone in a room with an open window?

He mumbled some of the worst words he knew as he ran back the way he'd come.

LINDSAY BACKED INTO the closet after Daniel was gone. She'd be hard to spot here. If someone—say, a vicious killer—looked into the room without entering, he wouldn't see her.

The gun shook because her hands were trembling, but she held it ready to fire. She wished she could hear better, but the hiss of the sprinklers obscured any sound coming from outside. Would she even be able to hear sirens?

Please let help come fast, she begged silently.

Her vision kept blurring. She panted, blinking moisture from her eyes. When they opened, she saw a dark shape looming just outside the window. It might be Daniel...but if so, why wasn't he saying anything? And if it wasn't...

Just as the man started to climb in, awkwardly compared to Daniel's exit, she made out a dark, smooth covering on his head. And something covered most of his face.

Thoughts darted through her head as she pressed back in the open closet. Had he seen her? *Shoot him*, Daniel had said. But Lindsay had never imagined shooting a human being, or even an animal, with the intent of killing.

Staying silent, the figure paused with a leg over the sill.

"Stop!" she yelled, without having planned it.

"There you are."

At least, that's what she thought he said.

She shifted the barrel of the small handgun slightly to the side and pulled the trigger. *Bang!* Glass splintered.

He kept coming, not believing she would actually shoot him. Because he knew her. *Thought* he knew her.

Oh God, oh God. Lindsay pointed the gun at him and fired.

When he yelled, she discovered she'd closed her eyes when she pulled the trigger. She opened them just in time to see him fall back out the window. More gunshots sounded almost instantly.

Freaked, she crept toward the window even knowing Daniel wouldn't want her risking herself. But what if the killer had fired those shots and Daniel was down?

The first thing she saw was the man running away with a lurching gait. One leg didn't work right. Her shot might have hit his thigh.

She looked in the other direction and her breath caught. Daniel lay sprawled on the grass. Her heart stopped. But he wasn't dead, she realized in a second. He held his gun extended in both hands, and as she watched he fired it. The running man jerked as if he'd been hit but kept going.

Lindsay scrambled out the window, tumbling painfully to her hands and knees, but jumped up immediately and racing to Daniel.

"You're hurt!"

"Shoulder." He rolled and climbed to his feet. "Hell. I'm not letting him get away."

The moonlight let her see the blood spilling down his arm and over the Kevlar vest. Too much blood. Lindsay exclaimed, "You can't go after him."

"Watch me." He took two strides before stopping. "What am I thinking? We can head him off. You can't stay here alone."

She took that to mean she should follow him. He ran for the front of the house, never even turning his head toward the fire that illuminated the night so weirdly. He was intent on the garage. Reaching it, he tapped in a code on a keypad she hadn't even noticed was there and the door rose.

Sirens wailed in the distance, but he paid no more attention to those than he had the fire.

Within moments they were both in his truck. She thought the keys were surely in the house, but he took them from his pocket and started up the engine. He accelerated so fast her head snapped back.

"Can you see him?" he asked.

She searched the open ground. "No. But he could turn around once he knows we're gone."

"Why would he?"

"If he thinks you left me..." Because *she* was the target. She couldn't forget that.

"He stopped to see what we were going to do. He knows you're with me." Daniel's voice was gravel-rough. "He'll have heard the sirens, too. He's running."

The truck swayed as they rocketed toward the road.

DANIEL FOUGHT FOR control as he pushed his pickup to an unsafe speed. His arm would hurt like hell later, but right now it was numb. He could feel the weakness in it, though, and damned if it wasn't his right side. He couldn't believe he'd let that scumsucker wound him. In his fear for Lindsay, he'd come around the corner of the house too fast, incautiously. His own shots had hit the bastard's center mass, he'd swear they had, which must mean the killer wore a vest, too. Of course he did, Daniel thought in disgust. He'd planned for any eventuality before each murder, hadn't he? If he got away this time—

Daniel savagely pulled himself back to the here and now. He'd be at the road in seconds and have to make a decision.

"I heard a car not that long ago," Lindsay said suddenly.

He chanced a quick look at her to see that she gripped her seat belt in one hand, the armrest with the other. She sat so stiffly, her back didn't touch the seat.

"Could you tell where?" he asked.

"I can't be sure, but I think it was right." She had to be terrified, but she hadn't so much as whimpered.

"Smartest place for him to leave the car."

He did brake, but they were still moving fast when he swerved onto the paved two-lane road. The pickup truck rocked and tires squealed as he laid down rubber. Pain finally stabbed his shoulder and upper arm, but it wasn't so bad he couldn't ignore it. As he accelerated again, he saw the flashing lights of an approaching fire truck in his rearview mirror.

Using his injured arm, he reached for his phone. Patted the pocket, then the one on the other side.

He mumbled a profanity. "Lost my phone." And, damn, trying to lift his hand back to the wheel awakened a new bolt of pain. His hand and arm weren't following orders, either. He dismissed thoughts of nerve damage. Like so much else, they could wait.

Impatiently, he asked, "Can you call Melinda or Alvarez?"

She produced her phone and dialed. When a voice answered, she put the call on speaker.

He updated Melinda in a few words and asked her to get as many officers as were immediately available to blockade this corner of the county. "Don't know what he's driving, but I'm betting on the white sedan."

"On my way."

"Wait, are you still there? This guy's got a gun and he's wearing Kevlar. He won't hesitate to shoot."

Some corner of his attention noted that his right hand was covered in blood. He was probably dripping onto the upholstery, too.

A deer appeared in the headlights, leaping a ditch and disappearing before Daniel had to brake. First movement he'd seen.

Maybe he should slow down. What if he passed that white Corolla, tucked out of sight off the road? That piece of scum could wait until the sound of his engine receded, pull out and sedately drive home. Nice to think he'd be spotted by another officer, but in reality there would be only one or two patrolling at this time of night, and they could well be on the other side of town or even responding to a call. Chaney wouldn't do them any more good; at night, his department probably had only one deputy covering the entire county.

Daniel's foot eased up on the accelerator and the speed dropped. At least he had two sets of eyes. At the moment, he trusted Lindsay's more than his own. The pain, or maybe the blood loss, was getting to him.

If this monster escaped to kill again, Daniel might not be able to forgive himself.

"I see something," Lindsay said suddenly.

"What—" Red taillights appeared ahead. Low to the ground. A car, and not a big one. Plus, these had to be on an older model.

Daniel slammed the gas pedal to the floor. With V8

at his control, the truck charged forward. If he thought he could safely run in the dark, he would have. As it was, he saw that the car ahead of him had immediately accelerated, too. Any other car on the road would have maintained a steady speed, or even pulled over when the driver became aware of a larger vehicle bearing down on him at high speed.

Still Lindsay didn't say a word, although he was distantly aware that her body was completely rigid. She knew what was at stake here. She'd been courageous during events far outside her experience.

They were closing in. Near enough to see the car ahead was white, and so small he damn well could run right over it.

"What are you going to do?" she asked, her voice thin.

"Run him off the road." Later he'd be irked that he'd had to damage his own truck, but that wasn't even a consideration right now. He was more worried about what would happen once both vehicles came to a standstill. This wasn't a man who'd put his hands in the air and surrender. Daniel didn't even know if he'd prefer that. A part of him regretted Lindsay's presence, because the knowledge that she was watching would keep him from stepping over the line.

The sedan began to weave from one side of the road to the other in an attempt to keep him from pulling alongside.

"Hold on," Daniel warned, and tapped the other vehicle's bumper. Metal screeched. A small gasp was the only giveaway of Lindsay's tension.

The Corolla kept swerving, but erratically now, as though the driver had lost control. Daniel chose his moment and sped up again, this time scraping his fender alongside the smaller car's. Then he yanked the wheel to the right, and the Corolla flew off the road into a barbed wire fence that worked like an arresting wire on an aircraft carrier deck.

Fighting to keep the truck on the road, Daniel braked hard, but it took time to stop. The minute he did, he threw the gear into Reverse and sped backward.

"Get down," he ordered. "He might come out shooting."

She unsnapped her seat belt and slid to her knees on the floorboard. In a matter of seconds, he braked with the pickup slightly behind the sedan. Then he threw open his door and jumped out, bending over to take advantage of the protection the metal body of his Ford offered.

He pulled his Glock from his lower back but found he couldn't lift it with his right hand. Damn. He had a familiar sensation of time having slowed, as if the scene clicked forward like old-fashioned slides.

The car's driver wasn't moving. He seemed to be slumped forward. With luck his head had slammed into the windshield, but Daniel didn't buy it. Moonlight let him see that the glass hadn't cracked into the telltale spiderweb pattern. Weapon held out in a two-hand grip, his left hand bearing most of the weight, he jumped the ditch and advanced on the tilted white car.

"Police!" he yelled. "Put your hands on your head! Let me see them."

The man didn't move.

Hip against the fender and then the back door, Daniel stayed behind the driver, watching for any giveaways. When he reached the driver door, he had to brace his right hand against the glass of the passenger side back window to free his left hand to wrench open the door.

Not locked, was the last thing he thought before the man now only inches away exploded into motion.

LINDSAY HAD CALLED Melinda even before Daniel jumped out of the truck. She couldn't tell if he even heard her.

"The attacker was wounded, and he ran. Daniel and I pursued in his pickup truck. When we saw an older Toyota Corolla, it sped up. Daniel ran it off the road and he's approaching the driver door now." She named the road and gave Melinda her best guess of how far they'd driven, then ended the call without waiting for a response. She had to see what was happening.

She took out her own gun again, as alien as it felt in her hands, and cautiously raised her head to see Daniel's broad back. He was opening the sedan's driver door with one hand…when the killer twisted in his seat and a gun barked.

Daniel reeled back. Then, shot again or not, he lunged forward and wrapped his arms around the other man and yanked him out of the car.

By that time, Lindsay had jumped out and was scrambling toward the two men wrestling for control. Daniel was the bigger, the more powerful, she saw immediately, but his right arm hung at his side and his gun had disappeared. Had it fallen from his hand?

The truck headlights partially illuminated the scene, just as the car's headlights speared the darkness of what might be a pasture.

Daniel spun his adversary and used his weight and strength to pin him against the back door. But, on a spurt of terror, Lindsay saw the pistol still clutched in the other man's hand. He was struggling to turn it. He couldn't see her approaching, so she got within feet of the two men and cried, "Drop the gun or I'll shoot!"

The barrel swung toward her. She couldn't see most of him, but his arm would do. This close, she couldn't miss. Grimly willing her eyes to stay open, she aimed and squeezed the trigger. As she heard the scream, the gun dropped from his hand.

"I'm kicking his gun under the car," she told Daniel, sounding astonishingly collected.

With what had to be a massive effort, he spun the killer and slammed him face-first against the metal of the car.

"I have cuffs in the glove compartment." Daniel's voice was guttural.

She put the safety on her borrowed gun and tucked it back in her waistband, then made her way back up the bank to the truck. Within moments, she returned.

"I have them."

"Snap one cuff on this wrist." Daniel pulled the man's right hand back despite another agonized scream.

The cuffs were metal ones, thank goodness; she didn't even know how the plastic ones worked. But she closed first one cuff on the wrist Daniel forced into view, then the second.

In moments, the man who'd tried to burn them out of Daniel's house tonight and killed so many people lay facedown on the ground. Daniel drilled one knee between his shoulder blades. "You're under arrest. You have the right to remain silent. Anything you say can and will be used against you in a court of law."

He went on, every word in that same raw, angry voice. Not until he finished did he raise his head.

His expression was nothing Lindsay had ever seen or ever wanted to see again. And yet, for all the rage there, he'd continued to do his job. He would have died to stop this man, both because of the atrocities he'd committed and to keep her safe. Her heart squeezed with love too painful to give joy.

Only then did she lower her gaze to the now diminished man who kept his head turned away from her. She circled behind Daniel, around the feet wearing white athletic shoes stained with blood, until she saw the face.

She wanted to be surprised, but couldn't.

"How could you do such terrible things?" she asked her mentor, her friend.

"I'd have done anything for you." Bitterness corroded his low voice. Without trying to meet her eyes, Glenn turned his head away.

She pressed her hand against her stomach to try to contain the nausea. He'd tortured and killed for her. What had she ever done or said to make him think she'd want any such thing?

She suddenly realized that Daniel was looking at her. Despite his pain and the banked anger, what his eyes held was understanding.

"It was never about you."

She managed a nod and backed away just as a police car screamed to a stop right behind Daniel's truck.

Epilogue

Every time Daniel surfaced from the anesthesia-induced grogginess, he asked for Lindsay. If he got answers, he didn't remember them the next time he awakened.

This time, he opened his eyes, worked his mouth and understood from the curtains pulled around the bed that he was in the hospital and no longer in recovery.

"Lindsay," he mumbled.

Like an angel, she appeared beside the bed. "You're awake." She gave him some sips of water and slivers of ice to roll around in his mouth.

"You're here," he managed. Brilliant.

"Because you kept asking for me." She smiled. "Otherwise they might not have let me in because I'm not family."

He groaned. His family would descend on the hospital room like a plague of locusts once they heard he'd been injured again.

"Melinda called and spoke to your mother. They'll be here in the next hour or two."

He reached across his body with his left hand and seized her wrist. "Don't leave."

She sat on the edge of the bed. "I don't know if I'll be allowed to stay."

"Fianceé."

Her eyes widened. "What?"

He repeated himself.

"I'm…not a very good liar."

"No lie." He worked his mouth until he could speak a little more coherently. "Doesn't have to be."

"You're asking…"

"Please." He took a deep breath that hinted at oncoming pain. "We don't have to hurry, but I don't want you to move out."

"Oh." She nibbled on her lip. "You know your house suffered some damage?"

He hadn't given his house a thought yet. And, damn, then there was his truck. "Bad?"

"According to the fire chief, no. A good part of one wall will need to be replaced, the kitchen door, and some work on the eaves. But with the sprinklers, the fire didn't progress, even fueled by gasoline."

"Good." He ought to release her but didn't want to. "You know what they did to me?"

What she told him rang a bell. The nurse in recovery had probably said the same. The surgeon had removed a bullet from his shoulder, and he had broken ribs from the two bullets that had struck his Kevlar vest.

He looked down at his right hand. The response was sluggish when he commanded it to ball into a fist, but eventually he managed it. He closed his eyes briefly in relief.

A hand cupped his jaw. "You'll have to do some physical therapy to get back full function, but the surgeon is confident that if you do your part, it will happen."

"Good." His jaw was probably scratching the palm of her hand, but he let go of her wrist to lay his left hand atop hers, pressing it to his cheek. He turned his head enough to kiss her palm. Daniel couldn't help noticing she hadn't given him an answer on the marriage/living together question. Or had he actually asked?

Probably not, he decided. He tried again. "Will you stay with me?"

"Here? Or...after they let you go home?"

"Both."

This time, she didn't look away. "The idea is scary for me. You know that. But... I loved living with you. I want to do that. To find out if we both keep feeling the same. So...yes."

"Love you," he whispered.

Lindsay bent forward to touch her forehead to his. "I love you, too."

"You can trust me."

As if startled, she straightened up, searching his eyes. "I know that! How can you think..." And then emotions crossed her face too quickly for him to identify, although bewilderment was in there somewhere. At the end came an unfamiliar softness. "Of course I trust you. You would have given everything to protect me, wouldn't you?"

If by everything, she meant his life, the answer was yes.

A smile bloomed slowly on her face, making him think of dawn. But all she said was, "They'll have to drag me out of here kicking and screaming."

That constituted all the promise he needed. He wrapped his working hand around her nape and drew her down again, until he felt her breath on his neck.

Then he fell asleep again.

* * * * *

COLTON'S UNDERCOVER REUNION

LARA LACOMBE

This one is for my mom,
who helps make it all possible.

Chapter One

Ainsley Colton closed her eyes and let the soothing sounds of ocean waves wash over her.

Deep breath in. Exhale.

Again.

Her muscles relaxed as she repeated the breathing exercises, and gradually, she felt the knots in her stomach ease.

She wasn't normally one for meditation. But with all the stress in her life, she was willing to try anything if it meant staving off a stomach ulcer, or worse.

"You've got to find some way to unplug," Dr. Bleaker had said. She'd looked up at Ainsley during her last visit, dark brown eyes serious behind her gold wire-rimmed glasses. "I mean it, Ainsley. These headaches, your stomach pain—all the tests show there's nothing wrong with you physically. Which means these issues are due to stress. Are you getting enough sleep? Are you exercising at all?"

Ainsley had bit her tongue to keep from laughing at the doctor. She knew the older woman meant well, but seriously? Her father had been shot and her brother Ace was the prime suspect, thanks to an anonymous email someone had sent to the board of her family's company, Colton Oil, that said Ace wasn't a biological Colton. Normally, something like that wouldn't matter, but there was a small clause in the bylaws of the corporation that stated the CEO of the company had to be a Colton by blood. Her father, never one for subtleties, didn't hesitate to oust Ace when the DNA test confirmed that Ace was in fact not a Colton. Her father had been shot soon after his decision, and there were a lot of fingers pointing at her brother.

As the corporate attorney for Colton Oil, she was right in the middle of the legal issues surrounding the company's change in leadership. And as a sister and daughter, her heart had been bruised and battered by the events of the past few months. Ace might not be her brother by blood, but she'd grown up with him. He'd always be her family. It pained her to think of how he must be feeling right now, especially after the things their father had said and done to him. And Ace couldn't have shot Payne. As for the old man, she loved him, too. He wasn't perfect, but he was her dad. Payne Colton was such a force of nature, she couldn't imagine the world without him in it. If only he'd wake up from his coma!

"I mean it, Ainsley," the doctor had said, interrupting her thoughts. "I know you're busy. But if you don't make time for your health, you're going to wind up with an ulcer or a heart attack. Don't work yourself to death. You're only thirty-seven. Your best years are still ahead of you."

Ainsley had smiled and thanked the woman, then hurried back to her office to deal with the latest crisis. But as she'd washed down her fifth antacid of the day with a gulp of stale coffee, she'd been forced to admit Dr. Bleaker was right. She did need to find a way to relax.

So she'd done a little research and decided meditation might be a good option. She didn't have time for yoga classes or a gym membership. But she could carve out fifteen minutes a day to listen to ocean sounds and breathe deeply.

Her cell phone vibrated on her desk, a soft buzz she registered over the meditation soundtrack. She cracked one eye open and stared at it, considering. Should she—?

No, she decided firmly. This meditation stuff wasn't going to help her unless she actually took it seriously. That meant no interruptions. It was only fifteen minutes of her day—the world could wait.

The buzzing stopped. Almost immediately, she heard the muted ring of her secretary's office phone. Someone really wanted to talk to her. Oh, well. Candace would take a message.

Deep breath in—

The door opened, making her jump. "Ms. Colton?"

Candace sounded deeply apologetic. "I know you don't want to be disturbed right now, but your brother is on the line and he says it's an emergency."

"Which brother?" Ainsley kept her eyes closed, tried to stay focused on her breathing. *I'm on a beach*, she told herself. If only that were true!

"It's Asa," Candace replied, using Ace's birth name rather than the nickname his friends and family had adopted.

Ainsley's eyes snapped open, all thoughts of relaxation disappearing between one heartbeat and the next. "I'll take the call," she said, forcing her voice to remain calm. She got to her feet and nodded at Candace, fighting the urge to lunge for the phone that sat on her desk a few feet away. "Thank you."

Candace nodded and backed out of the room, closing the door quietly behind her. Ainsley swore softly as she stepped over to her desk and picked up the receiver.

"Ace?"

"Ainsley, thank God! Why aren't you answering your cell?" He sounded flustered. Ainsley felt her muscles tense all over again. *So much for meditation*, she thought wryly.

"Never mind that. What's going on? You told Candace it was an emergency."

"It is! The police are here. They say they have a warrant."

"Wait, back up." She put her fingers to her forehead and began to massage the spot above her right eyebrow. "Where is here?"

"My condo," Ace said, his tone making it clear this should be obvious. "I came back here after a while. The police are here with a dog and a warrant. What do I do?"

"What are they looking for?" she asked, already walking around the desk to grab her purse from the bottom drawer.

"I don't know yet," he said. "No one's answering my questions."

"Just stay out of the way," she said. "I'm heading there now. I'll be there in a few minutes, and we'll get all this straightened out."

"Hurry," Ace commanded. He was clearly stressed, and she couldn't blame him. She'd be flustered, too, if the police showed up at her door with a K-9 and told her they were going to search the premises.

"I will. Keep your mouth shut," she instructed. "Tell them I'm coming and you'll answer questions once I'm there." With that, she hung up the phone and rushed to the door. "I'll be out for a bit," she said to Candace as she walked past the secretary's desk. "Clear my schedule for the afternoon, please."

"Yes, ma'am," Candace called after her.

Ainsley opted for the stairs, descending as fast as she dared. She was sure the police had their legal ducks in a row—it was highly unlikely they'd risk an illegal search, especially on a member of her family, and given their relation to an MVPD sergeant—but she still wanted to get to Ace quickly. He was already jumpy and freaked out over the events of the past few months, and the last thing she needed was for him to say or do anything that might be interpreted as incriminating.

"Hang on, Ace," she muttered as she climbed behind the wheel of her car. "I'm coming."

IT DIDN'T TAKE long to get there. Ainsley opted for the elevator, not wanting to arrive out of breath. As soon as the doors opened, she stepped into the foyer of Ace's condo and glanced around, looking for her brother.

She found him pacing along the far wall of the living room, in front of the stretch of windows that overlooked Mustang Valley. His hair was mussed, and as she watched, he lifted a hand to run through it in a nervous gesture.

He turned on his heel, caught sight of her. Relief flashed across his face, and for an instant, Ainsley felt ten feet tall. It meant a lot to know that her older brother had called her for help, even though technically he wasn't her brother anymore. Regardless, she was going to do everything in her power to prove he hadn't shot their father.

"Hey guys, she's here!" he yelled, alerting the officers to her arrival.

She crossed the room and hugged Ace, feeling the

tension in his body as she did. "Did anything happen since we last spoke?"

He shook his head, his brown eyes troubled. "I got out of the way, like you said. They're searching in the bedroom now."

"Did you say something, Ace?" a man's voice called out. Ainsley and Ace both turned to see Spencer Colton walk out of the bedroom. He stopped when he saw Ainsley. "Hey there," he said, offering her a nod.

Ainsley lifted one brow. "Spencer," she replied, greeting her cousin. "Or should I say, Sergeant Colton?" She put a bit of extra emphasis on his last name, and he ducked his head.

"I know it's awkward," he said, walking over to join them. "But I'm here in a professional capacity only."

She and Ace weren't close with their distant cousins, but it was still unorthodox that a family member should be here serving a warrant. She decided to let it slide. If there was an issue, she could always bring it up later.

"May I see the warrant?"

A hurt look flashed across Spencer's face, as though he couldn't believe she would doubt his motives. "Of course," he replied. He pulled a folded packet of papers from his back pocket and passed it to her.

Ainsley began to flip through the papers, scanning to find the information she sought. "A gun?"

She looked up at Spencer. "That's what you're hoping to find?"

He nodded, just as Ace interjected, "I don't have a gun!"

Ainsley placed one hand on her brother's arm, silently instructing him to remain quiet. "What's the basis for issuing this warrant?"

Spencer shifted on his feet. "I probably shouldn't tell you this, but..." He shrugged. "Seeing as how you guys are family." He leaned forward and lowered his voice. "We got a tip from someone who said Ace confessed to shooting his father and stashing the gun in his closet."

"That's ludicrous!" Ace said loudly. Ainsley tightened her grip on his arm, her nails digging slightly into his skin. He snapped his mouth shut.

"What's her name?"

Spencer started to shake his head. "Now you know I'm not supposed to—"

Ainsley merely arched her brow and stared him down. Spencer sighed. "All right. Given that Chief Barco approved me working on this case and it could otherwise be a conflict of interest... It was a woman named Destiny Jones."

Beside her, Ainsley felt Ace draw in a breath, preparing to defend himself. She gave his arm a little shake, and he backed down. "Did she say how she knows my client?" She deliberately used formal language, to remind everyone this wasn't a social call.

Spencer glanced at Ace, and twin spots of color appeared high on his cheeks. "She, uh, said it was during an encounter of a personal nature."

"She's lying!" Ace yelled. He shook off Ainsley's hand and stepped forward, bringing him closer to Spencer. "I don't even know a woman named Destiny!"

Spencer held up a hand, palm out to try to diffuse Ace's reaction. "No judgments, man. But we had to check it out."

"So I guess anyone can call you up and spread lies about me, is that it?" Ace threw his arms out in disgust. "This is such a crock of—"

"That seems pretty thin," Ainsley interjected. "How'd you get a judge to sign off on this?" She lifted the warrant, handed it back to Spencer.

"We had enough to get us in the door." His lips pressed together in a thin line. Clearly, her cousin was done talking.

Ace shook his head, still fuming. "Yeah, well, you're not going to find anything," he said. "That woman, whoever she is, is lying."

Seeming sympathy flashed in Spencer's blue eyes. "Between you and me, I hope so. But I still have to do my job."

"Spencer?" A voice called from the bedroom. "We need you back here. Looks like Boris has found something."

Ace sucked in a breath. Spencer shook his head slightly, then turned. "Coming."

Ainsley waited until her cousin had left the room. Then she grabbed Ace's arm and dragged him over to the foyer, as far away from the bedroom as she could get.

"You need to be straight with me, right now," she said, tugging his shirt for emphasis. "What are they going to find in your bedroom?"

"Nothing!" Ace whispered back urgently. "I swear to you, Ainsley, I didn't shoot Dad. You know I didn't. There is no gun in my room because I didn't do it." He met her eyes unflinchingly, his tone, his expression, everything about him absolutely sincere.

"Then what—"

"I don't know!" he interrupted. She heard the edge of panic in his voice and her heart went out to him. He ran a hand through his hair again, causing the strands to stand on end. "But I can tell you this much—I don't know a Destiny Jones. I haven't been with a woman since—" he cut himself off, the tips of his ears going pink as he looked away. "Well, that doesn't matter. What's important is that whoever this woman is, she's lying."

"Why would a stranger lie about you like that?" Ainsley wondered aloud.

"I don't know," he said. He shook his head. "Maybe it's a business thing? Someone trying to get back at me for something I did earlier? Or for money?"

Ainsley nodded slowly. That was definitely possible. Ace had a reputation as a ruthless businessman, and he had his fair share of professional enemies. Had one of them heard about the recent troubles over at Colton Oil and decided to make things harder on Ace?

She opened her mouth to respond, but before she could say anything, she saw Spencer walk out of the bedroom holding an evidence bag.

"Ace?" he called.

Ainsley and Ace returned to the living room. Her gaze zeroed in on the clear bag in Spencer's hand, and her stomach dropped as she saw its contents.

Spencer lifted his arm, showing Ace the gun. "We're going to need you to come down to the station and answer a few questions."

Three hours later...

AINSLEY SANK INTO her desk chair with a sigh, feeling wrung out. She was tired, both from the events of the afternoon and her struggles to manage Ace's reactions to everything.

Her brother had immediately and emphatically insisted the gun that Spencer's scent hound, Boris, had discovered was not his. She believed him, but the police weren't quite as willing to take him at his word. And why should they? A woman had called in a tip saying Ace had a gun in his closet, and lo and behold, they'd found it. It was a compelling piece of evidence, and possibly the weapon that had been used to shoot Payne Colton.

Except, it was all so very neat and tidy. Too neat,

in Ainsley's opinion. The more she thought about it, the more plausible Ace's theory about a business or personal rival sounded. It was the perfect way to punish Ace for his steamroller business strategy, and she was willing to bet there were a lot of disgruntled souls he'd left in his wake as CEO of Colton Oil.

But as much as she wanted to help her brother, she was going to have to call in reinforcements. It wouldn't be appropriate for her to handle Ace's legal issues while still working for Colton Oil. Besides, she wasn't a defense attorney, and after the discovery of the gun in Ace's closet, her brother had now become the prime suspect in their father's shooting.

"Don't leave town," Spencer had cautioned after he'd declared Ace was free to go.

"We'll definitely have more questions for you later," Detective Kerry Wilder, their adoptive brother Rafe's fiancée, had added.

"I'm sure you will," Ace had grumbled. "I've always been a suspect."

Ainsley had managed to drag her brother away before his temper had flared again. She understood why he was so upset, but every time he got emotional it only made him appear more guilty.

"Stay here," she'd told him, dropping him off at his condo. "I know the best defense attorney in the state. I'm going to call in a favor."

"I don't want someone else," Ace had said. "I want you."

"You can't have me," she'd told her brother. "This isn't my specialty. Trust me, this guy is good. You don't need to worry."

"I'm worried as hell," he'd grumbled. "But I do trust you."

She'd been touched by his admission, once again feeling a spurt of pride at the fact that her big brother was relying on her. Now, in the privacy of her office, she allowed herself a little smile.

Her cell phone sat on her desk. She reached out and traced her fingertip along the edge, gathering up her courage to take this next step. She'd promised her brother the best defense attorney in the state. She owed it to him to deliver.

Even if it meant calling the man who'd broken her heart.

She took a deep breath and picked up the phone before she could change her mind. She'd deleted Santiago's number years ago, but it didn't matter. Her fingers danced across the keypad without hesitation, punching in the numbers she still knew by heart.

He picked up on the first ring. "Ainsley." His voice was deep and smooth. A tingle shot down her spine and she closed her eyes, wishing he hadn't answered so quickly. She'd wanted a few more seconds to compose herself, to prepare to speak to him again.

She cleared her throat. "Hello, Santiago. How are you?"

"Better, now that I'm talking to you." He'd always

been so charismatic. It seemed the years had done nothing to diminish his charm. "To what do I owe this pleasant surprise?"

Ainsley swallowed hard, pushing down her pride. Ace. She was doing this for her brother. "I need your help."

"Of course," Santiago replied. "Are you in your office?"

She frowned. "Yes. But—"

"Excellent," Santiago said, cutting her off. "I'll be there in five minutes."

"You'll what?" she exclaimed. But he'd already ended the call, leaving her with nothing but a dial tone.

Ainsley hung up and placed the phone on her desk, her thoughts a jumbled mess. He couldn't be coming here. That wasn't the deal. She'd bargained on talking to him only, giving him Ace's information and letting him take things from there. She hadn't intended on seeing him again.

And what was he doing in town anyway? He didn't live in Mustang Valley. It was the only reason she'd been able to get over him after he'd broken her heart years ago. If she'd had to see him all the time, she'd still be pining for the man. His move to New York after their break-up had been a bit of a gift. She'd heard through the professional grapevine he'd returned to Phoenix, but she hadn't expected to find him in the comparatively sleepy town of Mustang Valley.

She lifted her hand, brushing it over her hair. This was really happening. In a few minutes, Santiago Morales was going to walk through her door.

Would her heart be able to handle it?

DAMN. SHE LOOKS GOOD.

Santiago pushed the thought aside and offered a smile to Ainsley's secretary. The woman blushed prettily and nodded before turning to leave. Normally, he'd take such a reaction as a compliment, maybe even an excuse to invite her to dinner. But now that he'd seen Ainsley again, he only had eyes for her.

Had it really been five years since their breakup? Five years since he'd left to chase his dreams in New York City, opting to prioritize his career over his personal life? In some ways, it felt like a lifetime ago. But standing in Ainsley's office, watching the play of emotions on her face as he drew closer, it suddenly seemed like only a few hours had passed since he'd made his choice.

She looked different now. Her brown hair was shorter, falling to her shoulders instead of down her back. God, how he'd loved to wrap those strands around his hands! Her hair had always felt like silk on his skin, a soft caress that had driven him mad. Even now, just thinking about it gave him goose bumps.

Ainsley watched him approach, her blue eyes guarded and her delicate features arranged in a carefully neutral expression. Her skin was still pale, a testament to the amount of time she spent in her office. She sported some fine lines at the corners of her eyes, and he hoped they were from laughing and not frowning. He'd always wanted the best for her, had always wanted her to be happy.

Which was why he'd left.

He wasn't husband material—never had been, never would be. It was something he'd always known about himself, and given his family history of miserable marriages, he wasn't looking to take on that particular role.

So he'd left, before he could disappoint Ainsley with his shortcomings.

Santiago forced himself to smile as he came to a stop in front of her desk. His arms ached to embrace her, to have her fill the Ainsley-shaped hollow space in his soul that he'd lived with over the past five years. But he could tell by her apprehensive air that such an overture would not be welcomed.

"Ainsley," he said. Just saying her name gave him a kind of relief. After he'd left, he'd done his best to push all thoughts of her to the side. He'd thrown himself into his work, and his efforts had paid off. He'd made a name for himself, first in New York City, then in Phoenix. Coming back to Arizona had never been part of his plan, but when the firm had called a year and a half ago, they'd made him an offer he simply couldn't refuse.

So he'd packed his things and moved back to the

land of sun. And Ainsley. He hadn't expected to hear from her—after all, things hadn't ended well between them. Even so, he couldn't deny he'd felt a spark of hope when he'd seen her name on his phone screen. He knew it had taken a lot for her to reach out to him. And while he knew she had zero interest in seeing him again in a personal capacity, part of him wondered if they couldn't find their way to being friends again.

"Hello, Santiago." She didn't offer her hand, so he didn't either. It was clear she didn't want him to touch her, and he always respected a woman's boundaries.

She gestured to the seat behind him. "Please, make yourself comfortable. Would you like something to drink?"

"No, thank you," he replied, lowering himself into the chair. He made an obvious show of studying her face. "You look wonderful," he said simply.

If she appreciated the compliment, she didn't show it. "Thank you," she said flatly. She leaned back a bit in her chair, evidently conducting her own appraisal. "I'm surprised you're in town," she said. "What's a big fish like you doing in such a small pond?"

Ouch. He tried not to wince at the barb. He hadn't used those exact words, but that had been the gist of his argument when he'd left five years ago. "I can't grow my career here," he'd said, gesturing to the window to encompass Mustang Valley. "I'm not going to spend the rest of my life working on drunken assault cases and DUIs." He'd needed to move to New York to take on the kind of high-profile cases that interested him. Given his childhood, he'd known marriage wasn't in his future. He hadn't enjoyed hurting her, but there had been no other way.

"I'm here on family business," he said, running his hand down the length of his tie. But he didn't want to talk about that just yet. First, he wanted to hear her story. "Why don't you tell me how I can help you?"

Ainsley pressed her lips together, and he got the impression that calling him had been a last resort. Worry flared to life in his belly. What was going on? Was she in some kind of trouble? He'd assumed she'd called him on behalf of someone else, but in the face of her obvious reluctance, he had to wonder if he'd been wrong.

"You know I'll help you," he said quietly. He'd never stopped caring for her, probably never would. He'd made it clear when he'd left that he would always be there for her. And even though he'd never expected her to turn to him again, he was pleased that she had now.

She nodded, emotion flashing in her eyes. "It's my brother," she said finally.

Bit by bit, she told him the whole story. The email to the company's board, the DNA test, her father's shooting. And the gun they'd found today in Ace's condo. He'd heard some of the details before, thanks to news coverage of the story. But she'd filled in several gaps in his knowledge and he realized how convoluted the whole thing actually was.

"He didn't do this," she said, leaning forward a bit. "I know it looks bad right now, but I also know my brother. He's not capable of doing something like this."

Santiago didn't argue. In his experience, people were often very capable of doing shocking things, and often for less motivation that what she'd just outlined. But he wasn't here to argue with Ainsley about the darker aspects of human nature. He'd only met Ace a few times before; he didn't know the man well enough to form an opinion on the matter.

"So are you asking me to advise you?" She wasn't a defense attorney, but he knew she could handle this case if she wanted to, especially with a little help.

She shook her head. "No. I'm asking you to take the case."

He leaned back, considering. What he'd told her earlier was true—he was in town on a family matter. But perhaps he could kill two birds with one stone?

"All right," he said slowly. "I'll take the case."

Relief flashed across Ainsley's face. "Thank you. I'll have a contract drawn up immediately. We will pay your full rate, plus expenses."

Santiago waved this away. "I'm not worried about the money. There's something else I need from you."

Ainsley's eyes filled with wariness, and he felt a wall go up between them. "Oh? What's that?"

"You're not the only one who has a sibling in trouble."

Ainsley arched an eyebrow, silently inviting him to continue.

"It's my sister, Gabriela," he began. "She married a real piece of work. She's been unhappy for a long time, and she agreed to try counseling. They went to this place called The Marriage Institute. It's a few miles outside town—have you heard of it?"

Ainsley shook her head. "No," she said. "Is it like a retreat of some kind?"

"That's exactly what it is," he said, relieved that she seemed to understand. "Gabriela and her husband Eric went, and after a week there, she agreed to sign some paperwork nullifying large sections of their prenuptial agreement, specifically the clauses regarding spousal infidelity and inheritance upon her death."

Ainsley frowned. "That doesn't sound right."

"No, it doesn't," he agreed. "But I looked at the documents and they appear to be solid, from a legal standpoint."

"Why would she sign such a thing? Your parents were always vigilant about your inheritance terms. I'm sure they treated your sister the same way."

Santiago nodded. "Believe me, they did. If anything, they were even more careful with Gabriela's share once she decided to get married." His family's wealth went back generations, thanks to careful stewardship from his great-grandfather and then grandfather. His own parents had added to the layers of protection guarding their money, wanting to ensure their family's future for decades to come. Gabriela's engagement had come with a veritable forest of paperwork for her would-be husband to sign, all in the interest of making sure he couldn't touch a penny of her share of the Morales fortune.

And then his sister had undermined most of it with a stroke of the pen.

"I think Gabriela was coerced into signing the paperwork," he said, leaning forward. "I think this Marriage Institute is a sham, that they don't really care about helping people at all. I think they take bribes from spouses and go to work brainwashing the unsuspecting partner until they agree to see things their spouse's way. That's the only reason Gabriela would sign those papers." He shook his head, frustration rising in his chest the way it always did when he thought about what had happened. "I've spoken to some other people who attended the retreat. They all tell the same story. Gabriela isn't the only one they took advantage of—there are several other people out there who noticed irregularities in their joint accounts that their exes never really explained. Missing funds that were probably used as bribes. My sister isn't stupid. She was tricked. And I'm going to prove it."

"How are you going to do that?" Ainsley asked. "I can't imagine they'll just let you poke around the retreat and ask accusatory questions."

"They won't," he agreed. "Which is why I'm going there undercover."

Ainsley frowned. "What do you mean?" There was a note of concern in her tone, and for a second, he wondered if she was worried about him getting into trouble.

"I'm going to pretend to be a client, there with my wife. We're both going to offer them a bribe, then find out which person they decide to help."

"Oh." Ainsley visibly relaxed, apparently assuming she'd deduced his request. "So do you need me to draw up some sham paperwork that your fake wife wants you to nullify?"

"Nope." Santiago shook his head, nerves tingling in his belly as he arrived at his real reason for coming to Ainsley's office. "I want you to be my wife."

Chapter Two

Ainsley stared at Santiago, certain she had misunderstood. Surely he wasn't really suggesting she play his wife for his little sting operation?

"Excuse me?"

His green gaze didn't waver. "I said I want you to be my wife. You're the only one who I can trust to help me with this."

So he was serious.

The initial shock faded as anger bubbled to the surface. The nerve of this man! To sit here in her office and casually suggest she play his wife, when he'd walked out on her five years ago, claiming he wasn't the marrying kind! It was a cruel joke; even he had to know that.

She shook her head. "That's not funny."

"I'm not joking," he said calmly. "I meant what I said, Ainsley. I trust you."

"Find someone else," she said flatly, determined not to let her emotions show.

"There is no one else," he replied.

"Don't you have a girlfriend who could do the job?"

He shook his head, opened his mouth to speak again. But she cut him off. "Hire someone, then."

"It's not the same," he said. Santiago leaned forward, his expression earnest. "I know this is awkward."

Ainsley snorted, and he had the grace to look embarrassed. "Believe me, I wouldn't ask you if it wasn't so important."

"I still don't understand why you can't hire someone. I'm sure there's at least one underworked actress in Phoenix looking for some extra cash."

"I'm sure there is, too," he replied. "But you and I have a history together. An intimacy that can't be faked. The people running the retreat aren't stupid. They'll know in an instant if I bring an actress with me. But you..." He trailed off, tipped his head to the side. "You know me."

It was true—she did. They'd met in law school and quickly become inseparable. She'd loved him with all her heart, had spent hours imagining their lives together, dreaming of what things would be like. She couldn't have children thanks to a childhood surgery that had resulted in massive internal scarring, leaving her infertile. Santiago knew that, and he'd assured her that wasn't a problem for him, that he didn't want kids. Everything had seemed so perfect—their future bright. She'd given him years, only to be cast aside so he could move to New York and become a big shot.

A part of her had always wondered if he'd told the truth. Had he really left to chase his professional dreams? Or had he wanted to find a woman who could give him children, in case he changed his mind later?

It was a question that still haunted Ainsley from time to time. She'd had years to accept the fact that she would never be pregnant, never have a baby come from her body. There were moments she still grieved the loss of possibility, but she'd made her peace with it. If she ever decided she had to be a mother, she'd look into adoption. Perhaps Santiago hadn't felt the same way. Maybe that had turned out to be a deal-breaker after all, despite his words to the contrary.

Eventually, Ainsley had decided it didn't matter. Whatever his motivations, he was gone from her life. She'd tried to move on, and for the most part, she'd done so successfully.

But now he was back, pouring salt in the wounds he'd inflicted, wearing an apologetic smile and shrugging as if to say, "What can I do?"

Why did he have to look so damn handsome, too? His charcoal suit fit him to perfection, and his crisp white button-down was open at the collar, providing a tantalizing glimpse of his golden tan skin. She knew from experience how warm he was, how solid he felt pressed up against her body. How he could read her moods with just a glance, know exactly what she needed from him at any given moment. He'd felt like an extension of her soul, and when he'd left she'd felt like her world had shifted overnight, never to be the same again. And just like the earthquake that had rocked Mustang Valley a few months ago, Santiago's departure had left permanent marks on her heart.

"Please, Ainsley," he said. His voice was low, but there was a subtle note of anxiety that cut through her anger. "I'm not trying to hurt you again. But I need you."

She knew how much the admission cost him. Santiago's pride ran deep, and he'd always hated to ask for help. It was a big deal for him to admit he needed her now.

But he was also asking for a huge favor.

Ainsley sighed, considering her options. Like it or not, she needed Santiago. Or rather, Ace needed Santiago. If she refused to play a part in his undercover operation, he might very well walk out of her office and leave her and her brother high and dry. It seemed the only way she was going to be able to help Ace was if she pushed aside her feelings and helped the man who'd broken her heart.

"All right," she said finally.

Relief flashed across his face and the breath gusted out of him. Ainsley was a little surprised at his reaction—apparently, he hadn't taken her agreement for granted.

"Thank you," he said. He moved his hands as though he wanted to reach across the desk and touch her, but stopped short of the gesture. "I can't tell you how much I appreciate this."

"Don't thank me yet," she cautioned. "This plan of yours might not work."

"It will. I know it will." He got to his feet, all traces of vulnerability gone as his confident facade slipped back into place. "I'm going to call and make the appointment at the center. I'm hoping to get in this weekend, and the retreat lasts a week. Will that work for your schedule?"

Ainsley stood and made a show of checking her calendar, though she knew it would be fine. "All right," she said. "I can clear some time."

"Excellent." Santiago smiled at her, flashing the dimples that never failed to make women sigh. "I will contact your brother. I should be able to make some headway on his case before our session at the center."

"Use my middle name and your fake surname when you register us," she said.

Santiago tilted his head to the side. "Grace Rodriguez?"

Ainsley nodded. "This place is close to Mustang Valley, so there's a chance people working there might recognize the name Ainsley Colton. If you want this sham to work, you'd better use my middle name so no one questions our relationship."

Santiago nodded. "Good idea. I was going to use a different last name, just to make sure no one connected me with my sister. That will also provide an extra layer of coverage for you as well."

He turned to go, moving across the room with that smooth gait she knew so well. "Santiago," she called, just before he reached the door.

At the sound of his name, Santiago stopped and looked back. "Yes?"

There was just one thing she had to know before he left. "If I had said no, would you still have taken my brother's case?" Was this simply a quid pro quo arrangement? Or would he have helped regardless of her answer?

He didn't hesitate. "Of course." He studied her for a few seconds, his gaze probing. "I once told you I would always be there for you. I meant it."

Ainsley sucked in a breath as a tingle shot down her spine. He'd said those words to her just before he'd moved to New York. At the time, she'd thought he was simply trying to make her feel better, to make it seem that even though he was blowing up her dreams of a future together, he still wanted to be friends.

Apparently, he'd been making a promise.

She nodded, her throat too tight to speak. Damn him! This would have been easier if he'd kept things transactional—a you scratch my back, I'll scratch yours kind of thing. But he had to go and bring up his parting words, stirring up all kinds of emotions she'd thought were long buried.

Santiago's expression changed, a knowing look

entering his eyes. For a second, she thought he was going to come back, to embrace her the way he'd always done in the past when she'd been upset. But he stayed by the door, apparently recognizing it wasn't his place to comfort her anymore.

He offered her a small nod. "I'll be in touch."

Ainsley tried to smile. "Great," she replied, trying to sound casual. "I'll clear my schedule starting on Friday for the next week."

He inclined his head in a nod of acknowledgment. Then he turned and walked out of her office.

Ainsley waited until the door shut behind him before dropping back into her chair. Seeing Santiago again had been challenging—he was still handsome, still charming.

Still her missing piece.

She shook her head, dismissing the romantic notion. She didn't need anyone to complete her. She was a strong, intelligent woman who had friends and family who loved her and a career she enjoyed. She wasn't broken or somehow less than simply because she was single.

But there were times when she was lonely.

Once upon a time, Santiago had felt like her other half. He'd been her safe place, the person she went to when she had joys to share or sorrows to grieve. He'd always been there for her, a steadfast, constant presence that she'd thought would always be part of her life. When he'd left, she had mourned as though he'd died. It had taken years, but she'd gotten to the point where she didn't think of him every day anymore, didn't feel that hollow ache in the center of her chest whenever something reminded her of him.

Now that she'd seen him again though, she felt bruised. All her hard work, all the time and energy she'd put into moving on—it wasn't enough. It was like the past five years hadn't happened, and she was back at square one, feeling raw and vulnerable and exposed all over again.

Playing the part of Santiago's wife would be a particularly ironic job since he'd left her because he hadn't wanted to commit. In the weeks after he'd moved, she'd sometimes fantasized about him coming back, metaphorical hat in hand, realizing he'd been wrong to let her go. He'd get down on his knees and beg her to take him back, plead for her forgiveness and grovel for his shortsighted mistake. The fantasy had helped her feel better, even though she'd known it would never happen.

And yet, in a strange twist of fate, he'd returned. Although he hadn't groveled, he did need her help.

At least this time, she knew the score from the beginning.

"It's business," she muttered to herself. "Only a business arrangement." No matter how personal it seemed, she had to remember that she was playing a part. Yes, they shared a past. But they didn't have a future together. She would do this favor for him, he would help her brother, and then they'd part ways and go back to their separate lives.

For a split second, she thought about backing out. Santiago had said he'd still help Ace even if she didn't help him. Why put herself through the emotional wringer if she didn't absolutely have to?

But she dismissed the idea with her next breath. If she didn't help Santiago, she'd feel like she owed him for taking Ace's case. At least this way, they were balanced. A few days of awkwardness was preferable to being indebted to Santiago.

And maybe in some ways this would be good for her. She'd spent so much time mourning what might have been, she'd lost sight of all the reasons why she and Santiago might not have worked out to begin with. All his annoying traits had faded into the recesses of her memories. Perhaps a reminder of his imperfections and bad habits was just what she needed to realize how lucky she was to still be single.

Ainsley straightened, warming to the thought. It was the perfect approach to take for this upcoming ordeal. Instead of focusing on what she'd lost, she'd think about what she'd avoided and what she had now. Best of all, it would help her keep Santiago at arm's length, which was what she needed to do for both her heart and the purposes of his ruse. It would be a win-win-win all around. Ace would get the best defense lawyer in the state; Santiago would help his sister; and she would have a renewed appreciation for her life.

She took a deep breath, recalling her interrupted meditation session earlier in the day. Everything would go back to normal soon. She just had to get through this first.

Friday morning.

"More coffee?"

Santiago glanced up at the waitress, who stood next to the table holding a full carafe. "Yes, please." He lifted his cup to make it easier for her to pour, then brought the brew to his face to inhale the fragrant steam. Bubba's Diner wasn't the fanciest place in town, but the coffee was hot and the pancakes were fluffy.

"You ready to order yet?"

"Another moment, please," Santiago said with a smile. "I'm sure my friend will be here shortly."

The waitress nodded and walked off to attend another table. Santiago glanced at his watch. Ace Colton was late.

He added a packet of sugar and a dollop of cream to his coffee, then stirred gently. Just as he brought the mug to his lips the door to the diner opened, setting a string of bells jingling.

Ace walked inside and stopped just past the threshold. Santiago threw up his arm and gave him a little wave, and Ace nodded.

"Sorry I'm late," he said as he slid into the booth across from Santiago. "I had a rough night."

He looked it, too, with his tousled hair, stubbled cheeks and red-rimmed eyes.

"I understand," Santiago said, offering his hand. It was the truth—he hadn't slept well either, but for different reasons. Seeing Ainsley again had been a shock to his system. He'd assumed the passage of time would have dulled his body's response to her, but he'd been wrong. He'd spent last night tossing and turning, wanting nothing more than to go back to her office and lay her back on that wide desk of hers. Or the coffee table he'd spied in the sitting area. Or any flat surface, really. He wasn't picky. He just ached to feel her again, to have her in his arms once more.

Ace shook his hand, pulling him out of his thoughts. "I remember you." His gaze turned assessing. "You dumped my sister to chase your career." He tilted his head to the side. "How'd that work out for you?"

Guilt speared Santiago's heart, but he ignored the uncomfortable sensation. "Depends on your perspective," he said, deliberately keeping his tone light. He wasn't about to get into the details of his past with Ainsley with her brother, and especially not here.

Ace studied him a moment, and Santiago got the impression the other man was debating on staying or going. "Ainsley says you're the best," he said finally.

Pleasure bloomed in Santiago's chest. It meant a lot to know that despite their past, Ainsley still thought highly of his professional skills and trusted him to defend her brother. "I'm glad she called me." *For more reasons than one.* "I think I can help you."

A look of relief flashed across Ace's face. "I trust my sister's judgment. If she thinks you're good, I do, too."

Smart man. Santiago knew from experience Ainsley had a brilliant legal mind. She'd had her pick of firms, but her loyalty to her family had led her to choose corporate law and Colton Oil.

"Ainsley told me about your situation. But I'd like to hear the details from you, if you don't mind." Santiago liked to hear his clients tell their stories firsthand, as often their body language and facial expressions told him just as much as their words.

Ace nodded, then started talking, pausing only to place an order for food and coffee when the waitress stopped by the table again. He told Santiago about the initial email and the board's reaction, the DNA test and Payne Colton's response to finding out Ace wasn't his biological son. Ace tried to hide it, but it was clear from the anguish in his eyes that Payne's actions had hurt him deeply.

He expressed shock over Payne's shooting, and even more disbelief at the fact the police had found a gun in his condo yesterday.

"It's not mine, I swear it," Ace said, leaning forward for emphasis. "I don't know where it came from, but someone must have planted it."

Santiago nodded, jotting down notes on a small pad. “Does anyone else have a key to your condo?”

Ace shook his head, but then stopped and frowned. “The cleaning lady,” he said. “And maybe the property management company?” He sounded uncertain about the last possibility.

“Let’s start with the cleaning lady first,” Santiago replied. “What’s her name?”

Ace rattled off the information, and Santiago dutifully recorded her name and number. “Any security tapes?” he asked.

“I do have some cameras installed inside,” Ace said. “And I know the building has some security cameras.”

“All right. I’ll want to see the footage from your cameras,” Santiago said.

“I can email the files to you, but the police already looked at everything,” Ace said. He sounded discouraged. “They said they didn’t find anything.”

Santiago smiled. “They may not have found evidence of a crime, but I have a different set of criteria for evaluation.”

Ace considered that for a second. “I like it,” he said, nodding slowly.

“What about this source? What did the police say her name was again?”

“Destiny Jones.” Ace practically spat the name. “I have no idea who she is.”

"The police told you she said she'd seen the gun during an intimate encounter?"

"Yeah. Except I've never seen the woman, much less slept with her!"

Santiago tilted his head to the side. "This is only going to work if you're 100 percent honest with me." He had to know everything about Ace's actions over the past few months, even the details that might be considered embarrassing.

Ace's eyes widened. "I'm telling you the truth! I have no idea who she is. She could walk right up to me and I wouldn't know her."

"Okay." He decided to take Ace at his word. The man didn't appear to be lying; in fact, the whole time he'd been talking he'd seemed genuine and sincere. It was still possible Santiago was being played, but if that was the case, Ace Colton was a terrific actor.

"Any chance you know her by a different name?"

Ace shook his head. "How would I know that?"

Santiago took a sip of coffee. "I'm asking you if you've taken a woman back to your condo for personal reasons. Maybe someone you don't know very well, or only just met? A professional, perhaps?" Ace looked aghast, so Santiago held up a hand. "I'm not here to judge you. I'm just trying to find out if this woman got inside your condo by pretending to be someone else."

"That's not possible," Ace said flatly. "I'm not in a relationship, and I don't need to pay for companionship. The only woman who has regular access to my place is the maid, and Maria has worked for me for years. I doubt she'd do something like this."

"Fair enough," Santiago said easily. "Let's switch gears. Who found Payne after he'd been shot?" He hadn't had time to pull the police reports this morning before coming to the diner. It was on his to-do list, but given the time crunch he was facing, he'd decided to prioritize talking to Ace and hearing his side of things. He wanted to gather as much information as possible before Saturday, when he and Ainsley had their appointment at The Marriage Institute. The two of them were going to have to share a room for the duration of the retreat, and bringing a pile of work was a surefire way to keep both his hands and his mind occupied.

"The Colton Oil cleaning lady found him," Ace said. "Her name is Joanne Bates. She's worked for the company for the past five years. I don't have her contact information with me, but I know Ainsley can get you her number."

Santiago nodded. "Sounds good."

The waitress delivered their food. Santiago asked Ace a few more questions between bites of pancakes and eggs, getting to know the man's temperament. He'd done some online research last night and had learned from several industry articles that Ace had a reputation as a ruthless businessman.

"Have you ever double-crossed someone in a deal?"

Ace shrugged. "I'm sure it probably felt that way to some people, but I'm always careful to do things by the book. My actions are always legal, even though they might not be nice."

"Can you think of anyone who would want to frame you for Payne's attempted murder? Any enemies in your personal or business life who want to see you suffer?"

Ace took a bite of bacon and chewed, his expression thoughtful. "Not off the top of my head," he said. "I've been thinking about it since yesterday, when the cops found that gun. Ainsley thinks maybe someone is trying to get me back for a business deal gone wrong, but I can't come up with any people who would feel that way." He took a sip of coffee and shrugged. "The people I deal with all know the score. I do what's necessary to advance my company. They're the same way." A shadow crossed his face. "At least, it *was* my company."

Santiago felt a pang of sympathy for the guy. It had to be hard, losing his job, his family, his identity all at the same time.

They finished up and Santiago signaled for the check. He had a lot of work ahead of him, and the sooner he got started, the better.

"Thanks for meeting me on such short notice," he said as he signed the credit card receipt.

"Of course," Ace said. "I appreciate you taking my case."

"I'll probably have some more questions for you," Santiago said. "I know the police already told you this, but you need to stay in town. Don't give them a reason to suspect you more than they already do."

Ace nodded. "I know. I'm just tired of getting blamed for something I didn't do."

"I can understand that," Santiago replied. "And I'll do my best to prove you're not the one who shot Payne."

They stood and headed for the door. "Let me know what you need from me," Ace said, shaking Santiago's hand once they'd stepped outside. "Anything I can do to help you, I will."

"Thank you," Santiago said. "I'll be in touch."

They parted ways, and Santiago glanced down the street. The police department was only a few blocks away, at the end of Mustang Boulevard. The sun was bright, but the heat of the day had yet to settle over the town. A walk would help him organize his thoughts, so he set off in the direction of the one-story brick building.

He walked past a few storefronts, his mind ticking through options and making a mental to-do list. A kid on a bicycle careened toward him, so he stepped to the side to let the child pass. The move brought him up against the display windows of a jewelry store, and he was confronted by the sight of dozens of diamond rings, all sparkling in the sun.

Santiago's stomach dropped as he realized he

needed to buy Ainsley—and himself—rings. They were supposed to be married, after all, and married people wore wedding bands. But would she do that for him? Or was that taking things one step too far?

He remained rooted to the spot, indecision keeping him from walking away but also preventing him from going into the store. They would make a more convincing couple if they had wedding rings. If he'd hired a woman to play the part of his wife, he wouldn't hesitate to supply the necessary prop. But Ainsley wasn't just any woman. And this wouldn't be just any ring.

Santiago shook his head, wishing for the millionth time there had been some way to preserve their relationship. But given his own dismal family history where love was concerned, he'd known his best option was to focus all his energy on his career and making a name for himself. At least he'd have some fulfillment in his life, even though legal briefs didn't exactly keep him warm at night.

There had been times he'd questioned his decision. But in those moments of doubt, he'd only had to think of his parents and their seemingly permanent state of misery to know he'd made the right choice. His actions had paid off, at least professionally. He'd done well for himself career-wise. And he hadn't lacked for company on a personal level. But he'd never truly connected with anyone the way he had with Ainsley. His relationships had been pleasant but superficial, and he'd been careful to ensure that the women he'd dated didn't get the wrong idea about a future with him.

He simply wasn't the marrying kind.

The men in his family were cursed when it came to marriage. He'd never met his grandparents, but his father had told him how unhappy they'd been together. And his own parents had made no secret of their disdain for each other. It was still a mystery to him why his parents had stayed together, but Gabriela had once told him she thought their mother and father wouldn't separate because they hated each other too much to want to risk the other finding happiness with someone else. It made a sick kind of sense—they were locked in a self-destructive cycle, where punishing each other was more important than their own joy.

Growing up, Santiago had simply assumed he'd be alone. But when he'd met Ainsley in law school, he hadn't been able to stay away from her. She was totally unlike his mother, her opposite in practically every way. Ainsley had taught him that relationships didn't have to be prisons of misery, that both people could and should be happy together. And they had been, for a while.

But as the years had passed, Santiago had known Ainsley wanted to settle down. She'd made no secret of her desire for marriage, just as he'd been up-front about the fact that he wasn't marriage material. When the job in New York had come up, he'd jumped at the chance to leave. Better to break it off while they still liked each other than let their affections wither and die because he couldn't give her what she wanted most. No way was he going to follow in his parents' footsteps.

He'd never thought he would be in the position of picking out a wedding ring. And yet here he was, standing outside a jewelry store and checking out the sparkling display.

A small part of him was curious about the process. Ainsley was the only woman in his life he might even imagine marrying, so it was somehow fitting he needed to pick out a wedding set for her. But not a diamond. Diamonds were significant—they meant commitment, a white dress, the whole nine yards. No, he needed something more subtle. Something that would look nice, but that wouldn't send her mixed signals. He knew she wasn't happy about doing him this favor, and he couldn't blame her. He'd broken her heart five years ago, was lucky she'd even agreed to speak with him. Buying her a diamond ring and asking her to wear it would just be cruel, and he never wanted to hurt her.

Santiago peered past the window display, trying to see deeper into the store. Surely they carried more than just diamonds?

Only one way to find out. With a sigh, he pulled open the door and stepped inside.

Chapter Three

Still at the office?

Ainsley read Santiago's text later that day and frowned. Yes, she was working late. But she wasn't really in the mood to talk right now.

Yes, she wrote back. Big project.

His reply was swift. Excellent. Be right there.

"Oh, come on," she muttered. Was he really going to barge into her office on such short notice two days in a row? She was grateful he'd taken Ace's case, but she had her limits.

Ten minutes later, there was a knock on her door.

She got to her feet and headed across the office, stopping for a second as she caught a glimpse of herself in the mirror on the wall. Her hair looked a bit frazzled, and her blouse was wrinkled. She couldn't fix her shirt, but she did a quick U-turn and snagged an elastic band off her desk. Working quickly, she smoothed her hair back into a short ponytail. Then she shrugged into her blazer, hoping it would hide the wrinkles. It was silly, she knew, but she wanted to look good in front of Santiago. Let him see what he'd been missing over the years. Her pride demanded nothing less.

He smiled when she opened the door, those dimples making an appearance once more. "Thanks for seeing me."

She arched a brow and stepped aside so he could enter. "You didn't give me much choice."

He chuckled, the low sound going straight to her belly. "That's true, I didn't." He held up a large paper bag as he walked past her. "Do you still like orange chicken?"

Ainsley caught a whiff of the hot Chinese food and her mouth watered. She was trying to cram in as much work as possible before the retreat, so she'd skipped lunch thanks to back-to-back meetings. The granola bar she'd snagged a few hours ago was a distant memory to her empty stomach.

"I do," she replied, restraining the urge to wrest the bag from his grasp. "But you didn't have to bring dinner." It was a thoughtful gesture. It also stung a little. How many nights had they spent together, poring over legal texts while munching on pizza or other takeout?

Santiago shrugged and placed the bag on the conference table set up on the right side of the office. "I needed to talk to you, and I'm hungry. Thought you might be, too. This seemed like the most efficient use of our time."

She couldn't fault his logic. Ainsley gathered paper plates from the cabinet next to the table and joined him as he removed box after box of food from the bag.

"I got a little of everything," he explained, pointing to each carton as he named the contents.

Ainsley took an egg roll. "Any mustard sauce?" she asked hopefully.

Santiago reached into the bag and pulled out a few packets with a grin. "Of course," he said. "I know better than to leave that behind."

Ainsley smiled, feeling a little touched that he'd remembered her preferences after so long apart.

They dished food onto their plates and for a few minutes, they were both quiet as they focused on those first bites.

"I met your brother this morning," he said after a bite.

"I know." She spoke around a mouthful of chicken and rice. "He called me after."

Santiago smiled at that. "I figured he would. For what it's worth, he thinks highly of your legal skills and judgment."

Ainsley's ego preened. "That's good to know."

"Smart of him," Santiago continued. "You've always been an amazing lawyer."

The unexpected praise caught her by surprise. She sucked in a breath, inhaling a grain of rice. Her throat spasmed, triggering a fit of coughing that caused her to lean forward in her chair.

"Are you okay?" Santiago looked alarmed, and he set his fork down. Ainsley waved away his concern, but she couldn't stop coughing. Santiago stood up and crouched next to her, placing his large hand flat on her back. He started to gently rub circles between her shoulder blades, leaning in close as though his proximity could help her.

Gradually, the coughing subsided. Santiago leaned over and grabbed a bottle of water off the counter of the low cabinets. He twisted off the cap and handed it to her, then resumed rubbing circles on her back.

Ainsley took a cautious sip, relieved when it didn't trigger a new coughing fit. "Thanks," she said, turning to look at him. "I think I'm good now." Her voice sounded a little hoarse, belying her words.

He was close enough that she could see the thin ring of gold that circled his pupils. His eyes had always reminded her of green turquoise, the color almost too beautiful to be real.

The breath caught in her throat as he leaned in, his gaze intent on hers. She was acutely aware of his touch on her back. The warmth of his body heated the space between them, and she had the sudden urge to press herself to him, to flatten her curves against his solid chest and breathe in his intoxicating scent. His pheromones were better than any drug, and their effects as potent now as they'd ever been. She'd already overcome that particular addiction once. If she wasn't careful, she'd get hooked again.

"Are you sure you're all right?"

Ainsley nodded, not trusting her voice.

Santiago held her gaze a few seconds more, assessing her condition for himself. Apparently convinced she was telling the truth, he leaned back and placed his hand on the table as he stood.

Ainsley immediately felt the loss of his touch. She looked away as he sat in his chair again, hoping her disappointment didn't show.

Get it together! she silently chided herself. She'd spent a grand total of an hour or so in Santiago's presence over the last twenty-four hours, and she was already melting for him again. How was she going to survive this marriage retreat if she couldn't keep her emotions and body in check?

"So what did you think of Ace?" Change the subject, focus on something else. By engaging her mind, maybe she could forget about the effect he was having on her body...

Santiago tilted his head to the side as he pinched a bit of chicken between his chopsticks. "I think he's telling the truth."

Some of the knots in Ainsley's chest loosened at his words. "I think so, too," she confessed. "But part of me was worried I wasn't thinking clearly because he's my brother—even if not biologically. It's good to know you have the same impression."

Santiago shot her a grin. "Always trust your instincts," he advised. "I asked him a lot of questions this morning. I could tell by the way he answered that he was being truthful—he didn't prevaricate, or hesitate to respond. And his words didn't sound rehearsed, either."

"This has been hard on him," Ainsley said. A shadow passed over her heart as she thought about the events of the last several months. It felt like her family was coming apart at the seams, and no matter how hard she tried, she couldn't fix everything.

"I don't think he's the only one having trouble," Santiago said softly. She looked up to find him watching her, his expression kind.

She smiled absently and pushed away her thoughts. "It's been a shock to us all," she said, striving to make her tone light. If he kept looking at her like that, she was going to break down and cry. And while Santiago had once been her safe harbor, she had to remember he wasn't anymore.

"I spoke with the police after I talked to Ace," he said, smoothly steering the conversation away from troubled waters. "One of the officers was helpful. Spencer Colton was his name—another family member?"

"A cousin," Ainsley confirmed. "I'm glad he was cooperative."

"Very," Santiago said. "He put me in touch with the D.A.'s office, and they gave me the names and contact information of the witnesses in the case. I've already made appointments to speak to your brother's housekeeper and the cleaner who discovered your father."

Ainsley nodded. "That was fast."

"No point in waiting," he said. "Besides, you're helping me out for the next week. I wanted to make a good faith effort on your brother's case, so you wouldn't think I was taking advantage of your cooperation."

"I know you wouldn't do that." It was true. She might not be able to trust him with her heart, but she knew he was a man of his word. He'd told her he'd represent Ace. There was no doubt in her mind that he would follow through.

"I, uh, did want to talk to you about the retreat." He shifted in his seat, looking uncharacteristically uncertain.

Interesting, she thought. Perhaps Santiago was having second thoughts about his plan? Maybe she wouldn't have to spend the next seven days pretending to be the wife of the man who'd broken her heart?

"All right." She pushed her plate away, no longer hungry. "We should probably come up with a strategy. Make sure we're on the same page."

He nodded. "I'm working on an email that outlines everything. I'll finish it tonight and send it to you. We can talk about any questions you have in the car tomorrow, on the way to the retreat."

Ainsley's stomach did a little flip-flop. They were

really going to do this. It was time for her to fulfill her promise.

"I'll look for it later," she said. She was curious to know what Santiago had in mind and how he was going to get the information he needed to prove The Marriage Institute was scamming people. But she hoped she'd be able to keep a professional distance from him while they worked.

"There's one more thing." He looked down, clearly uncomfortable. A stone of dread formed in Ainsley's stomach. Was he going to change the deal? Did he need her to do more than just pretend to be his wife?

"I did a little shopping today," he continued. He sighed, then withdrew something from his jacket pocket. He placed it on the table, exactly in the middle of the space separating them.

Ainsley stared at the small black velvet box as though it were a bomb. She glanced up and Santiago offered her a shrug and a slight wince. "I just thought..." he trailed off. "I mean, we *are* supposed to be married."

She shook her head, not knowing whether to laugh or to cry. How many times had she dreamed of this man giving her a ring? How many times had she fantasized about him proposing to her? How he'd look, how he'd sound. How the love he had for her would shine on his face as he asked her to spend the rest of her life with him. And the joy that she'd feel, the unmitigated happiness she'd experience when he slipped the ring on her finger, a tangible symbol of their commitment to each other.

Instead, she was sitting in her office, her dinner forming a cold lump in her stomach while Santiago had trouble meeting her eyes.

She reached for the box without conscious thought. Might as well get this over with.

The ring was beautiful. A round emerald surrounded by a halo of tiny diamonds sat on a thin band of white gold. Additional small diamonds decorated the sides of the band. Even in the soft light of her office, she could see the stone was a deep, verdant green, the color of summer grass. The diamonds sparkled like tiny stars, making the ring glitter as though lit from within. There was a thin wedding band nestled under the ring, carved with an intricate scroll filigree that was exquisitely delicate.

Ainsley swallowed hard, trying to keep her emotions at bay. "It's lovely," she said, her heart aching as she stared at it.

Santiago cleared his throat. "Under the circumstances, I didn't think a big diamond would be appropriate."

"No," she agreed, tearing her gaze away to meet his eyes. "This is fine."

"I had to pick something that looked like a wedding set," he said, sounding nervous. "This wasn't being sold as an engagement ring, but when I saw the emerald, I thought it was fitting."

"Your family," she murmured. Santiago's parents were from Colombia, a country famous for its emeralds.

"Exactly." He looked relieved that she understood. "And then I saw the thin band, and I thought they looked good together."

If the circumstances were different, Ainsley would have sworn Santiago was worried about her liking the rings. "They're very nice," she said. Her fingers were stiff as she pulled the rings from the box and slid them on. They fit perfectly. Of course.

"I had to guess your size," he said, watching her movements. "Looks like I got it right."

"You did," she said flatly. Ainsley stared at her left hand for a moment, trying to adjust to the sight of the jewelry. It looked like a stranger's hand, one she'd never seen before.

The surreal image was too much. She tugged the rings off and put them back in the box, feeling shaken.

"You don't have to wear them," Santiago said hastily. "It's fine if you'd rather not."

She shook her head. "No, I'll do it." He wasn't the only one who kept promises. She'd told him she would pretend to be his wife for the retreat. "What about you?" she asked. "Do I need to find a band for you?" Just the thought of walking into a jewelry store to buy Santiago a wedding band was enough to make her heart hurt, but she'd play her part.

"No," he said emphatically. He stuck his hand into his pocket again and held up a gold ring. "I'm all set."

Ainsley nodded, relief stealing over her. "What time are we leaving tomorrow?"

Santiago returned the band to his pocket. "I was thinking we could go around four. That way we can both get some work done and it won't be a totally wasted day."

"That works for me." She stood and began to gather up the remains of their meal. She needed him to leave now, needed to be alone so she could process her feelings in private and get her emotions locked down before the retreat started. The wedding rings had been an unexpected surprise, and she wasn't sure how she felt about them.

Apparently recognizing his cue, Santiago pushed back in his chair and helped her clean off the table. She left the small velvet box alone, not ready to touch it again just yet.

"Where should I pick you up tomorrow?" he asked. "Here at the office, or at your home?"

"Here is fine," she replied. She didn't want him coming to the house she shared with her siblings and father. She might have her own wing of rooms, but the house was never empty. If anyone saw him there they'd have questions, and she wasn't in the mood to provide answers. Besides, the last thing she wanted was to have Santiago in her private living quarters. His very presence would forever alter the character of the space, and she'd feel like a stranger in her own home. The rooms were her escape from the demands of her career and her family, her safe haven where she could relax and recharge. She didn't need to be haunted by memories of Santiago in her home, examining her personal items and studying the private side of her life.

Santiago nodded, oblivious to her thoughts. "Very good," he said. "I'll come here then."

Before she could react, he took a step forward and leaned down to press a kiss to her cheek. Ainsley sucked in a breath at the contact. Santiago drew back, then froze as their eyes met.

It was clear from the look on his face he'd acted without thinking. She knew she shouldn't read into the gesture, that he'd been moving on autopilot and the kiss had simply been offered out of habit. But her cheek tingled from the contact, and her heart thumped hard against her ribs. With this man, her body wasn't capable of ignoring any contact, no matter how innocent.

Something flashed in his green gaze—heat? Awareness? His eyes dropped to her lips. Unconsciously, her tongue darted out to moisten them. *What are you doing?* she screamed silently to herself. She didn't want to seduce him, didn't want him to think she was interested. But her brain was no longer in charge. Ainsley felt her skin warm as his scent filled her nose—starch, coffee and that intangible note that belonged to him alone.

His head dipped closer, making her breath stutter in her chest. Was he really going to kiss her? More importantly, was she going to stop him?

Apparently not. Without conscious thought, she leaned forward, reducing the distance between them. Santiago smiled faintly, and then she felt the warmth of his mouth as he brushed his lips against her own.

It was a gentle caress, the pressure like the stroke of a butterfly's wings. But it started a fire in her belly that shot tendrils of heat through her limbs and triggered an ache in her heart.

Santiago pulled back, his lips shining and a bewildered look in his eyes.

"I—" He broke off, shaking his head. "I'm sorry," he said finally.

Ainsley took a deep breath, trying to regain her equilibrium. "It's fine," she said. She glanced away, unable to meet his eyes. "I'll see you tomorrow."

Santiago hesitated, then moved away. The tension in her body eased as the distance between them increased. "Yes, of course," he said, his tone professional now, as if he hadn't just kissed her for the first time in more than five years. "Thank you again for your help."

"Likewise," she said. She stood and walked to her desk, placing her hand on it for support. "I appreciate you getting started on Ace's case so quickly."

"It was the least I could do." He paused by the door, and she got the feeling there was more he wanted to say. But she kept her eyes on her desk, not wanting to engage him further.

He got the hint. She heard him sigh quietly. "Have a good evening."

"You, too," she said automatically. She waited until the door shut behind him before sinking into her desk chair. What had she done?

She rubbed absently at her mouth, her lips still tingling from the contact with his. Twenty-four hours, and she'd already kissed him.

"Technically, he kissed me," she muttered. But that didn't matter. The kiss had happened, and now she was going to have to forget about it.

They had a long week of close contact coming up. She couldn't afford to get distracted, to let her body run the show.

If she was going to get through this with her heart intact, she couldn't let things get personal between them again.

THE NEXT AFTERNOON, Santiago pulled into the parking lot in front of the offices of Colton Oil and cut the engine. A quick glance at his watch confirmed he was a little early, so he decided to wait a few minutes before heading up to Ainsley's office.

Nerves crackled in his stomach, making him feel unsettled. It was a strange sensation, one he didn't experience often. He could count on one hand the number of times he'd been nervous in his adult life, and he'd still have fingers left over. What was it about this situation that had him feeling out of sorts?

A flash of light caught his eye and he focused on the gold band on his left hand. The metal gleamed in the afternoon sun, as bright as a flame. He stared at the ring for a moment, having a hard time believing what he was seeing even though he'd put the band on his own finger earlier in the day.

After a childhood spent living in the shadows of his parents' contentious relationship, Santiago had known marriage was not in his future. Even though his relationship with Ainsley had been good—better than he'd ever thought possible—a part of him had always known it wouldn't last. Couldn't last. After all, his own parents had started out madly in love with each other. But somewhere along the way, their affection had withered into mutual contempt. It was a pattern that had been repeated throughout the generations of his family, one he was determined to stop.

So when he'd had an opportunity to move to New York to launch his career after law school, he'd said goodbye to Ainsley, knowing he was really doing her a favor. Better to leave now, while they still liked each other, than to let things disintegrate into the inevitable unpleasantness that would come.

He'd missed her terribly at first. Still did, if he was being honest with himself. Not that he lacked for company. He'd dated several women in New York, all of them beautiful and pleasant. But despite the affection he'd felt for each one, he'd never experienced the soul-deep connection that he'd had with Ainsley. Seeing her again had stirred up latent emotions, feelings he thought he'd processed long ago. But it turned out he'd simply buried his emotions in work rather than deal with them. Now he was going to have to pay the price.

Could he really go through with this? Could he really handle this sham marriage for the week? They'd be living in the same cottage, spending most of their time together. Her scent would be in his nose, her voice in his ears. His body already wanted her again—it had taken all of thirty seconds for his libido to sit up and take notice after walking into her office. And then that moment last night, when he'd kissed her…

It had been the wrong thing to do, he knew that. But it had felt so very right.

"It wasn't even a real kiss," he muttered to himself. No, that had been more like a prelude to a kiss, a teasing promise of things to come. The barest brush of his lips against hers, nothing more.

And yet he'd had to take a cold shower last night before he'd been able to fall asleep.

Santiago shook his head at his own foolishness. Here he was, acting like a randy teenager when really, nothing had happened. To make matters worse, he was certain his feelings were all one-sided. Ainsley had looked shocked after the almost-kiss, but she'd quickly regained her composure. Probably because it wasn't even a blip on her radar. He'd been burning for her after one brief taste, but she'd clearly felt nothing beyond annoyance.

Not that he blamed her. He didn't know why he'd gotten so familiar with her last night. It certainly wasn't something he'd planned. He'd meant to keep things strictly professional between them. But something about that moment had made him forget where they were and what they were doing. He'd gotten distracted by her nearness and the years apart had melted away, making him think they were still together. He'd acted on instinct, moving in to touch her the way he'd done a million times before. Back when he'd still had that privilege.

"It won't happen again," he told himself sternly. It couldn't. He had to expose this marriage retreat for the fraud it was, and the only way to do that was with Ainsley's help. If he messed things up between them, she'd walk away and he wouldn't be able to help his sister, or the other couples who had made the mistake of trusting these people.

"Eyes on the prize," he muttered. This week would be difficult, but he simply had to shove his feelings and attraction to Ainsley to the side so he could focus on the important job ahead.

He reached for the door handle, only to startle as

someone rapped on the passenger side window. Ainsley gave him a little wave and he unlocked the door.

She tossed a bag in the back seat, then opened the door and slid in next to him. "Hey," she said. "I saw you from my office window so I decided to come down. Save you a trip up."

He gawked at her, staring at her hair. It was no longer brown—she'd added honey-blonde highlights throughout, changing her appearance completely.

"You look different," he managed.

She reached up and touched her hair. "Yeah, I did it last night. I think it turned out okay, for a home job."

"It looks good." He'd never thought of her as a blonde, but she carried it well.

"Thanks," she said.

"What possessed you to do it?"

She frowned. "I worried people at the retreat might recognize me. This place is pretty close to Mustang Valley, and I didn't want anyone there to see me and doubt our story."

"Good thinking," he said.

"I do occasionally have good ideas," she said, offering a lop-sided smile.

"So, just the one bag?" he asked, glancing back at the small duffel she'd brought.

"Yep," she confirmed. "I pack light."

"That's right, you do," he murmured. "I'd forgotten."

He caught her eye as he turned around and smiled

faintly. She glanced away, lifting her hand to push a strand of hair behind her ear.

Santiago sucked in a breath as he saw the rings on her finger. A shock went through him, an electric zap down his spine that radiated through his limbs. She was wearing the emerald he'd given her.

It shouldn't have been a surprise—she had said she would wear the wedding set. Logically, he'd known he'd see the rings on her finger.

But there was something about the sight of his ring on her left hand that hit him hard. A wave of possessiveness washed over him, his thoughts congealing into a single word: *mine*.

The rational part of his brain recognized he was being ridiculous. The rings were a fake symbol, a prop for the roles they were playing. But some caveman impulse deep inside of him swelled with pleasure to see Ainsley sporting a visible sign of their connection. The whole world would know at a glance that this woman was taken, that she was his.

Even though it wasn't true.

"Are you all right?"

She was studying him with a concerned expression, clearly worried. What must he look like to elicit that question?

Santiago cleared his throat and schooled his features into a neutral mask. "I'm fine. Just thinking about this week."

Ainsley nodded, apparently satisfied by his response. "I'm worried, too. What do you think it will be like?"

He shifted the car into gear and pulled onto the road, starting their journey toward The Marriage Institute retreat center. "Gabriela told me there's a lot of group sessions. For most of them, the husband goes to one, while the wife goes to another."

"They must separate the couples according to who they've rigged to 'win,'" Ainsley said. "How do they decide that?"

"Bribery," Santiago replied. "Has to be."

"It's always about money," she muttered.

Santiago nodded. She'd apparently been thinking about what he'd said, and he appreciated she was taking this seriously. Though he wasn't surprised—he knew from experience that Ainsley Colton was a woman of her word.

"Makes sense," he said. "I have one of my research assistants digging into their financial records. It seems the Woods have some off-shore accounts, which in and of itself isn't so suspicious. But it definitely raises questions."

"You think they've got a tax shelter?"

"Probably," he said. "Once we gather our evidence, I'm hoping the D.A. will be able to open a case and pry into those secrets."

Ainsley was quiet a moment. "So what else should we expect from this thing?"

"Gabriela said there were some joint counseling

sessions, but looking back on it, she sees now they were one-sided."

"Like she was being manipulated?" Ainsley asked.

"Exactly," Santiago confirmed. "She said it felt like the counselor and her husband were a team, and she was on the outside."

"Oh, man." From the edges of his vision, he saw Ainsley shake her head. "That's terrible. I feel so bad for her. Not to mention the rest of the innocent people who went there looking for help. Do you think they took bribes from everybody?"

"Probably not," Santiago said. "But I think they're probably known in certain circles for helping people get the result they want."

"Rich people, you mean," she muttered.

"Yeah," he said. Anger simmered on a low boil in his chest, a sensation he'd felt ever since Gabriela had come to him in tears, confessing her worries and asking him for help. "It makes me sick to think of what these people have done."

"They won't get away with it for much longer," Ainsley said quietly. "We'll make sure of that."

His spirits lifted at her use of the word *we*. It was good to know he wasn't in this alone, despite the personal issues still lurking between them.

"I think the best way to do this is for both of us to offer them a bribe, separately. We'll see if they accept the money."

"Are we offering them the same amount?"

Santiago shook his head. "No. Your envelope has two thousand dollars, with the promise of three thousand more after the retreat is over, provided you get what you want. My bribe will be four thousand dollars, with the promise of six thousand more after the retreat is over."

Ainsley whistled softly. "That's a lot of cash."

"It is," he agreed. "Hopefully too much for them to pass up."

"What about other evidence?" she asked. "Taking bribes is unethical, but it might not be enough to shut this place down."

"That's true," he said. "Which is why we're going to record everything."

He glanced over in time to see her wrinkle her nose. "Is that legal?"

"Technically speaking, yes," he said. "Arizona is a single-party consent state, so as long as you and I know the conversations are being recorded, we're in the clear."

"That's true, so long as the other parties don't have a reasonable expectation of privacy," Ainsley pointed out. "I'm fine with recording our conversations with the Woodses, since they're the ones running this thing and scamming people. But I'm not comfortable recording any of the group counseling sessions. Those other people don't deserve to have their privacy violated like that."

Santiago smiled, enjoying the display of both her

intellect and her moral code. He'd definitely picked the right woman to help him bring these charlatans down.

"I totally agree with you," he said. "I wasn't planning on having us record any group counseling sessions. But I do want to record our private sessions with them, and any one-on-one conversations we have with either of them."

She nodded, accepting his response. "I suppose we'll just use our phones?"

"Better," he said. "I have some devices for us to wear." Keeping one hand on the wheel, he reached into the back of the car and grabbed his leather messenger bag. He placed it in Ainsley's lap. "You'll find a flat white box inside," he said.

She hesitated a second, then opened the bag and began to rummage inside. A faint tingle tickled the base of his spine. Seeing Ainsley riffle through his bag felt intimate somehow, though there was really nothing personal inside. The contents were all work-related. If it had been any other person, he would have worried about breaking attorney-client privilege. But he trusted Ainsley and knew she wouldn't examine anything other than the box he'd described.

A few seconds later she withdrew the item in question. "Is this it?"

"That's the one."

She opened the lid and he glanced over to see her

press her lips together in a thin line. "More jewelry," she said flatly.

He winced, wishing there had been another option. "I know," he said, his tone apologetic. "But it was my only option."

"It's fine," she said. She studied the necklace, one brow lifted. "Not really my style, but that's all right."

"Believe it or not, that was the best one." Santiago shook his head as he recalled the truly garish pieces he'd seen while searching the internet for something for Ainsley to wear.

She pulled the pendant from the box and clasped the chain around her neck. The silver locket hung just above the neckline of her shirt, perfectly positioned to capture the activity around her. The scrollwork design on the front of the pendant was a bit ostentatious, but it did a good job of disguising the small opening for the camera lens.

"If anyone asks, you can tell them it's a family heirloom," he suggested.

"That works," she said. "It does have an old-fashioned look to it."

"It's touch activated," he told her. "You just have to slide your finger over the surface of the locket to start recording."

"That seems easy enough," she said. She fiddled with it for a few seconds, then placed her hands in her lap again.

"So what's our story?"

He frowned, not entirely sure what she was asking. “Pardon?”

“You know. Why are we there? Why is our marriage in trouble? We’ve got to have a good reason for wanting to split up.”

“Oh.” He’d sent her an email earlier with some options for their cover story. Now it seemed they needed to decide what they were going to say.

“I work too much,” he said. “No time for the relationship.”

She laughed. The sound was unexpected, and it made him smile. “What? Doesn’t that sound convincing?”

“Oh, completely,” Ainsley said, humor in her voice. “But what about me? Is there any reason you’re unhappy with me?”

No, he thought automatically. But he shrugged. “You work a lot, too?” he suggested.

“I think we can do better than that,” she said. She was silent a moment. When she spoke again, her voice was quiet. “Maybe we should tell the truth.”

“What do you mean?” In some ways, they were being honest. He’d broken up with her so he could pursue his career. He truly was a workaholic—he wouldn’t have to pretend to play that part.

“We can tell them that you want biological children. I can’t give them to you.”

His heart cracked at her words. “Ainsley, no. That’s not the reason.”

"Are you sure?" she whispered.

"No," he said firmly. Taking a chance, he reached over and took her hand in his. "You know that's not why I left…before."

She turned to look out the window so he couldn't see her face, but didn't speak. A sense of urgency gripped him, desperation clawing at the edges of his thoughts. Did she really think he'd broken up with her because they couldn't have children together? Had she spent the last five years believing she was somehow to blame for his actions?

He had to make it clear that wasn't the case. But what could he say to convince her he was telling the truth? That he'd left because the fault was within him, not with her?

"Ainsley, I told you the truth. I broke up with you because I needed to move to New York to pursue my career, and I knew you didn't want to leave your family here.

"Please believe me," he said. "The kid thing didn't matter to me. We could have always adopted, if that's what we both wanted." He was telling the truth. Part of him had been disappointed when she'd told him she was unable to have children. But he'd never felt compelled to become a father, never had that all-consuming desire to have children. Santiago had always thought that kids deserved to be born into a family that wanted them more than anything. Since he didn't want kids more than anything that way, he was happy remaining child-free.

"All right," she said finally, but it was clear from her tone she still had doubts. "It's fine. We can still use it as part of our story, if you want."

"No," he said, putting a little steel into his voice. "I'm not going to ask you to expose yourself to these people. They don't deserve your pain. Besides, it wasn't true then, and it isn't true now. We'll just stick with the original script." He searched for something else to say, hoping to lighten the mood. "You can say you hate my family, too."

She turned to look at him and he glimpsed the curiosity on her face before returning his gaze to the road. "I never met your parents," she said.

He huffed out a laugh. "Trust me. That was for a reason." He didn't enjoy spending time with his family. Gabriela was fine, but his mom and dad had spent so many years antagonizing each other they didn't know how else to behave. Even if he got them one-on-one, they spent the entire visit complaining about the other person so that there was no way to have a real conversation. For the sake of his own mental health, Santiago limited his contact with his parents to emails and the occasional phone call.

"It seems wrong that this is all your fault," she mused. "I mean it makes sense from my perspective that I would blame you for everything. But they're going to want to know why you're happy to end things. We need to come up with some issues that you have with me, so it seems realistic that you'd be willing to walk away as well. Otherwise, why wouldn't you want to fight for us?"

He considered her words as he took the next freeway exit and maneuvered the car onto the access road. What she said made sense—it would be a little suspicious if the impetus for the breakup was all one-sided. "Do you have any ideas?" he asked.

"What if we told them I had an affair?" she suggested. "I blamed you for working too much and being out of town all the time, so I cheated on you."

The idea of Ainsley with another man triggered a reflexive spurt of jealousy, but he quickly tamped it down. He had no claim on her, no right to be offended or hurt if she was with someone else. Her relationship status was a question he hadn't thought to ask earlier. Was that because he didn't want to know the answer?

"That's a good idea," he said. "Um, I probably should have asked you this before, but are you seeing anyone right now?" He held his breath, waiting for her to reply.

"No."

Santiago relaxed as some of the tension left his body. Her answer shouldn't have mattered to him, but it did. The small, selfish part of him didn't want to think about her with another man. No one was good enough for her—he could say that with authority. Even he had spent many an hour wondering what he'd done to deserve her affections. Her love was a gift, one he hadn't taken for granted. But in the end, he'd had to acknowledge she'd be better off without him.

"What about you? I know you're single now, but has there been anyone special since you moved to New York?"

Her question caught him off guard. He hadn't expected her to be curious about his own personal life, since she'd made it clear she was only helping him because he'd agreed to take her brother's case. Did she feel the same twinge of jealousy at the thought of another woman in his life? Or was she simply curious, wondering about his path since they'd parted ways?

"Ah, no," he said, deciding not to elaborate. He hadn't exactly been living the life of a monk, but he hadn't found anyone he really clicked with, either.

She didn't reply, and he couldn't see her expression so he didn't know what she was thinking. Hopefully, his single status would help convince her that he really had been telling the truth five years ago—he'd left to work on his career, not because he wanted to trade her in for a different model. He'd should have made that clear years ago, but he just hadn't been able to talk about his fears regarding commitment with her. At the time, it had seemed easier to use his career aspirations as the excuse to end their relationship.

They were silent the rest of the drive, which wasn't

very long. In a matter of minutes, he turned off the two-lane country road onto a gravel drive. The car bounced along for about a hundred yards until the drive ended in a small paved parking lot. He pulled into a spot and turned off the engine, and together, they stared at the large log cabin situated about twenty yards away.

"Nice," Ainsley observed, turning her head to look at the smaller cabins nestled among the trees nearby. It was clear the large cabin was the main gathering center, and Santiago imagined the smaller ones were lodgings for the couples at the retreat.

The whole thing had a slick, polished feel to it. Flowerbeds lined the sidewalk to the main cabin, bursting with color. The grass was green and clipped, and the trees cast dappled shade on everything. Under any other circumstances, he would have enjoyed staying at a place like this.

"It seems cheating people pays well," he observed. If the grounds looked this nice, the interior must be amazing as well. The Woodses had an image to maintain, after all.

Santiago turned to look at Ainsley. "Last chance." He wasn't going to force her to stay and play the part of his wife, especially after her earlier tears. He had no intention of letting the Woodses get away with their fraudulent behavior, but he also wasn't willing to emotionally torture Ainsley to expose them as cheats and liars.

A glint of determination shone in her eyes. "I'm ready. Are you?"

He smiled, relieved to know she was on his team. "Let's do this."

Chapter Four

Ainsley took a deep breath, trying to calm the nerves jangling in her stomach. She'd never been much of an actress. Hopefully she could pull this off. Spencer hadn't been thrilled when she'd told him what she was doing, but then again, she hadn't been looking for his approval. She'd simply wanted to let him know what was going on, in case there was any trouble.

Santiago walked next to her as they moved up the path, side by side. The sunlight glinted off the emerald she wore on her left hand, the stone the same color as the trees around them. She still wasn't used to the feel of the band around her finger. But it was a gorgeous set, and a small, girlish part of her felt a little thrill every time she glanced down and caught sight of the jewelry.

Since when have I been distracted by shiny things? she mused silently, tearing her gaze away from the ring.

She jumped when Santiago took her hand. Without thinking, she pulled away. He slid her a glance. "We're splitting up, remember?" she whispered.

"I know," he replied in a low voice. "Nice job."

He held open the door to the main building, and she walked past him. The truth was, she hadn't been thinking of their facade when she'd pulled away. She'd simply reacted on instinct; it had been five years since he'd tried to hold her hand, and the men she'd dated after him hadn't been interested in public displays of affection. Ainsley simply wasn't used to casual physical contact.

But part of her wished she hadn't rejected his touch. Her skin tingled where they'd made contact. The sensation was a nice distraction from her nerves, and his gesture was a timely reminder that they were in this together.

Still, she probably shouldn't look to Santiago for reassurance. They *were* supposed to be splitting up. Her awkwardness and discomfort would help make them appear like a genuine couple in trouble. If she was too comfortable, too relaxed in his presence people would wonder why they were ending things.

She paused at the entrance, glancing around the foyer of the building. The air was cool and smelled of flowers, thanks to a large bouquet sitting on a table to the right. The walls were painted a soft green that paired nicely with hardwood floors the color of honey. She heard the soothing sounds of running water and spied a fountain just past the hospitality desk that was located straight ahead.

She felt the warmth of Santiago's body at her back, but he was careful not to touch her. *Good*, she thought, trying not to be disappointed. Her brain knew there couldn't be anything between them again, but that kiss in her office had convinced her body there was still hope. As a result, she felt conflicted, her baser wants at war with her logical self. This week would be an exhausting struggle, but she knew which side had to win.

"Do you see anyone here?" he said softly.

"No," she replied, glancing around as though an employee might jump out from behind the flowers. "Maybe we just sign in?"

They approached the tall desk together, their footsteps tapping on the floor and echoing slightly in the otherwise quiet room. Just as they reached the counter, a young man stepped forward from a room off to the left that they hadn't seen from the front door.

"Hello, and welcome to The Marriage Institute." He smiled politely, revealing straight, white teeth. "My name is Brett. You must be Mr. and Mrs. Rodriguez." It was the pseudonym Santiago had chosen for this retreat, not wanting anyone to make the connection between him and his sister Gabriela.

Ainsley frowned slightly, taken aback by this young man's familiarity. "How did you know that?"

He nodded in her direction. "You're the last ones to arrive for this week's retreat."

"Are we late?" Santiago asked. "I was told we should get here at five."

Brett chuckled. "Not to worry. Everything is fine. Please, let's get you checked in." He gestured to the tall counter and motioned for them to follow him over.

Ainsley let Santiago take care of the details. There was something about this young man that seemed off to her, though she couldn't quite put her finger on what, exactly, bothered her. He was pleasant and polite, and he looked like a model employee in his pressed khaki pants and light blue oxford shirt. Even his hair was on its best behavior, with none of the golden strands out of place. Why, then, did he make her uncomfortable?

"All right, Mr. and Mrs. Rodriguez. We're all set. Allow me to show you to your cabin."

They walked out of the main lodge, back onto the path. "Do you have any luggage?" Brett asked.

"Just two bags," Santiago replied.

"Let me help you with them."

Ainsley hung back, allowing Brett to carry her bag. She didn't want to get close to him, didn't want to risk touching him.

The path split close to the main building, with one path branching off to the left. Brett led them down this walk, which took them deeper into the trees.

Ainsley looked around as they walked, trying to

get a sense of the layout of the place. She knew from her online research there were five cabins arranged behind the main building, and she'd seen another small building on the map that wasn't identified. *Storage?* she'd wondered. *Or something else?*

Now that she was seeing the compound in person, she was surprised at how spread out everything was. The map had made it look like the cabins were close to each other, but she realized that wasn't the case at all. There were at least fifty yards between each cabin, and as they moved deeper into the trees, the main building seemed to recede into the distance.

"Here we are," Brett said cheerfully. He walked up the porch steps and unlocked the door, gesturing for them to precede him inside. Ainsley stepped onto the porch and cast a last look around before stepping inside—their cabin appeared to be the farthest away from the main building.

Brett placed her bag on the floor by the door. "Welcome to your home for the week," he said. "As you can see, there is a small kitchen area, which we've outfitted with a coffee maker and a teakettle. We've stocked the fridge with cream, but we ask that you enjoy your meals at the main house." He smiled at each of them in turn, as though this was a perfectly natural request.

"There are two bedrooms and two bathrooms," he continued, gesturing to the hallway off the main room. "One set on each side of the cabin. Each bedroom is large enough for two people. We understand you each might need your space during this time, but we encourage you to come together as often as possible to discuss your feelings and process the important work you'll be doing during your sessions."

Okay, this was getting a little too weird. Ainsley had never before had someone suggest how she should spend her time, and she didn't appreciate Brett's thoughts on the matter of her bed.

"Finally," he continued, "you'll find we have some amenities at the main cabin, such as an exercise room and a sauna. The main cabin is open from six in the morning to eleven at night every day, and we serve meals at eight thirty, noon and six. Follow the path from your cabin, and you'll have no trouble making your way back."

"What about the Woodses?" Santiago asked. "When will we meet them?"

Brett smiled, and Ainsley realized why she didn't like him: he was putting on an act. Everything about his behavior was fake, his bland pleasantness a front that gave no hint of real human emotion. He was like a Ken doll come to life, an automaton rather than an actual person.

"Alva and Brody will stop by your cabin after you've had a chance to settle in. They make it a point to greet every couple personally after they arrive."

"Wonderful," Ainsley murmured. She was ready

for this man to leave, so she and Santiago could talk in private.

Brett turned his smile on her, making her uncomfortable. "Thanks for your help," she said, hoping he would take his cue.

He did. "My pleasure. Please, don't hesitate to reach out if I can make your stay more pleasant. Just dial 9 from the phone, and you'll connect to the front desk."

"Thank you," Santiago said.

They were silent as Brett walked to the door and let himself out. Ainsley waited until she heard his footsteps fade on the gravel of the path before turning to Santiago.

He lifted a hand before she could speak, silently bidding her to remain quiet. As she watched, he took a small black device from his pocket and pressed a button. A green light appeared on top of the device, and Santiago began to walk around the cabin.

She followed him as he entered every room, holding the device in front of him as though it were some kind of divining rod. He led her back into the main room of the cabin and sat on the overstuffed cream sofa, then patted the cushion next to him.

Ainsley lowered herself onto the plush seat, watching as he turned the device off. "Did you just sweep the place for listening devices?" She was part astonished, part impressed. She'd never considered the possibility the place might be bugged.

Santiago nodded. "Yep. And I'll do it again after the Woodses leave, in case they turn them on later."

"Do you really think they spy on the couples here?"

He shrugged. "Who knows? Although I wouldn't be surprised. They're probably looking for any advantage to scam these people."

"I didn't like Brett," she said. "He's just too…" she trailed off, trying to articulate her thoughts.

"Brainwashed," Santiago supplied.

"Yes!" She nodded, glad he'd seen it, too. "That's exactly it."

"Yeah, he's definitely drunk the Kool-Aid," Santiago said. He shook his head. "I almost feel bad for the kid."

"Do you think the Woodses will have that same vibe?" Ainsley shuddered at the thought of having to spend the next week in this atmosphere. It was like the beginning of a horror movie, where everything was just a little bit skewed.

"I hope not," Santiago said. "Since they're the ones in charge, hopefully they're a little more natural." He glanced around the room. "Seems like a nice enough place to spend the week."

Ainsley nodded. "Yeah. If the circumstances were different, this would be a pretty little vacation spot."

The room was spacious, outfitted in shades of cream and forest green. The back wall and hallway were mostly windows, looking out on the trees beyond. She'd glimpsed the kitchenette when they'd walked in, spying cream counter tops and honey-blond cabinets.

"Which bedroom do you want?"

Their quick tour had revealed the bedrooms were arranged as mirror opposites, containing a queen-size bed, a chair and a simple wooden dresser. One had been decorated in shades of purple, the other in shades of blue.

"I'll take the purple one," she said.

She laughed as a look of relief crossed Santiago's face. "Not a fan?"

"It's not my favorite color," he admitted. "But if you wanted the blue room I'd deal."

"I'm not going to torture you," she said. She stood and walked over to pick up her bag. "I guess I'll unpack while we wait."

"Good idea," Santiago took his bag and followed her down the hall. They reached the end, and she turned right while he turned left.

Ainsley paused in the doorway to the bedroom and glanced back. "Santiago?"

He turned to face her. "Yeah?"

"I hope we bring these guys down." They hadn't even started the retreat yet, hadn't offered their bribes or been subject to the dubious therapy sessions. But she already disliked the place and had a feeling it was even worse than his sister had described.

He grinned, teeth flashing white in the shadows of the hallway. "We will."

THE KNOCK CAME shortly after six.

Ainsley had just finished brewing a cup of tea in the small kitchen. Santiago glanced at her, and she nodded.

Ready to meet the enemy.

He opened the door to find a middle-aged couple standing on the porch. "Welcome to The Marriage Institute. I'm Brody Woods, and this is my wife, Alva."

"Santiago Rodriguez," he replied, automatically sticking out his hand.

Brody had a firm handshake, strong but not painfully so. Alva offered him a smile and held up a brown paper bag. "May we come in for a moment?" she asked.

"Of course." Santiago stepped aside to let them past, though what he really wanted to do was drag them to a jail cell.

Easy does it, he reminded himself. As satisfying as it would be to unleash his anger on these two, he needed to keep the end goal in mind. Gather evidence, then bring them down.

They looked like a nice couple, a stereotypical middle-class pair. He wore khakis and a button-down shirt, his blond hair shot through with silver. She was a plump, matronly type, her short hair permed and teased to perfection. Her large glasses magnified her eyes, making her look a bit like an owl.

"We brought food," she said in a singsong announcement. She placed it on the small table in the kitchen area and smiled, looking pleased with herself. "It's not fancy, but we wanted to make sure you both had something to eat tonight. The kitchen in the main cabin doesn't open until tomorrow morning."

"Thank you." Ainsley spoke softly, and Santiago could tell by her tone that she was struggling to appear friendly. He couldn't blame her, and hopefully if the Woodses picked up on her negativity, they'd assume it was directed at him. After all, their marriage was in trouble, right?

Alva nodded. "Our pleasure. We're so glad you're here."

Santiago nearly snorted. Of course they were. As far as the Woodses were concerned, he and Ainsley were two more marks to swindle.

"I'm glad we could fit this into our schedule," he said. "And even happier you had room for us at the retreat."

Brody spread his arms out, and for a split second, Santiago was afraid the other man was going to try for a hug. "Our mission is to help couples in trouble. As licensed counselors, we've made it our life's work to teach other people how to effectively communicate and save their relationships." His tone was earnest;

if Santiago hadn't known better, he might have believed the older man.

Alva stepped forward and placed what he supposed was meant to be a comforting hand on his arm. Santiago fought the urge to recoil from her touch. "You've both taken the first step, which is often the most difficult." She glanced to Ainsley and back to him, clearly speaking to them both. "Your presence here means you're both committed to doing the hard work of repairing your relationship. We are so happy to help with that."

Ainsley merely nodded. Alva aimed a smile at her. "We're looking forward to getting to know you both over the next week. Remember, if you need anything, we're here to help."

"Thank you," Santiago said.

Brody tilted his head toward Ainsley. "We hope you enjoy your evening. The facilities at the main cabin are closed for the evening—we want everyone to wait to meet each other until our first session in the morning. Please get some rest, and we'll see you at breakfast."

"That sounds good," Santiago replied. "Let me walk you out." He stepped to the door and held it open. As the Woodses passed him, he shot Ainsley a look.

She nodded, understanding his silent signal.

Santiago closed the door behind him and indicated Alva and Brody should walk down the porch steps with him. While their backs were turned, he ran a finger over the surface of his own hidden camera, disguised as a coin he wore on a chain around his neck. "I was hoping to have a word in private?"

"Of course." Brody's tone was friendly, but he'd dropped his voice to match Santiago's volume. "What's on your mind?"

Santiago stopped and lifted his hand to scratch the back of his head. "Here's the thing," he said. He made a point of glancing back at the cabin, as if he was worried Ainsley was spying on them. "This isn't going to work. I'm only here so that I can tell the divorce lawyer I tried everything. We have a prenup agreement that states we have to try counseling before we split or else she gets half of everything. Since we're both lawyers, it's not going to be easy to divorce. But I want out of this marriage."

The Woodses exchanged a look. "I see," Alva said carefully.

"Is there something you can do to help me?" he asked. "Maybe you can convince Grace that she'd be better off without me? If she initiates the divorce, I'll be able to argue down the amount of alimony she should get." It felt strange to use Ainsley's middle name, but he needed to get used to saying it around these people.

Brody nodded, his expression thoughtful. "You're not the first man to ask us this."

Santiago lifted his eyebrows, trying to look earnest. "That's why I came here. A friend of a friend said you guys work magic in these situations."

Alva and Brody exchanged a look. She nodded imperceptibly, and he turned to Santiago. "I think we can help you, if this is really what you want."

Santiago sighed as though relieved. "It is. What's it going to take?"

"We'll talk to your wife," Alva said. "We'll make sure she realizes she would be happier on her own. But to do that, we're going to have to paint you in an unflattering light. Are you going to be okay with that?"

Santiago nodded vigorously. "I don't care what you say about me. Just get me free."

"Funny you should use that word," Brody said. "I hope you can appreciate that when we take on a special project like this, it goes beyond the scope of the fees that you paid to attend the marriage retreat."

Santiago reached into his back pocket and pulled out an envelope. He passed it to Brody, who opened it and flipped through the bills.

"Four thousand now. Six thousand when she signs the divorce papers at the end of the week."

Brody passed the envelope to Alva, then smiled at him. "That's fair," he said.

"We can't offer any guarantees," Alva said firmly. "We will do our best, but for obvious reasons we make no promises."

"I understand," Santiago said.

"That means no refunds," Alva continued. She arched one brow, as though daring him to challenge her on this. "And we ask that you are discreet about our arrangement during the retreat."

"Of course." Santiago nodded. "I won't say a word. I don't want her suspecting anything."

"She won't," Brody said confidently. "Like I said before, you're not the only one we've helped. The spouses never know."

He smiled smugly, and Santiago fought the urge to punch the man in the nose. How many people had they hurt, all for the sake of a few dollars?

"Excellent," Santiago replied. "Thank you."

"Thank *you*, Mr. Rodriguez," Alva said. She tucked the envelope into her pocket with a smile. "I'm glad we'll be able to help you with your problem."

"Me, too," he said. "I'll see you in the morning." He waved goodbye and walked back to the cabin, his body shaking with anger. He swiped across the surface of his camera, turning it off again.

Ainsley took one look at his face when he walked in and stood up from where she'd been sitting on the sofa. "What happened?"

He shook his head. "They accepted the bribe."

She pressed her lips together, her expression disgusted. "Of course they did."

"They were so casual about it," he said, reliving the conversation in his mind. He felt strangely disconnected from the events, even though they had happened only a few minutes ago. "Like it was the kind of thing they do every day."

"They probably do," she pointed out.

"Who does that?" he asked, trying to wrap his brain around their casual, callous disregard for the welfare of others. He looked at her, hoping she had some insight as to what made these people tick.

Ainsley's eyes were full of warmth as she stared up at him. "I don't know." She stepped closer and placed her hand on his arm, almost in the same spot where Alva had touched him earlier. Her warmth burned away the hidden stain Alva had left behind, and he felt himself relax. "Try not to waste your time trying to understand them. It's not worth your emotional energy. All that matters is their actions, and they've proven they aren't trustworthy or decent people."

"I know, I just…" he trailed off, shaking his head. "I guess I'm trying to make sense of this. Don't get me wrong—I hate what they did to my sister, and to everyone else they hurt. I wish there had been enough evidence for the other people to press charges. I'm not trying to make excuses for them. I just want to know how two normal-looking people decided to go down this path. Did they wake up one day, look at each other and say, 'Let's start taking bribes!' Were they desperate for money? What do they tell themselves so they can sleep at night?"

Ainsley gave him a crooked smile, amusement dancing in her eyes.

"What?" he asked. "Why are you giving me that look?"

She shook her head. "Just remembering law school, and all those times in mock trial when you persuaded the jury to cut your client some slack. You'd always weave a detailed story about their actions, their life, their motivations. You could make even the most hardened killer seem sympathetic when you were done."

"Hey now," he protested. "You know I'm very selective about my clients. I don't do image rehabilitation for true monsters."

"I'm not saying you do," she replied. "But you're very good at presenting the human side of people, of making juries think about why your clients make the choices they do. I don't think you try to make the truly guilty appear innocent. You just offer a nuanced perspective to ensure the jury doesn't make a knee-jerk decision without first accepting the humanity of your client."

He tilted his head to the side. "Are you saying that's a bad thing?"

"Not at all." She squeezed his arm and dropped her hand. "I admire that about you, the way you can see the good in people who, at first glance, don't seem to have any inside. But I think in this instance, your empathy is misplaced."

Santiago frowned. "What do you mean?"

Ainsley sighed softly. "When you're working, you're able to maintain a professional distance from your clients. It's just a job. But this is personal. The Woodses hurt your sister, and who knows how many others. This isn't just a case you can set aside at the end of the day. We're going to be around them all week, watching them work up close, all the while knowing they're lying and cheating and hurting people. It's going to be hard to do that, to bear witness to their behavior without trying to stop them. But we have to."

"I know," he said quietly. In truth, he'd thought he'd be able to handle it. But after spending only a few minutes around Brody and Alva, he knew Ainsley was right. It was going to take all his self-control to keep his anger in check during the week.

"Hey." Ainsley's voice was soft in the otherwise silent cabin. She touched his arm again, this time laying her hand flat against the side of his biceps. When he met her eyes, he saw her gaze was filled with understanding. "We're in this together, remember?"

Her words warmed him from the inside, making him feel less alone. If only that were really true! Sure, she was here with him now, helping him as he sought to expose the Woodses for the frauds they were. But that was as far as their partnership went. After the week was up, they'd go their separate ways, back to their individual lives with their own problems.

It was fine. It's what he'd wanted five years ago. Still wanted, come to that.

So why did the thought give him a twinge of regret?

He frowned, pushing aside his internal disquiet. He had one job this week: gather the evidence needed to tear down this sham of a marriage retreat and bring the Woodses to justice. His own emotional turmoil would have to wait.

Besides, once he got away from Ainsley, he would no longer feel that old familiar pull.

Right?

"We can do this," Ainsley said, misinterpreting the cause of his frown. "You and me. No time for second thoughts now."

He forced himself to smile. "I can't tell you how much I appreciate your help."

"Don't mention it," she replied. "I'll admit, I was skeptical at first. But now that I've met them and they've already taken your bribe, I know we're doing the right thing." She slid her arms around him, squeezing tightly in a fierce hug.

The movement caused her breasts to flatten against his chest. Santiago sucked in a breath as a zing of lust shot through him, igniting a fire of need in his belly. *Cool it*, he thought. It was clear Ainsley wasn't making a come-on; she was simply trying to offer him comfort. What kind of cad would he be if he responded to her innocent gesture with arousal?

After a few endless seconds, she pulled back, gazing up at him with a smile. It was the first truly unguarded look she'd given him since he'd stepped into her office earlier in the week, and the sight of it nearly took his breath away. This was the Ainsley he'd missed; full of life, a little mischievous, a lot passionate. He knew from experience that when she turned her focus on something or someone, she devoted herself entirely. It was a hell of a thing, to be on the receiving end of her attentions.

He cleared his throat, needing to shift his own mental focus before he let himself get carried away. "Are you hungry?"

She wrinkled her nose. "Kind of. But do you think we can trust the food they brought?"

"It's probably fine," he said. "I can't imagine they're in the business of poisoning their clients. Can't get money out of dead people, right?"

She laughed. "True. That reminds me—why don't you do another sweep of the place? Make sure they haven't turned anything on now that they paid us a visit."

"Good call." Santiago collected the detector from his room and walked around the cabin, double-checking their privacy. Once again, the place came up clear.

"Still nothing," he said, walking back into the kitchenette.

Ainsley nodded as she rummaged in the bag Alva had left behind. "Looks like sandwiches in here," she said, pulling out a few plastic cartons. "Along with some chips."

"Works for me," Santiago said. He was still too keyed up to eat, his emotions suppressing his hunger.

She placed everything on the table and sat in one of the chairs. He took the seat opposite hers and pulled one of the sandwiches in front of him. "In a twisted way, I suppose we're off to a good start," he remarked.

Ainsley took a bite and eyed him over the top of her sandwich. "Because they took the bribe?" she asked around her mouthful of food.

Santiago took his own bite and nodded. "It was so easy. Almost too easy." He frowned, seeing their conversation in a new light. He'd thought he was trapping them, but did the Woodses have something up their own sleeves?

"I wouldn't read too much into that," Ainsley said. "I'm sure they won't hesitate to throw you under the bus and tell me you bribed them if they think it will help them, but since I'm in on it, it doesn't matter."

"That's true," Santiago replied. "They probably think I'm just as compromised as they are."

"How are you going to get the money back, anyway?"

He shrugged. "I expect the judge who hears the case will order them to repay me, since I have them on tape taking the bribe."

"Fair enough." Ainsley shook her head and laughed.

"You know, it's kind of nice feeling like the smartest one in the room."

Santiago nearly choked on his food. "Aren't you used to that already?"

"Hardly." Her tone was dry, the aural equivalent of rolling her eyes.

"Oh, come on," he insisted. "You were the smartest one in our class at law school. And no offense to your family, but I doubt any of your relatives are anywhere close to your level of intelligence."

"Flattery isn't necessary," she said, raising one eyebrow in a clear expression of skepticism. "I'm already here. No need to keep trying to convince me."

"It's not flattery, it's the truth," he shot back. "You're the smartest person I know."

She shifted in her chair and he knew she was uncomfortable. She'd always had a hard time accepting praise, a habit he'd never understood. When they'd been together, he'd tried to help her see just how amazing she was. He was willing to bet that once they'd separated, she'd had no one in her life to hold up a mirror so she would recognize her own accomplishments.

The thought made him sad. Ainsley was special, but she'd always minimized her own gifts, preferring the shadows to the spotlight.

It's not your problem, he reminded himself. A part of him would always care for Ainsley—he was smart enough not to deny or fight it. But he couldn't be there for her, not in the way a true partner was. And if he let himself get too close, if he started to forget why he'd left her in the first place, he'd only hurt them both in the end.

She cleared her throat. "Maybe I can get them one-on-one tomorrow morning after breakfast," she said. "Offer them my bribe and see what happens."

"That sounds like a plan." Santiago nodded, glad the conversation was moving on. Best to focus on why they were here and ignore any other distractions.

It was the only way he was going to get through this.

Chapter Five

"Welcome to breakfast." The young woman smiled at them, nodding first at Santiago, then at Ainsley, the following morning. "If you'll please follow me, I'll show you to your table. This is where you both will eat your meals for the duration of your stay with us."

Interesting, Ainsley thought as they followed the staffer into a dining room off the main lobby. It seemed the Woodses didn't want the couples at the marriage retreat speaking to each other outside of any group sessions. Was that because they didn't want people comparing notes? It was definitely easier to manipulate people if you isolated them. Given the fact the Woodses had insisted they stay in their cabins last night, and were now assigning them all to separate tables, it seemed they were starting the process early.

The dark-haired woman stopped at a two-top and flashed that Stepford smile once more. "Here you are."

"Thank you," Santiago said quietly. They sat

across from each other, and Ainsley glanced around the room.

There were nine other tables, all of them set for only two people. Six couples were here already, sipping coffee or eating scrambled eggs. There was a quiet hum of conversation in the air, but she couldn't make out any individual words.

The room itself matched the subtle, classy decor of their cabin and the lobby they'd seen yesterday. The sound of a fountain tinkled through the room, the soothing noise providing additional privacy for speech.

Not that it mattered. The tables were set far apart, islands scattered throughout the room. The better to discourage casual socialization, she supposed.

Santiago caught her eye. "Interesting setup," he said softly.

She nodded. "For a couple who claims to be all about encouraging communication, it sure doesn't seem that way."

A twentyish-looking man appeared at their table, looking like a catalog model. "Coffee?" he asked brightly.

Santiago and Ainsley both nodded, and he filled their cups. "I'll tell the kitchen you're here. The food will be out momentarily."

"We don't get to order from a menu?" Ainsley asked.

The waiter shook his head. "No, ma'am. The

Woodses have carefully curated the menu for this retreat, choosing foods specially designed to help you focus and cleanse your body. Since neither of you indicated any food allergies in your application paperwork, you're able to partake of every meal."

"Wonderful," Ainsley said dryly.

The young man didn't appear to pick up on her sarcasm. His smile brightened, an event Ainsley hadn't thought possible. "I think you'll find the food to be delicious."

He disappeared, and Ainsley shot Santiago a look. "The brainwashing seems to have already begun."

A spark of amusement flared in his dark eyes, making her stomach do a little flip. "Gotta start early," he said.

His voice was deep and soft. Ainsley took a deep breath, determined to ignore the physical reaction. It was a reflex, nothing more.

She reached for the coffee and took a fortifying sip. Truth be told, she hadn't slept well last night, and not just because of the unfamiliar surroundings.

Being around Santiago was unsettling. Hugging him last night had been a mistake. The last thing she needed was a visceral reminder of the way their bodies fit together. The kiss in her office had thrown her for a loop, but she'd pushed aside the emotions that had stirred up. But that hug? Feeling her body press against his, her breasts flattening against the solid plane of his chest, the way his arms had circled round her…that was harder to ignore.

And then there was the way he'd looked at her last night, when he'd told her she was the smartest person he knew. The statement had nearly made her cry, though she shouldn't have been surprised. Santiago had always been supportive of her endeavors. He wasn't the type of man who had to put others down in order to feel superior, and he'd never been threatened by her intelligence. He was one of the only men she knew who seemed to enjoy her brains, rather than merely tolerate them.

Each event, taken on its own, would be tolerable. But all together? It was adding up to be trouble.

Her thoughts were interrupted by the waiter, who slid a plate in front of her. She eyed the food, expecting something unusual after that nonsense about "focus and cleansing" the waiter had spouted earlier. But everything looked normal: eggs, whole-grain toast and a side of fresh fruit. A sliced avocado sat off to the side, along with a small pot of jelly.

"This looks…decent." She poked at the eggs with her fork and reached for the pepper.

"Tastes okay, too," Santiago said around a mouthful.

Ainsley glanced up, surprised he was already chowing down. "You trust them?"

He lifted one shoulder in a shrug. "Like I said last night, it's not in their best interest to poison us."

"That's true." She forked up a bite of eggs, pleased to find they were fluffy. Despite their flaws, it seemed the Woodses hired decent chefs.

Movement from the side of the room caught her eye, and she turned to see the couple was here.

Brody and Alva made their way to a small platform at the front of the room, smiling and nodding to people as they moved through the room. The remaining couples had filed in while she and Santiago hadn't been looking, and now it seemed they were all present and accounted for.

"Welcome, welcome," Brody said, spreading his arms wide, a smile on his face. "We're so glad you're here for our marriage retreat."

Standing at his side, Alva beamed up at him, the very picture of wifely devotion.

Ainsley refrained from rolling her eyes. Barely.

"Alva and I have been married for forty years," Brody continued. He looked down at his wife with an affectionate smile. "I think we've learned a thing or two, wouldn't you say, dear?"

The older woman giggled, the sound like nails on a chalkboard to Ainsley's ears. "We do have degrees in counseling as well, dear."

Brody smiled indulgently at his wife. "We are so excited to have you all join us. The fact that you're here means you've taken the first, most difficult step. And it also shows that, despite your troubles, you each still value your marriage."

He paused to let that sink in. Ainsley saw several people nod, and noticed a few looks of surprise throughout the room, as though Brody's words had made these people realize something they hadn't considered before.

Her heart squeezed in empathy. Much as she hated to agree with him, Brody was right. These people were here because they were trying to get their relationships back on track. Or most of them were, at least. The fact that Brody and Alva were all too happy to cheat and lie and take advantage of their vulnerabilities made her blood boil.

"Now, this isn't going to be easy," Alva said. "We have a lot of work to do, and we're going to ask a lot of you. You're going to have to open your hearts and minds, and you're going to have to be vulnerable to each other. We're going to work to rebuild trust in your marriages, something that may have been lacking in the recent past."

There were a few rueful chuckles throughout the room. Alva nodded, apparently encouraged. "We can't promise results," she continued. "But Brody and I are proud of our track record. Over the last decade that we've been doing this retreat, 95 percent of the couples who attend go on to have stronger marriages after their time with us."

A few gasps of surprise punctuated this announcement. Ainsley kept her expression neutral, but inside, her BS detector was blaring. That seemed like an awfully inflated number, but with no way to verify the data, the Woodses could make whatever claims they wanted.

"We're going to be with you every step of the way," Brody chimed in. "We aren't asking you to do anything we haven't done. And we're going to be sharing with you, as well. We believe that experience is the best teacher. But we don't want you to have to experience all the trials and tribulations we've gone through. So we're going to take the lessons we've learned and share them with you."

"In all their embarrassing detail," Alva said.

Brody chuckled, along with the other couples in the room. As Ainsley scanned the faces in the room, she realized they were buying this spiel hook, line and sinker.

She glanced at Santiago, who was also smiling. If she hadn't known better, she would think he was swallowing this drivel as well.

His reaction made her realize she, too, had a part to play. So she pushed her true feelings aside and tried to act like she was happy to be here.

"If there's one thing I've learned," Brody said. "It's that pride will get you into a lot of trouble. I hope one of the things you'll all learn during the retreat is how to put your own selfish pride aside and focus on the good of your partner and your relationship. If you can learn that lesson, you'll be ready to face whatever life throws at you."

"But it won't be easy," Alva cautioned the room. "That's why we have so many sessions during this retreat. You'll each experience two individual counseling sessions per day, along with two couple's sessions. We also have one group session and one seminar every day."

Ainsley felt her eyebrows lift, and judging from the other expressions in the room, she wasn't the only one surprised by this schedule.

Alva held up a hand, anticipating objections. "I know that sounds like a lot. It is." She glanced up at Brody with a smile. "You've all made a significant financial investment to be here. Now we're asking you to match that with your time and effort. If you truly commit to the experience and put in the work, you will reap the rewards."

"She's right." Brody stepped forward, his avuncular demeanor making it seem like he was about to impart a nugget of wisdom. "That means put away your distractions—no phones, no work. I'm sure you've already noticed there are no televisions in your cabins."

"It's important you set aside the routines of your daily life in order to truly focus on healing the damages in your marriage," Alva added. "Only by breaking free of the chains of past habits and patterns can you truly move forward together."

Ainsley had to admit, they talked a good game. And some of what they said actually made sense. She knew from her own experience that she'd had to let go of some of her habits after Santiago had left—going to the same stores, the same restaurants had been too hard, a painful reminder that what they'd once done together she was now doing alone. So she'd started trying new things, building a new set of memories that didn't contain Santiago. It had been difficult, but she'd done it. Moving back to Mustang Valley after law school had helped with that, as he'd never lived there. It only stood to reason that couples in trouble would have to learn new ways of relating to each other, since their existing strategies had brought them here in the first place.

"Your server will bring your personal schedules to your tables shortly," Brody said. "Take a few moments to look them over, and we will see you soon for your first session. All of you will be there, and we will assign the smaller groups at that time."

With that, the pair stepped down from the stage and began to make their way out of the room. Ainsley looked at Santiago. "I guess it's time for me to offer my bribe," she said quietly.

He nodded. "Act like you're looking for the bathroom," he suggested.

"Good idea." She got to her feet and made a show of looking around the room. Fortunately for her, there wasn't a clearly marked sign identifying the facilities, so it didn't look too odd that she was wandering around.

Ainsley made sure she gave them a minute or two

to leave the room, so she didn't appear to be chasing after them. She slipped out of the room and caught sight of their backs as they reached the end of the hallway.

Picking up the pace, she raced after them. As she ran, she ran a finger over the front of her necklace to activate the camera. "Excuse me!" she called out.

Brody turned, followed by Alva. "Yes?" Brody asked. "Did you need something?"

She came to a stop in front of them, panting slightly. "Yes," she said. "I was hoping to have a private word?"

Impatience flitted across Alva's face, so she quickly added, "I don't need much of your time."

The couple exchanged a cryptic look. "Of course," Brody said, his tone friendly. "What can we do for you? It's Grace Rodriguez, right?"

Ainsley nodded and stepped closer, dropping her voice. "It's my husband, Santiago," she said. "I have to get out of this marriage."

Alva's brows drew together, her expression one of maternal concern. "Oh my dear," she said. "What makes you say that?"

Ainsley glanced around, as though worried someone would overhear. "He's cheating on me," she nearly whispered. "Has been for years. I have proof, but he doesn't know that. I agreed to this retreat because he thinks he can use these sessions as an excuse to shortchange me on the alimony."

"I'm so sorry." Brody looked genuinely sympathetic.

"How can we help?" Alva asked.

"I need him to admit to his infidelity," Ainsley said. "If he confesses in one of the counseling sessions, then according to the terms of our prenup, I'll get everything."

Alva nodded gravely. "I see. Well," she trailed off, shaking her head. "We're sympathetic to your situation of course, but I'm sure you can appreciate that what happens in the individual counseling sessions must remain private. This is a safe space, and if people don't trust that what they say will be held in confidence, then they won't participate fully. It undermines our mission to bring people together."

Ainsley locked eyes with the older woman. "I understand," she said. "But I only want to know what Santiago says, not what anyone else talks about. And I'm willing to pay for the information." She slipped her hand into the back pocket of her pants and withdrew an envelope.

Alva and Brody exchanged another look, this one assessing. For a moment, Ainsley thought they were going to refuse her bribe. But then Brody extended his hand and took the envelope.

He handed it to Alva, who opened it and flipped through the bills inside. The older woman glanced up, the look on her face making it clear she wasn't impressed with the offer.

"Half now, half after you tell me what he says,"

Ainsley said, injecting a defensive note into her voice. "Do we have a deal?"

Brody looked at Alva, who gave a subtle nod. "Yes, Mrs. Rodriguez," he said, sticking his hand out to shake hers. "It would seem that we do."

"Excellent." Ainsley smiled. "Thank you for your help."

"Normally, we don't operate like this," Alva said. "But in cases of infidelity…"

"I understand," Ainsley said, offering the absolution the other woman seemed to be asking for. "I wouldn't have asked, but after what he's done, I'll never trust him again."

"There are some things that can't be fixed," Brody said seriously.

"I trust you'll remain discreet?" Alva asked. She seemed a little anxious, but there was a calculating glint in her eyes that made Ainsley think this was all just an act designed to make it look like they'd never taken a bribe before.

"Of course," Ainsley replied. "If Santiago's lawyer were to find out I paid to get this information, it would only hurt my case during the divorce."

Alva nodded, apparently satisfied by her response. "All right. We'll do what we can for you. Mind you, we can't force him to admit to anything. We can only encourage total honesty."

"I'll take any help you can give me," Ainsley said, trying to sound relieved.

"I think we'll be able to get you what you need," Brody said. He reached out to give her shoulder a pat, and Ainsley steeled herself not to flinch away from the contact. "Just relax and try to enjoy your time here. Even though your marriage is over, you might still find the seminars useful."

"That's true," she forced herself to say. "Maybe I can learn how not to make the same mistakes twice."

Brody smiled, a teacher pleased with his pupil's response. "Exactly." He dropped his hand, making Ainsley sigh internally with relief. "We'll see you at the first seminar," he said.

Ainsley nodded. "Looking forward to it," she replied.

The Woodses began walking away, and Ainsley turned and started back down the hallway that led into the dining room. After a few steps, she drew up short.

Brett was standing in the doorway to the dining room, that perma-smile fixed on his face. It was clear he'd been watching them, and a shiver ran down Ainsley's spine at the knowledge he'd been spying.

"Did you get the help you needed?" His voice was perfectly pleasant, his demeanor calm. But just as before, Ainsley's skin crawled at his proximity.

"Yes, thank you," she said.

He stepped to the side, his hand out to indicate she should precede him into the dining room. "May I escort you back to your table?"

"No, thanks," she replied quickly. "I can find it just fine on my own."

He nodded as she slipped past him, fighting the urge to contort her body to get as far away from him as possible. This time, she felt his eyes on her back as she headed toward Santiago.

She took her seat across from him, and he nodded at her. He lifted his coffee cup and held it in front of his mouth while he spoke. "You appear to have a shadow," he said softly.

Ainsley tried not to shudder. "I know."

"It's not just you," he added. "I've noticed that one of the employees follows anyone who has gotten up from the table. They stay at a distance, but it's clear they're watching where people are going."

"Making sure we don't talk to each other?" she wondered aloud. "Or keeping people from snooping?"

"Maybe a bit of both," he said. "Everything go okay?"

"Yep," she said shortly. "They took the bait. Now we just wait and see how this plays out."

Santiago nodded. "Good work." The note of approval in his voice made her want to preen, but she pushed down the inconvenient reaction. She didn't need his appreciation, damn it.

"It didn't take much effort on my part," she said. "I told them you'd been unfaithful, and they went with it." It was the story they'd agreed upon last night, one that would make it easy for them to track how the Woodses behaved. If they encouraged Santiago to confess his marital sins, they'd know her bribe had worked. If they tried to convince Ainsley she was better off on her own, they'd know Santiago's bribe held sway. Either way, they both had the Woodses on camera accepting bribes to skew the results of the marriage retreat.

It was the start of a rock-solid case. If only they could end things now and go back to their normal lives…

"Come on," Santiago suggested. He got to his feet, throwing his napkin on the table. "The first session starts in five minutes. We should head to the room."

"Sounds good." Ainsley rose as well and moved to stand by him. Together, they set off for the entrance, where one of the ever-present smiling employees stood to direct them to their next stop.

She stole a glance across the room as they left, back in the direction of where she'd pursued the Woodses. Brett still stood in the doorway, his eyes fixed on her. He noticed her look and nodded, his smile slipping a bit.

Ainsley swallowed, bile rising up the back of her throat. Something was going on behind the scenes here, she just knew it.

But did she really want to find out what it was?

HE WAS GOING to go insane.

After two days at the marriage retreat, Santiago

had just about reached his limits. He didn't think he could sit through one more group discussion, participate in another self-reflection, or handle an additional couple's therapy session.

It was all so…slick. So carefully crafted to manipulate the thoughts and feelings of the "chosen victim," as he'd taken to thinking about it. By now, it was clear the Woodses had picked his side and were actively working to wear down Ainsley so she would agree to an easy divorce. It was enough to turn his stomach, and the only thing that kept him going was the knowledge that Ainsley was here with him, and that she knew the truth.

She sat across from him now as they ate lunch together. He stole glances at her face between bites and wondered how anyone who had vowed to love, honor and respect someone could have their heart turned so drastically. He and Ainsley had never married, but he had loved her and he still cared deeply for her. He couldn't imagine getting to a point in their relationship where he would pay people to deliberately hurt her.

But that seemed to be what half the people in this room had done. Unless he missed his guess, most of the couples in the room had at least one person who had paid to sway the outcome of this retreat. He knew in his own group sessions, the counselor had focused on tips and tricks to manage the divorce process, everything from hiding assets to choosing an attorney.

And wouldn't you know it, they just so happened to have a list of lawyers they could recommend if anyone was interested. He hadn't recognized any of the names on the list, but he'd definitely pass the info along to the police later. The whole thing made Santiago wonder just how big this racket really was—were the bribes simply limited to the Woodses, or was there a network of people ready and waiting to profit off the misery of others?

Ainsley's experience had been quite the opposite, as though she was in a totally different retreat. She'd told him that members of her group were being counseled to move on, to maintain their dignity and let go without a fight. Based on what she'd told him, her group sessions had encouraged people to look inward, to blame themselves for the problems in their marriages. As he glanced at the faces around the room, he could tell based on the pinched, anxious expressions that the message seemed to be taking hold.

It was enough to make him want to end things now, to stop this charade and tell the Woodses he and Ainsley had them on camera accepting bribes. But that wasn't quite enough. They had to collect evidence proving the bribes had made a difference in how he and Ainsley were being treated, in the things that were said to them. Only then would he have the strongest case against them. Anything less, and there was a very real risk that the Woodses would be able to argue their way out of the lawsuit he planned to file as soon as this retreat was over.

"Are you okay?"

Ainsley's voice broke into his thoughts, and he looked up to find her watching him, concern shining in her eyes.

Santiago nodded. "Just thinking."

The corner of her mouth lifted in a wry smile. "Try not to," she advised. "You'll just get angry."

"How are you holding up?" he asked. "You're the one getting the short end of the stick here. At least in my sessions, the counselors are validating everything I say. I know it's fake, but it's got to be exhausting to be told you're in the wrong all the time."

She shrugged and dropped her eyes to her plate. "It's not fun," she said. "But I know not to take it personally. I'm worried for the people who actually believe what we're being told."

"No kidding." That's what kept him up at night; the innocent people in this situation who, through no fault of their own, were being manipulated into thinking they'd done something wrong.

"Five more days, right?" she said softly. "We can get through five more days."

Santiago nodded, knowing they had no other choice. "Eyes on the prize," he muttered.

Chapter Six

Three days later...

The thought kept circling around Ainsley's mind, a mantra she was silently chanting to herself to get through the current group counseling session. It was unbelievable, the way the other members in her "circle" were being told to let go and move on with their lives, or to forgive and forget, even though their spouses had been treating them badly for months, or even years.

"...so you see, Jenny," continued Alexa, one of the counselors Ainsley was quickly growing to hate, "while it's tempting to blame your husband for his infidelity, it's important to examine your emotional and sexual availability over the last several months. Have you been a true partner to him, or have you let the demands of your life intrude in your marriage?"

Jenny, a thirtysomething woman with limp blond hair and a long face, nodded. Her lower lip trembled as she stared up at Alexa, her eyes shiny with unshed tears.

"I know I've changed a lot since the baby came," Jenny said, her voice thick with emotion. "I went into survival mode right after the birth, and I was too exhausted to do anything more than take care of little George. I guess I just fell into the habit of focusing solely on him, since he was the most vocal about needing my attention."

Ainsley very nearly snorted in disgust. What kind of man cheated on his wife while she was taking care of their newborn son? What kind of narcissistic psychopath broke his marriage vows because his wife wasn't stroking his ego (or other bits) while recovering from childbirth?

Alexa nodded sagely, her expression patient. "That's exactly right," she said, her voice pitched low in a soothing cadence. "Your marriage existed before your son came along. You need to nurture the connection with your husband so he doesn't feel shut out of the new family dynamic."

"I'm, uh, still recovering from the birth." Jenny looked down at her lap and blushed. "I know it's been nine months, but there was a lot of stitching involved, and my doctor told me the kind of repairs I had will affect...things."

Alexa nodded again, like she understood exactly was Jenny was going through. In reality, the woman didn't have children—she'd said as much when she'd introduced herself at the beginning of the week.

"I know having a baby can be a physically traumatic experience," the counselor said. "But you've got to try to rekindle the flame for your husband."

"Even if it hurts?" Jenny's voice was impossibly small and Ainsley's heart broke for her. Her husband was even worse than she'd initially thought.

Alexa smiled brightly. "I'm sure the pain is partly in your mind. Besides, there are things you can do to help. Have you seen a therapist?"

Ainsley bit her lip to keep from screaming. The woman was clearly exhausted from the demands of caring for her baby, in addition to healing from what sounded like a difficult birth. She needed to ditch the man-child—in her case, she'd be better off alone than tied to a guy who pressured her for sex despite her pain, and cheated on her when she didn't fulfill all his needs.

"I don't know where to start with that," Jenny said.

"That's why we're here," Alexa replied. "You're already starting the process. At the end of the week, I can give you some recommendations so you can continue this important work of self-improvement for your husband and marriage."

Ainsley glanced around, wondering if anyone else thought Alexa was way out of line with the advice she gave to Jenny. But all she saw was a circle of nodding heads, everyone apparently on board with this casual display of cruelty toward a new mother.

"Well, we seem to be out of time at the moment. We'll take a break and pick things up again tomorrow. In the meantime, I want you all to reflect on the ways your behavior has contributed to the troubles in your marriage. Have you been emotionally and sexually unavailable, like Jenny? Or have you put your work above your partner?" She glanced around the room, smiling at everyone in turn. "Tomorrow, we'll start digging deeper into these common mistakes and learn about ways to make amends."

Ainsley grabbed her clutch and got to her feet, positioning herself so she was close to Jenny. As they filed out of the room, she gently touched the other woman's elbow.

Jenny looked back, startled. Ainsley offered her a small smile. "Do you have a minute to chat?"

"Okay." Jenny nodded, but she looked uncertain.

Ainsley led her into a small alcove off the hall, near a ficus tree standing in a nut-brown pot.

"I'm worried about you," Ainsley said softly.

Jenny's eyes widened. "Me? Why?"

Ainsley tilted her head to the side. "You're taking care of a new baby, probably on your own, am I right?"

Jenny looked down. "My husband works hard at his job. He deserves a break when he gets home at the end of the day."

Anger bubbled through Ainsley's veins, making her feel hot. Those sounded like her husband's words coming out of her mouth. "And what about you? Don't you deserve a break?"

Jenny blinked, as though she hadn't thought about it that way.

"You're still healing from the birth," Ainsley continued. "He should not be pressuring you for sex, especially when he knows it causes you pain."

"I think I just need to relax," Jenny started.

Ainsley held up a hand. "I'm not a doctor. But do you have one you can trust? Maybe something didn't heal properly? It's worth getting checked out, for your own sake."

Jenny nodded, and Ainsley saw a light come into her eyes. "I think you're right." She studied Ainsley for a few seconds. "You seem to know a lot about this. Do you have kids?"

Ainsley shook her head, ignoring the prick of pain in her heart. "No." She debated telling Jenny the truth—that she couldn't have children, wasn't even sure if she wanted them, in fact—but decided against it.

"I have several close friends with kids, and my half sister just had one," she said instead. "So I've heard a lot about the delivery and recovery process."

"It's been really hard," Jenny said. She sounded almost confessional, as though she'd kept her doubts and struggles to herself for so long, she wasn't sure she should be talking about them now.

"I've heard," Ainsley said. And Jenny's situation was apparently made even more difficult thanks to her cad of a husband.

"He shouldn't be cheating on you," Ainsley said, feeling bolder now that they'd been talking on their own. "You don't deserve that."

Jenny looked down again, but not before Ainsley caught the sheen of tears in her eyes. "You don't think it's my fault?"

"Not at all," Ainsley conformed. "You shouldn't have to put up with that. If I were you, I'd leave him." She lowered her voice. "My husband is cheating on me, too. I know what it's like. But trust me, there's someone better out there for you, someone who won't sleep with other women and then try to blame you for his actions."

"I don't know," Jenny said sadly. "Steve says my body isn't what it used to be. He's right—I still haven't lost all of the baby weight."

Screw him! Ainsley screamed in her head. This guy had really done a number on Jenny's sense of self-worth. It was going to take more than one pep talk to help Jenny feel better about herself. But Ainsley had to try.

"Any true man would be lucky to have you," she said.

Jenny glanced up, a shy smile forming at the corners of her mouth. "Do you really think that?"

Ainsley nodded. "I wouldn't have said it otherwise."

"Maybe you're right," Jenny said, sounding tentative. "Maybe I—"

"Babe? Jenny, what are you doing back here?"

As soon as the male voice interrupted their conversation, Jenny retreated back into her shell. She seemed to grow smaller before Ainsley's eyes as her shoulders drew up and her head lowered.

"Hi, honey," she said. "I was just taking to one of the women from my group."

A man walked up and put a possessive hand on Jenny's arm. Even if Ainsley didn't know what he'd said and done to his wife, she would have disliked him on sight. He was a few inches taller than she was, with an arrogant air about him. His blond hair was combed to the side and shiny with gel. He sported khaki pants and a tucked-in polo shirt, the business casual uniform of corporate drones the world over. But it was his eyes that she found so repulsive—small, blue and mean.

He gave Ainsley the once-over, clearly suspicious. "Oh yeah? You know we're not supposed to talk to others outside of sessions." He tugged on Jenny's arm. "Come on. We don't want to be late for lunch."

Jenny gave Ainsley an apologetic glance before turning away. "Okay, Steve."

Steve released Jenny's arm and hung back while his wife walked away. He glared at Ainsley.

"What the hell do you think you're doing?" His voice was low and full of malice.

Ainsley bit her lip, stifling a knee-jerk reply. As satisfying as it would be to bring this man down to size, he was liable to take his anger out on Jenny. The other woman hadn't said there was any physical abuse going on, but as Ainsley took note of Steve's red face and clenched hands, she didn't trust that he wouldn't start beating his wife for talking out of turn.

"We were just chatting," Ainsley said. "We have some things in common. Jenny looked like she could use a friend."

Steve relaxed a bit, though he didn't quite seem to believe her. "She's fine," he said shortly. "She doesn't need any friends. She's got enough already."

"Why don't you let her decide that for herself?"

Steve took a small step forward. Ainsley stood her ground, refusing to be bullied. "Stay away from my wife," he said quietly.

Any other time, Ainsley would have pushed forward, ignoring this man's blatant intimidation tactics and doing what she wanted. But she just couldn't bring herself to make things harder for Jenny. The other woman had enough trouble as it was—the last thing Ainsley wanted was to add to the new mom's difficulties.

"I won't talk to her," Ainsley said, hating the words even though she knew they were necessary. It wasn't in her nature to back down from a bully, but she had to do what was best for Jenny.

"But," she added, "if Jenny speaks to me, I'm not going to ignore her."

"She won't," Steve said shortly. "She knows better than to do that."

He gave her one final glare and turned on his heel, walking quickly to catch up with his wife.

Ainsley watched them go, wincing in sympathy as she saw Steve's tight grip on the back of Jenny's arm. That was a man with control issues, and likely anger management problems as well. Unless she missed her guess, he'd very likely bribed the Woodses to help gaslight Jenny so she wouldn't leave him.

But why? Why hang on to a marriage he himself was disrespecting? Was it just for the image? Or something more?

Whatever his motivation, Ainsley hoped that when she and Santiago brought down the Woodses, this guy got what was coming to him as well.

SANTIAGO SHUT THE door of the cabin with a sigh and leaned back against the cool, wooden surface. He was physically exhausted, which made no sense at all. He'd spent most of his time over the past few days sitting—in group counseling sessions, in couple's therapy sessions, in one-on-one sessions. So. Much. Talking.

His body was stiff from disuse, his muscles achy with a need to move. If only he could muster the energy!

On some level, he'd known this would be an emotionally challenging week. What he hadn't predicted was the effort required to control his reactions, to sell his performance as a dissatisfied husband looking for a way out. No amount of time spent at the gym could provide that kind of conditioning.

He felt a touch on his arm and looked down to find Ainsley watching him, her brows drawn together in a slight frown. "Talk to me," she said. "I'm worried about you."

The corner of his mouth twitched. "I'm okay." Her concern warmed him from the inside, restoring some of his equilibrium. Her presence anchored him in reality, helping him shrug off the facade he wore all day during the retreat. He'd quickly come to look forward to their evenings in the cabin, the time they spent alone together giving him a chance to recharge and prepare for the next day of lies.

Their evenings had already fallen into a pattern, one that seemed to suit them both. They retired to the cabin after dinner and both changed into casual clothes. Ainsley made herself a cup of decaf coffee while he sipped on tea. Then they sat on the sofa and talked. Mostly about the events of the day, but other things, too. Like her brother's case. The interviews he'd managed to conduct before the retreat. What she thought might be going on, who could have sent that first, shocking email about her brother's parentage.

Occasionally, they would flirt with something more personal. But they usually skated around those topics, as if by silent mutual agreement. This week was already complicated enough. No need to make things more difficult.

The way she was watching him now, Santiago feared she was about to break their unspoken understanding. So he pushed off the door and headed for the kitchenette. “Just a long day,” he said over his shoulder. “Want me to start your coffee?”

“That’d be great, thanks,” she replied. “I’m going to go change.”

“Take your time,” Santiago said. The longer she was in the bedroom, the more time he’d have to regain his composure. It would be so, so easy to really open up and talk to Ainsley. But he couldn’t let himself get emotionally involved with her again. It wouldn’t be fair to either one of them.

He grabbed the small carafe and filled it with water from the tap, then poured it into the coffee maker. Once he got the coffee brewing, he started gathering the things for his tea. After a few minutes, he heard the soft sounds of Ainsley’s slippered feet on the wood floor and knew she’d returned.

“So how was your day?” she asked around a yawn. “Learn anything new?”

Santiago turned around and leaned against the counter, crossing his arms over his chest. “Not really,” he said. “Just more confirmation that some people are total monsters.”

“Tell me about it,” she said. She shook her head

as she dropped into one of the chairs at the small table. "There's this woman in my group—her name is Jenny. She opened up today during our group counseling session." She launched into the story of this poor woman and her emotionally abusive husband. Santiago felt his heart break for Jenny, and wished there was something he could do to help her and her son. Having grown up in a house with two parents who hated each other, he knew firsthand the difficult childhood that was surely in store for the baby.

"I tried to talk to her after the session, but her husband interrupted us," Ainsley continued. "He was a real jerk about it, too. Makes me wonder how much worse he is behind closed doors, when he's not worried about making an impression on other people."

Santiago frowned. "What's his name again?"

"Steve." Her disdain practically dripped from the word.

A tingle of worry shot down Santiago's spine. "I know him from my sessions. He's a total ass."

"Yeah, I figured that out pretty quickly."

The coffee maker gurgled, signaling its completion. Santiago poured Ainsley a cup and placed a tea bag in his own mug of steaming water. He carried both to the table and took the chair opposite her. "No, I mean he's got a temper."

Ainsley's eyes flashed with anger. "Is he hitting her? She didn't mention physical abuse, but after what I saw today, I wouldn't put it past him."

Santiago shook his head. “He hasn’t mentioned that, and I doubt he’d admit it. It’s one thing to say you’re cheating on your wife because she’s not interested in sex anymore. It’s quite another to confess to beating her.”

Ainsley sipped her coffee with a frown. “I suppose you’re right.” She was silent a moment, then leaned forward. “I’m convinced he bribed the Woodses as well. Is there anything we can do to bring him down, too?”

Santiago couldn’t help but laugh; despite her faded sweatshirt, threadbare flannel pants and messy ponytail, there was a fierce air about Ainsley that only a fool would dismiss.

“We can expose his lies, for sure. And I will personally offer my services to his wife, if she decides to divorce him, after all this is wrapped up. Pro bono, of course.”

Ainsley nodded and leaned back, apparently satisfied for now.

“I know you want to help this woman,” Santiago said, growing serious. “But please, don’t do anything to antagonize Steve. If he sees you as a threat, he might lash out and hurt you.”

Ainsley flapped her hand in the air, dismissing his concern. “I’m not afraid of him. I can take care of myself.”

“I’m not suggesting otherwise,” Santiago replied,

digging deep for patience. "I just don't want you to take any unnecessary chances."

Ainsley narrowed her eyes. "I'm not going to turn my back on this woman on the off chance her husband might lose his temper with me. She needs a friend."

"I agree with you." Santiago decided to try a different tack. "But if he's half as bad as we think, he's liable to take his anger out on her."

Ainsley's expression softened. "Yeah, I'm worried about that, too. I told him I wouldn't initiate a conversation with her, but if she talks to me first I'm not going to ignore her."

He could tell her mind was made up. Recognizing the futility of further argument, Santiago nodded. "That seems reasonable." Privately though, he was still worried. It wasn't in Ainsley's nature to walk away from a problem. He could imagine any number of scenarios where she reached out to Jenny, then took the blame if her husband found out they were talking. As far as he knew, Ainsley had never been touched in anger. It seemed as though she simply didn't think it was possible that a man would attack her for speaking to his wife. Unfortunately, thanks to his line of work as a defense attorney, Santiago knew differently.

He watched her now, saw the wheels turning as she tried to figure out a way to help Jenny without tipping off her husband. Admiration filled his chest, but he couldn't shake the twinge of fear for her safety. Ainsley wasn't a rash person—he knew she wouldn't do anything impulsive. But he also understood she wasn't going to stop worrying about Jenny and her situation.

In a way, he was glad she had something to focus on. All the people in his group were unrepentant jerks who lacked the self-awareness of a goldfish. Sitting around listening to these people deny, deflect and blame others for their bad behavior was enough to make him want to tear his hair out. At least Ainsley seemed to have some good people in her group, even though their plights tugged on her heartstrings. At this point, he wasn't sure which scenario was worse: his hating everyone, or her guilt over not being able to save the others.

"What?"

Her question pulled him out of his reverie, and he focused on her again. "I'm sorry?" he asked.

"You have a strange look on your face. What's going on?" she said.

He shook his head to clear his thoughts. "I was just thinking," he said.

She took another sip of coffee. "Penny for your thoughts."

Santiago debated on what to tell her. If he confessed he was worried about her, she'd shrug off his concern and tell him he was overreacting. And perhaps he was. He certainly hoped that was the case. Still, it was probably better he not mention it.

"The baby," he said instead. "I feel bad for their

child. I know what it's like to grow up in a home with that kind of tension."

Ainsley's face softened with understanding. "It can't have been easy for you or Gabriela."

He'd told her a little about his family when they'd been dating. It wasn't a topic he liked to discuss, so he tried not to bring it up. But he could tell Ainsley was curious.

"It was tough," he admitted. "I'm lucky, though—I had my sister, so I wasn't totally alone."

"Did you ever learn why your parents hated each other so much?"

Santiago shook his head. "No. And at some point, I stopped caring about the reason. Either figure it out, or split up, you know? Stop torturing the rest of us."

"I bet you couldn't wait to move out."

"As soon as I could," he confirmed. "I tried to take Gabriela with me, but..." he trailed off, remembering the fight. "They told her if she moved in with me, they'd cut us both off financially. At that point, they were paying for my college, and they'd promised to do the same for her. I was willing to go it on my own, but Gabby was afraid. She told me to leave her, that she'd be fine."

Ainsley reached across the table and placed her hand on his own. "How many years did she have until graduation?"

Her touch was soft and warm, and Santiago wanted to flip his hand over and thread his fingers through hers. But that seemed like too intimate a gesture, so he didn't move. Instead, he squinted, searching his memory. "At that point she was a sophomore in high school, so it was two years until she could get out."

"Man." Ainsley shook her head in sympathy. "I can't imagine being so vindictive toward someone I loved."

He laughed, but there was no humor in it. "Oh, that was the tip of the iceberg, believe me."

"Do you think if your parents had done something like this—I mean a real marriage retreat, not this fake garbage—that it would have made a difference in their relationship?"

Santiago considered her question. He'd wondered the same thing from time to time, but had never really come up with an answer. "Probably not," he said. "I think they're determined to hate each other, and nothing is going to change that. I've learned that some people are only happy when they're unhappy, if that makes any sense. I think my parents are like that."

Ainsley nodded. "I think I know what you mean. My father's ex-wife, Selina, is a real piece of work. I'm not sure why they were ever together. Well," she amended quickly, "I'm pretty sure she was only in it for the money, but I don't know what Dad ever saw in her."

Santiago raised one eyebrow, prompting Ainsley to ask, "What?"

"Is she pretty?"

Ainsley scoffed and gently smacked his hand as she pulled away. "Men."

He shrugged. "It's a valid question. I mean, put yourself in his shoes for a minute. His first wife has died, he's got three kids at home and a company to run. A beautiful woman shows up and lavishes him with attention, making him forget the stress of his life for a little while. It's only natural he'd fall for her."

Ainsley crossed her arms. "Is that what happened to you? You fell for a pretty face in New York, someone to distract you from the pressures of the big city?"

Santiago shook his head. "Hardly. I haven't gotten seriously involved with anyone."

"Why's that?"

Because they're not you, his brain supplied helpfully. He shifted in his seat, uncomfortable with the direction of his conversation. Talking to Ainsley was a pleasure, but he didn't want her to know that he still missed her in that way.

"Just haven't found the right person, I guess," he said lamely.

She studied him for a moment, her expression sympathetic. "Are you afraid of turning into your parents?" she asked quietly.

The question hit him like a punch to the gut, an

unexpected blow that stunned him for a few seconds. He'd never told her that. Never been able to work up the courage to share the truth with her. Even though it was his greatest fear, he knew how ridiculous it sounded and he hadn't wanted Ainsley to think he was lying to her when he'd left. But perhaps he should have given her more credit.

Santiago struggled to find his voice, knowing she deserved a response. "I haven't exactly had the best role models," he admitted.

"No," she murmured. "You haven't."

Unable to bear her scrutiny any longer, he changed the subject. "What about you?" he asked. "Why is there no ring on your finger?"

Ainsley held out her left hand and looked at it appraisingly. "Actually, there is," she teased.

"You know what I mean."

The smile faded from her face and she shrugged. "Same reason, I suppose. Not the parent thing. The finding the right person thing." She looked down, tracing the rim of her cup with the tip of her forefinger. "Men aren't exactly lining up around the block to date a workaholic who can't have babies."

Santiago's heart cracked at her words. He'd known she couldn't have children—she'd made that clear from the beginning of their relationship. An emergency surgery during Ainsley's childhood had resulted in massive internal scarring, encasing her ovaries and rendering her infertile. She'd always been matter-of-fact about it, and truth be told, he hadn't been bothered by the news. He was attracted to Ainsley for who she was, not for the hypothetical children she could provide. But it seemed that perhaps her outwardly calm acceptance of her condition hid an inner turmoil she'd never shown him before.

"Has anyone ever said that to you?" He tried to keep his voice even, but just the thought of a man making her feel bad because of her inability to have children made Santiago's blood boil. She didn't deserve to be treated like that; she was a vibrant, amazing woman, not someone's broodmare.

Ainsley shrugged one shoulder, not meeting his eyes. "I can read between the lines. I usually wait to tell people until we've gotten to know each other a bit. When they stop returning my calls, I get the message."

He remembered when she'd told him. How she'd seemed nervous and preoccupied. He'd asked her about it, but she'd said everything was fine. Then, in the middle of dinner, she'd set her fork down and announced she couldn't have children.

He could still see the defensive light in her eyes, the way her chin had been turned up, as though daring him to challenge her. He'd asked a few questions and that was that. She'd seemed a little deflated by his underwhelming reaction, but as time had passed, she'd come to accept he'd spoken the truth when he'd told her he didn't need to have biological children.

Was she still at peace with the limitations of her body? Or had something changed?

"How do you feel about it?" he asked softly.

She glanced up, meeting his eyes for a second before looking away again. "I thought I was okay, but as the years have passed, it's gotten a little harder to accept that I can't have kids. When I was younger, I thought I wouldn't care. I'd create this amazing career and fill my life with friends and dogs. But the older I get, the more I feel like I'm missing out." Her hands tightened on the cup, her knuckles going white. "I see my friends having kids and I wonder what it's like."

"You can still be a mom, if that's what you want," he said. "There's always adoption, or perhaps IVF."

"Yeah." She nodded. "I've considered that. I guess part of me is just curious to know what it's like to be pregnant and to give birth. To have this new little person that is a part of me, you know?"

"I do." Santiago had wondered the same, from time to time. But in the end, he always circled back to the same conclusion: fatherhood was great, but it wasn't something he felt compelled to do with his life.

"I think I like the idea of children more than I'd like the reality," she continued. "I know I don't have to be a mother to lead a fulfilling life. But I think a part of me will always be curious as to what things might have been like, if I could have gotten pregnant. Kind of like the way I wonder how things would have ended up if I'd chosen to be a doctor or a writer or a chef instead of a lawyer."

Seeking to lighten the mood, he decided to tease her a bit. "Those are some wildly diverse career choices."

She smiled. "They were all on the list when I was a kid. Along with ballerina and cowgirl."

His brain conjured up an image of her now in a pale pink leotard and tutu, the fabric clinging to her curves. *Idiot*, he told himself. But it was too late. His imagination had taken off, picturing her dancing, her body moving in front of him as she treated him to a private show. Unfortunately, he knew all too well what she would look like, as she'd once worn a ballerina costume for a Halloween party in law school. He'd barely been able to keep his hands off her at the party, and once they'd gotten home, she hadn't worn the outfit long enough to treat him to a dance performance.

He shifted in the chair, trying to find a distraction before his body took the mental image and ran with it, all the way to an embarrassing conclusion. "If it's any consolation, you're an amazing lawyer."

She smiled. "You have to say that because I'm helping you."

Santiago shook his head. "You know that's not why."

Ainsley grew serious. "You're not so bad yourself," she said softly. "Why do you think I called you?"

"Because you knew I'd help?"

She shook her head. "I didn't know that, actually. I hoped you would, but I wasn't taking anything for granted."

It hurt to know she hadn't believed him when he'd told her he'd always be there for her, but could he really blame her? It was the kind of thing people said all the time when they were breaking up with someone. But in his case, he'd truly meant it.

"Well, now you know," he said. "It wasn't an empty promise."

Ainsley nodded, her blue eyes luminous from the glow of the overhead light. "Thank you."

Her gratitude made Santiago uncomfortable. He didn't deserve it, for one thing. They were both helping each other, so there was no need for her to feel like she owed him something for taking her brother's case.

Besides, after the way he'd hurt her five years ago, it was the least he could do.

"Don't mention it," he said. "Please. I don't deserve your thanks. You're helping me too, remember?"

She nodded and looked away, breaking the connection between them. "On that note, I'm going to turn in early. It's been a long day."

"I understand," he said. "I think I'm going to do the same. Maybe we can talk about Ace's case tomorrow, after we've both had some rest? I emailed him yesterday. Hopefully he'll reply soon."

"That sounds good." She pushed away from the table and took her now empty cup to the sink. Santiago got to his feet and followed, intending to set his mug on the counter. But just as he reached out, Ainsley turned and moved forward, pulling up short just before she ran into him.

"Oh!" The small sound of surprise escaped on a breath, and she blinked up at him, her cheeks going pink.

"Sorry," he murmured. "Didn't mean to sneak up on you."

"It's okay," she replied, her voice low.

They stayed like that, close but not touching, staring into each other's eyes. *What are you doing?* his brain demanded. *Move!*

On some level, Santiago knew he was playing with fire. He should step back, give Ainsley some space and let her walk out of the kitchen. But his feet wouldn't obey his brain's commands. Being so close to her stilled the restlessness inside of him, quieting the low-level anxiety that had plagued him ever since they'd started this damn retreat of lies. Logically, he understood this proximity to Ainsley was a bad idea. But emotionally?

He needed her.

Ainsley stared up at him, her eyes large and inviting. He saw no trace of fear, no hint of apprehension in her gaze. She made no move to leave, and it wasn't because he had her pinned—she was free to step back, to put distance between them.

If that's what she wanted.

Santiago waited, giving her time to decide. His mind was made up, but he wasn't going to force himself on her. As he watched her, the tip of her tongue darted out to wet her bottom lip. Any other time, he would have taken that as a clear invitation to kiss her. Now, though? He remained still, giving them both one last chance to walk away.

A smile flitted across her mouth, and she nodded slightly. She reached out and grasped the fabric of his shirt, then tugged gently.

She didn't have to ask him twice.

Santiago dropped his head and fit his mouth to hers. Her lips were warm and soft, absolutely perfect. As soon as they connected, he felt something click into place inside his chest as every cell in his body seemed to sigh with relief.

Yes. This is right. This is what I need.

It was a sensation more than an actual thought, a sense that this woman was his match in every way. His world shifted, as though things that had once been a little off-kilter were now in perfect alignment. It was a powerful feeling, a rush that left him a little light-headed.

Ainsley pressed herself against him, the added contact sending tendrils of warmth throughout his body. Santiago ran his tongue along her bottom lip, coaxing her mouth open.

He'd barely registered the taste of her coffee when the window behind them shattered.

Chapter Seven

Everything seemed to happen in a blur.

One minute, Ainsley was sinking into Santiago's kiss, relishing the feel of her curves pressed against his chest. The next thing she knew, there was a crash from somewhere behind her. Before she could fully register the sound, Santiago's arms came around her in a tight embrace and he pulled her to the floor. The back of her head made contact with the tile floor, and she cried out as pain pierced her skull.

"Are you okay?" Santiago's breath was warm on her cheek; she blinked, slowly registering he was on top of her.

"Uh, yeah, I think so. What happened?" Her head was still spinning from the sudden change in position, and the throbbing of her skull made it difficult to organize her thoughts.

"The window." He shifted, his eyes looking past her as he searched for something. "It shattered behind you."

A jolt of alarm shot down her spine. "Were you

hurt?" She hadn't felt anything, but she'd been so caught up in the moment it might not have registered. She took a mental inventory now, trying to determine if she'd been cut or injured by flying glass.

Santiago was quiet for a few seconds, apparently performing his own silent survey. "No, I think I'm fine."

He planted his knees on either side of her thighs, taking some of his weight off her. They waited a few more seconds, but the cabin was silent.

"Do you think we're safe?" She felt a little silly whispering, but windows didn't break themselves. Something had caused the glass to explode.

Or someone.

The image of Steve flashed through her mind as she recalled the dark glare he given her before walking away with Jenny. He hadn't threatened her outright, but he'd made it clear he didn't want her speaking to his wife.

Had he decided to underline his warning with a little vandalism?

"I'll take a look," Santiago said. "Stay down until I know it's okay."

Ainsley opened her mouth to protest, but Santiago looked down and met her eyes. "Just stay down," he repeated, anticipating her objection.

He waited for her to nod before sliding off her. She registered the loss of his body heat immediately, but pushed the inconvenient observation aside. Now was not the time to think about the implications of that kiss, or the direction they'd been heading before the surprise interruption…

Wanting to keep him in sight, Ainsley rolled onto her stomach and craned her neck. Santiago moved cautiously toward the window at the other end of the room, his head swiveling from side to side as he searched for any signs of an intruder or a threat. She held her breath, willing him to remain safe. The chances that someone was out there waiting to take a shot were slim, but she couldn't get Steve's menacing expression out of her mind. Even though he was upset with her, he might lash out and hurt Santiago by mistake. If Santiago was injured because of her actions…she'd never forgive herself.

After an endless moment, Santiago called out. "I don't see anyone." The glass crunched under his shoes as he walked back to her and reached down to help her up. "I think we're safe."

"What happened?" Ainsley kept her hands on Santiago's arms, unwilling to let go just yet. Her stomach still roiled from adrenaline and she felt a little shaky. He was solid and strong, and his closeness provided a reassurance that transcended words.

Santiago seemed to understand her need for touch, as he drew her close. "I'm not 100 percent sure," he said, looking at the scene at the other end of the room. "As best I can tell, it seems like a tree branch crashed through the window."

"So it wasn't a person trying to hurt us?" *That* was a relief.

"Doesn't look like it, no," he said.

Together, they walked over to the mess on the floor. Ainsley could see he was right—a large branch was hanging half-out of the room, and both the small table and floor were littered with shards of glass and a few pieces of bark and leaves. From this angle, she could see the jagged end of the branch, which looked like it had been ripped off the tree. She reflexively glanced up, but it was impossible to tell which tree the branch had come from.

"That's quite a mess," she said.

"I'll see if I can find a broom," Santiago replied. She released her hold on him as he stepped away. Rather than watch him walk, she turned back to the scene in the kitchen. Even if Santiago was able to find something they could use to clean up, they would need help blocking the empty space where the window had once been.

With a sigh, she walked over to the phone and pressed 9 to dial the front desk of the main building. *Please, not Brett*, she thought silently as she listened to the phone ring. He was one of the last people she wanted to talk to right now, and with her nerves still on edge, she didn't want him coming over to inspect the damage to the cabin.

"Marriage Institute, this is Carmen speaking," answered a woman's voice.

Ainsley identified herself and explained the situation. Carmen tutted sympathetically, and assured Ainsley that someone would arrive momentarily with plywood to cover the broken window and help clean up.

After thanking the woman, Ainsley hung up. Did nothing faze these people? Carmen's chipper tone hadn't varied throughout the call. Ainsley imagined that no matter the reason for her call, Carmen's response would have been the same.

I'm calling because my arm just fell off.

Oh, that's okay! I'll send someone over to help you clean up!

She shook her head at the thought, and Santiago drew up short as he returned to the kitchen.

"You okay?"

"Yeah," she said. "Just got off the phone with the main cabin. They're sending someone to help us."

"Good, because I couldn't find a broom." He held up his empty hands in illustration and moved to stand next to her.

"I'm sure they'll have everything we need," Ainsley commented. "And I know they'll be cheerful about it."

Santiago chuckled. "I take it you spoke with Brett?"

She shuddered at the mention of the man's name. "No. Thank God. It was someone else. But she sounded just as perfect."

Santiago ran his hand down her arm. "Try not to let them get to you. We'll be out of here soon."

Ainsley nodded, knowing he was right. "Let's get started." She gestured to the mess on the floor. "We can at least pull the branch out of the room."

"Good call." They headed for the front door and stepped out onto the porch. As soon as she walked out of the house, Ainsley froze.

Santiago paused on the steps, glancing back with a worried expression. "Hey. What's wrong?"

She shook her head, searching for the words. The whole thing felt very wrong, but she couldn't quite put her finger on why…

Then it snapped into place. She pointed up with her index finger. "This porch is covered."

Santiago glanced at the roof in question and looked back at her. "Yes." He drew the word out, as though he was waiting for her to realize she was being silly.

"That branch couldn't have fallen through the kitchen window on its own." She gestured to the side, where the branch in question still hung from the frame.

Santiago followed her movement, his eyes tracing the lines of the roof and then the window frame. The porch roof extended to cover half of the width of the window, so it was feasible a branch could have fallen from a tree and busted through the unprotected side.

But that wasn't the case here. The wood had clearly punctured the half of the glass that was shaded by the porch, leaving large shards still attached to the side of the frame that was uncovered.

There was only one way to explain that pattern.

Someone had rammed the branch through the window, wanting it to look like an accident.

Santiago looked back at her, his eyes widening as understanding dawned.

"I think you should go back inside."

Ainsley bristled at his words. "And leave you out here alone? I don't think so."

Santiago shot her an exasperated glare and moved to grab the branch. "How did I know you were going to say that?" he sighed. "Come on then, let's get this done quickly."

Working together, they carefully pulled the branch free and tossed it on the ground in front of the cabin. Then they both walked inside to wait for the cleanup crew to arrive.

"So it wasn't an accident," he said softly.

"Nope," she replied.

He nodded, as though this confirmed a private suspicion. "I thought it was strange. There haven't been any storms, and I didn't hear a gust of wind that might have caused the branch to tear free."

"I have seen some downed branches by the running trail," Ainsley said. "Whoever did this probably picked one up there." Given the forest nearby, pieces of wood weren't hard to find. And it was an ideal tool for vandalism—after all, any reasonable person would assume the branch had fallen from one of the trees close to the house.

It was a mistake they'd made at first, until she'd realized things didn't quite add up.

But…who would do this? And why?

Another thought came swiftly, making her skin crawl with revulsion; how long had someone been standing outside, watching them?

Santiago placed his hand on her arm. "Your face—what is it?"

She shuddered. "I just realized, whoever did this was probably standing outside the window, watching us kiss."

A shadow crossed his face. "Yes," he said shortly.

That safe feeling she'd had after assuming this had all been an accident evaporated, leaving her exposed and vulnerable. What other private moments had this person seen? How long had they been spying?

Santiago drew her close once more, wrapping his arms loosely around her. "It's okay," he said, dropping his mouth to her ear. "Whoever did this, they won't hurt you. I won't let them."

She hadn't started to worry about her personal safety yet, but Santiago's assurance helped soothe her nerves. "Should we say something? When help arrives?"

She felt his head move against her hair. "I don't think so," he said. "It's not like we can trust them, you know?"

"Yeah." Brett's face flashed through her mind, and she tightened her grip around Santiago's waist. She'd been thinking Steve had done this, or perhaps one of the other spouses trying to intimidate them. But what if it was an employee? Maybe the Woodses had figured out she and Santiago weren't really married at all? Perhaps this was the start of a campaign to get them to leave, or worse still, they'd uncovered Ainsley and Santiago's investigation and wanted to scare them into dropping it.

She said as much to Santiago. He stroked one hand down the valley of her spine; she focused on his touch, drawing comfort from the gesture. "That's possible," he said. He was quiet for a few seconds, then spoke again. "What do you want to do?"

Ainsley pulled back to look up at him. "What do you mean?"

His green eyes were clear. "I'm not going to ask you to risk yourself for this project." He reached up to brush a strand of hair behind her ear. "And I don't want you to spend the remainder of the week living in fear that someone is spying on us or going to hurt us. If you want to leave, we can."

His consideration was like a warm balm on her soul, spreading over her and making her feel cherished. She knew how much this investigation meant to him, how passionate he was about helping his sister and the other people who had been conned. The fact that he was willing to walk away just so she wouldn't be scared showed how much he cared about her.

Even as she appreciated his concern, a small part of her heart ached. Santiago still thought highly of her, that much was clear. But did it really matter? All the affection in the world hadn't stopped him from leaving five years ago.

Ainsley slowly extracted herself from his embrace, being careful not to make it seem like she was rejecting him. That would only raise questions, and she didn't want to let him know that her heart was still bleeding from his actions.

"I'm fine," she said decisively. "I want to finish this. I'm not going to let some coward with a tree branch scare me away from doing the right thing."

Santiago nodded, a smile tugging the corners of his mouth. "I figured you'd be stubborn. But don't be afraid to change your mind—if you decide you're done, we'll leave. No questions asked."

"I won't. I'm going to see this through to the end." She owed him that much, since he was helping Ace. Besides, if she was to walk away now, part of her would always wonder if these stolen kisses and subtle touches would have led to something more. Her heart was already fluttering with the idea of a second chance for both of them. No, staying here would prove those encounters were nothing but blips, moments of weakness brought on by stress and worry. They weren't the beginning of something new, they were a maladaptive coping strategy she had to shake off.

Her brain understood there was no future for the two of them. Santiago had made that clear five years ago, and nothing had changed.

Ainsley just had to make sure her heart got the message.

SANTIAGO FLIPPED HIS pillow over with a sigh that night, punching it into the shape he liked before flopping back down on the bed.

He should sleep. He knew this. His body was tired. But his mind wouldn't shut down.

The events of this evening played on an endless loop, a movie reel he couldn't turn off. Making Ainsley's coffee. Talking with her at the table. Kissing her by the sink…

In some ways, he was grateful the window had broken at that moment. He hadn't meant to kiss Ainsley, but once he'd started, he hadn't wanted to stop. And given his determination to keep his distance, kissing her was the last thing he needed to be doing.

It was strange, though. The more group discussions and couple's therapy sessions they attended together, the more he realized how good their relationship had been. Listening to other people talk about the problems in their marriages made him realize he and Ainsley had been lucky—they hadn't argued all the time, hadn't had big, fundamental disagreements about life, the kind that tore a couple apart. He'd never been tempted to cheat on her, and as far as he could tell, she'd never wanted to cheat on him. Compared to these unhappy couples at the retreat, he and Ainsley had had a charmed relationship.

It was enough to make him wonder if he'd made the right choice five years ago.

He flipped onto his back with a sigh. On the other hand, perhaps the past seemed so good because he was currently surrounded by people contemplating divorce. After all, happy couples didn't consider breaking up. It was easy to think their relationship had been ideal compared to the stories he'd heard over the last several days.

Though he couldn't deny they had worked well together…still did, come to that.

There was no one he'd rather have by his side this week. Ainsley was the best partner he could ask for; not only was she helping him gather evidence against the Woodses and their cronies, but she provided him with the emotional support he'd unexpectedly needed to continue this deception.

Santiago only hoped he was helping her the same way she was helping him.

Which led him to a new set of worries; now that they knew the broken window had been no accident, was he doing the right thing by keeping them here?

He'd never forgive himself if Ainsley was hurt. He knew, too, that she wasn't going to walk away. She was too stubborn to give in to intimidation, especially now that she'd seen firsthand the people who were being hurt by the Woodses. He could tell by the way she'd talked about Jenny that she had a soft spot for the other woman, and he couldn't blame her.

That didn't mean he wanted her risking her own neck to help. It was one thing to provide moral support and to be there as a friend, even if it annoyed Jenny's husband. But now that someone had thrown a tree branch through the cabin window, Santiago feared the stakes were considerably higher.

There was no guarantee the disgruntled husband was responsible for the act of vandalism, though Santiago didn't know who else it could be. It was possible the Woodses had figured out he and Ainsley were not who they seemed—perhaps they were trying to send a message? Though it must be an awfully subtle one, if that was the case. No, if the Woodses suspected their real motives, he doubted they would bother with something as small as a broken window. They'd simply force them out of the retreat and that would be that.

He doubted it was anyone on their staff, either. The employee who had come out to help clean up was perfectly pleasant, apologizing for the accident, saying it happened sometimes. The young woman had definitely stuck to the script, just as all the other staffers had during the week. And while that made them seem a little...creepy, it also made Santiago think they wouldn't do anything unless the Woodses ordered it. So the idea that an employee had broken the window didn't make sense, either.

Which brought him back to Steve, Jenny's husband. He was the only logical suspect so far.

Thanks to the two of them being in the same group, Santiago had seen flashes of the other man's temper. It was easy for him to imagine Steve picking up the branch and thrusting it through the window—it was just the kind of hotheaded, impulsive move men like Steve specialized in. The only question was, now that he'd gotten the anger out of his system for the moment, was he going to leave them alone?

Or would he escalate his behavior?

Santiago wasn't afraid for himself. Steve and his ilk were bullies, only picking on people they viewed as weaker. Even though Ainsley was smarter and stronger than Steve could ever hope to be, she was physically smaller and therefore, in his eyes, vulnerable. That made her an easy target.

And since Santiago couldn't be by her side every minute of the day, it posed a dilemma for him.

Carry on with the operation and risk Ainsley's safety?

Or leave now before someone was seriously hurt?

He knew what he wanted to do. If it was up to him, they'd leave in the morning. As much as he wanted to bring these guys down, to make them pay for their deceptions, the fact was that Ainsley's well-being meant more to him than anything else.

Feeling uncomfortably warm, he flipped the pillow over once more, searching for a cooler spot on the fabric. *It shouldn't be this hard*, he told himself. He didn't want to risk Ainsley, so they should leave. But she'd made it clear she wasn't going anywhere.

And…ultimately, he had to respect her choice.

Even though he hated the risk she was taking, it was hers to assume. He'd do everything in his power to keep her safe, for as long as possible. It wasn't in her nature to rely on someone to take care of her, but hopefully she'd have the sense to accept his help.

Because the only way they were going to get through the rest of this retreat was if they acted as a team.

Chapter Eight

At six in the morning, Ainsley decided she'd had enough. Rather than stay in bed, tossing and turning in a vain search for rest, she slipped out from under the covers and began to dress. An early morning run was her usual solution to the problem of an overactive brain. Hopefully, it would work today.

She tiptoed down the hall, careful not to make too much noise. Gentle snoring drifted from behind the closed door of Santiago's room. At least one of them had gotten sleep last night.

The air was refreshingly cool as she stepped onto the porch. She stretched a bit, using the stairs for leverage. Then she set off at a brisk walk under the blue-gray sky.

When she reached the trailhead she started to run, taking off down the dirt path that led into the trees. It was darker in the woods, the large branches overhead blocking the tendrils of sunlight that had begun to peer over the eastern horizon. A few enterprising birds were getting an early start to the day, but aside from their tentative songs, it was quiet.

The path was soft underfoot, absorbing the sounds of her steps. She focused on the rhythm of her breathing and let her mind wander.

The kiss last night had been a mistake. Her brain knew it, even as her body denied the truth. This retreat was turning out to be more difficult than she'd expected. Not just because of the Woodses and their con, though she did feel terrible for innocent people like Jenny. No, it was Santiago's presence that she found troubling.

He hadn't done anything objectionable—he was an honorable man, and she trusted him. But being around him every day, sharing the cabin together, the couple's sessions…she was having a hard time resisting the pull of their familiar groove. Without realizing it, she'd fallen into a shared closeness with him, like putting on a favorite pair of jeans. He fit in her life, just as he had before.

And the worst part? Ainsley had thought she'd moved on after their breakup. In many ways, she had. But being around Santiago made it clear there were things still missing from her life. Something as simple as having someone to talk to in the evenings. In a matter of days, Santiago's presence had expanded to fill the cracks in her life, making her aware of the missing pieces for the first time.

She jumped over a fallen tree, the obstacle slowing

her down for a few steps. Her heart pounded in her ears as she picked up the pace again, and her thoughts turned back to Santiago.

Why wasn't she angry with him? He'd left her five years ago, using the age-old excuse of "it's not you, it's me." No one would blame her for still being upset—with just a few words, Santiago had crushed her dreams for their future and caused her to question their past. But when Ainsley searched her heart, she found no resentment toward him.

Maybe it was because enough time had passed that the wounds to her heart had healed. Or maybe it was because he hadn't hesitated to help when she'd called.

Or maybe, just maybe, it was because he was still single.

The last possibility was the most dangerous. Why should she care if he was with someone else? She had no claim on him. But the truth of the matter was that she did care.

A lot.

Even though Santiago had assured her he was leaving for the sake of his career, a part of Ainsley had wondered if he was really dumping her because of her infertility. She'd sat with that thought for the past five years, imagining him finding a woman, marrying her and having a houseful of cute babies.

Except, he hadn't done that. And the fact that he was still single and without children forced her to re-evaluate things. It seemed he had told her the truth—it wasn't her after all.

Ainsley made the last turn and slowed to a walk, wanting to cool down a bit before returning to the cabin. The more she thought about the situation, the more she wondered about Santiago's reasons for leaving. He'd built a successful career, yes. But had he really expected her to hold him back? Or was there something more that had caused him to leave?

Leaved crunched under her feet as snippets of last night's conversation floated through her mind…

I haven't exactly had the best role models.

She'd known his childhood had been tumultuous. He'd talked about it in bits and pieces while they'd been dating, but he'd never gone into much detail. Just enough for her to know his parents should never have stayed married.

Was that the problem? Did he think he was doomed to repeat his parents' mistakes?

It made a certain kind of sense. Growing up with miserable parents had to have affected him and shaped his ideas about what a marriage looked like. But she'd foolishly thought that their own relationship had been proof enough that not every couple was doomed to fail.

Now she realized she'd been wrong.

She'd asked him last night if he thought he was worried about turning into his parents. He'd dodged the question, but she could read between the lines.

It was clear now that Santiago had left because of his fears, not because of her physical shortcomings.

The realization brought relief, along with a profound sense of peace. She stopped in the middle of the trail and bent at the waist, exhaling heavily as tears sprang to her eyes. For the last five years, she'd doubted the truth of his words, convinced he'd been trying to spare her feelings. Her fears had eaten away at her self-esteem like an acid drip on her soul, triggering a constant, low-level ache that she'd believed was just going to be a part of her life.

But now she saw the truth. And the doubt and heartache brought on by years of second-guessing drained out of her, leaving her feeling both empty and new.

She crouched on her heels and let the tears come, let them wash away the toxic emotions she'd been unknowingly carrying for so long. Ainsley had never been much of a crier, but these tears were cathartic, a fitting end to this chapter of her life.

She wasn't sure how long she stayed there, watching her tears speckle the dirt beneath her feet. Eventually, she stood and wiped her cheeks. Her nose was stuffy and her eyes felt swollen, but it was nothing a hot shower couldn't fix.

Dawn had broken during her run, and from this distance, it was easy to see the plywood covering the broken panes of the kitchen window. Ainsley started walking back to the cabin, hoping Santiago was still asleep. If he saw her face, he'd immediately know she'd been crying. At the moment, her emotions were still close to the surface and she wouldn't be able to deflect his inevitable questions.

She had questions of her own. Like why he'd never told her about his fears before. Why he hadn't trusted her with that information. Maybe they could talk about it now, since they were no longer a couple. It wouldn't change the past, but it would help her understand his actions.

The plywood was a blight on the front of the cabin, its unfinished surface a stark contrast to the polished look of the house. Ainsley eyed it as she got closer, expecting to feel a resurgence of the fear she'd experienced last night when the window had been broken. But the emotions never came.

In the face of her recent self-discoveries, the petty actions of last night's unknown assailant seemed unimportant and insignificant. What did she care if the window was broken? She'd just cast off the subtle despondency that had shaded her life for the past five years. The petty actions of a jealous husband were the farthest thing from her mind.

Pushing thoughts of Jenny's husband aside, she circled back to her own concerns. Now that she recognized the truth behind why Santiago had left, what was she going to do about it? Should she try to get him to see that he wasn't his father, and she wasn't his mother? That he wasn't destined to repeat his parents' sad history? Or should she leave the issue alone? They'd had their chance, after all. Maybe they weren't supposed to get another?

Lost in thought, her steps slowed as she approached the cabin. She stopped on the path, standing just inside the tree line. Perhaps she was being silly, but she was reluctant to go back to this temporary home without some kind of plan in place for how she was going to deal with her emotions. There were three days left in the marriage retreat. Three days of close contact with Santiago. Given the effect he'd already had on her, it might as well be an eternity.

How was she going to protect her heart? Even now, she felt it soften toward him as she considered his own misguided assumptions. She knew what it was like to live with mistaken impressions. Could she help him realize the truth—that he could have a healthy, happy relationship?

More importantly, since he'd left due to his fears did that mean he still loved her? They hadn't split up due to an argument or because of the long, slow death of passion that plagued so many couples. There had been real affection between them, genuine love.

Was it still there? Her heart said yes. Her love for him was dormant, perhaps. But salvageable.

If that's what they both wanted.

She tilted her head to the side, considering her options. But just as she began to organize her thoughts, a noise sounded on the path behind her.

Footsteps.

Ainsley started to turn around, intending to greet the other early morning riser. But before she could complete the rotation, there was a grunt of effort from someone close by and her world exploded in a starburst of pain.

SANTIAGO EMERGED FROM his room, the ends of his hair still a little damp from his shower. He walked into the kitchenette and stopped in the doorway, frowning.

Where was Ainsley?

Normally, she was an early riser. She got up at dawn for a run, then returned to the cabin to shower and dress. By the time Santiago was ready to start the day, he usually found her sitting at the small table sipping her coffee.

But today the room was dark and quiet.

He flipped on the lights, started the water for his tea. Maybe she had overslept. It was possible.

But not likely.

Ainsley was a creature of habit. If she wasn't here, then something was wrong.

Hesitating only a second, Santiago walked down the hall and turned right. The door to her bedroom suite was closed, so he rapped loudly on the wood. "Ainsley. Are you okay?"

There was no reply. He knocked a second time, then decided to try the handle.

The door swung open easily and he stepped inside

her room. Morning light streamed in from the window, illuminating the bed with its rumpled covers. He walked through to the bathroom, half-afraid he might find her on the floor. Was she ill?

But the place was empty.

He stood in place for a second, his thoughts churning as a sense of foreboding stole over him. It wasn't like Ainsley to disappear. Even if she'd been upset about something or angry with him, she would have told him if she was going somewhere.

He glanced at the window on the far wall, echoes of last night ringing through his mind. Had someone gained access to her bedroom through the window?

Probably not. It was closed, and the items on the small table that sat underneath the window were still in place.

No, wherever she was, Ainsley had left under her own power.

Was she still running? He glanced at his watch. Normally, she'd returned by now. They usually walked over to breakfast together, and she'd never been late before. But perhaps she'd taken a longer route today? There was an extensive set of trails around and through the woods. Maybe she'd opted for a change of scenery?

That had to be it. Santiago nodded to himself, trying to quash the nerves jangling in his stomach. No sense in imagining the worst when the ordinary was the most likely explanation.

He walked back into the kitchenette and brewed his tea on autopilot, his mind still focused on Ainsley. Should he go looking for her? What if she'd fallen and injured herself? The trails were uneven, with lots of forest debris like branches and even logs bisecting some of the paths. If she'd tripped or wrenched her ankle or knee, she'd need help getting back.

Abandoning his mug of tea, Santiago set off for the front door. Even though he knew she could have taken any number of routes, he had to at least try to find her. He yanked the front door open and stepped out onto the porch, then drew up short at the sight that greeted him.

Ainsley was stumbling toward the cabin, her hand on her head and her face twisting in pain with every lurching step she took.

"Ainsley!"

Santiago practically jumped off the porch and ran toward her, pulling her into his arms when he reached her. She sucked in a breath at the contact, but didn't pull away.

"What happened? Where are you hurt?" He leaned back and looked at her, noting the dirt on her skin and clothes. He didn't notice any blood, but he hadn't seen all of her yet…

Ainsley winced as she looked up at him. "My head," she said, drawing his attention to her hand, which was still cupped around the back of her skull.

"Did you fall?" It seemed his fears hadn't been

unfounded. Moving carefully, he released his hold on her and moved to the side so he could get a better look. She allowed him to remove her hand, but he saw no signs of an injury. With gentle fingers, he brushed past the pieces of dead leaves tangled in her hair and touched her scalp. There was a sizeable lump present, and when he removed his fingers, he saw the tips were pink with a stain of blood.

Ainsley shook her head and winced at the movement. "No, I didn't fall," she said. She met his eyes, her gaze intense. "Someone hit me."

A chill flowed over Santiago, followed swiftly by a rush of heat as anger pumped through his system. "Who?" The word escaped on a snarl, though he already knew the answer.

It must have been Steve, Jenny's husband. Who else could it be?

"I'm not sure," she said. "They hit me from behind so I never saw their face."

Santiago clenched his hands as another wave of anger swept through his body. Not only was Steve a coward who hurt women verbally and emotionally, he evidently attacked them physically—and from behind, as well.

"I see," he said quietly. "Let's get you inside."

Santiago's movements were stiff as he moved to help Ainsley walk the remaining steps to the cabin. His muscles were so tense it felt like they might snap at any moment, but he couldn't lose control. Not now, not while Ainsley still needed him.

She leaned against him as they navigated the stairs. Once inside the cabin, Santiago steered her toward the sofa and she sank down onto the cushion with a sigh.

He knelt in front of her, worry temporarily overcoming his anger. "Are you hurt anywhere else? Do you need a doctor?" There was a disturbing amount of dirt on her clothes, making him wonder if whoever had attacked her had stopped with just a blow to the head. His breath stalled in his chest as he considered additional possibilities, each one worse than the last.

"I think it's just my head." Ainsley gingerly touched the knot on her skull again, wincing as her fingers made contact with the swollen spot. She glanced down and he saw surprise flicker across her face. "Oh man, I'm a mess."

"You must have fallen to the ground."

"I did," she said. "I just didn't realize how dirty I'd gotten."

Convinced she would be all right for at least the next few minutes, Santiago got to his feet. "Stay here," he said unnecessarily. "I'll be right back."

He went to the kitchen and pulled some paper towels free from the roll, then stood at the sink and waited for the water to warm up. He glanced down, surprised to find his hands were shaking.

Santiago dropped his head and focused on his breathing. Deep inhale. Let it out.

Again.

This was getting out of control. The window breaking last night had been bad enough. But now, Ainsley was being physically attacked. It was unacceptable. This had to stop—as much as he loved his sister, Ainsley's safety was worth more than this investigation.

Feeling marginally calmer, he soaked the paper towels in warm water and turned off the tap. Wringing out the excess liquid, he took another deep breath and prepared himself to go back into the other room. He couldn't let his temper get the best of him. The last thing he wanted to do was alarm Ainsley—she didn't need to worry about his emotions while she was hurting.

She glanced up as he approached, a questioning look on her face. He extended the damp towels, and she took them with a small smile. "Thanks."

Santiago sank onto the cushion next to her as she set about wiping the worst of the dirt from her face and the skin of her arms and legs. "We need to call the police."

"What?" Ainsley's head jerked around, making her grimace. "No. We're not doing that."

Santiago felt his jaw drop. "Are you kidding me? You've just been assaulted. Why don't you want to report that?"

"Because." She continued to wipe at the dirt. "If the police show up and start investigating, we'll be exposed. We can't let that happen, not when we're so close to the end of this thing."

He reached out to touch her but stopped before making contact. She was probably bruised from the fall, and he didn't want to add to her pain right now. But he had to get her attention and make her understand that his personal vendetta no longer mattered. Not when she was at risk like this.

"Ainsley." He waited for her to look at him again. After a moment, she finally met his eyes. "Please, listen to me. I don't care about the Woodses. I don't care about any of this anymore. I just need you to be safe."

"I'm fine."

Her flippant tone made him clench his jaw. "No, you're not. Someone attacked you from behind—I can't ignore that, and you shouldn't either. I want whoever did this to pay." In reality, he wanted to spend a little one-on-one time with whoever had done this so he could work out his frustrations with his fists. His imagination turned up a quick fantasy of beating Steve into submission, an idea that was deeply appealing right now.

"He will." Ainsley's tone was grim. "Look, I know this is bad and getting worse. But it's personal to me now. And I'm not going to give up. I want to take them all down."

Santiago opened his mouth to respond, but she cut him off. "Please." She grabbed his hand and squeezed. "I know you don't like it. I don't, either. But we need to finish this."

His doubts must have shown on his face because Ainsley's expression hardened. "It's my decision," she announced, her tone making it clear she would tolerate no further argument.

Santiago sighed, knowing she was right. He could beg, plead and cajole all he wanted, but in the end, Ainsley was the one who had to press charges. And if she wasn't willing to do so, there was no point in calling the police.

"Will you at least let me take you to a doctor?" That bump on her head felt large, and had to hurt. She could have a concussion, or maybe something worse.

She smiled sweetly. "No." She gave his hand a pat before withdrawing her touch. "I really am fine. Besides, we're going to pretend like nothing happened."

"We are?" This was news to him. What was she planning?

"Yep." Ainsley leaned forward and placed the now-filthy paper towels on the coffee table. "I'm going to take a quick shower, and then we're going to go to breakfast."

"Why—" the word stuck in his throat, so Santiago coughed and tried again. "Why are you doing this?"

Ainsley stood and he noticed a scrape on her knee that he hadn't seen before. "I told you," she said patiently. "I'm going to win this thing. If we act like nothing out of the ordinary has happened, it will drive my attacker crazy. They're bound to slip up and reveal what they've done."

"This isn't a mystery," Santiago protested. "I know it was Steve who hurt you." How could she have any doubts at this point? It's not like there was anyone else it could be…

Ainsley frowned. "Actually, I'm not so sure about that."

"What do you mean?" A chill went down Santiago's spine. Was there something she wasn't telling him? Had someone else threatened her lately?

"I've never seen Steve on those trails," she said. "In fact, Jenny's mentioned in group sessions that he sleeps in all the time rather than helping her with the baby."

"Yeah, but now that they're at this retreat with no baby, his sleeping habits might have changed."

"I don't think so." Ainsley shook her head. "But even if it has, he's not a runner."

"What makes you say that?" Despite his frustration, Santiago was curious to hear her logic. Ainsley's conclusions were generally sound, even though in this case he thought she was mistaken.

"Haven't you noticed his stuffy head and frequent sneezing? Jenny mentioned his allergies are terrible right now. I find it hard to believe he'd choose to spend time outside when he already doesn't feel good."

She did have a point, though it was circumstantial at best. "All right," he said, spreading his hands palms up. "For the sake of argument, let's say you're right. We'll pretend Steve didn't do this. In that case, who did?"

"My money's on Brett," she said promptly. "I think the Woodses use him to intimidate spouses who aren't cooperating with their plans, the ones who resist the gaslighting and manipulation. He makes them feel unsafe and uncertain, making them more susceptible to the Woodses and their suggestions."

"They probably act like nothing is going on," Santiago said slowly, thinking out loud. "Brett terrorizes the spouse, but everyone around them acts like nothing is happening."

Ainsley nodded. "So they think they're going crazy. They can't trust their own perceptions. Maybe they really would be better off alone? And they're getting such a good deal..."

A little shock went through Santiago as he realized she might be right. "I can believe that," he said. "But in your case, you've been attacked. You have injuries that prove you were assaulted. You can't talk a person out of physical signs like that."

"True, but I never saw who hit me," she pointed out. "I imagine if I said something, they'd tell me I'd been hit by a falling branch. And since I didn't actually glimpse anyone behind me, I can't deny it's possible. If I were on my own here, with a husband who was actively trying to get rid of me, isolated from other people… I might question my own reality."

"My God," Santiago whispered. "I think you're on to something."

She smiled wryly. "Don't act so shocked."

He shook his head. "I just can't believe it. Every time I think these people couldn't go any lower, they find another level."

"Now you see why I'm not going to walk away. We're going to finish this and nail these bastards, once and for all. If we made a stink now, they'd find some way to get out of it and go back to hurting innocent people. We can't let that happen."

Santiago nodded, a renewed sense of determination filling him. "You're right," he said simply. How had he gotten so lucky? How had he picked the one woman in the world who was determined to see this through to the end, despite the personal cost?

More importantly, would he ever be able to repay her?

Ainsley nodded, satisfied with his response. "Just do me a favor," he said as she turned to go.

She glanced back. "What's that?"

He got to his feet, bracing for the battle his request was sure to provoke. "No more early morning runs alone. In fact, no more going anywhere alone."

Her brows drew together and she took a breath. He held up his hand, forestalling her objection. "Ainsley, you got lucky this morning. That bump on your head could have been something much worse. Next time, it will be. Please don't put yourself in danger. I'm begging you."

Her eyes softened and she finally nodded. "All right," she said quietly. "We'll stick together from here on out." She started walking away, then paused at the door. "I guess that means you'll be getting up early, because I'm not about to start skipping my morning run."

Even from this distance, he could see the mischievous glint in her eyes. He let out a dramatic sigh, knowing it was the reaction she was looking for. "Must you torture me, woman?"

She laughed, the sound curling in his chest and warming his heart. "Oh yes. And I'm going to enjoy every minute of it."

Chapter Nine

Ainsley let the hot water flow over her hands, enjoying the soothing sensation for a moment. What she wouldn't give for a relaxing soak in the bathtub! It would be the ideal way to ease the aches and pains she'd been dealing with since this morning's attack, but there simply hadn't been enough time. After convincing Santiago to stay the course, she'd had to squeeze in a shower before they'd headed to the main cabin for breakfast and the start of their day of counseling sessions.

The first group session had just concluded, and Ainsley had taken the opportunity for a bathroom break. She'd tried to catch Jenny's eye during the meeting, but the other woman had repeatedly dodged her. Was that because she felt guilty or embarrassed over what her husband had said yesterday, or was she too afraid to cross him by speaking to Ainsley? Either way, it looked like she wasn't going to get another chance to connect with the beleaguered new mother. Perhaps that was for the best, at least right now. If Ainsley drew too much attention to Jenny, it was possible the Woodses would order Brett to terrorize the poor woman, the same way Ainsley suspected she was being targeted.

She glanced in the bathroom mirror, studying her appearance with a critical eye. There were no signs of the attack this morning, at least not on her face. And as long as no one put their hands on the back of her head, they'd never know she had a big lump under her hair. As far as anyone knew, she was fine. It was just another normal day.

A toilet flushed in one of the stalls behind her, and a young lady wearing the uniform of a Marriage Institute employee stepped out and walked to the sink. She smiled pleasantly at Ainsley as she turned on the tap and squirted soap into her hands.

"How are you this morning?"

Ainsley offered her a polite nod. "I'm fine, thank you."

"Are you enjoying the retreat?"

How to answer that? Ainsley had no illusions that anything she said to this person would remain between them. If she indicated she was experiencing any problems, the information would likely be used against her in some way. So she decided to play it cool, in keeping with what she'd asked Santiago to do earlier.

"I'm learning a lot," she said truthfully.

The young woman smiled and turned off the tap.

"That's wonderful!" She reached for the paper towels as Ainsley shut off her own water. After a few seconds, the employee tossed her damp towels into the trash and nodded at Ainsley. "Have a good day!"

"You, too," Ainsley said automatically. Then the words sank in and she frowned, staring after her as she walked away.

Have a good day.

The phrase buzzed around in Ainsley's head, stirring a memory. She strained to identify it, but to no avail.

What was it about those words that bothered her? It was a throwaway phrase, the type of empty platitude people spouted all the time. Totally in keeping with the too-polished, too-perfect behavior of the other Institute employees.

And yet for some reason, the phrase struck Ainsley as disturbing.

She shook her head, wondering if the blow she'd taken that morning had knocked something loose inside her brain. It was silly to be so fixated on such a common, innocent sentiment.

But as the day wore on, she couldn't dismiss the feeling that those words revealed a hidden truth.

She sat through the counseling sessions on autopilot, nodding when appropriate, speaking when expected. But though she appeared fine, her brain was busily trying to figure out where that phrase fit into the bigger picture. She felt like she'd been given a piece of a puzzle, but with no idea as to what the final product was supposed to look like, she didn't have the first clue how to start putting it all together.

Santiago noticed her distraction. "What's going on?" he asked at lunch. They sat by themselves, as usual, their table far enough away from the other couples that there was no chance of their conversation being overheard.

"Something happened in the bathroom today."

He tensed, clearly expecting the worst, so she hurried to reassure him. "I'm fine," she said. Some of the tension left his shoulders and she explained her encounter with the Institute employee.

To his credit, he listened closely and didn't immediately laugh in her face. "I know it's probably nothing," she finished. "But something about that phrase hit me. Like a moment of déjà vu or something, you know?"

"It sounds unsettling," Santiago said. "Have you been able to find a connection to anything?"

She shook her head. "Not yet," she admitted. "But I just can't stop thinking about it."

He reached for her hand on the table, but she pulled away before he could touch her. "We're splitting up, remember?"

Annoyance flashed across his face. "Oh. Right."

"I appreciate the gesture." It was sweet of him to try to offer support. Even though he'd never mentioned it, Ainsley was absolutely certain his father had never emotionally supported his mother. The fact that his first instinct was to try to help her was yet one more reason why she knew Santiago was in no danger of turning into either one of his parents. But now was not the time to share her realizations with him.

"I can't help jog your memory, but I can offer some distraction," he said. "I don't know about you, but I need to get some work done tonight. I don't even want to think about how many emails I have now."

"No kidding," she said. Her own in-box was likely bursting at the seams.

Emails... In-box... Good day...

"That's it!" She sat up and gripped the table, excitement thrumming through her.

Santiago glanced to the side, and she realized people were looking at her. Heat washed over her, concentrating in her cheeks. *Way to be subtle*, she thought.

"Uh, I take it you made a connection about something?" he asked quietly.

Ainsley nodded, unwilling to speak until she was certain she was no longer the focus of the dining room. After a few seconds, she leaned forward. "The email that was sent to the board in January—the one that started this whole mess?"

Santiago nodded. "The message that claimed your brother isn't a true Colton."

"Exactly," she replied. "The email sign-off was just two words—*Good day.*"

"Okay." Santiago drew the word out, his tone making it clear he didn't put as much stock in this coincidence as she did.

"There's more," she said. "Have you heard of the Affirmation Alliance Group?"

Santiago frowned. "The name is vaguely familiar. Refresh my memory?"

"It's an organization run by a woman named Micheline Anderson. They claim to be a wellness group, focused on self-help and self-awareness, basically any self-thing you can think of that they can monetize."

"I take it you're not a fan?" he asked dryly.

"Not at all," she replied. "The whole group strikes me as being predatory, a way of taking advantage of people's insecurities to sell them something."

"That sounds familiar," Santiago murmured.

"Exactly." Now that she thought about it, Ainsley wondered if the Woodses knew Micheline. Didn't all grifters know each other, if only tangentially?

"Tell me why this group matters." Santiago's question broke into her thoughts, and Ainsley mentally refocused on the issue at hand. Later, when there was time, she'd explore the possibility of a connection between AAG and the Woodses.

"That email was sent by a member of AAG," she said, filling him in on the convoluted twists and turns in the police investigation. "Micheline's hands appear to be clean, but I just know she's neck-deep in all of this."

"She sounds pretty shifty."

"Oh, most definitely. And the worst thing? I think she might actually be Ace's biological mother." She described what they knew—that a nurse named Luella Smith had given birth right around the time of Ace's birthday; that both she and her baby had disappeared the next day, ostensibly so she could get specialized medical treatment for her ailing son. Then, nothing. The woman and her child, Jake, had apparently vanished.

"So you think this woman, Luella, switched her baby with the real Colton baby? Why would she do that?" Santiago's frown mirrored Ainsley's own internal feelings regarding this mystery.

"I'm not sure," she admitted. "My father said that when Ace was born, he was in pretty rough shape. They actually weren't sure he would make it, but the next morning, they said he was like a new baby." Goose bumps broke out along her arms as she heard Payne's voice in her head, telling the family story. If they'd only known at the time!

"I think Luella switched the babies out because she thought the Colton baby was going to die. I mean, think about it—if you don't want to be a mother, why not swap your perfectly healthy baby for one who looks like he won't live very long?"

"Except he didn't," Santiago pointed out. "If what you're saying is true, her gamble didn't pay off."

"Didn't it, though?" Ainsley asked. "If this theory

is correct, then Luella has raised the true Colton son as her own for all these years. Now's her chance to cash in on the deception."

"And you think Luella and Micheline are the same person?"

Ainsley nodded, pleased he was keeping up. "Yeah. Luella's trail went cold forty years ago, shortly after she left the hospital with 'her' baby. And according to Holden and Spencer, Micheline didn't exist until forty years ago." Spencer's Army buddy, FBI Agent Holden St. Clair, had protected Spencer's sister Bella, an undercover reporter, from threats at a recent beauty pageant. The two had caught a serial killer together—and fallen in love.

"That's quite a coincidence."

"It would be, if I believed in coincidences."

Santiago dabbed at his mouth with his napkin. "It's a good story. And I can tell you want it to be true. But I have to say, right now, it's all conjecture."

Ainsley pressed her lips together. "I know," she said, trying to keep the annoyance out of her voice. Santiago was right—she didn't have any real proof, just a gut feeling that this whole complicated situation was Micheline's fault. Still, she didn't like to be reminded of the fact.

He tilted his head to the side, his expression sympathetic. "Sorry," he offered. "I didn't mean to burst your balloon. I just want you to keep an open mind for other possibilities."

It was good advice, and she wasn't too proud to admit it. "You're right," she said. "I can't let my pet theory blind me to other explanations." Still, there had to be a connection between The Marriage Institute and AAG. When she'd seen Spencer recently, he'd told her about a run-in he'd had with Micheline. The woman had denied AAG was a cult, and had left after saying "Good day." It was a little thing, but sometimes the smallest incidents had the biggest impact.

"What are you thinking?" She glanced up to find Santiago watching her. "I can practically see the wheels turning in your mind."

She gave him a half smile. "I'm just wondering if there's a connection between AAG and The Marriage Institute. When we get back to the cabin, I'm going to text Spencer and tell him my suspicions." It was possible he and Holden could answer that question for her—perhaps they had identified the Woodses as known associates of Micheline?

"You think the staff members are members of AAG?"

"It would help explain their demeanor, don't you think?" she asked. "There's something off about these workers, I've felt it from the beginning. Like they were automatons, rather than actual humans. If they've been brainwashed by Micheline and the Woodses, it makes sense they'll only act according to their programming."

"Let's say you're right," Santiago said. He took

a sip of his water and continued. "Do you think the Woodses share the bribes with Micheline, or are they operating on their own?"

"I'm not sure," Ainsley said. "If they're true believers, I think they'd have to share the profits with her."

"Making her an accomplice," Santiago concluded.

Ainsley leaned back in her chair, letting the repercussions sink in. "This might be bigger than we originally thought."

Santiago nodded, his expression grim. "Yeah. We've got to be careful going forward. If what you say is true, Micheline sounds like a real piece of work. If she gets wind of what we're doing here, she'll feel threatened. I don't imagine she's the type to sit back and let the chips fall where they may."

"Probably not," Ainsley said. If Micheline was in on the bribes, she had a vested interest in keeping The Marriage Institute open for business. She wouldn't appreciate Ainsley and Santiago's efforts to turn off the flow of easy money she collected from them after every retreat.

Did she already know? Was that why Ainsley had been attacked this morning? She'd spent the last several hours thinking Alva and Brody were behind the assault, wanting to scare her into accepting Santiago's terms for a divorce. But what if Micheline was driving the bus? What if the Institute employees reported back to her, and took their orders from her?

It was enough to make her already aching head start pounding in earnest.

"Hey." Santiago touched her hand, and she opened her eyes to find him watching her. "I know things seem to be getting more complicated, but I'm still here. And I'm not going anywhere."

Ainsley nodded, not trusting herself to speak. She was grateful for Santiago's presence, and she knew he was the only person she could trust right now. But his words set off a dull ache in her chest. She wanted to believe him when he said he wasn't going anywhere. But he'd left her before. And she knew, once this was over, he'd leave her again.

Only this time, she wasn't going to let him walk away with her heart.

SANTIAGO MANAGED TO get through the afternoon without incident, though it took all of his self-control not to confront Steve during their group session. Even though Ainsley thought Brett was behind the attacks, he wasn't quite ready to declare Steve innocent. Especially after the man in question shot him a smug look as the session wrapped up.

"Saw your cabin this morning," Steve said, walking alongside Santiago as they made their way to the dining area for dinner. "What happened?"

Santiago clenched his jaw and forced himself to respond. "We had a tree branch come through the window last night. Glass was everywhere."

"Yikes. Hope no one was hurt."

Santiago studied the man's face, but saw no signs of either deception or amusement. Perhaps he wasn't responsible after all.

"No, my wife and I were both fine." It felt a little strange, saying the word *wife*. But not in a bad way. If things had been different, he and Ainsley probably would have been married for years by now. And happily so—no way would they have needed this retreat, where relationships apparently came to die.

"That's good. I'm glad no one was injured. Bet it was scary, though."

Now *that* was an interesting remark, and consistent with Santiago's theory that the incident had been aimed at intimidating them.

"It was unexpected, that's for sure."

They reached the entrance to the dining hall. Steve stopped, standing in such a way that Santiago was forced to stop as well. "Accidents are the worst." His gaze was level and steady and full of meaning. "If only there was something you could do to prevent them."

Just like that, Santiago went from calm to enraged. For a few seconds, he forgot how to breathe as white-hot anger consumed him. His muscles tensed, ready to fight. His vision tunneled, until the only thing he saw was Steve's eminently punchable face.

He wasn't conscious of moving. Didn't realize

he had, until he registered Steve leaning back, eyes going wide.

"Threaten my wife again, and I will put you into the ground."

Fear flashed in Steve's eyes, quickly replaced by the gleam of bravado. "You're bluffing." He gave Santiago a once-over and scoffed. "You're a desk jockey. Probably never even thrown a punch in your life. You don't have it in you."

Santiago surged forward and grinned as Steve flinched. "Try me," he said darkly. "Please. Give me an excuse."

Steve held his gaze for a second, then looked away. "Whatever," he muttered. "Just keep your wife away from my Jenny."

"My wife does what she wants, when she wants. I don't try to control her. Unlike you, I'm not threatened by a woman who knows her own mind."

Steve glared at him, but didn't respond. He turned and stomped into the dining room, leaving Santiago standing at the entrance, adrenaline still coursing through him.

Had he really just threatened Steve? It wasn't like him to lose control of his temper; it was even more out of character for him to promise physical violence. Normally, he fought his battles with wits and facts, not his fists. But in Steve's case, he was willing to make an exception.

No one threatened Ainsley. Not as long as he was

around. Aside from his sister, she was the most important person in his life. He wasn't about to stand by and let some bully take his anger issues out on her.

And if that meant he had to protect her with his body, then that's what he'd do.

He took a deep breath, feeling some of his anger ebb out on the exhale. It was strange, the feeling of anticipation that had come over him, along with the willingness to strike out at another human being. It was a rush like he'd never experienced before. No wonder some men seemed to like fighting—he could see how the endorphin rush might become addicting.

Motion in the dining room caught his eye, and he focused to see Ainsley giving him a wave. A small shock went through him as he realized he was still standing in place, as though rooted to the spot. With a little shake, he cast off the last of this strange mood and walked in to meet her.

Should he tell her about his conversation with Steve? She might want to know their first guess had been correct, at least as far as the window was concerned. Santiago didn't think Steve had attacked her this morning—he wouldn't have been able to keep from bragging about it if he had.

But as he approached the table and saw the fine lines of strain around her eyes, Santiago decided not to share this information. It would only upset her, and if he told her how he'd threatened the other man, she'd worry about his response and fret about the likelihood of his flying off the handle. The last thing he wanted was to add to the stress in her life. He was supposed to protect her, not add to her problems.

"Everything okay?" she asked as he sat across from her.

He smiled. "Yeah. Just lost in thought out there."

"I saw you talking to Steve." She took a sip of water, watching him carefully. "Did he have anything important to say?"

Santiago shook his head. "Not at all. Just bluster. He's not worth your energy."

"That's good." Relief flashed across her face, and he realized he'd made the right decision. "How were your sessions? Learn anything new?"

They fell into an easy conversation, sharing the events of their respective afternoons and moving on to other, more pleasant topics. She was so easy to talk to—she always had been. It was a characteristic he'd taken for granted during their relationship. Fortunately, he was older and wiser now.

He watched her face as she spoke, tracked the play of emotions across her features. Everything about her interested him—her thoughts, her reactions, her emotions. Would he ever grow tired of talking to her? Was that even possible?

She smiled, and he couldn't help but smile in return. Had his parents ever felt this way? Had his father ever sat across from his mother and gotten lost in her smile, felt himself drowning in the depths of her eyes? Had his mother ever looked at his father and felt a warm glow in her chest? Had they ever, in the history of their relationship, loved each other?

He wanted to hope so, for their sakes.

But even if they had started out with affection, somewhere along the way, they'd lost it. The same fate would have awaited him and Ainsley, had they stayed together. And even though he still loved her, he didn't trust the future. No one in his family had ever been lucky in relationships. As much as he wished otherwise, Santiago knew he wasn't special enough to be the exception.

And in the end, wasn't it better to be lonely than to hurt the person you loved?

Chapter Ten

Something was going on with Santiago—Ainsley could tell by his demeanor. He smiled and kept up with their conversation, but his body language was a little stiff, and there was a note of reserve in his voice that told her he was worried. Perhaps it had to do with Steve. She'd watched the two of them as they'd stood in the doorway, and she'd seen Santiago's anger rise to the surface. For a few seconds, his normally calm and cool demeanor had disappeared as rage had bubbled up. When he'd suddenly jerked forward, she'd half stood from her seat, convinced he was about to start using his fists. But based on his reaction to Steve's flinch, Santiago had only been trying to intimidate the man.

It wasn't like Santiago to use his height and his body to scare someone. For him to do so now meant Steve had done something to truly anger him.

The window, she thought. *Steve's the one who broke the window.*

No wonder Santiago was upset—either one of them

could have been hurt last night, thanks to Steve's temper tantrum. Had he also attacked her this morning?

She studied Santiago's face as they walked back to the cabin together. *No*, she decided. If Steve had hit her with the branch, he would be stupid enough to brag about it. And if Santiago had heard that, he wouldn't have pulled any punches. She would have had to peel him off the other man, and they would be sitting in a police station giving their statements, rather than walking into the cabin.

She waited for Santiago to close and lock the door before sharing her revelation. "It was Steve, wasn't it? He broke the window."

Santiago's body went still, reminding her of a deer caught out in the open. "How did you know?"

"I saw the two of you talking before you came into the dining hall. It's not like you to lose your temper the way you almost did. I figured Steve had said something to set you off, and I figured the window was the reason."

Santiago nodded. "He basically admitted to it, then issued a thinly veiled threat. I don't know what came over me, but in the moment I was angry enough to hit him." He sounded puzzled by his own reaction, an academic trying to apply logic to an emotional situation.

"But you didn't," she pointed out.

"No. I didn't. Probably for the best." He grinned at her. "He's definitely the type to press charges."

"Oh yeah," Ainsley agreed. "Speaking of charges, do you think he's the one who hit me this morning?"

Santiago shook his head. "I wondered that myself, but based on what he said, I don't think so. If I had any doubts, I'd probably be in jail right now for attempted murder."

His words confirmed her earlier thoughts, making her even more convinced Brett was her mystery morning attacker. "I'm glad that's not the case," she said, trying to lighten the mood. "I already have one man in my life in trouble with the legal system. Let's not make it two."

Santiago chuckled. "It would be hard to help your brother from behind bars."

"Do you still want to talk about the case tonight?"

"Absolutely. Are you sure you feel up to it?"

Ainsley nodded. "Yes. But I want to take a bath first. I'm a little achy from this morning, and I think the hot water will help with that."

A dark expression flashed across Santiago's face at the mention of her attack. "Of course," he said. "Take your time. I'll get set up here, and I'll have a cup of decaf coffee waiting for you when you get out."

Ainsley groaned in anticipation. "That sounds wonderful. I shouldn't be long."

She headed for her bedroom, closing the door behind her with a soft snick. Then she walked into the bathroom and turned on the taps.

The water ran as she undressed. She fired off a

text to Spencer, asking about a connection between Micheline and the Woodses. Then she ran her hand under the water to check the temperature: it was hot, exactly the way she wanted it. Ainsley sat on the edge of the tub and added a dollop of bath gel, smiling at the resulting explosion of bubbles. Once the tub was full, she switched off the water and slipped inside, leaning back with a sigh of pleasure.

The heat felt amazing on her tired, achy muscles. She closed her eyes and let her mind wander as the bath worked its magic, the warmth of the water radiating down to her bones.

Two days. That's all that was left of the retreat. Forty-eight more hours of putting on a mask and pretending like she and Santiago were a couple in trouble, of acting like she didn't know the Woodses were con artists hurting innocent people.

She wouldn't miss it, that much was certain. It was hard being so passive, seeing a crime happening in real time but doing nothing to stop it. Sure, in the larger scheme of things she and Santiago were doing the right thing. But all the micro-insults, the little digs at people like Jenny, were wearing on her soul. Ainsley had the benefit of knowing she was a target, so it was easy for her to dismiss the suggestions that she was wrong, or that Santiago would be better off without her. But the other people in her group didn't have that advantage. They were internalizing everything the counselors said, blaming themselves for the problems in their marriages, even though their spouses were the ones who had created this particular situation. Only the knowledge that she and Santiago were going to expose the dishonest actions of everyone—the Woodses and the bribing significant others both—kept her going.

But…there were some things she would miss about this week. Spending time with Santiago again had been wonderful, even though the circumstances had been less than ideal. They'd made the best of it, though, falling into a routine of sorts. It wasn't the same rhythm their lives had taken on when they'd been together, but it still felt familiar. She'd grown to enjoy their evening talks, of hearing more about his work and how his career had taken him from New York City back to Phoenix. While she wouldn't trade her work at Colton Oil, it was interesting to learn about the variety of clients Santiago had dealt with over the years.

He still felt like her other half. The time they'd spent apart hadn't changed that. The problem was, she didn't know what to do with this information. Based on things he'd said recently, it seemed his stance on marriage hadn't changed. He truly seemed to believe he was better off alone. While she understood his fears about repeating the mistakes of his parents, she also knew he wasn't the type of man to stay in a bad relationship simply to torture the other person. That took a level of spite that he didn't possess. And while

Ainsley wanted so badly for him to understand that, she couldn't make him see the truth.

In the end, it was probably for the best that they were going to go their separate ways after this was over. Being with Santiago again had been a nice reminder of what was possible, with the right person. But as much as it hurt her heart, she had to admit he wasn't for her. Sure, they got along well and were compatible in all the right ways. It just wasn't enough. She wasn't going to beg him to be with her—her pride wouldn't allow it. And since he refused to believe that they wouldn't turn into his parents, well… There was nothing more to be done.

Clearing her mind, Ainsley sank deeper into the water, feeling it brush against the bottom of her chin. Relaxation stole over her as the minutes ticked by. She knew she should finish up and get dressed. After all, she and Santiago didn't have much time left together, and she did want to work on her brother's case tonight while they were still at the retreat and the interruptions of the real world were held at bay.

He was probably still making her coffee, though. She'd get out soon. Just a few more minutes…

HE WAS STARTING to get worried.

It had been more than an hour since Ainsley had gone to her suite for a bath. He'd heard the water rushing through the pipes, but that sound had stopped long ago. The cabin was utterly quiet; if he hadn't known better, he would have thought he was the only one here.

Was she okay? He didn't want to disturb her, but his imagination kept creating scenarios that made him worry. Perhaps this morning's blow to the head had left her with a concussion and she'd passed out in the tub? What if she'd slipped getting into or out of the bath and was lying on the floor, out cold?

For the sake of his mental health, Santiago decided to check on her. She might not appreciate the interruption, but he needed to know she was all right.

Giving up all pretense of work—not that he'd been able to focus in the face of his distracting thoughts—he set aside his laptop and got to his feet.

It didn't take long to walk down the hall and arrive at the door to Ainsley's suite. He rapped softly on the wood. "Doing okay in there?"

She didn't respond, so he knocked again, a little louder this time. Still nothing.

Worried now, he tried the handle. It turned easily, and he stepped inside the bedroom.

He paused at the threshold. It seemed wrong to walk in uninvited, like he was crossing some invisible line. But he had to make sure she was okay. As soon as he confirmed Ainsley was fine, he'd leave.

Wanting to respect her privacy, he called out her name before venturing in farther. "Ainsley?"

Still no response. And she should have heard him easily, since the door to the bathroom was open.

Anxiety made Santiago's heart pound. Casting aside all considerations of privacy, he rushed across the room and stepped inside the bathroom, only to draw up short at the sight that greeted him.

Ainsley was reclined in the large tub, the back of her head resting against the wall. Her eyes were closed, her lips slightly parted as she breathed softly. A smattering of bubbles floating on the surface of the water did nothing to hide her curves from his view. Santiago's mouth went dry as he ran his eyes down the length of her body. His hands itched to touch her, to trace her peaks and valleys, to explore her sensitive spots. Would she still feel the same, or would she be a stranger to him now?

He forced his gaze back to her face, guilt flashing through him. She didn't deserve to be ogled, especially when she didn't know it was happening. He felt like the worst kind of voyeur.

Concern warred with shame as he watched her. Was she asleep, or had she passed out due to her head injury? He vaguely remembered watching some medical drama, where the doctor had told a husband not to let his wife fall asleep after a concussion or she might slip into a coma. Oh, was that what Ainsley had done? Had the heat of the water lulled her into a dangerous sleep?

Only one way to know for sure. With his heart

pounding against his breastbone, Santiago leaned down and placed his hands on her bare shoulders. He gave her a little shake, hoping she'd forgive this intrusion.

"Ainsley?" he said loudly. "Wake up, please."

He held his breath as he waited for her to respond. When she didn't move right away, he tried again, a sense of despair building in his chest. If something was wrong with her, he'd never forgive himself. He should have forced her to go to the hospital this morning, should have refused to move until she'd agreed to see a doctor…

She stirred in the water, her face scrunching up into a slight frown. Santiago swallowed a yelp of triumph, not wanting to scare her. Her eyelids fluttered open, and she stared up at him.

"Am I late?"

He leaned back and chuckled. "You might say that."

"Oh."

It took a few seconds for her to fully wake up. He could tell she was still groggy as she looked around. "What are we doing in the bathroom?"

"You came in to take a hot bath. It's been over an hour, so I was worried. I came to check on you."

She looked down, seeming to register the water for the first time. "I'm naked."

Santiago's cheeks heated. "Ah, yes. You are."

He expected her to cover herself, but she didn't.

Instead, she turned her head and looked him up and down. "Why aren't you?"

Her question was so unexpected it knocked the thoughts right out of his head. "Um…what?"

"You heard me." Her eyes were clear, all traces of sleep gone.

"I… I…" He was reduced to sputtering, his mind frantically trying to keep up with current events. Was he dreaming? Was he imagining things? Or had the blow to her head been so severe it had caused brain damage that was now manifesting in this unusual way?

Ainsley got to her feet and stepped out of the tub, totally unselfconscious about her nudity. She bent to pull the stopper, presenting Santiago with a view that nearly stopped his heart. His blood raced south, making it even harder to think.

She wrapped a towel around her body and took his hand. "Come on." With a gentle tug, she pulled him into the bedroom.

"What is happening here?" he whispered as she pushed him down on the mattress.

She straddled his lap, pressing the heat of her core against the fly of his pants. "I'm tired," she said, rubbing against him. The friction made his eyes roll back in his head, and he gasped for breath.

"The last few days have been so hard," she continued. She licked the side of his neck, her tongue leaving a hot trail that immediately cooled in the air of the room. Goose bumps broke out across his skin and the hair on the back of his neck stood on end.

"I'm tired of hearing about pain. I'm tired of seeing people hurt each other. You're a good man, Santiago. I know you don't see it, but I do. I know we don't have a future, but please, just give me tonight. Help me forget all of this, if only for a few hours."

She cast off the towel, sending it to the floor. Then she took his hands and placed them on her breasts. Her nipples hardened against his palms, and his fingers curled reflexively to cup her.

Everything she said made sense, and echoed his own internal feelings about the retreat. He'd drawn comfort from her presence this week, but perhaps they could give each other more. Maybe she was right—maybe they could lose themselves in pleasure and forget about the world for a little while.

It wasn't the smartest idea, at least where his heart was concerned. Santiago knew that if they slept together, he'd fall back in love with her again. Still, it was a price worth paying. And in a way, he owed her. He would have helped with her brother's case even if she'd refused to attend the retreat. But she was here, and she'd suffered for her efforts. If he could help her he would, even though he knew it was going to cost him.

Still, he had to make sure they were on the same page. He wasn't prepared to offer her something long-term. All he could do was give her tonight. She'd said she understood, but was that just her arousal talking? Or did she truly know he wasn't good for anything but this impulsive encounter?

"Ainsley." Thanks to the roar of blood in his ears, his voice sounded like it was coming from far away.

She leaned back, biting her bottom lip. "Mmm?"

God, she was beautiful! What was he going to ask again…?

She rocked against him and he couldn't contain a moan of need. His thoughts were circling the drain, his brain on the verge of ceding control to his body. Think, he had to think while he still could!

Ainsley placed her hands over his, causing him to tighten his hold on her breasts. "What do you need?" she whispered, her breath hot against his ear.

With the last of his willpower, Santiago slipped his hands free and placed them on her hips, halting her movement. "Are you sure?"

She paused, and he took the opportunity to breathe. She'd asked what he needed from her, and the truth was, he had to know she was certain about this. The last thing he wanted was to hurt her, even inadvertently.

Seconds ticked by, feeling like an eternity. Then she shifted, wriggling back. "I'm sorry. I shouldn't have…you don't want me."

Santiago kept his hands where they were, knowing if he let her go he'd never get her back, not even as a friend. "That's not it," he said, hating the note of hurt he'd put in her voice. "That's not it at all. I just want to make sure you're going into this with a clear head."

She looked at him, her blue gaze steady. "I know what I want. Do you?"

He couldn't help but smile at the subtle challenge in her tone. "I've always known," he said softly. Surprise flashed in her eyes—didn't she know how much he still cared for her? He wanted nothing more than to surrender to the need arcing between them, but he had to make sure they both understood the rules first.

"But you have to know that I can't give you what you want."

A shadow crossed her face. *This is it*, he thought. *She's done.* Disappointment flared in his chest, but he knew he'd done the right thing. Sex with Ainsley had always been mind-blowing, but at least this way he'd still be able to live with himself tomorrow.

To his surprise, she didn't move. She offered him a sad smile, then reached for his hands and put them back onto her breasts. Her skin was chilly against his palms, her nipples hard points he couldn't ignore. "This is what I want. Just you. One night only."

Santiago exhaled hard, the breath gusting out of him along with the rest of his reservations. Truth be told, this was still probably a bad idea. But he'd had worse.

Letting go of his doubts, Santiago dropped his head and took what she was offering.

Chapter Eleven

Ainsley let her head fall back and surrendered to the feel of Santiago's hands on her breasts and his mouth on her neck. This impulsivity was out of character for her, and it felt equal parts scary and thrilling to ignore the little voice in her head that always preached reserve and self-control. Even now, that little voice squawked in alarm, frantically insisting this was a mistake. And it probably was. But Ainsley was so desperate for Santiago's familiar comfort that she couldn't bring herself to care.

When she'd opened her eyes and seen his face above her, something had clicked deep inside her chest. She couldn't find the right words to describe how he made her feel, but she recognized the sensation: it was like coming home after the end of a long day. It wasn't fair that five years after he'd walked out of her life she still associated him with solace and security, but perhaps that was one of life's jokes.

Despite their years apart, Santiago still knew just how to touch her to drive her wild. His hands moved over her now, squeezing here, caressing there, his fingers skillfully building her arousal with a few well-placed strokes. And his mouth! The heat of it left a blazing trail of sensation across her skin that soon had her writhing in an unconscious expression of need and desire.

Needing to touch him, wanting to know if he still felt the same under her hands, Ainsley fumbled at the buttons of his shirt. Santiago captured her mouth with his own and tried to help her. Their fingers and tongues tangled together as they worked, and eventually, the two halves of his shirt opened to reveal the skin of his chest. Ainsley sighed as her fingertips made contact with the soft hair that dusted his pecs, and her thumbs brushed over his nipples. They hardened beneath her touch and she smiled against his mouth.

Santiago shifted, shrugging off his shirt before touching her again. He slid his hands from her hips to her bottom, cupping her curves with an air of possession that thrilled her. Without warning, he tightened his grip and pulled her up and forward, pressing her against his chest and settling her bare core on top of the bulge in his pants.

Heat suffused her body, the skin-on-skin contact nearly overwhelming her system. Ainsley threaded her fingers through Santiago's hair, loving the feel of it but also needing an anchor to keep her upright.

His erection throbbed under her, her sensitive tissues feeling every one of his heartbeats.

Ainsley's need built, the pressure inside her searching for an outlet. Unable to keep still any longer, she rocked her hips, dragging her core along the hard ridge tucked behind the fly of his pants. More, she needed more.

A small whimper sounded from somewhere in the room. With a shock, Ainsley realized the sound had come from her. "Please," she whispered, the word ragged even to her own ears.

"You don't have to beg." Santiago's voice was gravelly, his breath hitched. "You never have to beg me."

He slid his hand between them, working the button of his pants. With every movement, his fingers brushed against her sensitive nub. Ainsley bit her lip and clenched his shoulders, trying to stave off her orgasm. She didn't want to find release until they were joined together, their bodies moving as one.

Santiago's movements were jerky and uncoordinated, his usual dexterity impaired by arousal. Finally, she heard the rasp of his zipper and then she felt his flesh against hers, smooth and hot and hard.

She reached down to position him, but he put his hand over hers, stalling her movements. Ainsley looked up and found worry in his green gaze.

"I don't have a condom," he said. "I should have thought of it before, but well… I got distracted."

Ainsley shook her head. "I don't care." Pregnancy

wasn't a concern for her—doctors had made it clear she could never have a baby, and after the beginning stages of their relationship, they hadn't used protection. She hadn't gotten pregnant then, had never even experienced a scare. It simply wasn't going to happen.

"I know we never used condoms before. I just didn't want you to think I assumed… I mean, it's been a while, and…" he trailed off, clearly at a loss.

"My last round of tests came back normal," she said. "But if you'd feel better—"

"No, it's okay," he said quickly. "My last screen was normal, too."

She smiled at him, touched by his consideration. Under any other circumstances, she would have initiated the protection discussion long before things had escalated to this point. But given their history and what she knew of his character, she trusted Santiago. His display of concern at this charged moment was yet more proof that her trust in him wasn't misplaced.

"That's good to know," she said. She leaned forward and ran the tip of her tongue up the side of his neck, pressing a kiss at the corner of his jaw. Then she moved to nibble on his ear lobe and was rewarded by his sharp inhale.

Ainsley lightly raked her nails down his chest to his stomach, then wrapped her hand around his erection once more. She rose up onto her knees, but just as she was about to sink down, Santiago gripped her hips.

Before she could ask what was wrong, the world spun and she found herself flat on her back, staring up at the ceiling. "Santia—" His name died in her throat as he moved down her body. She felt his large hands on the inside of her thighs, pushing her legs apart. Then his mouth was on her, his tongue exploring her most sensitive parts with a skill that sent her eyes rolling back in her head.

The tension built in her body with every stroke, a spring coiling tighter and tighter inside her. Ainsley moaned, thrashing about as the sensations buffeted her from all sides. But Santiago never wavered in his attentions. His hands held her in place as he ravished her with single-minded focus.

Unable to hold back any longer, Ainsley stopped trying to control her body and let the waves of pleasure wash over her. The orgasm rolled through her, her muscles contracting and relaxing in a timeless rhythm that seemed to consume her.

She wasn't sure how long it lasted. The satisfaction of completion erased all sense of time and place, leaving her unmoored in an abyss of sensation. Gradually though, she became aware of Santiago's presence.

He kissed his way up her body, his hair tickling her skin as it brushed over her. "I've been wanting to do that since I walked into your office and saw you standing behind your desk." His voice was low in her ear, his tone smugly satisfied.

"What took you so long?" she croaked.

He laughed, the sound sending residual shocks through her core. “My perfect Ainsley, always so prim and proper. Do you know how much I love mussing you up?”

She couldn’t find the words to reply. His eyes bored into hers, his arousal making them glow like green fire.

“Do you like it when I make you lose control?”

She opened her mouth to respond, but before she could speak, he slid inside her. She moaned as her sensitive tissues parted to allow his entry, his erection filling and stretching her in all the right ways.

“That’s what I thought.” He paused, buried deep inside her. His eyes searched her face, his expression one of intense focus. “Did you miss me?” he whispered. “Did you miss this?” He punctuated the question with a little thrust of his hips, touching a spot inside of her that only he had ever been able to find.

“Yes,” she gasped, urging him to move with her hands and her hips. But he settled his weight onto her, holding her in place. It was clear Santiago wanted to be in charge, and for the moment, she was happy to let him.

“Good.” The satisfaction in his voice was unmistakable. “Because I missed you, too.”

Before he’d finished speaking the words, he started to move, his hips settling into a rhythm that was at once familiar and new. Ainsley wrapped her legs around his waist and gripped his shoulders, relishing the feel of his big body over hers. Yes, she'd missed this. He'd always felt like her other half, and now that they were joined together again, her heart was full for the first time in five years. Sex with Santiago had always been more than just a physical experience for her. Their bodies, their breath, even their souls entwined, linking them in a way that transcended time and space. Ainsley had never found this connection with anyone else. For a while, after Santiago had left, she'd wondered if she'd simply imagined it. Maybe her broken heart had conjured it in a fit of desperate loneliness. But now that they were together again, she knew she hadn't been wrong. This man truly was her equal and other half.

She felt him tense above her, knew he was close to his own release. Acting on a combination of instinct and habit, she lifted her head and gently bit his shoulder, pressing just hard enough to leave marks in his skin. He cried out, then shuddered as he found his completion. She held him as his body kicked inside hers, her own core squeezing as she climaxed in response to his passion.

Breathing hard, Santiago lowered himself until he was flush against her. Ainsley welcomed his weight, loving the way he made her feel surrounded and safe and small in comparison. She stroked her hand up and down his back as they returned to earth together.

Eventually, he stirred and lifted his head. "That was..."

She smiled at his shell-shocked expression. "I know."

"You always know just what to do."

"I could say the same for you," she replied, enjoying the compliment.

A look that could only be described as pure masculine satisfaction crossed his face, and she laughed. "Hey, now. This cabin isn't big enough for the two of us and your ego."

He waggled his eyebrows. "Are you sure?"

Ainsley nodded, pleased to see him so happy. The events of this week had put lines of stress around his eyes and mouth, but at the moment, they were gone.

Santiago rolled onto his back and reached for her, pulling her against his side. "That's too bad," he remarked, his hand drifting lazily down her arm. "I always love it when you stroke my...ego."

She groaned at the bad joke, making him laugh. "Oh, come on. It was a little funny."

"Nope," she said, resting her head on his shoulder. "I'm not going to encourage you."

They lay in silence for a time, their bodies growing cool in the air of the room. Ainsley wondered if Santiago was going to leave, but she didn't want to ask the question. She was happy for him to stay, happy to spend the night in his arms, the way they used to sleep together. They'd already broken so many rules tonight; what was one more?

She felt him relax against her, heard his breathing deepen as he slipped into his dreams. A sense of peace stole over her as the seconds ticked by. She reached down and pulled the covers over them, the way she'd done a million times before.

The regrets would come; she knew that. Maybe not tomorrow, maybe not even the day after, but some day she knew she would wish that she'd had the strength to resist falling back into bed with Santiago. Now that she'd slept with him again, reaffirming their connection in every way that mattered, it was going to be that much harder to walk away when this was over.

But she'd worry about that later. Right now, with the man she still loved beside her, Ainsley closed her eyes and drifted off to sleep, warm and safe in Santiago's arms.

IT WAS DAWN when she woke, the room growing lighter by degrees as the sun began to peek over the horizon. Ainsley stretched, then froze as she remembered she wasn't alone.

She turned her head, expecting to see Santiago sleeping next to her. But the bed was empty, the rumpled sheets the only evidence of his presence.

Ignoring the ache in her heart, Ainsley slipped out of bed and walked to the bathroom. She turned on the shower and brushed her teeth, pushing down her disappointment. What did she expect? They'd made no promises to each other last night. Both of them had known the score—the sex was a one-off, not the start of something new. Of course Santiago had returned to his own bed to sleep last night.

Still, she couldn't ignore the slight pang in her chest as she washed the last of his scent from her skin. Logically, she understood their encounter had been a moment out of time, a temporary respite they'd created for themselves. But her emotional side wished it could have lasted a little longer. Was a few more hours away from the real world too much to ask? Apparently so.

She toweled off and pulled her still-wet hair back into a ponytail. Then she dressed in running clothes and stepped out of her bedroom suite.

The light in the kitchenette was on. She frowned; Santiago must have left it on last night before he'd come to check on her in the bath. But as she walked down the hall, she smelled coffee…

She stepped into the kitchenette, surprised to find Santiago standing at the counter, his back to her. He was dressed in a T-shirt and sweatpants, and he was wearing an old pair of sneakers. Ainsley drew up short, frowning. Santiago was not a morning person. What was he doing here, and wearing something other than a bathrobe?

He must have heard her, because he turned around and handed her a cup of coffee. "Good morning." His tone made it sound like he met her all the time at dawn with coffee in hand.

"Morning," Ainsley replied, taking a sip from the mug. "I'm surprised you're up so early."

He shrugged. "I told you, we're sticking together from here on out. That means if you go for a run, so do I."

A smile tugged at the corners of her mouth. Truth be told, she'd forgotten about his promise to accompany her. "I didn't think you were serious about that."

"Oh yes. I'm not about to risk you getting attacked again."

The mention of yesterday's events made the back of her head ache, and she reached up to touch the still-tender spot. The swelling was almost completely gone, but she was certain the bruise would linger for a while. "I appreciate it."

He nodded. "I wasn't sure you were going to get up this morning, after..." he trailed off, his cheeks going pink. He cleared his throat and continued. "Anyway, I got up early and took a shower in my bathroom so as not to disturb you. Then I went to the car and dug out an old gym bag I had in the trunk." He gestured to his clothes. "Now I'm dressed for the occasion."

The hurt and disappointment she'd felt at waking to find him gone melted away. He hadn't left because the sex was over and he'd wanted to sleep alone. No, he'd left to get ready to go running with her, if that's what she wanted to do. Santiago might not realize it, but given his dislike of both mornings and running, Ainsley recognized his efforts as a gesture of love.

Warmth filled her chest, suffusing through her body until she thought she might actually be glowing. "We don't have to go." The offer was enough—she didn't want to torture him.

"No, no, I want to," he assured her. "Though we might need to do more walking than running. I don't know if I can match your pace."

"That's okay," she told him. "It'll be nice to just be outdoors."

"I agree." He reached for her cup and put it on the counter. "I usually stick to the rowing machine at the gym, and since there's a shortage of rivers in Phoenix, I never get to row outside. This will be a nice change of scenery for me."

They walked out of the cabin together, and she led him through her usual stretching routine. "Did you row in New York?" He'd enjoyed racquetball when they'd been together, but it sounded like he'd found a new exercise in the time they'd been apart.

"Yes," he said. "There was a club at my firm that I joined shortly after moving there. Seemed like a good way to make new friends, and I actually enjoyed it."

He told her about it as they set off. Ainsley deliberately slowed her pace, prioritizing conversation over aerobic achievements. They fell into an easy flow, the time passing quickly as they ran in unison.

After what seemed like only a few minutes, they were back at the cabin, having finished the main trail loop. In silent agreement, they slowed to a walk as soon as they came out of the woods.

"How'd you like it?" Ainsley asked. Santiago hadn't had any trouble keeping up, thanks to his long legs and his rowing habit. If he wanted to join her again in the morning, she'd push him to go a little faster.

He grinned, sweat gleaming on his forehead. "It was good," he said. "But I think I need different shoes if this is going to be a regular thing."

Ainsley smiled, but inside, she felt a pang at his mention of the future. It was nice to think they could remain like this, lovers who went running together every morning. But that wasn't going to happen. As soon as this retreat was over, she'd go back to her offices in Mustang Valley and he'd go back to Phoenix. Even though the two cities weren't that far apart, they might as well be in different galaxies.

Still, she wasn't going to let future pain rob her of her current joy. So she pasted on a smile and patted his shoulder. "Don't worry," she said. "I packed a few bandages. With a little TLC, your blisters won't last more than a few days."

"Does this mean we can take the morning off tomorrow?" He sounded so hopeful Ainsley couldn't help but laugh.

"Not a chance," she told him.

Santiago shook his head, but she saw the glimmer

of amusement in his eyes. "I'll get you back for this, just you wait."

Heat flared to life in her belly as she heard the unspoken promise in his voice. "Is that right?"

"Oh, yes," he said, his voice warm and low. "I have all kinds of ideas."

"Is that right?" She leaned against his side as they walked, needing to touch him. "What'd you have in mind?"

"It would take too long to explain." Santiago dropped his head, his breath warm across her ear. "I'll just have to show you."

Goose bumps broke out along her arms and legs, and Ainsley shivered in anticipation. Santiago must have felt the movement, because he chuckled with satisfaction.

"You tease," she said.

He put his arm around her shoulders and pulled her in closer. "It's only a tease if I don't follow through. But I have every intention of keeping my word."

A growing sense of arousal sent tingles through her breasts and core. She knew from experience, both historical and recent, that Santiago was an inventive lover. She hadn't expected their reunion would last longer than one night, but she wasn't opposed to the idea, either. It sounded like Santiago felt the same way.

"Morning, folks."

The new voice broke into their private moment,

and the pair of them drew up short. Ainsley turned to find Brody Woods standing on the porch of their cabin, eyeing them speculatively.

"Brody, what a surprise." Santiago dropped his arm from her shoulders and stepped forward to shake the man's hand. "What brings you to our cabin this morning?"

"I wanted to check out the damage from the broken window and make sure the temporary repair was taking care of things for you," he said. "I would have come out sooner, but we've been so busy I haven't had a chance."

"I understand," Santiago said smoothly. "As you can see, the plywood is keeping out the raccoons."

Brody laughed, though it sounded a little forced. "Good, good. Seems the window people won't be able to come out and replace it until Monday, which means you folks are going to have to deal with this eyesore for the rest of the retreat."

"That's okay," Ainsley said. "We can live with it for the next forty-eight hours."

Brody looked her up and down, his eyes lingering a little too long on her bare legs. "That's good," he said, sounding somewhat absent. "I was sorry to hear about the accident. Bet it was scary for you."

"It was unexpected," Santiago said, stepping to the side as if to partially block her from Brody's view. "But your employee was most helpful with the cleanup."

Brody shook his head slightly, as though to clear his mind. "Glad to hear it," he said. "I'll leave you two now. Got to get back to the big house. We've got a special speaker today at lunch, and Alva needs my help to make sure everything's ready."

"Oh?" Ainsley said. "What's the topic?"

"Being Your Best You," Brody said.

A chill shot down Ainsley's spine at his reply. "That sounds interesting," she said, hoping she didn't sound as wooden as she suddenly felt.

Brody nodded. "It is. Micheline is a fantastic speaker. You guys are going to love her."

"Can't wait," Santiago said.

Brody stepped off the porch and walked past them. Santiago offered Ainsley his hand and led her up the steps. "Breathe," he instructed quietly.

She waited until he'd shut the door behind them. "I knew it!" she exclaimed, spinning around to face him. "I told you they're connected."

"Probably," Santiago agreed. "But we have a more immediate problem—does Micheline know who you are?"

"You mean, will she recognize me if she sees me?" Ainsley asked. Santiago nodded.

"I'm not sure," Ainsley said. "I've seen her a few times around town, but we've never been officially introduced. Still, she probably knows I'm Ace's sister, and she definitely knows some of my other family members."

Santiago's expression was serious. "What do you want to do?"

Ainsley considered the question, mentally reviewing her options. They could both leave, today, before Micheline saw her and blew their cover with the Woodses. But they were so close to the end of the retreat, and with the couples all slated to share their decision to stay together or split up tomorrow during the closing session, they needed to stick this out. It was the final piece of evidence they wanted to connect the bribes and the retreat outcomes, and Ainsley didn't want to walk away without getting it.

"Why don't you go to the seminar?" she suggested. "I'll pretend to have food poisoning, so they won't suspect anything. That way, we'll still be able to finish the retreat."

"Are you sure? I don't like the thought of leaving you alone."

"I'll be fine," she assured him. "I'll hang out here and lock the door. Nothing to worry about."

She could tell by the set of Santiago's mouth that he didn't agree with her, but he didn't argue. "All right," he said. "What about this morning? Are you going to attend the morning sessions, or would you rather stay here?"

"No, I'll go," she said. "The counselors are really

putting on the pressure now that we're so close to the end. I need to record all the evidence I can get."

"Okay." Santiago nodded in agreement. "Let's get cleaned up, then. We've got work to do."

Chapter Twelve

The news that Micheline was making an appcarance at the retreat had put a damper on the morning. But despite this unforeseen complication, Santiago still walked into his first group counseling session with a spring in his step. It wasn't just last night's sex or this morning's run that had put him in a good mood, though he couldn't deny that both activities had been thoroughly enjoyable. No, he was riding the residual high of having fully reconnected, physically and emotionally, with Ainsley.

Santiago was happy to be with her now. In some ways, the knowledge that this liaison was temporary felt freeing, and allowed him to fully enjoy their chemistry. He'd be sad when the retreat ended and they went their separate ways, but that didn't mean they couldn't appreciate each other's company now. If only they'd surrendered to the attraction earlier in the week! They could have had more time together, rather than the scant hours they had left. But it was probably better this way, he told himself. Walking away from Ainsley was going to hurt, he knew that. If they'd started sleeping together on day one of the retreat, he probably wouldn't have been able to let her go again when this was all over.

Brody sidled up to him as the first session ended. "You and the missus looked awfully cozy this morning," he remarked.

Warning bells started clanging in Santiago's head. Brody sounded nonchalant, but Santiago recognized his comment was more than just a casual observation.

"Did we?" Santiago replied. He shrugged, as if he didn't care one way or another.

"Mmm-hmm." Brody waited until the rest of the group had cleared the room. Then he fixed Santiago with a dark stare. "Have you had a change of heart since we last spoke? Because I can tell you, if you have, you're not getting your money back."

Santiago's heart kicked into a higher gear and he sent up a silent prayer of thanks to the universe that he hadn't yet shut off his hidden camera. The spy cam around his neck was picking up everything, and at this point, Brody was only deepening his own grave. This evidence, combined with the research one of his paralegals was doing into the financial records of the Woods and The Marriage Institute, would make the case against the Woods air-tight. As soon as he heard from his paralegal, he was going to contact the police and give them all the evidence.

"I haven't changed my mind," Santiago replied.

"But from what I've seen this week, it'll be easier to get her to initiate the divorce if she thinks we're going to part as friends. Isn't that what you've taught us? To play nice until we get what we want?"

Brody nodded. "That's true. But most people aren't that good at acting the part. You need to be careful. I could tell by the way she was looking at you that your wife still loves you."

The observation landed like a blow, and for a second, Santiago couldn't breathe. Ainsley had told him last night that she knew this wasn't going to turn into anything. He'd believed she was telling the truth, had convinced himself it was okay to sleep with her because she wasn't going to let herself get hurt.

But had she been lying? Not to him, but to herself?

Was he going to break her heart all over again?

He forced himself to smile, hoping he didn't look as pained as he felt. "Trust me, Grace knows the score." It felt strange to use Ainsley's middle name, but he had to keep their cover intact for a little while longer. "My wife is aware that we don't have a future together." He hated saying the words aloud, and especially to this man, a relative stranger who had no business hearing about their relationship, fake or not.

Brody looked skeptical. "If you say so. Just remember, we told you there are no guarantees. If she doesn't sign the papers, it's not our fault."

"I understand," Santiago said, trying to hide his

disgust. Brody and Alva were even worse than he thought! If they truly cared about people, they'd be happy to see one of the couples at the retreat looking stronger and more connected. Instead, they were only worried about their bottom line and the possibility he might demand his bribe money back. Taking them down was going to be one of the most satisfying moments of his career, possibly even his life.

Brody nodded. "I'll check in with Alva, see what she's been saying in her group sessions. Hopefully you're right, and she really is getting ready to let go of your marriage."

Santiago wanted to protest the invasion of Ainsley's privacy, but he stopped himself just in time. For one thing, it didn't really matter since they weren't married and she was playing a part to help him. She hadn't been baring her soul in the group sessions, so he didn't have to worry about learning any secrets. Also, he had to keep his own role in mind: a husband who bribed the coordinators of a marriage retreat and asked for their help to convince his wife to get a divorce was not the kind of man who would worry about his spouse's privacy in the first place.

"That'd be great," he said instead. "I definitely don't want any surprises, especially so late in the game."

Brody clapped him on the back with a friendly smile. "We don't either, son. Now, get on to your couple's session. I'm sure she's waiting for you."

AINSLEY LEFT THE room where the group session had just been held and stepped into the hall. She was due for a couple's session with Santiago in a few minutes, but after one too many cups of coffee this morning, she needed a bathroom break first.

She stepped into the restroom and entered a stall. Only after she'd locked the door behind her did she realize the other one was occupied.

"That's right," she heard the other woman say. Apparently, she was on the phone and had no problem multitasking. "Yes, I'm here now."

Ainsley tried to tune her out as she relieved herself. The lady chatted on, talking over the noise as Ainsley flushed the toilet.

She exited the stall and walked to the sink, shaking her head. She'd never understood people who talked on the phone while they were using the bathroom. Just the idea of it grossed her out.

She started to wash her hands as the woman flushed her own toilet. "Well, like I said before," she said, metal rattling as she unlocked the door. "It's time to put the big plan in motion."

Ainsley glanced in the mirror as the woman walked out of the stall. *Oh my God*, she thought, freezing in place, her hands still under the stream of water.

Micheline Anderson stood behind her, her blonde hair teased to perfection, her makeup flawless, and her blue eyes narrowed as she stared at Ainsley.

"I'll call you back later," she said into her phone. She dropped it into her purse and tilted her head to the side. "Well, well, well," she said, sauntering forward. "Look what the cat dragged in."

Ainsley glanced away and turned off the faucet, then grabbed for the paper towels.

"What brings you here, Ms. Colton?" Micheline stepped close, leaning one hip against the counter.

"I'm here to see a friend," Ainsley lied, avoiding Micheline's gaze. She tossed the crumpled paper towels into the trash can and moved to leave, but Micheline leaned out and blocked her path, forcing her to stop or run into the other woman.

"Are you now?" Micheline asked softly.

Ainsley looked up and met her eyes, and the malice she saw glowing in those blue depths nearly made her take a step back. If she'd had any remaining doubts as to what this woman was capable of, they were gone now. The woman put on a good front, and a lot of people might think she was inspiring, but Ainsley knew she was looking at the real Micheline.

Or should she say, Luella?

Curiosity burned in her chest, and Ainsley wanted to ask Micheline what she knew about the email to the Colton Oil board members. After all, Harley Watts, the man who sent the email, was a member of AAG. And according to her cousin Spencer, Harley hadn't acted on his own initiative. He was clearly a pawn in someone else's game, and Ainsley knew in her bones she was face-to-face with the puppet master.

Something flickered in Micheline's eyes—a note of challenge, perhaps? If so, Ainsley was sorely tempted to take her up on it.

But before she could ask her first question, the restroom door opened and in walked a Marriage Institute employee. "Oh! Ms. Anderson, there you are. Mrs. Woods asked me to escort you to her office for a visit before your seminar."

Just like that, Micheline's mask slipped back into place. She turned and beamed a winning smile at the young woman. "Of course, honey. I'd be happy to follow you."

She patted Ainsley's shoulder like they were old friends. "I hope to see you again real soon." Her tone was sunny, but Ainsley recognized the statement for what it was: a threat.

Micheline and the employee left, and Ainsley leaned back against the cool tile wall, her heart racing. What were they going to do now? She'd hoped that by skipping the seminar, Micheline wouldn't see her and they could finish collecting evidence at the retreat. But clearly, that wasn't going to be the case. Her cover was as good as blown—as soon as Micheline saw Alva and Brody, she'd reveal Ainsley's true identity. She and Santiago had to get out of here, before the Woodses discovered the truth.

She left the bathroom and practically jogged down

the hall toward the room where they usually had their couple's counseling session. He was probably already inside with the facilitator, waiting for her to arrive. The therapist would think it was strange when she insisted he step into the hall to talk to her, but they didn't have to worry about keeping up appearances anymore. It was time to cut their losses and get out of here.

She slowed as she approached the room, frowning when she noticed the door was closed. That was strange. Usually, the door remained open until both she and Santiago arrived. She tried the handle. Locked.

"I'm afraid we had a room change," Brody said from behind her.

Ainsley whirled around, startled by his sudden appearance. He put up a hand and took a step back. "Sorry, I didn't mean to scare you," he said with a smile. "I was just coming to put a sign on the door. The lights aren't working in this room, so you and Santiago are now meeting in the Pine Room. Do you know where that is?"

She nodded. "The other side of the building, right?"

"Yes," Brody confirmed. "Just across from the main office, in fact."

Ainsley's stomach sank. Wonderful. She'd have to walk past Alva and Brody's office to get to Santiago. Past Micheline, who was probably even now telling Alva about her discovery in the bathroom.

There was no help for it. It had to be done. Ainsley drew up her shoulders and nodded at Brody. "Thanks." At least he didn't appear to know who she really was yet.

"No problem."

Ainsley turned and walked back down the hall, feeling Brody's eyes on her the whole way. He might not be aware that she was playing a part, but she could tell he suspected her of something.

She rounded the corner and crossed the main lobby, headed in the direction of the office. But just as she passed the reception desk, she heard someone call her name.

Ainsley turned, horrified to find Alva Woods standing by the main entrance. "Grace, can you help me for a minute?" The older woman was holding a squirming puppy and trying to carry a bag of dog food.

Ainsley approached cautiously, searching Alva's face for signs of anger. But there was no hint of malice, no indication she'd spoken to Micheline yet. Maybe her secret was still safe…

"Where did you get this little one?" she asked, reaching instinctively for the puppy. She had a soft spot in her heart for dogs of all kinds, and she'd been thinking about adopting one for a while. Maybe it was time to do so?

Alva passed the dog into Ainsley's willing arms with a smile. "Brett found her nosing around one of the outbuildings about an hour ago," Alva said. "I just ran to the store to pick up some dog food, and after the retreat Brody and I will take her to the vet." She started to walk down the hall, and Ainsley followed, cuddling the small ball of brown fur.

"She's adorable," Ainsley said. The puppy wiggled in her arms, her tongue lapping frantically at Ainsley's chin.

"Yes, she is," Alva agreed. She unlocked a room and swung the door open into the dark space. "We can keep her in here for now."

Ainsley walked past Alva, intending to set the puppy on the ground. But a sudden, sharp sting in her thigh made her cry out and jerk forward.

Almost immediately, her head began to swim. Ainsley felt her limbs grow heavy, and she set the dog on the floor before she dropped her. Lurching awkwardly, she slapped a hand onto the table in an effort to keep her balance.

Alva's face floated into her field of vision, the older woman's expression one of pure hatred. "Did you think you could get away with it?" she asked, her once-friendly tone now dripping with acid. "Did you think we wouldn't find out?"

Ainsley tried to speak, but her voice wouldn't work. She dropped to her knees, unable to stand any longer. With a grunt of effort, she lifted her hand and swiped her finger across the locket around her neck, activating the hidden camera.

Alva smiled as Ainsley sank to the floor. "That's right," she taunted, standing over her. "You're not going to get away with revealing our secrets."

Ainsley moved her lips, working to summon the strength to call for Santiago. But all that came out was a whisper.

"Don't worry," Alva said. "You won't be here long. I'm off to find Santiago now. The two of you will soon be together again."

The announcement filled Ainsley with horror. Alva's actions made it clear she and Brody had no boundaries when it came to protecting their scam. If they got their hands on Santiago, the couple could kill them both. Given the blind loyalty of their employees, they'd have no trouble covering up the crime.

Ainsley tried to reach out, tried to stop Alva from walking away. But her fingers curled around air. Alva laughed as she stepped out of the room, and the sound echoed in Ainsley's ears as her vision faded to black.

Chapter Thirteen

Where was she?

Santiago paced down the hall, heading for the room where they normally met for their couple's session. The lights hadn't been working, so Brody had poked his head in and told them to move to another location. He'd said he'd post a note for Ainsley, but as the minutes ticked by and Ainsley didn't arrive, Santiago had grown worried. He'd told the counselor he was going to go find her, then stepped out to do just that.

He arrived at the regular room to find the door shut and a note posted, directing Ainsley to the new spot. So why hadn't she shown up yet?

Was she back at the cabin? They'd planned for her to leave after the couple's session, so as not to arouse too much suspicion. But had she decided to go into hiding early? And if so, why?

He set off down the hall again, his pace slower as he considered other possibilities. Had she been attacked again? He'd figured she was safe here in the main cabin, with the other retreat attendees and the Institute's employees around. Now that he thought about it though, the employees probably weren't much use in his safety-in-numbers calculations. If they were truly as brainwashed as Ainsley suspected, they were just as likely to harm her as help her.

He glanced into the rooms he passed, looking out of habit. Ainsley wasn't the type to hide without telling him; the fact that she was gone now meant something was very wrong.

Santiago walked through the lobby and toward the Woodses' office. Maybe they'd seen Ainsley. If not, he'd check the cabin and if he still couldn't find her, he'd call the police.

He stuck his head in their office, but it was empty. "Hello?" he called out. Where was everyone?

"Probably getting ready for the seminar," he muttered to himself. He stepped back into the hall, intending to leave. But just as he took a step, a low, soft sound caught his attention.

Was that a…moan?

He spun on his heel and listened hard, hoping to hear the noise again. After a few seconds passed with only silence, he called out again. "Hello?"

There it was—a definite sound of a woman in pain.

Santiago stepped forward, zeroing in on a room several feet down the hall. The door was cracked, the interior dark. But he swore the sound was coming from inside.

He carefully pushed open the door, his free hand swiping along the wall in search of a light switch. His fingers made contact with the plastic nub and he flipped it up, flooding the room with light.

He blinked as his eyes adjusted to the brightness. A large conference table dominated the room, leaving little space for much else. He glanced around, but nothing seemed out of place.

As Santiago turned to go, something on the floor caught his eye. He bent over to get a better look. Was that a trash can, or…

Ice water filled his veins as he realized what he'd mistaken for office furniture was actually someone's feet. But not just anyone's.

Ainsley's.

He rushed forward, dropping to his knees next to her. She was lying facedown, her body completely limp. He pulled her into his arms, and she moaned at the movement.

"Ainsley, come on, wake up for me," he said frantically. He felt her neck for a pulse, calming only slightly when he found the steady, strong rhythm. She wasn't dying—not yet, anyway.

She stirred, her eyelids fluttering. "That's it," he said encouragingly. "Time to get up."

"Santiago," she whispered. "They know."

"I don't care," he said, all thoughts of the Woodses and his mission to take them down flying out of his head. All that mattered was getting Ainsley to safety.

She'd already been through so much for his sake—he couldn't let her suffer through more.

"Come on," he said, pulling her into a sitting position. "We're going to get you up."

Her head lolled back against his chest, but she remained awake. "I can't walk. Alva injected me with something and now I can't really move my legs." There was a note of panic in her voice, and he cupped her cheek with his hand.

"It's okay, baby," he assured her. "You will. It'll come back, I promise." He didn't know what drugs she'd been given, but they appeared to be wearing off now. Hopefully it wouldn't take much longer before she could move on her own again.

Santiago got to his feet, then bent down and gathered Ainsley into his arms. "I'm going to put you in this chair," he told her. He couldn't bear the sight of her on the floor any longer.

She tried to help him as he maneuvered her into the seat. She leaned forward, using the table to support herself. "It was Alva," she told him. "She's looking for you."

"I hope she finds me," he said darkly. He retrieved his cell phone and quickly dialed 911. Then, against the dispatcher's instructions, he hung up and called Spencer Colton's cell.

"Come quickly," he said. "Ainsley's in trouble." He rattled off the address of The Marriage Institute and hung up the phone. He didn't have time for Spencer's questions right now; he had to get Ainsley out of here before someone found them.

Santiago leaned down and slung her arm across his shoulders. “Come on, Ainsley. We need to move.” The keys to the car were in his pocket; all he had to do was get her inside and they could take off and wait for the police at the turnoff to the main road.

Ainsley grunted with effort as she tried to stand. Just as he got her to her feet, she clutched his shirt with her free hand. “Santiago,” she said.

He heard the note of fear in her voice and turned to follow her gaze.

Alva stepped into the room wearing a smile, Brody on her heels. The older man sized up the situation and lifted his arm, pointing a small pistol at Santiago’s chest.

“Now, where do you think you’re going?” he asked.

WHEN AINSLEY SAW the gun in Brody’s hand, she wanted to scream. Fortunately, her throat was too tight to allow any sound to escape.

Brody gestured with his free hand. “You go ahead and put her back down.”

Santiago did as instructed, depositing her gently onto the seat. She didn’t want him to move away, but her arms were too heavy to lift and she couldn’t grab him to keep him close.

“I think there’s been a misunderstanding,” Santiago said. He raised his hands to show he wasn’t a threat. "Why don't we just go our separate ways now? No harm, no foul, am I right?"

Brody shook his head. "I don't think so. We've come too far for that now."

"What do you mean?" Santiago asked.

Alva sneered. "We know who you are. Micheline confirmed it. She ran into this one here in the bathroom." She pointed at Ainsley with a look of undisguised contempt. "Thought you could fool us, didn't you?"

"Honestly, I don't know why it took us as long as it did to figure out you two were frauds. You're not a couple in trouble. I've seen the way you look at each other. It's clear you're in love."

Brody's words sent a shock through Ainsley and she glanced at Santiago. Was he right? Did Santiago love her?

"Our relationship is none of your business," Santiago said, his voice low and tight. "But you're right about one thing—we're stronger together than you'll ever know."

The ferocity of Santiago's response brought tears to her eyes. Was he speaking from the heart or bluffing? Either way, it sounded like he thought their relationship was on solid ground. And in some ways, perhaps it was. They might not have a romantic future together, but Ainsley knew they would always be friends at least.

"Whatever," Brody said. "Let's go."

Santiago made no move to follow the command. "No. You're going to have to shoot me here."

Brody stared at Santiago for a moment, as if judging his sincerity. Then he shrugged. "All right. Have it your way." He turned, pointing the gun at Ainsley.

The breath stalled in her chest as she stared at the black hole facing her. Her heart beat frantically against her ribs, as though trying to escape her body.

"I'm going to count to three," Brody said calmly.

He opened his mouth again, but before he could say "one," Santiago interrupted him. "Okay, okay!" he shouted. "Whatever you want. Just leave her alone."

Brody smirked. "That's what I thought."

"It's not too late to walk away." Santiago glanced from Brody to Alva. "The police are coming. I called them as soon as I found Ainsley. They'll be here in a matter of minutes. If you let us walk out of here, I'll tell them I made a mistake."

The Woodses looked at each other. "Guess we need to move fast, then," Brody said. Alva nodded.

"I'll get her," she said, taking a step toward Ainsley. "You deal with him."

"Wait, what's happening here?" Santiago asked, alarm sounding in his voice. He blocked Alva, preventing her from reaching Ainsley. "You don't have to do this."

"We're going to take a little walk," Brody said. "Back to your cabin."

"So you can shoot us there?" Santiago spoke

loudly, and Ainsley realized he was trying to draw attention to them.

Brody realized it, too. "Son, you can yell all you want," he said with a chuckle. "There's nobody around to hear you. We canceled the seminar and sent the other couples off on a guided nature meditation. It's just us here now."

"Don't you think the police will realize what you've done when they arrive and find us dead?"

"You mean, when we take them to your cabin and unlock the door to find the pair of you slumped on the sofa, killed in an apparent murder-suicide?" Brody asked.

Alva tsk-tsked. "There was such animosity between them all week, wasn't there, dear? Everyone saw it. We had complaints about your loud arguments in the middle of the night, and one of our employees had to go out there after you tossed a chair through the window."

Ainsley's blood ran cold as the woman smiled evilly. "Don't you see?" she asked. "You've been leading up to this all week. The only tragedy is that we didn't see the signs in time to stop you from killing your wife and then turning the gun on yourself."

Brody aimed the pistol at Ainsley again, his mouth set in a hard line. "Move," he ordered Santiago. "I'm not going to ask you again."

Santiago reluctantly stepped to the side. Ainsley could practically see the wheels turning in his mind and knew he was searching for a way out of this situation. Her own thoughts were a jumbled mess, thanks to the drugs and her own panic.

She glanced around the room, trying to find something, anything they could use as a weapon. But all she saw was the table in front of her and a few plastic chairs. Nothing that would offer protection from a bullet or a means of defense. Maybe they'd have better luck at the cabin?

But as Alva approached her, a glint of violence in her eyes, Ainsley knew they couldn't let themselves be taken to the cabin. If they cooperated at this point, the Woodses would slaughter them like spring lambs. Hell, she wouldn't put it past the couple to shoot her and Santiago in the back and make up a story later. No, she decided, her resolve growing with every heartbeat. Ainsley wasn't about to let this woman win. She might die today, but she wasn't going to go down without a fight.

Alva reached her side and leaned over, wrapping her arms around Ainsley's torso. "Come on," she said, grunting as she tried to pull Ainsley out of the chair. "Let's go."

Ainsley got to her feet, pleased to find she was rapidly regaining control of her limbs. She leaned on Alva, but not too much. She didn't want her to know just how much she weighed.

Alva took a step forward, tugging Ainsley along with her. Ainsley cooperated, looking over the top of the other woman's head to meet Santiago's eyes. She lifted one brow in a subtle gesture, and was rewarded with a flicker of recognition in his green eyes. He moved to let the pair of them pass, stepping to the side.

Once she was clear of Santiago, Ainsley wrapped her arms around Alva and let her body go limp. The smaller woman staggered under the sudden, unexpected weight, and Ainsley tightened her grip on Alva's shoulders. Alva cried out in alarm as the pair of them crashed to the ground, Ainsley landing on top of her with a satisfying thud.

Brody yelped, his attention now focused on his wife. He reached out to try to help her, remembering a split second too late that Santiago was still in the room.

It was all the time Santiago needed. Ainsley watched as Santiago picked up a chair and flung it into Brody's chest. Brody lifted his arm in defense and the gun clattered to the floor. The two men hit the ground, each one vying for the weapon. In the meantime, Alva struggled underneath Ainsley, trying to free herself. The older woman kicked and punched, but Ainsley refused to yield. She managed to grab Alva's wrists, but Ainsley's hands still weren't 100 percent on board with responding to her brain's commands, so her grip kept slipping.

Suddenly, the two men stopped grappling. Ainsley heard a muffled yelp, then someone scrambled to his feet. She looked up to see Santiago with the gun in his hand and Brody tripping for the door.

Don't do it, she silently pleaded. She knew how angry he was—the emotion was written all over his face. He hated the Woodses for what they'd done to his sister, for what they'd done to her. But shooting Brody wasn't going to fix things. If Santiago pulled the trigger, she knew it would haunt him for the rest of his life.

For a brief second, she thought he was going to let his anger rule. He lifted his arm, pointing the gun at Brody's back. Then she saw the shock wash over his face as he evidently realized what he was doing. To her relief, Santiago lowered the pistol.

Brody had just made it to the doorway when Santiago grabbed him from behind. He spun the man around, drew back his arm and landed a right hook to the jaw. Brody went down like a sack of potatoes. Alva started screaming, making Ainsley wince.

Santiago helped Ainsley off Alva, giving the woman a glare that would strip the paint off a car. "Don't you even think about leaving this room," he said darkly. "After what you've done to Ainsley, I could shoot you and not lose any sleep afterward."

Alva practically snarled as she knelt by Brody. "You won't get away with this! Just you wait—I'll make sure you both pay!"

Ainsley couldn't resist taunting the woman. "I don't think so, Alva. I have a recording of you threat-ing me after you drugged me. And of Brody pointing the gun at me, and you two describing your plans for our deaths."

The color drained from Alva's face. "How is that possible?" she sputtered.

Ainsley touched the chain around her neck. "Smile," she said sweetly. "You're on Candid Camera."

Santiago laughed and pressed a kiss to the side of her head. "God, you're the best."

A commotion sounded from the lobby, shouts of "Police!" echoing down the hall.

"In here," Santiago yelled.

A few seconds later, the room was full of officers and emergency personnel. Santiago told them about the gun, and someone collected it and locked it away. Ainsley breathed a sigh of relief, allowing herself to relax now that she knew they were no longer in danger. The Woodses were taken into custody, and Santiago waved over an EMT, insisting he evaluate Ainsley.

Spencer pushed his way through the crowd. "What the hell happened here?" he asked, looking from Ainsley to Santiago and then back again. "You two mind filling me in?"

Ainsley looked at her cousin and very nearly started crying. She didn't think she'd ever been so happy to see him. She tried to speak, but the words wouldn't come.

Someone squeezed her hand, and she glanced down to find Santiago's fingers were laced with hers. She glanced up into his warm green eyes, and in that moment, she knew they were going to be okay. She didn't have to be afraid any longer. He was here, by her side, and they were safe.

Taking a deep breath, she turned back to Spencer. "It's kind of a long story..."

Chapter Fourteen

Two weeks later

Ainsley closed her eyes and took a deep breath, counting silently to herself. *In, one, two, three. Out, one, two, three.*

The faint sounds of birdsong played from her phone. She'd ditched the ocean waves soon after coming home from the retreat; it was too similar to the background noise one of The Marriage Institute counselors had used at the beginning of the group sessions.

Things had moved quickly in the aftermath of the retreat. After explaining everything to Spencer and showing him and the other officers the footage her hidden camera had recorded, the Woodses had been arrested and charged with attempted murder. In the following days, she and Santiago had spent hours speaking to the district attorney, laying out all their evidence and sharing their stories. As a consequence, additional charges had been filed, including fraud and several other white-collar crimes. It was exactly the outcome they'd hoped for, the one they'd worked so hard to achieve.

And then Santiago had left.

It hadn't been a surprise—Ainsley had known he would return to Phoenix once everything was over. But a small, irrational part of her had hoped that maybe, just maybe, he would change his mind.

She should have known better. After all, she'd told him she wasn't expecting more than just one night. It wasn't Santiago's fault her heart had disobeyed her mind's orders to stay out of it.

To his credit, Santiago hadn't left without saying goodbye. He'd stopped by her office about a week ago to give her an update on Ace's case.

"I spoke with Ace again," he'd said, settling into the chair across from her desk. "He didn't have anything new to share with me."

"That's a bit of a relief." Ainsley herself hadn't had a chance to connect with Ace since arriving home. She'd been focused on catching up at work and finding new ways to distract herself from missing Santiago. It was good to know her brother hadn't gotten into more trouble in her absence.

"I'm speaking with the cleaning lady in an hour, and Ace is going to send me the security camera footage from his condo. Hopefully I'll be able to find something useful."

"So this is goodbye?" Her heart had started to pound, emotions swirling in her chest as she'd fought to keep her expression neutral. *Don't cry*, she'd told herself. The last thing she wanted was for Santiago to know how much she wished things could be different between them.

"For now," he'd replied easily. "I'll be in and out of Mustang Valley as I work on the case. I hope you won't mind if I stop by?"

"Of course not," she'd said. As long as he gave her advance warning, she'd be able to control her emotions when she saw him again.

His expression had changed then, a faint smile playing at the corners of his mouth. "That was a hell of a ride, wasn't it?"

She'd nodded, a strange sense of nostalgia growing as she recalled the events of the past week. She wouldn't miss the retreat or the people there. But Santiago? She'd miss their time together very much. Once again, he'd upended her life and she was going to have to figure out a new way of moving forward without him.

"I can't tell you how much your help means to me. I couldn't have done this without you, and I want you to know how much I appreciate everything you did for me."

"It was no problem," she'd lied. "I'm just glad the Woodses are behind bars and the innocent people they hurt now know the truth."

"Because of you," he'd said.

"Because of us," she'd corrected.

He'd watched her silently for a moment. Ainsley had known by the look in his eyes and the set of his mouth that there was more he'd wanted to say. She'd sat across from him, mentally urging him to speak, hoping he'd confess to a change of heart. They were perfect together—the retreat had proven the years apart hadn't broken their bond. Why couldn't he see that? Why wasn't he willing to take a chance with her? Didn't he think she was worth it?

Whatever he'd been thinking, he hadn't shared it with her. He'd gotten to his feet and she'd done the same, walking him to the door of her office. They paused to say goodbye, and then he'd dropped his head.

Ainsley's heart had jumped into her throat. Was he going to kiss her? She'd sucked in a breath, anticipating the feel of his mouth against hers.

But his lips had landed on her forehead. A chaste gesture of affection, the kind a brother might offer to his sister. Not the kiss of lovers.

She'd waited until she was certain he'd left. Then she'd returned to her chair and quietly cried.

He hadn't called since that final visit. And while she still missed him, still ached to be near him, it was for the best. If they stayed in regular contact, it would only prolong her heartbreak. Better to rip the bandage off now and start healing than to draw out the inevitable.

So Ainsley had returned to her work and the family drama, trying to sort through all the issues surrounding the mystery of who had shot her father and where her biological brother actually was. At least Payne's condition was stable. She didn't think she could handle any more stress at this point.

Which was why she'd taken up meditation again. It wasn't a foolproof strategy, but it was better than nothing.

In, one, two, three. Out, one, two, three.

"Ms. Colton?"

Ainsley opened her eyes and pressed the button on the intercom sitting on her desk. "Yes?"

"They're ready for you."

"Thank you."

After a final set of counts, Ainsley closed the meditation app on her phone and got to her feet. She smoothed a hand down her blouse, then picked up a file folder and headed for the door.

The conference room was adjacent to her office, a small space that was furnished more like a living room than a meeting location. Two sofas bracketed a low coffee table, and a set of chairs at the far end of the space provided additional seating. There was a narrow table along the wall closest to the door, a variety of bottled waters, teas and sodas arranged on its surface.

Ainsley walked in and smiled at the scene. Most of her siblings were there; she'd called a family meeting of sorts, wanting to give everyone an update on the investigation into Payne's shooting and Ace's history.

Marlowe noticed her first and jumped to her feet. "Ainsley! Oh my goodness—how are you? I heard about the marriage retreat. What on earth were you doing there?"

Ainsley hugged her half sister, who, despite having a newborn at home, looked as beautiful as ever. "It's a long story," she said. "I'll fill you in later when we have time."

Rafe came over to greet her next, concern shining in his blue eyes. Even though he'd been adopted by Payne as a child, as far as Ainsley was concerned he was her brother in all the ways that counted. "Kerry told me some of the details," he said softly, referring to his fiancée, who was also one of the detectives working Payne's case. "Are you sure you're okay?"

Ainsley nodded, touched by his concern. "I'm fine," she assured him. "Really, I am."

"You'd better be," Grayson said. He stepped forward and wrapped her in a bear hug. Ainsley closed her eyes and soaked up her brother's strength. They were only a year apart, and out of all her siblings, Grayson was her favorite. Though she'd never admit it out loud, especially not in front of Ace.

Ainsley gestured for everyone to sit. Marlowe and Rafe sat on one sofa, and she and Grayson took the other. "I asked you all here today so we could talk about the case. I learned a few things while at the retreat, and I wanted to fill you in."

Over the next several minutes, Ainsley told her siblings about the connection between AAG and The Marriage Institute, and her run-in with Micheline Anderson. The three of them listened intently as she spoke, clearly interested in what she had to say.

The room was silent for a moment after she finished, each of her siblings processing this new information. Finally, Grayson spoke.

"What do you think she meant by 'putting the big plan into motion?'"

Ainsley shook her head. "I have no idea. But it's been bothering me ever since. She's clearly planning something. The question is, what? Does it involve us?"

"I'm sure it does," Marlowe said. "Even though Harley Watts hasn't admitted it, we all know Micheline is the one who told him to send that email to the board."

"I'm more convinced than ever that she's really Luella Smith," Ainsley said. Her siblings all nodded in agreement.

"I think that's the most likely explanation," Rafe said. "It's all too coincidental—Luella disappears into the night and a few weeks later, boom. Micheline Anderson is born."

"But where is that baby now?" Grayson asked. It

was the question they'd all been asking. "If we find him, we'll have all the answers."

"That's the problem," Rafe said. "Luella Smith's son, Jake Anderson, hasn't been seen or heard from since he left town at the age of seventeen. I'm not supposed to talk about this, but Kerry said they're having a hard time finding him."

Ainsley frowned. "Do they think he's in hiding?"

Rafe shrugged. "Hiding. Dead. Who knows?"

"Is it really that hard to find a person?" Grayson asked skeptically. "Don't the cops have that fancy software that locates people in a matter of minutes?"

Rafe fixed Grayson with a droll stare. "They do on TV. But not in real life. Besides, do you know how many Jake Andersons are out there, both in and outside Arizona? Mustang Valley PD simply doesn't have the resources to track them all down."

"Which means we'll just have to wait," Ainsley said. "Maybe we can hire a private investigator to work on behalf of the company."

Marlowe nodded. "We should definitely consider it. Anything to get this wrapped up."

"What about Micheline?" Grayson asked. "Are the police going to do anything about her?"

"Not at this time," Ainsley said. "I told Spencer what she said about the big plan and that I knew she was up to something. He agrees with me, but there isn't enough evidence to justify launching a full investigation."

Marlowe shook her head. "This lady is bad news."

"I agree," Ainsley said. "But until she actually does something illegal, we can't do anything about it."

"What about Ace?" Grayson asked. "How is he holding up?"

Ainsley shrugged. "About as well as can be expected." She filled them in on the search of his apartment and the gun that had been planted there. "Some woman named Destiny Jones said he showed her the gun and bragged about shooting Dad."

Grayson snorted. "Ace was never one for subtleties, but even that is too over the top for him."

"Tell me about it," Ainsley agreed. "But it gets better—the police tried to bring her in for more questioning, but she skipped town."

"Of course she did," Rafe said dryly. "I'm sure whoever hired her made sure she was on the first bus out of Mustang Valley after the police found the gun. Can't have her talking and undoing the frame job."

"Who do you think hired her?" Marlowe asked.

"I don't know," Ainsley admitted. "But whoever it was, I think we can assume they're connected to the one who actually shot Dad."

The group was silent for a moment, each person considering their own list of suspects.

"My money's on Selina," Grayson said. "I bet Payne told her the gravy train was running dry and she flipped out."

Ainsley tilted her head to the side in acknowledgment. "It's possible." There was no love lost between Payne's children and his ex-wife, Selina Barnes Colton. Unfortunately, Selina was an executive and served on the board of Colton Oil, so they all had to deal with her on a regular basis. Ainsley always tried to be polite, but it was difficult at times.

Marlowe looked at Rafe. "Is she a suspect?"

He shrugged. "I can't really comment."

Grayson snorted, and Rafe held up his hands in defense. "I'm not trying to be vague. I genuinely don't know. Kerry plays things close to the vest—she doesn't want the investigation overshadowed by conflict of interest claims. But I can tell you that they are exploring every angle."

A muffled commotion outside interrupted the conversation. Suddenly, the door burst open and Selina stomped inside, Candace trailing after her.

"What the hell is this?" Selina demanded.

"I'm so sorry, Ms. Colton," Ainsley's secretary said. "I tried to stop her."

"It's all right, Candace," Ainsley said. "Don't worry about it."

Selina fixed Ainsley with a glare. "What are you all doing here? I didn't get a notice about a board meeting."

"That's because we're not *having* a board meeting," Ainsley said evenly. "This is a family discussion."

Malice burned in Selina's blue eyes. "You always were such a spoiled bitch, you know that? You and your brothers." She indicated Grayson with a toss of her head. "You just couldn't stand to see your father happy."

"Sure, Selina," Grayson said sarcastically. "Whatever you say."

She sniffed. "Ace has always been out of control. I tried to warn your father about him, but he never wanted to hear it. And now look what's happened. He shot Payne. He's guilty, and you all know it."

Ainsley bared her teeth in a fierce smile. "You're the last person who should be lecturing anyone about guilt, Selina. You're the one who's been blackmailing our father for the last twenty years. Tell me, how do you sleep at night?"

"Like a baby," Selina said. She grinned, the cat who'd gotten the cream. "Believe me, sweetie, I could tell you stories that would make your hair curl. Why do you think your father keeps me around?" She laughed. "I'm not going anywhere."

"Well, we are," Marlowe announced. She got to her feet, and everyone else followed suit. "Ainsley, call me later, okay? You need to stop by the house and visit Reed. He missed his aunt."

"Will do," Ainsley promised. She followed her siblings as they all brushed past Selina and left the room. Ignoring their erstwhile stepmother, she embraced Marlowe, then Rafe and Grayson. "Love you guys."

"Love you, too, sis," Grayson said, ruffling her hair.

"Be careful," Rafe said quietly. "If you even see Micheline in town, I want you to walk the other way."

"I will," she promised. She wasn't taking any chances. If the retreat had taught her anything, it was that the people involved with AAG were unhinged. It was possible Micheline was angry that her friends, the Woodses, had been arrested. Since Ainsley had been involved in bringing them down, Micheline might target her for revenge.

"I mean it," Rafe insisted. "Do we need to get you a bodyguard?"

Santiago had wondered the same thing, but Ainsley had brushed away his concern. "I don't think that's necessary," she said, echoing what she'd told Santiago. "Micheline might be crazy, but she's not stupid. She's playing the long con here, and I don't think she's going to get distracted."

"If you say so," Rafe replied.

Ainsley watched her siblings leave. Selina walked out of the conference room and opened her mouth to speak, but before she could make a sound, Ainsley turned her back on the woman and walked into her office. She shut the door behind her with a thud and flipped the lock into place.

She heard Selina's muffled squawk of indignation, and smiled. Yes, she was being petty. But given the events of the past few weeks, Ainsley would take her pleasure where she could find it.

SANTIAGO LEANED BACK in his chair and sighed, surveying the stacks of paper on his desk. He'd been working on Ace Colton's case for the last few days, hardly stopping to sleep or eat. He was tired, hungry and missed Ainsley desperately.

Leaving her had been agonizing. He'd wanted so badly to return to that little cabin in the woods, shut the door and spend the rest of his life making love to her. But that simply wasn't an option. And as she'd sat across from him behind her desk, looking so professional and proper, he'd known that the magic they'd found at the retreat was gone. No matter how good things had been between them, the distance between them was back.

He never should have slept with her again.

But he was so glad he had.

The emotional dichotomy was enough to make his head spin. Things would be so much easier right now if his heart didn't ache with every breath, but at the same time, he cherished the time they'd spent together. Ainsley had given him a gift, and he would treasure it forever.

But for now, he had to make progress on this case. He owed it to Ainsley to save her brother—after everything she'd gone through for his sake, clearing Ace's name was the least he could do.

He skimmed his notes again, mentally reviewing the conversations he'd had with various people. Before leaving Mustang Valley, he'd interviewed the cleaning lady who had found Payne after the shooting. She'd been a lovely woman who had reiterated the story she'd already told the police: she'd been vacuuming in the other room, so she hadn't seen anyone leave Payne's office. Still, she'd heard the word *mom* and someone had cursed just before the gunshot. She thought it was a man's voice, but not one she recognized.

And then there was the Arizona State Sun Devils pin that had been found near Payne's prone form. According to pretty much everyone, Payne wasn't a big sports fan. Why, then, was the pin in his office? It had to be from the shooter, Santiago figured.

Mom. The pin. And Payne Colton. The three were connected, though for the life of him, Santiago couldn't see how.

As for the gun in Ace's condo? He'd reviewed the security footage and seen a figure skulking through the rooms. The camera angle didn't show their face though, so he couldn't rule out the cleaning lady. Still, he'd spoken to the police and had been told, unofficially, of course, that the body type on the surveillance from the condo matched the body type seen on Colton Oil security tapes the night of Payne's shooting.

It was far from conclusive evidence, but taken together, Santiago was convinced Ace was not the shooter. He was, however, the victim of a frame job. The fact that Destiny Jones, the tipster who had told the police about the gun in Ace's condo, had skipped town was just the cherry on top. Santiago knew once he found her, the whole house of cards would come tumbling down.

A sharp rap on his door broke into his thoughts, and he looked up to find his sister, Gabriela, standing at the entrance to his office. "Hey, there!" He smiled for the first time since leaving Ainsley, and stood up to greet her.

She met him halfway to his desk, and he pulled her in for a hug. She squeezed him tightly, then leaned back with a frown. "Santiago," she said disapprovingly. "When was the last time you had a shower?"

"Ah..." He ran a hand through his hair, trying to remember. "The day before yesterday, I think?"

Gabriela wrinkled her nose and shook her head. "You're a mess. I came by to see if I could take you to dinner, but you're not fit for public company."

"We could order in," he suggested.

She nodded. "We'll have to."

Forty-five minutes later, they sat across from each other at the small conference table tucked into the corner of his office. She twirled spaghetti on her fork, while he lifted a piece of pizza to his lips.

"How are you?" he asked around a bite.

She grinned. "Better, now that you exposed the Woodses as the criminals they are." She pointed at him with her fork. "My attorney and I had a meeting with the judge today. She ruled that in light of the fraud committed by the Woodses, the paperwork I signed was null and void." Happiness gleamed in her eyes as she spoke. "She reinstated the original prenup, and now Eric isn't getting a dime!"

Satisfaction bloomed in Santiago's chest. This was it—this was why he'd done what he had, why he'd talked Ainsley into helping him. Gabriela was free from her jerk of a husband, and the man who had tried to scam her was now facing some tough questions. The stress of the retreat, the danger he'd been in, it all melted away in the face of his sister's joy. Her natural sparkle was back, and he could tell she was back to her old self again.

"I'm glad to hear it," Santiago said. "I hope you're considering pressing charges against Eric?"

Gabriela nodded. "Oh, yes. My attorney says I have a solid case. Thanks to you."

He shrugged. "You don't have to thank me. Besides, I didn't act alone."

"Who helped you?" Gabriela leaned forward, obviously curious. "I've been wanting to ask you about it. I know you didn't go there alone—they wouldn't have let you stay. So who pretended to be your wife?"

"A friend of mine. Ainsley."

Gabriela's eyes widened. "Ainsley, as in your law school girlfriend, Ainsley? The woman it seemed like you were going to marry?"

Santiago shrugged, wishing his sister hadn't made the connection. "Yes."

"Wow." Gabriela leaned back, eyeing him speculatively. "I'm surprise she still talks to you, after what you did."

"What do you mean?" He sounded a little defensive, even to his own ears, but he didn't care. His own sense of curiosity wanted to know what his sister had to say.

She tilted her head to the side. "You dumped her, remember?"

"I didn't dump her, I moved for my career."

"Whatever." Gabriela waved her hand, dismissing his clarification. "The fact remains that the two of you dated for years. Dad was ready to get the family diamonds out of the safe. But then you walked away."

"It was the right thing to do," he muttered.

"Are you kidding me?"

Santiago looked up to find his sister staring at him incredulously. "What?" he asked.

"How was leaving her the right thing to do? You'd never been so happy."

"What makes you so sure that was because of her? You never met her."

"Yeah, you made sure of that, didn't you?"

Santiago looked away. "You know why I kept her away. I wasn't going to expose her to our parents."

"Because you loved her," Gabriela said, her tone making it clear he'd just proven her point.

"What does it matter now?" he asked, pushing away his plate. "That was a long time ago."

Gabriela was silent a moment, chewing a bite of her pasta. "It was. But I think you still love her."

Santiago choked on a sip of water. "Excuse me?" His sister was right, but how had she figured that out?

Gabriela nodded. "You do," she said. "And I'm willing to bet she still loves you, too."

"What makes you say that?" He heard the note of hope in his voice and hoped his sister didn't pick up on it.

She shook her head, clearly exasperated. "She helped you at the retreat, didn't she?"

"Well, yes, but only because I agreed to take her brother's case."

Gabriela leveled him with a stare. "Oh, please. Not even you are that dumb."

Santiago's face heated and he looked away. "It doesn't matter," he muttered. "We don't have a future together."

"Why not?"

He whipped his head around to look at his sister. "You know why."

She gaped at him. "Because of Mom and Dad?"

He nodded, not bothering to elaborate.

Gabriela scoffed. "You've got to be kidding me."

"I'm not." Santiago pulled a pepperoni free from its nest of cheese and popped it into his mouth. "Our family has a terrible track record when it comes to marriage. Why would I want to go down that road, when it only leads to heartache?"

He felt his sister's eyes on him and looked up to find her staring at him, her expression a mixture of shock, disbelief and confusion. "So you're telling me," she said slowly. "That you walked away from a woman who loves you, and who you love in return, because you're afraid your relationship will wind up like our parents'?"

"Well, yeah. Look at how well things worked out for you."

Gabriela shook her head. "That's because I married the wrong person! Eric wasn't right for me—I married him to get away from Mom and Dad. You and Ainsley were nothing like that."

Santiago didn't respond. He'd never before considered the possibility that Gabriela had seen Eric as a way out of the family home. He'd thought his sister had married for love, only to have it turn sour.

"Oh my God," Gabriela said softly. "You have got to be both the smartest and the stupidest person I know. How is that possible? How can you be so intelligent, and yet so clueless when it comes to relationships?"

"Hey," he said sharply. "I don't need a lecture."

"Apparently, you do," she shot back. "You found love. Do you have any idea how rare that is? But rather than hold on to it, you threw it away because you were afraid."

"Aren't you?" Santiago asked. "No one in our family has had a good relationship. No one."

"So what?" Gabriela shrugged. "You think I'm

going to let other people's failures dictate how I live my life?" She shook her head. "Hell, no. Mom and Dad made our childhood miserable. I'm not about to let them steal the joy from my future, and you shouldn't, either."

Santiago didn't reply. Gabriela's words washed over him, sinking into his mind and taking root. He hated to admit it, but she made some good points.

His mind drifted back to the retreat. Ainsley had said as much to him, hadn't she?

You're a good man, Santiago. I know you don't see it, but I do.

She'd been so understanding that night, when he'd told her about his parents and the troubles in their marriage. He'd never talked about his childhood with anyone else, never opened up like that before. Partly because he didn't like thinking about his childhood, but mostly out of fear. He'd always assumed that once people heard about his family, they'd know he was damaged.

But Ainsley hadn't thought that.

"You're not Dad." Gabriela's voice broke into his thoughts. "And even though I've never met her, Ainsley isn't Mom. You guys aren't doomed to repeat history."

"I..." Santiago trailed off, shaking his head as a new memory popped into his brain.

I could tell by the way she was looking at you that your wife still loves you.

It's clear you're in love.

Brody's words echoed in his ears. His parents had never looked at each other with love, never shown affection of any kind. What did it say about him and Ainsley that Brody Woods, of all people, thought they were in love?

"I'm going to head out," Gabriela said. She gathered up the remnants of her meal and stood. "It's clear you have some thinking to do."

Santiago nodded, feeling shell-shocked. "Thanks for stopping by."

"Of course." She kissed him on the cheek. "Thanks again for everything. You and Ainsley make a great team."

"We do, don't we?" He'd always thought so, but he liked hearing his sister say it. And now, for the first time, he began to hope there might be a way for them to stay together…

Gabriela nodded. "Not everyone gets a second chance," she said. "I'd hate to see you throw away yours."

Santiago smiled, a sense of peace filling him as he thought about Ainsley and allowed himself to dream of a future with her. Gabriela was right; he wasn't his father. She wasn't his mother. And he wasn't going to give his parents any more control over his life.

"I'm not going to," he assured her. "I'm going to make this right."

"Good," she said, moving to the door. She stopped and turned back. "Oh, and one more thing."

"What's that?"

Gabriela wrinkled her nose. "Take a shower."

Three days later

AINSLEY SCROLLED DOWN the computer screen, looking at the pictures and reading the short descriptions attached.

He's cute, she thought. *A little on the young side, though.*

She moved the mouse down, bringing up a new image.

Oh, now she's beautiful.

The picture showed a golden retriever, her long hair shiny and her brown eyes bright. Ainsley read the description provided by the shelter, falling more in love with every word.

Four years old. Owner surrender due to new baby. Good with pets and people.

She was perfect.

Ainsley jotted down her identification number. As soon as she got off work, she was going to the animal shelter to check out the dogs. She'd decided adopting a pet was the best cure for her loneliness in the evenings, and this pretty girl looked like she'd be a wonderful companion.

She continued to scroll through the images, but none of the other dogs captured her attention the way the golden had. Hopefully she'd still be there this evening. Maybe she should call, just to make sure…

She reached for her phone, eyes on the screen as she searched for the number to the animal shelter. A knock sounded on her door, but she didn't look up.

"Come in," she said absently.

She found the number and punched it into her phone as the door opened. She took one last look at the golden, then glanced over to see who had come into her office.

"Mustang Valley Animal Shelter." A receptionist answered the shelter phone.

Ainsley couldn't speak. Santiago stood in the doorway, holding a bouquet of flowers.

"Hello? Hello?"

Ainsley shook her head and tried to focus on the call. "Ah, yes. Hello. I'm calling about one of the dogs on your website. Is she still available?" She provided the ID number and waited while the woman checked her system.

"Yes," she said after a few seconds. "That dog is still up for adoption. Are you interested?"

"I am," Ainsley said. Her eyes never left Santiago's face. "I'm going to stop by after work."

"Wonderful," the woman replied. "You can take her for a walk if you like."

"That sounds great," Ainsley said. "Thanks." She hung up the phone and nodded at Santiago. "You're back."

"I am," he said. He walked forward and placed the flowers on her desk. "For you."

She glanced at them. "They're lovely. Thank you." What was he playing at? He'd never brought her flowers, not even when they'd been dating.

"They're from my sister," he said. "She wanted to thank you for your help with The Marriage Institute."

Ah, that explained it. Ainsley reached for the bouquet and brought it to her nose. "That's very kind of her," she said, inhaling the fragrant blooms. The potent scent was enough to make her head spin, so she placed the flowers back on her desk. She needed a clear mind to deal with Santiago.

"What brings you here?" she asked. "I'm sure you have better things to do than act as a courier for your sister."

He shrugged. "I was hoping to talk to you."

"All right." She took a deep breath. "I have time." Hopefully he'd made a break in Ace's case. She was ready for this to be over, ready to go back to her normal life.

"I owe you an apology."

Ainsley blinked. "What?" That was…not what she'd expected him to say.

"I made a mistake. Lots of mistakes, actually."

"I see," she said carefully.

He offered her a lopsided smile. "See, that's the thing. You do see me. Like no one ever has, really."

Ainsley frowned. This conversation was getting dangerously close to being personal, and she wasn't emotionally prepared for that. "Santiago—"

He held up a hand, forestalling her objection. "Please, just let me say this." He took a deep breath, then met her gaze. His green eyes shone with vulnerability, and she sucked in a breath. Never, in all the years she'd known him, had he looked so…exposed. Her heart beat hard in her chest, and a sense of anticipation slammed into her. Santiago hadn't come here to talk shop. There was something on his mind. Something big.

"Ainsley, I love you."

His declaration knocked the wind out of her, and she leaned back in her chair.

"I always have. I realize now that I always will. You're the one for me, the only one for me. I think I've known it all along, but I was too afraid to do anything about it. I walked away from you because I thought I was protecting you. Now I realize I was only trying to protect myself."

Ainsley gaped at him. She'd dreamed about this moment for years, imagining the day when Santiago would come to her and admit he'd made a mistake letting her go. Was this really happening now, or was this simply a product of her overactive imagination?

He shook his head. "You don't owe me anything. And I certainly don't deserve another chance with you. But I'm going to ask anyway. Do you think we could try again?"

"Try again?" she echoed weakly.

Santiago nodded. "I've been doing a lot of soul-searching. I realize now that I spent too many years letting my past dictate my future. I don't want to do that anymore. I want to build a life, with you. I want to marry you, if you'll have me," he said shyly.

Say yes! her heart screamed. *Do it now!*

But her brain wasn't so impulsive.

"This is quite a change of heart," she said, unable to keep the emotion from her voice. Oh, how she wanted this to be real! But Santiago had spent years feeling like marriage wasn't for him, and that they didn't have a future together. "How can I be sure you're not going to change your mind again?"

"You can't," he said simply. "Just like I can't be sure you won't change yours. But I can promise you this—if you're willing to give me another chance, I won't make the same mistakes again."

Tears welled in her eyes as emotions warred in her chest. "I want to believe you," she whispered. "I do. But..." She shook her head. "You've walked away from me twice. I don't know if I can survive a third time."

Santiago circled the desk and gathered her into his arms. She went willingly, her body desperate to be close to him even as her mind insisted on keeping him at arm's length. "Oh, Ainsley," he said. "I'm so sorry. Please believe me when I say I thought I was protecting you."

"I know that," she sniffed. "I know you still care

for me. Your actions during the retreat proved it time and time again."

He ran his hand down her hair. "Tell me to go, and I will. Ask me to stay, and I will. I know I have a lot of work to do to regain your trust. But I'm going to put in the time, however long it takes."

She sniffed and leaned back. "How do you feel about couple's counseling?"

He nodded. "I think it's a good idea. Just as long as we find someone reputable."

She laughed. "That goes without saying."

"So…is that a yes?"

Ainsley smiled, feeling her world click into place. "It means, if you're willing to do the work, then so am I."

Relief stole across Santiago's face. "I am," he breathed. "We're a team. I'm just sorry it's taken me so long to realize it."

"Better late than never, I suppose," Ainsley teased.

He leaned forward and pressed his mouth to hers. His kiss was full of promise, the start of a new chapter in their story. Ainsley cupped his face in her hands and gave herself over to this man, feeling him take his place in her heart once more.

"It's always been you," he whispered against her lips.

Ainsley smiled, her tears falling freely now. Santiago leaned back and wiped them away, the pads of his thumbs caressing her cheeks. “Beautiful,” he said softly.

“I don’t have a ring,” he said, sounding a little shy. “Unless… well, what do you think about the emerald for now?”

Ainsley smiled. “Yes. It’s perfect.”

He pulled the ring from his pocket and slipped it on her finger. “I’ll buy you a big diamond, if that’s what you want.”

Ainsley shook her head, staring down at the green stone. In some ways, it felt familiar, like seeing an old friend again. “No,” she said. “This is perfect.” Santiago had put a lot of thought into picking this ring out, and even though she’d initially worn it as a prop, it had made her feel connected to him. It seemed fitting to use it as a symbol of their commitment now, since the marriage retreat had brought them together again.

Santiago glanced at her monitor. “Going to adopt a dog?”

Ainsley smiled. “That’s the plan.”

Emotion flickered in his eyes. “Any other adoptions in the works?”

She sucked in a breath. “Maybe,” she said, drawing out the word. “Is that what you want?”

Santiago smiled. “I want to be with you, and for you to be happy. I told you before I don’t have to be a father. But if you want to be a mother, I am one-hundred percent on board.”

Ainsley’s heart swelled as his words sank in. She

opened her mouth to respond, but her phone buzzed on the desk, interrupting their moment. Santiago glanced at the display. "It's your brother," he said.

Ainsley bit her lip, feeling torn. "Answer it," Santiago said gently. "I'm not going anywhere."

His words warmed her from within, and she picked up her phone. "Ace? Did you get my message?"

"Yeah, I did." Ace sounded bone-tired, and she couldn't blame him. The ballistics report had come back on the gun found in Ace's condo: it was the same weapon that shot Payne.

"We need to talk about your statement," she said. She put him on speakerphone. "I've got Santiago here with me now. Can you come to my office? We can go over the details and walk you through what's going to happen next."

"Now's not really a good time for me," Ace said.

Ainsley exchanged a look with Santiago, a kernel of worry forming in her stomach. "Ace, this is important."

"I know, Ainsley. But I'm a little busy at the moment."

"Ace," Santiago said. "The police are going to arrest you soon. You don't want them to come after you. It will look much better for you if you meet us here at Ainsley's office. Then we can all go to the police station together."

"I'm sure you're right, but that's not going to happen," Ace replied. "Look, I've got to go. Ainsley,

I want you to know I appreciate everything you're doing for me. I love you."

Alarm bells started clanging in her head. "Ace, please don't do anything stupid," she pleaded. Santiago placed his hand on her shoulder and squeezed in a silent gesture of support.

"I'll try not to, but you know me. Can't be helped."

"Ace—" she said, but the line went dead before she could get another word out.

Ainsley hung up and turned to Santiago. "What is he doing?" she moaned. "This will only make things worse."

Santiago rubbed her back. "It's going to be okay," he said. "We'll clear his name and this will all blow over."

"I hope you're right."

The phone rang again, and this time, Spencer's name flashed across the display. Ainsley answered it, putting the call on speaker once more.

"Hello?"

Spencer didn't bother with the niceties. "Where's your brother, Ainsley?"

"I don't know. Why?"

Her cousin sighed heavily. "You know why. We need to arrest him."

"Go ahead. I'm not stopping you."

"He's not here," Spencer said wearily. "His condo is empty. No sign of him. It looks like Ace has skipped town."

Ainsley closed her eyes, silently cursing her brother and his impulsivity. "Maybe he's just running some errands?"

"Nope," Spencer said. "We've been looking for him all day. His condo hasn't been lived in for a few days at least. Ace is gone."

"Great."

"Yeah." Spencer sighed again. "Look, I know this is awkward, but if you hear from him…?" He trailed off, his question clear.

"If I hear from him in the future, I will encourage him to turn himself in," Ainsley said.

"All right." She could tell from Spencer's tone he'd been hoping for more than the standard legal response. But Ainsley wasn't about to make a promise she wasn't sure she could keep.

"Take care of yourself, Spencer," she said. It was clear he was burning the candle at both ends, trying to solve this case.

"You, too, Ainsley."

She hung up and looked at Santiago. "Well, he's gone and done it now."

"It doesn't look good," Santiago admitted. "But like I said before, I know the truth will come out in the end."

She shook her head. "Such confidence."

He grinned. "Hey, can you blame me? Now that I've got you by my side, I can take on the world. Proving your brother's innocence is just the first thing on my to-do list."

Ainsley smiled and leaned in for another kiss. “I guess we’d better get started then.”

Santiago brushed a strand of hair off her cheek, his green eyes alight with love. “Together.”

* * * * *

COMING SOON!

We really hope you enjoyed reading this book. If you're looking for more romance, be sure to head to the shops when new books are available on

Thursday 14th May

To see which titles are coming soon, please visit

millsandboon.co.uk/nextmonth